JAMES
FENIMORE COOPER

THE LAST OF
THE MOHICANS

In writing *The Last of the Mohicans*, James Fenimore Cooper was not simply attempting an exciting adventure story. He was alarmed and disgusted by the neglect of public and private virtue and by the inability of most of his fellow men to find pleasure in the commendable aspects of life. In many ways, this book is a moral tale in which Magua, the essence of all that is evil – treacherous, cruel, greedy and lustful – is contrasted with the soft and gentle virtues of Cora and Alice, the manly tenderness of Major Heyworth, the simple religion of David Gamut and the practicality, born of necessity, of Chingachgook, Uncas and Hawk-eye. Between the heroes and heroines of the tale the author has created a subtler difference. The British travellers show a compassion for their enemies (apart from Magua) which is almost totally lacking among the Indians and Hawk-eye. Hawk-eye understands this Christian compassion, but knows that for reasons of safety he cannot indulge it. The Indians are unaware of it. They live by a strict and honourable code, but in its killing and scalping it is far harsher, and repugnant to those not brought up under it.

Cooper continually moves the action of the story from one attitude to another, subtly pointing and embroidering the basic differences.

This present edition has been edited, abridged and annotated by Robin S. Wright B.A. (Oxon.)

JAMES FENIMORE COOPER

THE LAST OF THE MOHICANS

David McKay Company, Inc. New York

THE LAST OF THE MOHICANS

Annotations and illustrations © 1973 by The Felix Gluck Press, Ltd., Twickenham.
All rights reserved, including the right to reproduce this book, or parts thereof, in any form,
except for the inclusion of brief quotations in a review.
Illustrations by Christopher Bradbury. Based on a concept by René Simmen.
Historical consultant: Cottie Burland, F.R.A.I.

First American Edition, 1976.
Library of Congress Catalog Card Number: 76-13132.

ISBN 0 679 20372 9
Printed in Great Britain

CONTENTS

Preparations for a Journey   8
Danger in the Thicket   11
Rifle and Bow   13
Deception and desertion   15
Hawk-eye Takes Charge   18
The Harboring Place   21
The Maquas Attack   24
No Gunpowder, No Canoe   28
Le Renard Subtil Returns   31
Prisoners   34
Alice Shows Her Courage   37
Battle   41
A Night Among the Dead   45
Through Enemy Lines   48
Heyward Becomes An Envoy   52
Colonel Munro Surrenders   54
Massacre   57
The Pursuit Begins . . .   62
. . . And Continues   65
A Water Chase   68
Duncan is Deceived   71
David Regains his Pitch Pipe   75
Into the Enemy Camp   79
Uncas in Danger   82
A Bear Triumphs   86
Uncas in Disguise   89
Magua Makes a Speech   91
The Cunning of the Huron   94
Duncan Shields Hawk-eye   98
The Verdict of the Delawares   102
Uncas in Charge   105
The Final Battle   107
The Last Warrior   111

Characters in *The Last of the Mohicans*   116
Glossary   117
Books for further reading and sources of illustrations   120

LIST OF ILLUSTRATIONS

page

8 British Grenadier's Mitre Cap – without brim to avoid obstruction when throwing a grenade.

9 Indian drums

10 Fife and fife case – regimental musical instrument used in conjunction with drum to aid keeping time when marching.

11 Log cabin – notches in the logs arranged so as not to retain rain water, thus preventing wood from rotting at the corner joints.

12 Costume – typical male dress of mid 18th century.

15 Trade tomahawk – traded by Europeans for furs and other Indian goods. Indian club tomahawk – a popular weapon before the advent of European influence – often used to display enemy scalps.

17 Indian bag – porcupine quills were used for decorative purposes before the widespread introduction of beads from Europe.

18 Horned rattlesnake – not found in Eastern Woodlands – a native of the Plains.

20 Bow and accoutrements. Trade iron arrow heads superceded native flint heads. Bird bolt protected carcass from damage. A wooden sheath was slipped over an ordinary arrow head, thus only stunning the bird.

22 Wooden keg – used by woodsmen, and Indians in their service.

25 Sassafras – an infusion of the roots was a popular beverage.

27 Knives. The woodsman's knife served both domestic and defensive purposes.

29 Powder horn – carved design depicts New York during conquest of Canada.

31 Flintlock or horse pistol – muzzle-loaded (see chart p. 80). Silver mounts denoted a quality gun, brass mounts being more common.

32 Holster – mounted on left side of saddle, pistol butt curving forward for easy access by right hand, left hand controlling reins. Officers often carried two pistols, one each side.

33 Musket. The Brown Bess was standard issue to British

page

Army *c*. 1715–1840. Four major models had progressively shorter barrel lengths, ranging from 46″ in the original Long Land musket (62″ overall), to 39″ in the final version, the New Land (58″ overall). 0.75 calibre. Walnut stock, brass fittings, metal ramrod.

34 Detail of lock – stamped with royal cipher.

35 Proof marks. To proof, a gun was loaded with double the recommended charge, fired, checked for damage, and if passed, proof-marked.

36 Decorations. The gorget was originally a piece of European armour to protect the throat, but later became purely ornamental and was given to Indians as a token of favour. The medal, however, was specifically produced for this latter purpose.

38 Scalping knife – traded by Europeans and colonists who paid for Indian scalps as well as wolf scalps, thus initiating the practice.

39 Scalping pole – used to display enemy scalps. Stretcher was for drying and preserving the scalp.

42 Indian knife. Indians added their own handles to metal blades given in trade.

44 Moccasins. Made of hide or straw and varying in design from tribe to tribe. Eastern Woodland version had large ankle flaps as protection against snakes. Adopted by Europeans as well-suited to the terrain.

45 Whip-poor-will

47 Swords. Decorative dress swords carried by officers and civilian gentlemen.

48 Block house. A fortified building inside a stockade, access by one door only. Of stone and brick except for two levels of timber equipped with firing slits.

49 Marquis of Montcalm

50 Military dress. The 60th Foot (Royal American) Regiment, founded in New York in 1755, became the first British rifle regiment. Its fifth Battalion was trained in skirmishing and given green camouflage uniform.

51 French musket. Fastened to stock by brass bands. 0.69 calibre and lighter than the Brown Bess. Throat-hole cocks (hammer) as opposed to the English goose-neck.

page

53 Military drum

56 Union Jack. Original was composed of the red Cross of St. George (England) and the blue saltire of St. Andrew (Scotland). In 1801 the red saltire of St. Patrick (Ireland) was added to complete the modern flag.

57 Cross of the Order of St. Louis. Founded by Louis XIV in 1693.

58 French flag – mid 18th century.

59 Wagon

60 Female dress – of necessity simple, due to conditions.

63 Humming-bird

64 Deer

65 Wolf

66 Owl

67 Indian pipes. Used by Indians long before tobacco was introduced into Europe.

69 Loon – Great Northern Diver

72 Beaver

73 Beaver lodge

75 Moose

77 Tribal totems. Pine tree marks special chief (not hereditary) and denotes the League of Six Nations.

80 Iroquois war club. A weapon carved from a single piece of ironwood, about 20″ long, weighing $1\frac{3}{4}$ lbs. Still used on ceremonial occasions.

83 Tomahawk pipes. Popular with both French and English traders. French design was more flamboyant. The bowl counterbalanced the axe head, and the handle was hollow to allow smoke to be drawn through.

85 Black bear

87 Chair. Originally an English design, more popular in the colonies than at home.

89 Head of black bear.

91 Tricorn hat. Most popular headwear of 18th century, worn by civilians and officers alike.

page

92 European pipe. Clay pipes have been used in England since the early 17th century. This Georgian style has a squatter bowl and shorter stem than the better-known Victorian Navy and Churchwarden pipes.

95 Indian designs on trade silver

97 Indian hat. Beads of European origin here used to decorate a typically Indian garment.

99 Panther, buffalo (Plains) and ermine.

100 Pigeon and wildcat.

101 Fox and hare.

102 Woodpecker and blue jay.

104 Wampum belt. Made of beads derived from shells of periwinkle and hard clam (quahaug). White wampum, symbol of joy, relatively common and used as personal adornment. Purple wampum, symbol of mourning, more scarce and therefore highly prized for trading.

105 Red pine and cone

108 British socket bayonet. Widely used during 18th century, replacing earlier plug bayonet. Socket bayonet, unlike latter, allowed firing when still in position, as it slotted on to outside of muzzle over the foresight.

111 Raven

CHARTS (numbers indicate page next to set of charts)

8 Map of area covered by the story
 Early forts in America
 Map of Indian tribal distribution
40 American Indian canoes
 Dress and equipment of a woodsman
 Indian food recipes
56 British and French uniforms
 How to load and fire a flintlock
 Uniforms, continued
88 American Indian tipi
 Woodland and plains Indians
 Iroquois longhouse

PREPARATIONS
FOR A JOURNEY

It was a feature peculiar to the colonial wars of North America, that the toils and dangers of the wilderness were to be encountered before the adverse hosts could meet. A wide and apparently an impervious boundary of forests severed the possessions of the hostile provinces of France and England. The hardy colonist, and the trained European who fought at his side, frequently expended months in struggling against the rapids of the streams, or in effecting the rugged passes of the mountains, in quest of an opportunity to exhibit their courage in a more martial conflict.

Perhaps no district throughout the wide extent of the intermediate frontiers can furnish a livelier picture of the cruelty and fierceness of the savage warfare of those periods than the country which lies between the headwaters of the Hudson and the adjacent lakes.

The facilities which nature had there offered to the march of the combatants were too obvious to be neglected. The lengthened sheet of the Champlain stretched from the frontiers of Canada, deep within the borders of the neighboring province of New York, forming a natural passage across half the distance that the French were compelled to master in order to strike their enemies. Near its southern termination, it received the contributions of another lake, whose waters were so limpid as to have been exclusively selected by the Jesuit missionaries to perform the typical purification of baptism, and to obtain for it the title of lake "du Saint Sacrement."

Winding its way among countless islands, and imbedded in mountains, the "holy lake" extended a dozen leagues still further to the south. With the high plain that there interposed itself to the further passage of the water, commenced a portage of as many miles, which conducted the adventurer to the banks of the Hudson, at a point where, with the usual obstructions of the rapids, or rifts, as they were then termed in the language of the country, the river became navigable to the tide.

While, in the pursuit of their daring plans of annoyance, the restless enterprise of the French even attempted the distant and difficult gorges of the Allegheny, it may easily be imagined that their proverbial acuteness would not overlook the natural advantages of the district we have just described. It became, emphatically, the bloody arena in which most of the battles for the mastery of the colonies were contested.

It was in this scene of strife and bloodshed that the incidents we shall attempt to relate occurred, during the third year of the war which England and France last waged for the possession of a country that neither was destined to retain.

When intelligence was received at the fort which covered the southern termination of the portage between the Hudson and the lakes, that Montcalm had been seen moving up the Champlain, with an army "numerous as the leaves on the trees," its truth was admitted with more of the craven reluctance of fear than with the stern joy that a warrior should feel in finding an enemy within reach of his blow. The news had been brought, towards the decline of a day in midsummer, by an Indian runner who also bore an urgent request from Munro, the commander of a work on the shore of the "holy lake," for a speedy and powerful reinforcement. The loyal servants of the British crown had given to one of these forest fastnesses the name of William Henry, and to the other that of Fort Edward; calling each after a favorite prince of the reigning family. The veteran Scotchman just named held the first, with a regiment of regulars and a few provincials; a force really by far too small to make headway against the formidable power that Montcalm was leading to the foot of his earthen mounds. At the latter, however, lay General Webb, who commanded the armies of the king in the northern provinces, with a body of more than five thousand men. By uniting the several detachments of his command, this officer might have arrayed nearly double that number of combatants against the enterprising Frenchman, who had ventured so far from his reinforcements, with an army but little superior in numbers.

After the first surprise of the intelligence had a little abated, a rumor was spread through the entrenched camp, which stretched along the margin of the Hudson, forming a chain of outworks to the body of the fort itself, that a chosen detachment of fifteen hundred men was to depart, with the dawn, for William Henry, the post at the northern ex-

BRITISH GRENADIER'S
MITRE CAP (48TH FOOT)

THE
UPPER
LAKE

QUEBEC

ST. LAWRENCE
RIVER

CHAMPLAIN
LAKE

LAKE OF
THE HURONS

1 2 3 4 5
6

ONTARIO LAKE

A HIGH PLACE

THE COUNTRIES
CONQUERED
BY THE
FIVE NATIONS

THE COUNTRY OF
THE FIVE NATIONS

ALBANY

PART OF
NEW ENGLAND

HUDSON RIVER

LAKE ERIE

LONG ISLAND

OHIO RIVER

MARYLAND

MAP OF AREA COVERED BY STORY MID C18TH

1 MOHAWK
2 ONEIDA
3 ONONDAGA } IROQUOIS 6
4 CAYUGA
5 SENECA

THESE FIVE AND LATER SIX TRIBES OR NATIONS
FORMED THE LEAGUE OF THE IROQUOIS ABOUT
1570. THE LEAGUE WAS FORMED PRIMARILY
FOR PROMOTING PEACE AND FOR STRENGTH. AFTER
THE EUROPEAN ARRIVAL DURING THE MID C18TH THE
POWER OF THE LEAGUE DECLINED.

EARLY FORTS IN AMERICA

BRITISH FORT· MID C18TH BECAUSE OF SPEED AND LIMITED MOST FORTS WERE CONSTRUCTED OF LOCAL MATERIALS, STONES AND EARTH. ONLY THE MORE IMPORTANT FORTIFICATIONS UTILISED MASONRY.

PALISADE WALL

AVERAGE LENGTH OF STAKE 14FT.

FIRING HOLES (PORTS)

DITCH

STOCKADE MADE FROM SODS OF EARTH LAID AGAINST AN EARTH WALL AND HELD IN PLACE BY WOODEN PICKETS

TURF SODS

METHODS OF CONSTRUCTING STOCKADE WALLS

WALL MADE FROM WOVEN SAPLINGS FILLED WITH EARTH FROM THE DITCH AND LOGS PLACED ALONG THE TOP THE REMAINING EARTH WAS PLACED INFRONT OF THE STRUCTURE.

TREES AND SCRUB WERE CLEARED AROUND THE FORT AS FAR AS CANNON RANGE (1000-1200 YARDS). THUS THE TIMBER WAS PROVIDED FOR BUILDERS NEEDS. FORTS WERE, WHEN POSSIBLE BUILT AROUND NATURAL SPRINGS

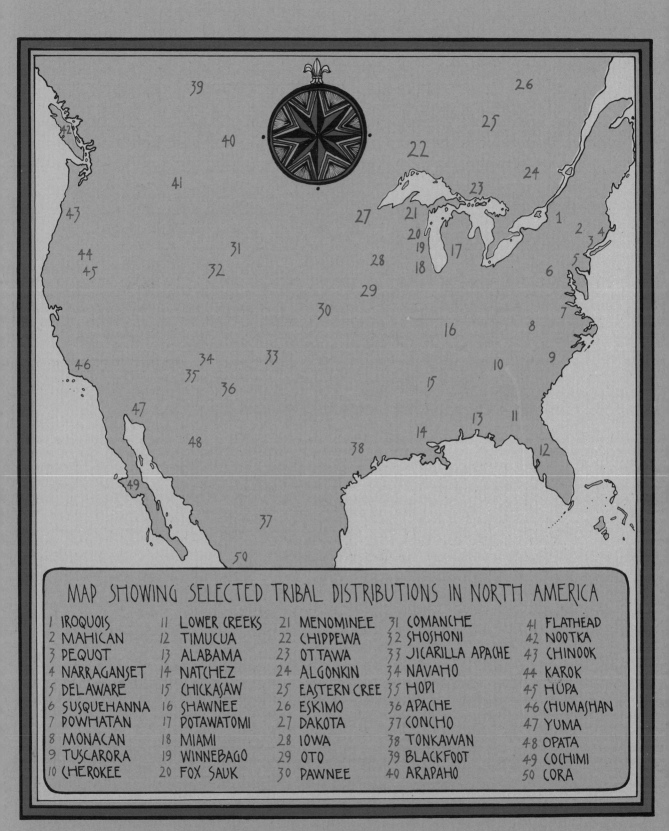

MAP SHOWING SELECTED TRIBAL DISTRIBUTIONS IN NORTH AMERICA

1 IROQUOIS	11 LOWER CREEKS	21 MENOMINEE	31 COMANCHE	41 FLATHEAD
2 MAHICAN	12 TIMUCUA	22 CHIPPEWA	32 SHOSHONI	42 NOOTKA
3 PEQUOT	13 ALABAMA	23 OTTAWA	33 JICARILLA APACHE	43 CHINOOK
4 NARRAGANSET	14 NATCHEZ	24 ALGONKIN	34 NAVAHO	44 KAROK
5 DELAWARE	15 CHICKASAW	25 EASTERN CREE	35 HOPI	45 HUPA
6 SUSQUEHANNA	16 SHAWNEE	26 ESKIMO	36 APACHE	46 CHUMASHAN
7 POWHATAN	17 POTAWATOMI	27 DAKOTA	37 CONCHO	47 YUMA
8 MONACAN	18 MIAMI	28 IOWA	38 TONKAWAN	48 OPATA
9 TUSCARORA	19 WINNEBAGO	29 OTO	39 BLACKFOOT	49 COCHIMI
10 CHEROKEE	20 FOX SAUK	30 PAWNEE	40 ARAPAHO	50 CORA

tremity of the portage. That which at first was only rumor soon became certainty, as orders passed from the quarters of the commander in chief to the several corps he had selected for this service, to prepare for their speedy departure.

According to the orders of the preceding night, the heavy sleep of the army was broken by the rolling of the warning drums, whose rattling echoes were heard issuing, on the damp morning air, out of every vista of the woods, just as day began to draw the shaggy outlines of some tall pines of the vicinity, on the opening brightness of a soft and cloudless eastern sky. In an instant the whole camp was in motion; the meanest soldier arousing from his lair to witness the departure of his comrades, and to share in the excitement and incidents of the hour. The simple array of the chosen band was soon completed. While the regular and trained hirelings of the king marched with haughtiness to the right of the line, the less pretending colonists took their humbler position on its left, with a docility that long practice had rendered easy. The scouts departed; strong guards preceded and followed the lumbering vehicles that bore the baggage; and before the gray light of the morning was mellowed by the rays of the sun, the main body of the combatants wheeled into column, and left the encampment with a show of high military bearing that served to drown the slumbering apprehensions of many a novice, who was now about to make his first essay in arms. While in view of their admiring comrades, the same proud front and ordered array was observed until, the notes of their fifes growing fainter in distance, the forest at length appeared to swallow up the living mass which had slowly entered its bosom.

The deepest sounds of the retiring and invisible column had ceased to be borne on the breeze to the listeners, and the latest straggler had already disappeared in pursuit; but there still remained the signs of another departure, before a log cabin of unusual size and accommodations, in front of which those sentinels paced their rounds who were known to guard the person of the English general. At this spot were gathered some half dozen horses, caparisoned in a manner which showed that

INDIAN DRUMS

two, at least, were destined to bear the persons of females, of a rank that it was not usual to meet so far in the wilds of the country. A third wore the trappings and arms of an officer of the staff; while the rest, from the plainness of the housings, and the traveling mails with which they were encumbered, were evidently fitted for the reception of as many menials, who were, seemingly, already awaiting the pleasure of those they served. At a respectful distance from this unusual show were gathered divers groups of curious idlers; some admiring the blood and bone of the high-mettled military charger, and others gazing at the preparations with the dull wonder of vulgar curiosity. There was one man, however, who, by his countenance and actions, formed a marked exception to those who composed the latter class of spectators, being neither idle, nor seemingly very ignorant.

The person of this individual was to the last degree ungainly without being in any particular manner deformed. He had all the bones and joints of other men, without any of their proportions. Erect, his stature surpassed that of his fellows; though, seated, he appeared reduced within the ordinary limits of the race. The same contrariety in his members seemed to exist throughout the whole man. His head was large; his shoulders narrow; his arms long and dangling; while his hands were small, if not delicate. His legs and thighs were thin, nearly to emaciation, but of extraordinary length; and his knees would have been considered tremendous, had they not been outdone by the broader foundations on which this false superstructure of blended human orders was so profanely reared.

While the common herd stood aloof, in deference to the quarters of Webb, the figure we have described stalked into the center of the domestics, freely expressing his censures or commendations on the merits of the horses, as by chance they displeased or satisfied his judgment. His eyes fell on the still, upright, and rigid form of the "Indian runner," who had borne to the camp the unwelcome tidings of the preceding evening. Although in a state of perfect repose, and apparently disregarding, with characteristic stoicism, the excitement and bustle around him, there was a

9

FIFE AND FIFE CASE

sullen fierceness mingled with the quiet of the savage that was likely to arrest the attention of much more experienced eyes than those which now scanned him, in unconcealed amazement. The native bore both the tomahawk and knife of his tribe; and yet his appearance was not altogether that of a warrior. On the contrary, there was an air of neglect about his person, like that which might have proceeded from great and recent exertion, which he had not yet found leisure to repair. His eye alone, which glistened like a fiery star amid lowering clouds, was to be seen in its state of native wildness. For a single instant, his searching and yet wary glance met the wondering look of the other, and then, changing its direction, partly in cunning and partly in disdain, it remained fixed, as if penetrating the distant air.

It is impossible to say what unlooked-for remark this short and silent communication, between two such singular men, might have elicited from the white man, had not his active curiosity been

again drawn to other objects. A general movement amongst the domestics, and a low sound of gentle voices, announced the approach of those whose presence alone was wanted to enable the cavalcade to move.

A young man in the dress of an officer conducted to their steeds two females who, as it was apparent by their dresses, were prepared to encounter the fatigues of a journey in the woods. One, and she was the most juvenile in her appearance, though both were young, permitted glimpses of her dazzling complexion, fair golden hair, and bright blue eyes to be caught, as she artlessly suffered the morning air to blow aside the green veil which descended low from her beaver. The flush which still lingered above the pines in the western sky was not more bright nor delicate than the bloom on her cheek; nor was the opening day more cheering than the animated smile which she bestowed on the youth, as he assisted her into the saddle. The other, who appeared to share equally in the

attentions of the young officer, concealed her charms from the gaze of the soldiery with a care that seemed better fitted to the experience of four or five additional years. It could be seen, however, that her person, though molded with the same exquisite proportions, of which none of the graces were lost by the traveling dress she wore, was rather fuller and more mature than that of her companion.

No sooner were these females seated than their attendant sprang lightly into the saddle of the war-horse, when the whole three bowed to Webb, who, in courtesy, awaited their parting on the threshold of his cabin, and turning their horses' heads, they proceeded at a slow amble, followed by their train, toward the northern entrance of the encampment. As they traversed that short distance, not a voice was heard amongst them; but a slight exclamation proceeded from the younger of the females as the Indian runner glided by her unexpectedly and led the way along the military road in her front. Though this sudden and startling movement of the Indian produced no sound from the other, in the surprise, her veil also was allowed to open its folds, and betrayed an indescribable look of pity, admiration, and horror, as her dark eye followed the easy motions of the savage. The tresses of this lady were shining and black, like the plumage of the raven. Her complexion was not brown, but it rather appeared charged with the color of the rich blood, that seemed ready to burst its bounds. And yet there was neither coarseness nor want of shadowing in a countenance that was exquisitely regular and dignified, and surpassingly beautiful. She smiled, as if in pity at her own momentary forgetfulness, discovering by the act a row of teeth that would have shamed the purest ivory; when, replacing the veil, she bowed her face and rode in silence, like one whose thoughts were abstracted from the scene around her.

DANGER IN THE THICKET

While one of the lovely beings we have so cursorily presented to the reader was thus lost in thought, the other quickly recovered from the alarm which induced the exclamation, and, laughing at her own weakness, she inquired of the youth who rode by her side:

"Are such specters frequent in the woods, Heyward; or is this sight an especial entertainment ordered on our behalf? If the latter, gratitude must close our mouths; but if the former, both Cora and I shall have need to draw largely on that stock of hereditary courage which we boast, even before we are made to encounter the redoubtable Montcalm."

"Yon Indian is a 'runner' of the army; and, after the fashion of his people, he may be accounted a hero," returned the officer. "He has volunteered to guide us to the lake, by a path but little known, sooner than if we followed the tardy movements of the column; and, by consequence, more agreeably."

"I like him not," said the lady, shuddering, partly in assumed, yet more in real terror. "You know him, Duncan, or you would not trust yourself so freely to his keeping?"

"Say, rather, Alice, that I would not trust you. I do know him, or he would not have my confidence, and least of all at this moment. He is said to be a Canadian too; and yet he served with our friends the Mohawks, who, as you know, are one of the six allied nations. He was brought amongst us, as I have heard, by some strange accident in which your father was interested, and

CORNER JOINT CONSTRUCTION OF A LOG CABIN

PIONEERS' LOG HOUSE

in which the savage was rigidly dealt by – but I forget the idle tale; it is enough that he is now our friend."

"If he has been my father's enemy, I like him still less!" exclaimed the now really anxious girl. "Will you not speak to him, Major Heyward, that I may hear his tones? Foolish though it may be, you have often heard me avow my faith in the tones of the human voice!"

"Should we distrust the man because his manners are not our manners, and that his skin is dark!" coldly asked Cora.

Alice hesitated no longer; but giving her Narraganset a smart cut of the whip, she was the first to dash aside the slight branches of the bushes, and to follow the runner along the dark and tangled pathway. For many minutes the intricacy of the route admitted of no further dialogue; after which they emerged from the broad border of underbrush which grew along the line of the highway, and entered under the high but dark arches of the forest. Here their progress was less interrupted; and the instant the guide perceived that the females could command their steeds, he moved on, at a pace between a trot and a walk, and at a rate which kept the sure-footed and peculiar animals they rode, at a fast yet easy amble. The youth had turned to speak to the dark-eyed Cora, when the distant sounds of horses' hoofs, clattering over the roots of the broken way in his rear, caused him to check his charger; and, as his companions drew their reins at the same instant, the whole party came to a halt, in order to obtain an explanation of the unlooked-for interruption.

In a few moments a colt was seen gliding, like a fallow deer, amongst the straight trunks of the pines; and, in another instant, the person of the ungainly man, described in the preceding chapter, came into view, with as much rapidity as he could excite his meager beast to endure without coming to an open rupture. Notwithstanding a constant application of his one armed heel to the flanks of the mare, the most confirmed gait that he could establish was a Canterbury gallop with the hind legs, in which those more forward assisted for doubtful moments, though generally content to maintain a loping trot.

The industry and movements of the rider were not less remarkable than those of the ridden. At each change in the evolutions of the latter, the former raised his tall person in the stirrups; producing, in this manner, by the undue elongation of his legs, such sudden growths and diminishings of the stature as baffled every conjecture that might be made as to his dimensions.

The frown which had gathered around the handsome, open, and manly brow of Heyward, gradually relaxed, and his lips curled into a slight smile, as he regarded the stranger. Alice made no very powerful effort to control her merriment; and even the dark thoughtful eye of Cora lighted with a humor that, it would seem, the habit, rather than the nature, of its mistress repressed.

The cavalcade had not long passed before the branches of the bushes that formed the thicket were cautiously moved asunder, and a human visage, as fiercely wild as savage art and unbridled passions could make it, peered out on the retiring footsteps of the travelers. A gleam of exultation shot across the darkly painted lineaments of the inhabitant of the forest as he traced the route of his intended victims, who rode unconsciously onward; the light and graceful forms of the females waving among the trees, in the curvatures of their path, followed at each bend by the manly figure of Heyward, until, finally, the shapeless person of the singing master was concealed behind the numberless trunks of trees, that rose, in dark lines, in the intermediate space.

MALE CIVILIAN DRESS

RIFLE AND BOW

Leaving the unsuspecting Heyward and his confiding companions to penetrate still deeper into a forest that contained such treacherous inmates, we must use an author's privilege and shift the scene a few miles to the westward of the place where we have last seen them.

On that day, two men were lingering on the banks of a small but rapid stream, within an hour's journey of the encampment of Webb, like those who awaited the appearance of an absent person, or the approach of some expected event. While one of these loiterers showed the red skin and wild accouterments of a native of the woods, the other exhibited, through the mask of his rude and nearly savage equipments, the brighter though sunburnt and long-faded complexion of one who might claim descent from a European parentage. The former was seated on the end of a mossy log, in a posture that permitted him to heighten the effect of his earnest language, by the calm but expressive gestures of an Indian engaged in debate. His body, which was nearly naked, presented a terrific emblem of death, drawn in intermingled colors of white and black. His closely shaved head, on which no other hair than the well-known and chivalrous scalping tuft was preserved, was without ornament of any kind, with the exception of a solitary eagle's plume that crossed his crown and depended over the left shoulder. A tomahawk and scalping knife, of English manufacture, were in his girdle; while a short military rifle, of that sort with which the policy of the whites armed their savage allies, lay carelessly across his bare and sinewy knee. The expanded chest, full-formed limbs, and grave countenance of this warrior would denote that he had reached the vigor of his days, though no symptoms of decay appeared to have yet weakened his manhood.

The frame of the white man, judging by such parts as were not concealed by his clothes, was like that of one who had known hardships and exertion from his earliest youth. His person, though muscular, was rather attenuated than full; but every nerve and muscle appeared strung and indurated by unremitted exposure and toil. He wore a hunting shirt of forest green, fringed with faded yellow, and a summer cap of skins which had been shorn of their fur. He also bore a knife in a girdle of wampum, like that which confined the scanty garments of the Indian, but no tomahawk. His moccasins were ornamented after the gay fashion of the natives, while the only part of his underdress which appeared below the hunting frock was a pair of buckskin leggings that laced at the sides, and which were gartered above the knees with the sinews of a deer. A pouch and horn completed his personal accouterments, though a rifle of great length, which the theory of the more ingenious whites had taught them was the most dangerous of all firearms, leaned against a neighboring sapling. The eye of the hunter or scout, whichever he might be, was small, quick, keen, and restless, roving while he spoke, on every side of him, as if in quest of game, or distrusting the sudden approach of some lurking enemy. Notwithstanding these symptoms of habitual suspicion, his countenance was not only without guile, but at the moment at which he is introduced, it was charged with an expression of sturdy honesty.

"Even your traditions make the case in my favor, Chingachgook," he said, speaking in the tongue which was known to all the natives who formerly inhabited the country between the Hudson and the Potomack, and of which we shall give a free translation for the benefit of the reader; endeavoring, at the same time, to preserve some of the peculiarities, both of the individual and of the language. "Your fathers came from the setting sun, crossed the big river, fought the people of the country, and took the land; and mine came from the red sky of the morning, over the salt lake, and did their work much after the fashion that had been set them by yours; then let God judge the matter between us, and friends spare their words!"

"My fathers fought with the naked Red Man!" returned the Indian, sternly, in the same language. "Is there no difference, Hawk-eye, between the stone-headed arrow of the warrior, and the leaden bullet with which you kill?"

"There is reason in an Indian, though nature has made him with a red skin!" said the white man, shaking his head like one on whom such an appeal to his justice was not thrown away. For a moment he appeared to be conscious of having the worst of the argument, then rallying again, he answered the objection of his antagonist in the best manner his limited information would allow: "I am no scholar, and I care not who knows it; but judging from what I have seen, at deer chases and squirrel hunts, of the sparks below, I should think a rifle in the hands of their grandfathers was not so dangerous as a hickory bow and a good flint-head might be, if drawn with Indian judgment, and sent by an Indian eye."

"You have the story told by your fathers," returned the other, coldly waving his hand. "What say your old men? Do they tell the young warriors that the palefaces met the Red Men, painted for war and armed with the stone hatchet and wooden gun?"

"I am not a prejudiced man, nor one who vaunts himself on his natural privileges, though the worst enemy I have on earth, and he is an Iroquois, daren't deny that I am genuine white," the scout replied, surveying with secret satisfaction the faded color of his bony and sinewy hand; "and I am willing to own that my people have many ways, of which, as an honest man, I can't approve. It is one of their customs to write in books what they have done and seen, instead of telling them in their villages, where the lie can be given to the face of a cowardly boaster, and the brave soldier can call on his comrades to witness for the truth of his words. In consequence of this bad fashion, a man who is too conscientious to misspend his days among the women, in learning the names of black marks, may never hear of the deeds of his fathers, nor feel a pride in striving to outdo them. For myself, I conclude all the Bumppos could shoot, for I have a natural turn with a rifle, which must have been handed down from generation to generation, as, our holy commandments tell us, all good and evil gifts are bestowed; though I should be loath to answer for other people in such a matter. But every story has its two sides: so I ask you, Chingachgook, what passed, according to the traditions of the Red Men, when our fathers first met?"

A silence of a minute succeeded, during which the Indian sat mute; then, full of the dignity of his office, he commenced his brief tale, with a solemnity that served to heighten its appearance of truth.

"Listen, Hawk-eye, and your ear shall drink no lie. 'Tis what my fathers have said, and what the Mohicans have done." He hesitated a single instant, and bending a cautious glance toward his companion, he continued, in a manner that was divided between interrogation and assertion: "Does not this stream at our feet run toward the summer, until its waters grow salt, and the current flows upward?"

"It can't be denied that your traditions tell you true in both these matters," said the white man; "for I have been there, and have seen them; though why water which is so sweet in the shade should become bitter in the sun, is an alteration for which I have never been able to account."

"And the current!" demanded the Indian, who expected his reply with that sort of interest that a man feels in the confirmation of testimony, at which he marvels even while he respects it; "the fathers of Chingachgook have not lied!

"My tribe is the grandfather of nations, but I am an unmixed man. The blood of chiefs is in my veins, where it must stay forever. The Dutch landed, and gave my people the firewater; they drank until the heavens and the earth seemed to meet, and they foolishly thought they had found the Great Spirit. Then they parted with their land. Foot by foot, they were driven back from the shores, until I, that am a chief and a Sagamore, have never seen the sun shine but through the trees, and have never visited the graves of my fathers!"

"Graves bring solemn feelings over the mind," returned the scout, a good deal touched at the calm suffering of his companion; "and they often aid a man in his good intentions; though, for myself, I expect to leave my own bones unburied, to bleach in the woods, or to be torn asunder by the wolves. But where are to be found those of your race who came to their kin in the Delaware country, so many summers since?"

"Where are the blossoms of those summers! Fallen, one by one. So all of my family departed, each in his turn, to the land of spirits. I am on the hilltop, and must go down into the valley; and when Uncas follows in my footsteps, there will no longer be any of the blood of the Sagamores, for my boy is the last of the Mohicans."

"Uncas is here!" said another voice, in the same, soft, guttural tones, near his elbow. "Who speaks to Uncas?"

The white man loosened his knife in his leathern sheath, and made an involuntary movement of the hand toward his rifle, at this sudden interruption; but the Indian sat composed, and without turning his head at the unexpected sounds.

At the next instant, a youthful warrior passed between them, with a noiseless step, and seated himself on the bank of the rapid stream. No exclamation of surprise escaped the father, nor was any question asked, or reply given, for several minutes. At length Chingachgook turned his eyes slowly toward his son, and demanded:

"Do the Maquas dare to leave the print of their moccasins in these woods?"

"I have been on their trail," replied the young Indian, "and know that they number as many as the fingers of my two hands; but they lie hid like cowards."

"The thieves are outlying for scalps and plunder!" said the white man, whom we shall call Hawk-eye, after the manner of his companions. "That busy Frenchman, Montcalm, will send his spies into our very camp, but he will know what road we travel!"

"'Tis enough!" returned the father, glancing his eye toward the setting sun. "They shall be driven like deer from their bushes. Hawk-eye, let us eat to-night, and show the Maquas that we are men tomorrow."

"I am as ready to do the one as the other: but to fight the Iroquois 'tis necessary to find the skulkers; and to eat, 'tis necessary to get the game – talk of the devil and he will come; there is a pair of the biggest antlers I have seen this season, moving the bushes below the hill! Now, Uncas," he continued in a half whisper, and laughing with a kind of inward sound, like one who had learnt to be watchful, "I will bet my charger three times full of powder, against a foot of wampum, that I take him atwix the eyes, and nearer to the right than to the left."

"It cannot be!" said the young Indian, springing to his feet with youthful eagerness. "All but the tips of his horns are hid!"

"He's a boy!" said the white man, shaking his head while he spoke, and addressing the father. "Does he think when a hunter sees a part of the creatur', he can't tell where the rest of him should be!"

Adjusting his rifle, he was about to make an exhibition of that skill on which he so much valued himself, when the warrior struck up the piece with his hand, saying, "Hawk-eye! will you fight the Maquas?"

"These Indians know the nature of the woods, as it might be by instinct!" returned the scout, dropping his rifle, and turning away like a man who was convinced of his error. "I must leave the buck to your arrow, Uncas, or we may kill a deer for the Iroquois, to eat."

The instant the father seconded this intimation by an expressive gesture of the hand, Uncas threw himself on the ground, and approached the animal with wary movements. When within a few yards of the cover, he fitted an arrow to his bow with the utmost care, while the antlers moved, as if their owner snuffed an enemy in the tainted air. In another moment the twang of the cord was heard, a white streak was seen glancing into the bushes, and the wounded buck plunged from the cover, to the very feet of his hidden enemy. Avoiding the horns of the infuriated animal, Uncas darted to his side, and passed his knife across the throat, when bounding to the edge of the river it fell, dyeing the waters with its blood.

"'Twas done with Indian skill," said the scout, laughing inwardly, but with vast satisfaction, "and 'twas a pretty sight to behold! Though an arrow is a near shot, and needs a knife to finish the work."

"Hugh!" ejaculated his companion, turning quickly, like a hound who scented game.

"By the Lord, there is a drove of them!" exclaimed the scout, whose eyes began to glisten with the ardor of his usual occupation.

"No. The horses of white men are coming!" returned the other, raising himself with dignity, and resuming his seat on the log with his former composure. "Hawk-eye, they are your brothers; speak to them."

"That will I, and in English that the king needn't be ashamed to answer," returned the hunter, speaking in the language of which he boasted.

DECEPTION AND DESERTION

TRADE TOMAHAWK

INDIAN CLUB TOMAHAWK

The words were still in the mouth of the scout when the leader of the party, whose approaching footsteps had caught the vigilant ear of the Indian, came openly into view. A beaten path, such as those made by the periodical passage of the deer, wound through a little glen at no great distance, and struck the river at the point where the white man and his red companions had posted themselves. Along this track the travelers, who had produced a surprise so unusual in the depths of the forest, advanced slowly toward the hunter, who was in front of his associates, in readiness to receive them.

"Who comes?" demanded the scout, throwing his rifle carelessly across his left arm, and keeping the forefinger of his right hand on the trigger, though he avoided all appearance of menace in the act. "Who comes hither, among the beasts and dangers of the wilderness?"

"Believers in religion, and friends to the law and to the king," returned he who rode foremost. "Men who have journeyed since the rising sun, in the shades of this forest, without nourishment, and are sadly tired of their wayfaring."

"You are, then, lost," interrupted the hunter, "and have found how helpless 'tis not to know whether to take the right hand or the left?"

"Even so; sucking babes are not more dependent on those who guide them than we who are of larger growth, and who may now be said to possess the stature without the knowledge of men. Know you the distance to a post of the crown called William Henry?"

"Hoot!" shouted the scout, who did not spare his open laughter, though, instantly checking the dangerous sounds, he indulged his merriment at less risk of being overheard by any lurking enemies. "You are as much off the scent as a hound would be, with Horican atwixt him and the deer! William Henry, man! If you are friends to the king, and have business with the army, your better way would be to follow the river down to Edward, and lay the matter before Webb; who tarries there, instead of pushing into the defiles, and driving this saucy Frenchman back across Champlain, into his den again."

Before the stranger could make any reply to this unexpected proposition, another horseman dashed the bushes aside, and leaped his charger into the pathways, in front of his companion.

"What, then, may be our distance from Fort Edward?" demanded a new speaker. "The place you advise us to seek we left this morning, and our destination is the head of the lake."

"Then you must have lost your eyesight afore losing your way, for the road across the portage is cut to a good two rods, and is as grand a path, I calculate, as any that runs into London, or even before the palace of the king himself."

"We will not dispute concerning the excellence of the passage," returned Heyward, smiling; for, as the reader has anticipated, it was he. "It is enough, for the present, that we trusted to an Indian guide to take us by a nearer, though blinder path, and that we are deceived in his knowledge. In plain words, we know not where we are."

"An Indian lost in the woods!" said the scout, shaking his head doubtingly. "When the sun is scorching the treetops, and the watercourses are full; when the moss on every beech he sees will tell him in which quarter the north star will shine at night! 'Tis strange that an Indian should be lost atwixt Horican and the bend in the river! Is he a Mohawk?"

"Not by birth, though adopted in that tribe; I think his birthplace was farther north, and he is one of those you call a Huron."

"Hugh!" exclaimed the two companions of the scout, who had continued until this part of the dialogue, seated immovable, and apparently indifferent to what passed, but who now sprang to their feet with an activity and interest that had evidently got the better of their reserve, by surprise.

"A Huron!" repeated the sturdy scout, once more shaking his head in open distrust. "They are a thievish race, nor do I care by whom they are adopted; you can never make anything of them but skulks and vagabonds. Since you trusted yourself to the care of one of that nation, I only wonder that you have not fallen in with more."

"Of that there is little danger, since William Henry is so many miles in our front. You forget that I have told you our guide is now a Mohawk, and that he serves with our forces as a friend."

"And I tell you that he who is born a Mingo will die a Mingo," returned the other, positively. "A Mohawk! No, give me a Delaware or a Mohican for honesty; and when they will fight, which they won't all do, having suffered their cunning enemies, the Maquas, to make them women – but when they will fight at all, look to a Delaware, or a Mohican, for a warrior!"

"Enough of this," said Heyward, impatiently. "You have not yet answered my question; what is our distance from the main army at Edward?"

"It seems that may depend on who is your guide. One would think such a horse as that might get over a good deal of ground atwixt sunup and sundown."

"I wish no contention of idle words with you, friend," said Heyward, curbing his dissatisfied manner, and speaking in a more gentle voice. "If you will tell me the distance to Fort Edward, and conduct me thither, your labor shall not go without its reward."

"And in so doing, how know I that I don't guide an enemy, and a spy of Montcalm, to the works of the army? It is not every man who can speak the English tongue that is an honest subject."

"If you serve with the troops, of whom I judge you to be a scout, you should know of such a regiment of the king as the 60th."

"The 60th! You can tell me little of the Royal Americans that I don't know, though I do wear a hunting shirt instead of a scarlet jacket."

"Well, then, among other things, you may know the name of its major?"

"I have heard that a young gentleman of vast riches, from one of the provinces far south, has got the place. He is over young, too, to hold such rank, and to be put above men whose heads are beginning to bleach; and yet they say he is a soldier in his knowledge, and a gallant gentleman!"

"Whatever he may be, or however he may be qualified for his rank, he now speaks to you, and of course can be no enemy to dread."

The scout regarded Heyward in surprise, and then lifting his cap, he answered, in a tone less confident than before – though still expressing doubt –

"I have heard a party was to leave the encampment this morning, for the lake shore?"

"You have heard the truth; but I preferred a nearer route, trusting to the knowledge of the Indian I mentioned."

"And he deceived you, and then deserted?"

"Neither, as I believe; certainly not the latter, for he is to be found in the rear."

"I should like to look at the creatur'; if it is a true Iroquois I can tell him by his knavish look, and by his paint," said the scout, stepping past the charger of Heyward, and entering the path behind the mare of the singing master, whose foal had taken advantage of the halt to exact the maternal contribution. After shoving aside the bushes, and proceeding a few paces, he encountered the females, who awaited the result of the conference with anxiety, and not entirely without apprehension. Behind these, the runner leaned against a tree, where he stood the close examination of the scout with an air unmoved, though with a look so dark and savage that it might in itself excite fear. Satisfied with his scrutiny, the hunter soon left him. As he repassed the females, he paused a moment to gaze upon their beauty, answering to the smile and nod of Alice with a look of open pleasure. Thence he went to the side of the motherly animal, and spending a minute in a fruitless inquiry into the character of her rider, he shook his head and returned to Heyward.

"A Mingo is a Mingo, and God having made him so, neither the Mohawks nor any other tribe can alter him," he said, when he had regained his former position. "If we were alone, and you would leave that noble horse at the mercy of the wolves tonight, I could show you the way to Edward, myself, within an hour, for it lies only about an hour's journey hence; but with such ladies in your company 'tis impossible!"

"And why? They are fatigued, but they are quite equal to a ride of a few more miles."

"'Tis a natural impossibility!" repeated the scout. "I wouldn't walk a mile in these woods after night gets into them, in company with that runner, for the best rifle in the colonies. They are full of outlying Iroquois, and your mongrel Mohawk knows where to find them too well, to be my companion."

"Think you so?" said Heyward, leaning forward in the saddle, and dropping his voice nearly to a whisper. "I confess I have not been without my own suspicions, though I have endeavored to conceal them, and affected a confidence I have not always felt, on account of my companions. It was because I suspected him that I would follow no longer; making him, as you see, follow me."

"I knew he was one of the cheats as soon as I laid eyes on him!" returned the scout, placing a finger on his nose, in sign of caution. "The thief is leaning against the foot of the sugar sapling, that you can see over them bushes; his right leg is in a line with the bark of the tree, and," tapping his rifle, "I can take him from where I stand, between the ankle and the knee, with a single shot."

"Hold!" interrupted Heyward. "It will not do – we must think of some other scheme – and yet, I have much reason to believe the rascal deceived me."

The hunter, who had already abandoned his intention of maiming the runner, mused a moment and then made a gesture, which instantly brought his two red companions to his side. They spoke together earnestly in the Delaware language. His companions were not long in comprehending his wishes, and laying aside their firearms, they parted, taking opposite sides of the path and burying themselves in the thicket, with such cautious movements that their steps were inaudible.

"Now, go you back," said the hunter, speaking again to Heyward, "and hold the imp in talk; these Mohicans here will take him without breaking his paint."

"Nay," said Heyward, proudly, "I will seize him myself."

"Hist! what could you do, mounted, against an Indian in the bushes?"

"I will dismount."

"And, think you, when he saw one of your feet out of the stirrup, he would wait for the other to be free? Whoever comes into the woods to deal with the natives, must use Indian fashions, if he would wish to prosper in his undertakings. Go, then; talk openly to the miscreant, and seem to believe him the truest friend you have on 'arth."

Heyward prepared to comply, though with strong disgust at the nature of the office he was compelled to execute. The sun had already disappeared, and the woods, suddenly deprived of his light, were assuming a dusky hue, which keenly reminded him that the hour the savage usually chose for his most barbarous and remorseless acts of vengeance or hostility, was speedily drawing near.. Stimulated by apprehension, he left the scout, who immediately entered into a loud conversation with the stranger that had so unceremoniously enlisted himself in the party of travelers that morning. He spurred his charger, and drew the reins again, when the animal had carried him within a few yards of the place where the sullen runner still stood, leaning against the tree.

"You may see, Magua," he said, endeavoring to assume an air of freedom and confidence, "that the night is closing around us, and yet we are no nearer to William Henry than when we left the encampment of Webb with the rising sun. You have missed the way, nor have

INDIAN QUILLED BAG

I been more fortunate. But, happily, we have fallen in with a hunter, he whom you hear talking to the singer, that is acquainted with the deer paths and by-ways of the woods, and who promises to lead us to a place where we may rest securely till the morning."

The Indian riveted his glowing eyes on Heyward as he asked, in his imperfect English, "Is he alone?"

"Alone!" hesitatingly answered Heyward, to whom deception was too new to be assumed without embarassment. "Oh! not alone, surely, Magua, for you know that we are with him."

"Then Le Renard Subtil will go," returned the runner, coolly raising his little wallet from the place where it had lain at his feet; "and the palefaces will see none but their own color."

"Go! Whom call you Le Renard?"

"'Tis the name his Canada fathers have given to Magua," returned the runner, with an air that manifested his pride at the distinction. "Night is the same as day to Le Subtil, when Munro waits for him."

"And what account will Le Renard give the chief of William Henry concerning his daughters? Will he dare to tell the hotblooded Scotsman that his children are left without a guide, though Magua promised to be one?"

"Though the gray head has a loud voice, and a long arm, Le Renard will not hear him, or feel him, in the woods."

"But what will the Mohawks say? They will make him petticoats, and bid him stay in the wigwam with the women, for he is no longer to be trusted with the business of a man."

"Le Subtil knows the path to the great lakes, and he can find the bones of his fathers," was the answer of the unmoved runner.

"Enough, Magua," said Heyward. "Are we not friends?"

The Indian then fastened his eyes keenly on the open countenance of Heyward, but meeting his glance, he turned them quickly away, and seating himself deliberately on the ground, he drew forth the remnant of some former repast, and began to eat, though not without first bending his looks slowly and cautiously around him.

"This is well," continued Heyward; "and Le Renard will have strength and sight to find the path in the morning."

Magua held out the wallet to the proffer of the other. He even suffered their hands to meet, without betraying the least emotion, or varying his riveted attitude of attention. But when he felt the fingers of Heyward moving gently along his own naked arm, he struck up the limb of the young man, and uttering a piercing cry as he darted beneath it, plunged, at a single bound, into the opposite thicket. At the next instant the form of Chingachgook appeared from the bushes, looking like a specter in its paint, and glided across the path in swift pursuit. Next followed the shout of Uncas, when the woods were lighted by a sudden flash that was accompanied by the sharp report of the hunter's rifle.

HORNED RATTLESNAKE

HAWK-EYE TAKES CHARGE

The suddenness of the flight of his guide, and the wild cries of the pursuers, caused Heyward to remain fixed for a few moments in inactive surprise. Then recollecting the importance of securing the fugitive, he dashed aside the surrounding bushes, and pressed eagerly forward to lend his aid in the chase. Before he had, however, proceeded a hundred yards, he met the three foresters already returning from their unsuccessful pursuit.

"Why so soon disheartened!" he exclaimed. "The scoundrel must be concealed behind some of these trees, and may yet be secured. We are not safe while he goes at large."

"Would you set a cloud to chase the wind?" returned the disappointed scout. "I heard the imp, brushing over the dry leaves, like a black snake, and blinking a glimpse of him, just over ag'in yon big pine, I pulled as it might be on the scent; but 'twouldn't do! And yet for a reasoning aim, if anybody but myself had touched the trigger, I should call it a quick sight; and I may be accounted to have experience in these matters, and one who ought to know. Look at this sumach; its leaves are red, though everybody knows the fruit is in the yellow blossom, in the month of July!"

"'Tis the blood of Le Subtil! He is hurt, and may yet fall!"

"No, no," returned the scout, in decided disapprobation of this opinion. "I rubbed the bark off a limb, perhaps, but the creature leaped the longer for it. A rifle bullet acts on a running animal, when it barks him, much the same as one of your spurs on a horse; that is, it quickens motion, and puts life into the flesh, instead of taking it away. But when it cuts the ragged hole, after a bound or two, there is, commonly, a stagnation of further leaping, be it Indian or be it deer!"

"We are four able bodies, to one wounded man!"

"Is life grievous to you?" interrupted the scout. "Yonder red devil would draw you within swing of the tomahawks of his comrades, before you were heated in the chase. It was an unthoughtful act in a man who has so often slept with the war whoop ringing in the air, to let off his piece within sound of an ambushment! But then it was a natural temptation! 'Twas very natural! Come, friends, let us move our station, and in such a fashion, too, as will throw the cunning of a Mingo on a wrong scent, or our scalps will be drying in the wind in front of Montcalm's marquee, ag'in this hour tomorrow."

This appalling declaration, which the scout uttered with the cool assurance of a man who fully comprehended, while he did not fear to face the danger, served to remind Heyward of the importance of the charge with which he himself had been intrusted.

"What is to be done?" he said, feeling the utter helplessness of doubt in such a pressing strait. "Desert me not, for God's sake! Remain to defend those I escort, and freely name your own reward?"

His companions, who conversed apart in the language of their tribe, heeded not this sudden and earnest appeal. Though their dialogue was maintained in low and cautious sounds, but little above a whisper, Heyward, who now approached, could easily distinguish the earnest tones of the younger warrior from the more deliberate speeches of his seniors. Heyward drew still nigher to the dusky group, with an intention of making his offers of compensation more definite, when the white man, motioning with his hand, as if he conceded the disputed point, turned away, saying in a sort of soliloquy, and in the English tongue:

"Uncas is right! It would not be the act of men to leave such harmless things to their fate, even though it breaks up the harboring place forever. If you would save these tender blossoms from the fangs of the worst of sarpents, gentleman, you have neither time to lose nor resolution to throw away!"

"How can such a wish be doubted! Have I not already offered – "

"Offer your prayers to Him who can give us wisdom to circumvent the cunning of the devils who fill these woods," calmly interrupted the scout, "but spare your offers of money, which neither you may live to realize, nor I to profit by. These Mohicans and I will do what man's thoughts can invent, to keep such flowers, which, though so sweet, were never made for the wilderness, from harm, and that without hope of any other recompense but such as God always gives to upright dealings. First, you must promise two things, both in your own name and for your friends, or without serving you, we shall only injure ourselves!"

"Name them."

"The one is, to be still as these sleeping woods, let what will happen; and the other is, to keep the place where we shall take you forever a secret from all mortal men."

"I will do my utmost to see both these conditions fulfilled."

"Then follow, for we are losing moments that are as precious as the heart's blood to a stricken deer!"

Heyward could distinguish the impatient gesture of the scout, through the increasing shadows of the evening, and he moved in his footsteps, swiftly, toward the place where he had left the remainder of his party. When they rejoined the expectant and anxious females, he briefly acquainted them with the conditions of their new guide, and with the necessity that existed for their hushing every apprehension, in instant and serious exertions. Although his alarming communication was not received without much secret terror by the listeners, his earnest and impressive manner, aided perhaps by the nature of the danger, succeeded in bracing their nerves to undergo some unlooked-for and unusual trial. Silently, and without a moment's delay, they permitted him to assist them from their saddles, when they descended quickly to the water's edge where the scout had collected the rest of the party, more by the agency of expressive gestures than by any use of words.

"What to do with these dumb creatures!" muttered the white man, on whom the sole control of their future movements appeared to devolve. "It would be time lost to cut their throats and cast them into the river; and to leave them here would be to tell the Mingoes that they have not far to seek to find their owners!"

"Then give them their bridles, and let them range the woods," Heyward ventured to suggest.

"No; it would be better to mislead the imps, and make them believe they must equal a horse's speed to run down their chase. Aye, aye, that will blind their fireballs of eyes! Chingach – Hist! what stirs the bush?"

"The colt."

"That colt, at least, must die," muttered the scout, grasping at the mane of the nimble beast, which easily eluded his hand. "Uncas, your arrows!"

"Hold!" exclaimed the proprietor of the condemned animal, aloud, without regard to the whispering tones used by the others. "Spare the foal of Miriam! It is the comely offspring of a faithful dam, and would willingly injure naught."

"When men struggle for the single life God has given them," said the scout sternly, "even their own kind seem no more than the beasts of the wood. If you speak again, I shall leave you to the mercy of the Maquas! Draw to your arrow's head, Uncas; we have no time for second blows."

The low, muttering sounds of his threatening voice were still audible, when the wounded foal, first rearing on

IRON · NOCK · FLINT ARROW HEAD.

AERIAL VIEW OF FLIGHTS.

BIRD BOLT · WAR ARROWS · QUIVER AND BOW

its hinder legs, plunged forward to its knees. It was met by Chingachgook, whose knife passed across its throat quicker than thought, and then precipitating the motions of the struggling victim, he dashed it into the river, down whose stream it glided away, gasping audibly for breath with its ebbing life. This deed of apparent cruelty, but of real necessity, fell upon the spirits of the travelers like a terrific warning of the peril in which they stood, heightened as it was by the calm though steady resolution of the actors in the scene.

The Indians, however, hesitated not a moment, but taking the bridles, they led the frightened and reluctant horses into the bed of the river.

At a short distance from the shore, they turned, and were soon concealed by the projection of the bank, under the brow of which they moved, in a direction opposite to the course of the waters. In the meantime, the scout drew a canoe of bark from its place of concealment beneath some low bushes whose branches were waving with the eddies of the current, into which he silently motioned for the females to enter. They complied without hesitation, though many a fearful and anxious glance was thrown behind them toward the thickening gloom which now lay like a dark barrier along the margin of the stream.

So soon as Cora and Alice were seated, the scout, without regarding the element, directed Heyward to support one side of the frail vessel, and posting himself at the other, they bore it up against the stream, followed by the dejected owner of the dead foal. At length they reached a point in the river where the roving eye of Heyward became riveted on a cluster of black objects, collected at a spot where the high bank threw a deeper shadow than usual on the dark waters. Hesitating to advance, he pointed out the place to the attention of his companion.

"Aye," returned the composed scout, "the Indians have hid the beasts with the judgment of natives! Water leaves no trail, and an owl's eyes would be blinded by the darkness of such a hole."

The whole party was soon reunited, and another consultation was held between the scout and his new comrades, during which they whose fates depended on the faith and ingenuity of these unknown foresters, had a little leisure to observe their situation more minutely.

The river was confined between high and cragged rocks, one of which impended above the spot where the canoe rested. As these, again, were surmounted by tall trees, which appeared to totter on the brows of the precipice, it gave the stream the appearance of running through a deep and narrow dell. The scout directed Heyward and his disconsolate fellow travelers to seat themselves in the forward end of the canoe, and took possession of the other himself, as erect and steady as if he floated in a vessel of much firmer materials. The Indians warily retraced their steps toward the place they had left, when the scout, placing his pole against a rock, by a powerful shove, sent his frail bark directly into the center of the turbulent stream. For many minutes the struggle between the light bubble in which they floated, and the swift current, was severe and doubtful. Forbidden to stir even a hand, and almost afraid to breathe lest they should expose the frail fabric to the fury of the stream, the passengers watched the glancing waters in feverish suspense. Twenty times they thought the whirling eddies were sweeping them to destruction, when the master hand of their pilot would bring the bows of the canoe to stem the rapid. A long, a vigorous, and, as it appeared to the females, a desperate effort, closed the struggle.

"Where are we? And what is next to be done?" demanded Heyward, perceiving that the exertions of the scout had ceased.

"You are at the foot of Glenn's," returned the other, speaking aloud without fear of consequences, within the roar of the cataract; "and the next thing is to make a steady landing, lest the canoe upset, and you should go down again the hard road we have traveled, faster than you came up; 'tis a hard rift to stem, when the river is a little swelled; and five is an unnatural number to keep dry, in the hurry-skurry, with a little birchen bark and gum. There, go you all on the rock, and I will bring up the Mohicans with the venison. A man had better sleep without his scalp than famish in the midst of plenty."

His passengers gladly complied with these directions. As the last foot touched the rock, the canoe whirled from its station, when the tall form of the scout was seen, for an instant, gliding above the waters, before it disappeared in the impenetrable darkness that rested on the bed of the river. Left by their guide, the travelers remained a few minutes in helpless ignorance, afraid even to move along the broken rocks, lest a false step should precipitate them down some one of the many deep and roaring caverns, into which the water seemed to tumble, on every side of them. Their suspense, however, was soon relieved; for aided by the skill of the natives, the canoe shot back into the eddy, and floated again at the side of the low rock, before they thought the scout had even time to rejoin his companions.

"The death of the colt sits heavy on the heart of its owner," said the scout; "but it's a good sign to see a man account upon his dumb friends. He has the religion of the matter, in believing what is to happen will happen; and with such a consolation, it won't be long afore he submits to the rationality of killing a four-footed beast, to save the lives of human men."

The scout, whilst making his remarks, was busied in collecting certain necessary implements; as he concluded, he moved silently by the group of travelers, accompanied by the Mohicans, who seemed to comprehend his intentions with instinctive readiness, when the whole three disappeared in succession, seeming to vanish against the dark face of a perpendicular rock, that rose to the height of a few yards, within as many feet of the water's edge.

THE HARBORING PLACE

Heyward and his female companions witnessed this mysterious movement with secret uneasiness; for, though the conduct of the white man had hitherto been above reproach, his rude equipments, blunt address, and strong antipathies, together with the character of his silent associates, were all causes for exciting distrust in minds that had been so recently alarmed by Indian treachery.

The stranger alone disregarded the passing incidents. He seated himself on a projection of the rocks, whence he gave no other signs of consciousness than by the struggles of his spirit, as manifested in frequent and heavy sighs. Smothered voices were next heard, as though men called to each other in the bowels of the earth, when a sudden light flashed upon those without, and laid bare the much prized secret of the place.

At the further extremity of a narrow, deep cavern in the rock, whose length appeared much extended by the perspective and the nature of the light by which it was seen, was seated the scout, holding a blazing knot of pine. The strong glare of the fire fell full upon his sturdy, weather-beaten countenance and forest attire, lending an air of romantic wildness to the aspect of an individual who, seen by the sober light of day, would have exhibited the peculiarities of a man remarkable for the strangeness of his dress, the ironlike inflexibility of his frame, and the singular compound of quick, vigilant sagacity and of exquisite simplicity that by turns usurped the possession of his muscular features. At a little distance in advance stood Uncas, his whole person thrown powerfully into view. The travelers anxiously regarded the upright, flexible figure of the young Mohican, graceful and unrestrained in the attitudes and movements of nature. Though his person was more than usually screened by a green and

fringed hunting shirt, like that of the white man, there was no concealment to his dark, glancing, fearless eye, alike terrible and calm; the bold outline of his high, haughty features, pure in their native red; or to the dignified elevation of his receding forehead, together with all the finest proportions of a noble head, bared to the generous scalping tuft. It was the first opportunity possessed by Duncan and his companions to view the marked lineaments of either of their Indian attendants, and each individual of the party felt relieved from a burden of doubt, as the proud and determined, though wild expression of the features of the young warrior forced itself on their notice. They felt it might be a being partially benighted in the vale of ignorance, but it could not be one who would willingly devote his rich natural gifts to the purposes of wanton treachery. The ingenuous Alice gazed at his free air and proud carriage as she would have looked upon some precious relic of the Grecian chisel, to which life had been imparted by the intervention of a miracle; while Heyward, though accustomed to see the perfection of form which abounds among the uncorrupted natives, openly expressed his admiration at such an unblemished specimen of the noblest proportions of man.

"I could sleep in peace," whispered Alice, in reply, "with such a fearless and generous looking youth for my sentinel. Surely, Duncan, those cruel murders, those terrific scenes of torture, of which we read and hear so much, are never acted in the presence of such as he!"

"This, certainly, is a rare and brilliant instance of those natural qualities in which these peculiar people are said to excel," he answered. "I agree with you, Alice, in thinking that such a front and eye were formed rather to intimidate than to deceive; but let us not practise a deception upon ourselves by expecting any other exhibition of what we esteem virtue than according to the fashion of a savage. As bright examples of great qualities are but too uncommon among Christians, so are they singular and solitary with the Indians; though, for the honor of our common nature, neither are incapable of producing them. Let us then hope that this Mohican may not disappoint our wishes, but prove, what his looks assert him to be, a brave and constant friend."

"Now Major Heyward speaks as Major Heyward should," said Cora. "Who that looks at this creature of nature, remembers the shade of his skin!"

A short, and apparently an embarrassed silence succeeded this remark, which was interrupted by the scout calling to them aloud, to enter.

"Are we quite safe in this cavern?" demanded Heyward. "Is there no danger of surprise? A single armed man, at its entrance, would hold us at his mercy."

A spectral-looking figure stalked from out the darkness behind the scout and, seizing a blazing brand, held it toward the further extremity of their place of retreat. Alice uttered a faint shriek, and even Cora rose to her feet, as this appalling object moved into the light; but a single word from Heyward calmed them, with the assurance it was only their attendant, Chingachgook who, lifting another blanket, discovered that the cavern had two outlets. Then, holding the brand, he crossed a deep, narrow chasm in the rocks, which ran at right angles with the passage they were in, but which, unlike that, was open to the heavens, and entered another cave, answering to the description of the first in every essential particular.

"Such old foxes as Chingachgook and myself are not often caught in a burrow with one hole," said Hawk-eye, laughing. "You can easily see the cunning of the place – the rock is black limestone, which everybody knows is soft; it makes no uncomfortable pillow, where brush and pinewood is scarce; well, the fall was once a few yards below us, and I dare to say was, in its time, as regular and as handsome a sheet of water as any along the Hudson. But old age is a great injury to good looks, as these sweet young ladies have yet to l'arn! The place is sadly changed! These rocks are full of cracks, and in some places they are softer than at othersome, and the water has worked out deep hollows for itself, until it has fallen back, aye, some hundred feet, breaking here and wearing there, until the falls have neither shape nor consistency."

"In what part of them are we?" asked Heyward.

"Why, we are nigh the spot that Providence first placed them at, but where, it seems, they were too rebellious to stay. The rock proved softer on each side of us, and so they left the center of the river bare and dry, first working out these two little holes for us to hide in."

"We are then on an island?"

"Aye! There are the falls on two sides of us, and the river above and below. If you had daylight, it would be worth the trouble to step up on the height of this rock, and look at the perversity of the water. It falls by no rule at all; sometimes it leaps, sometimes it tumbles; there, it skips; here, it shoots; in one place 'tis white as snow, and in another 'tis green as grass; hereabouts, it pitches into deep hollows, that rumble and quake the 'arth; and thereaway, it ripples and sings like a brook, fashioning whirlpools and gulleys in the old stone, as if 'twas no harder than trodden clay."

While his auditors received a cheering assurance of the security of their place of concealment from this untutored description of Glenn's, they were much inclined to judge differently from Hawk-eye of its wild beauties. But they were not in a situation to suffer their thoughts to dwell on the charms of natural objects; and, as the scout had not found it necessary to cease his culinary labors while he spoke, unless to point out with a broken fork the direction of some particularly obnoxious point in the rebellious stream, they now suffered their attention to be drawn to the necessary though more vulgar consideration of their supper.

The repast, which was greatly aided by the addition of a few delicacies that Heyward had the precaution to bring with him when they left their horses, was exceedingly refreshing to the wearied party. Uncas acted as attendant to the females, performing all the little offices within his power, with a mixture of dignity and anxious grace that served to amuse Heyward, who well knew that it was an utter innovation on the Indian customs, which forbid their warriors to descend to any menial employment, especially in favor of their women.

In the meanwhile, the gravity of Chingachgook remained immovable. He had seated himself more within the circle of light, where the frequent uneasy glances of his guests were better enabled to separate the natural expression of his face from the artificial terrors of the war paint. They found a strong resemblance between father and son, with the difference that might be expected from age and hardships. The fierceness of his countenance now seemed to slumber, and in its place was to be seen the quiet, vacant composure which distinguishes an Indian warrior when his faculties are not required for any of the greater purposes of his existence. On the other hand, the quick, roving eye of the scout seldom rested. He ate and drank with an appetite that no sense of danger could disturb, but his vigilance seemed never to desert him. Twenty times the gourd or the venison was suspended before his lips, while his head was turned aside, as though he listened to some distant and distrusted sounds – a movement that never failed to recall his guests from regarding the novelties of their situa-

WOODEN KEG CONTAINING SPIRITS OR WATER

tion, to a recollection of the alarming reasons that had driven them to seek it. As these frequent pauses were never followed by any remark, the momentary uneasiness they created quickly passed away, and for a time was forgotten.

"Come, friend," said Hawk-eye, drawing out a keg from beneath a cover of leaves, toward the close of the repast, and addressing the stranger who sat at his elbow, doing great justice to his culinary skill, "try a little spruce; 'twill wash away all thoughts of the colt, and quicken the life in your bosom. I drink to our better friendship, hoping that a little horseflesh may leave no heartburnings atween us. How do you name yourself?"

"Gamut – David Gamut," returned the singing master, preparing to wash down his sorrows in a powerful draught of the woodman's high-flavored and well-laced compound.

"A very good name, and, I dare say, handed down from honest forefathers. I'm an admirer of names, though the Christian fashions fall far below savage customs in this particular. The biggest coward I ever knew was called Lyon; and his wife, Patience, would scold you out of hearing in less time than a hunted deer would run a rod. With an Indian 'tis a matter of conscience; what he calls himself, he generally is – not that Chingachgook, which signifies big sarpent, is really a snake, big or little; but that he understands the windings and turnings of human natur', and is silent, and strikes his enemies when they least expect him. – What may be your calling?"

"I am an unworthy instructor in the art of psalmody."

"Anan!"

"I teach singing to the youths of the Connecticut levy."

"You might be better employed. The young hounds go laughing and singing too much already through the woods, when they ought not to breathe louder than a fox in his cover. Can you use the smooth bore, or handle the rifle?"

"Praised be God, I have never had occasion to meddle with murderous implements!"

"Perhaps you understand the compass, and lay down the watercourses and mountains of the wilderness on paper, in order that they who follow may find places by their given names?"

"I practise no such employment."

"You have a pair of legs that might make a long path seem short! You journey sometimes, I fancy, with tidings for the general."

"Never; I follow no other than my own high vocation, which is instruction in sacred music!"

"'Tis a strange calling," muttered Hawk-eye, with an inward laugh. "Let us hear what you can do in that way; 'twill be a friendly manner of saying good night, for 'tis time that these ladies should be getting strength for a hard and a long push, in the pride of the morning, afore the Maquas are stirring."

"With joyful pleasure do I consent," said David, adjusting his iron-rimmed spectacles, and producing his beloved little volume, which he immediately tendered to Alice. "What can be more fitting and consolatory, than to offer up evening praise, after a day of such exceeding jeopardy!"

Alice smiled; but regarding Heyward, she blushed and hesitated.

"Indulge yourself," he whispered. "Ought not the suggestion of the worthy namesake of the Psalmist to have its weight at such a moment?"

Encouraged by his opinion, Alice did what her pious inclinations and her keen relish for gentle sounds had before so strongly urged. The book was opened at a hymn not ill adapted to their situation, and in which the poet, no longer goaded by his desire to excel the inspired King of Israel, had discovered some chastened and respectable powers. Cora betrayed a disposition to support her sister, and the sacred song proceeded, after the indispensable preliminaries of the pitch pipe and the tune had been duly attended to by the methodical David.

The air was solemn and slow. At times it rose to the fullest compass of the rich voices of the females, who hung over their little book in holy excitement, and again it sank so low that the rushing of the waters ran through their melody, like a hollow accompaniment. The natural taste and true ear of David governed and modified the sounds to suit the confined cavern, every crevice and cranny of which was filled with the thrilling notes of their flexible voices. The Indians riveted their eyes on the rocks, and listened with an attention that seemed to turn them into stone.

But the scout, who had placed his chin in his hand, with an expression of cold indifference, gradually suffered his rigid features to relax until, as verse succeeded verse, he felt his iron nature subdued, while his recollection was carried back to boyhood, when his ears had been accustomed to listen to similar sounds of praise, in the settlements of the colony. The singers were dwelling on one of those low, dying chords, which the ear devours with such greedy rapture, as if conscious that it is about to lose them, when a cry that seemed neither human nor earthly rose in the outward air, penetrating not only the recesses of the cavern, but to the inmost hearts of all who heard it. It was followed by a stillness apparently as deep as if the waters had been checked in their furious progress at such a horrid and unusual interruption.

"What is it?" murmured Alice, after a few moments of terrible suspense.

"What is it?" repeated Heyward.

Neither Hawk-eye nor the Indians made any reply. They listened, as if expecting the sound would be repeated, with a manner that expressed their own astonishment. At length, they spoke together, earnestly, in the Delaware language, when Uncas, passing by the inner and most concealed aperture, cautiously left the cavern. When he had gone, the scout first spoke in English.

"What it is, or what it is not, none here can tell; though two of us have ranged the woods for more than thirty years! I did believe there was no cry that Indian or beast could make, that my ears had not heard; but this has proved that I was only a vain and conceited mortal!"

"Was it not, then, the shout the warriors make when they wish to intimidate their enemies?" asked Cora, who stood drawing her veil about her person, with a calmness to which her agitated sister was a stranger.

"No, no; this was bad, and shocking, and had a sort of unhuman sound; but when you once hear the war whoop, you will never mistake it for anything else! Well, Uncas!" speaking in Delaware to the young chief as he reentered, "what see you? Do our lights shine through the blankets?"

The answer was short, and apparently decided, being given in the same tongue.

"There is nothing to be seen without," continued Hawk-eye, shaking his head in discontent; "and our hiding place is still in darkness! Pass into the other cave, you that need it, and seek for sleep; we must be afoot long before the sun and make the most of our time to get to Edward, while the Mingoes are taking their morning nap."

Cora set the example of compliance, with a steadiness that taught the more timid Alice the necessity of obedience. Before leaving the place, however, she whispered a request to Duncan that he would follow. Uncas raised the blanket for their passage, and as the sisters turned to thank him for this act of attention, they saw the scout seated again before the dying embers, with his face resting on his hands, in a manner which showed how deeply he brooded on the unaccountable interruption which had broken up their evening devotions.

Heyward took with him a blazing knot, which threw a dim light through the narrow vista of their new apartment. Placing it in a favorable position, he joined the females, who now found themselves alone with him for the first time since they had left the friendly ramparts of Fort Edward.

"Leave us not, Duncan," said Alice. "We cannot sleep in such a place as this, with that horrid cry still ringing in our ears!"

"Nature has made an impenetrable barrier on this side," he said, pointing down the perpendicular declivity into the dark current, before he dropped the blanket; "and as you know that good men and true are on guard in front, I see no reason why the advice of our honest host should be disregarded. I am certain Cora will join me in saying that sleep is necessary to you both."

Duncan ceased speaking; for the same strong, horrid cry as before filled the air, and rendered him mute. A long, breathless silence succeeded, during which each looked at the others in fearful expectation of hearing the sound repeated. At length, the blanket was slowly raised, and the scout stood in the aperture with a countenance whose firmness evidently began to give way before a mystery that seemed to threaten some danger, against which all his cunning and experience might prove of no avail.

THE MAQUAS ATTACK

"'Twould be neglecting a warning that is given for our good to lie hid any longer," said Hawk-eye, "when such sounds are raised in the forest! These gentle ones may keep close, but the Mohicans and I will watch upon the rock, where I suppose a major of the 60th would wish to keep us company."

"Is then our danger so pressing?" asked Cora.

"He who makes strange sounds, and gives them out for man's information, alone knows our danger. I should think myself wicked, unto rebellion against his will, was I to burrow with such warnings in the air! Even the weak soul who passes his days in singing is stirred by the cry and, as he says, is 'ready to go forth to the battle.' If 'twere only a battle, it would be a thing understood by us all, and easily managed; but I have heard that when such shrieks are atween heaven and 'arth, it betokens another sort of warfare!"

"It is extraordinary!" said Heyward, taking his pistols from the place where he had laid them on entering. "Be it a sign of peace or a signal of war, it must be looked to. Lead the way, my friend; I follow."

On issuing from their place of confinement, the whole party instantly experienced a grateful renovation of spirits, by exchanging the pent air of the hiding place for the cool and invigorating atmosphere, which played around the whirlpools and pitches of the cataract. Their anxious and eager looks were baffled by the deceptive light, or rested only on naked rocks, and straight and immovable trees.

"Here is nothing to be seen but the gloom and quiet of a lovely evening," whispered Duncan. "How much should we prize such a scene, and all this breathing solitude, at any other moment, Cora! Fancy yourselves in security, and what now, perhaps, increases your terror, may be made conducive to enjoyment—".

"Listen!" interrupted Alice.

The caution was unnecessary. Once more the same sound arose, as if from the bed of the river, and having broken out of the narrow bounds of the cliffs, was heard undulating through the forest, in distant and dying cadences.

"Can any here give a name to such a cry?" demanded Hawk-eye, when the last echo was lost in the woods. "If so, let him speak; for myself, I judge it not to belong to 'arth!"

"Here, then, is one who can undeceive you," said Duncan. "I know the sound full well, for often have I heard it on the field of battle, and in situations which are frequent in a soldier's life. 'Tis the horrid shriek that a horse will give in his agony; oftener drawn from him in pain, though sometimes in terror. My charger

SASSAFRAS LEAVES

is either a prey to the beasts of the forest, or he sees his danger without the power to avoid it. The sound might deceive me in the cavern, but in the open air I know it too well to be wrong."

The scout and his companions listened to this simple explanation with the interest of men who imbibe new ideas, at the same time that they get rid of old ones which had proved disagreeable inmates. The two latter uttered their usual and expressive exclamation, "hugh!" as the truth first glanced upon their minds, while the former, after a short musing pause, took upon himself to reply.

"I cannot deny your words," he said; "for I am little skilled in horses, though born where they abound. The wolves must be hovering above their heads on the bank, and the timorsome creatures are calling on man for help, in the best manner they are able. Uncas" – he spoke in Delaware – "Uncas, drop down in the canoe, and whirl a brand among the pack; or fear may do what the wolves can't get at to perform, and leave us without horses in the morning, when we shall have so much need to journey swiftly!"

The young native had already descended to the water, to comply, when a long howl was raised on the edge of the river and was borne swiftly off into the depths of the forest, as though the beasts, of their own accord, were abandoning their prey in sudden terror. Uncas, with instinctive quickness, receded, and the three foresters held another of their low, earnest conferences.

"We have been like hunters who have lost the points of the heavens, and from whom the sun has been hid for days," said Hawk-eye, turning away from his companions. "Now we begin again to know the signs of our course, and the paths are cleared from briers! Seat yourselves in the shade which the moon throws from yonder beech – 'tis thicker than that of the pines – and let us wait for that which the Lord may choose to send next. Let all your conversation be in whispers; though it would be better, and perhaps, in the end, wiser, if each one held discourse with his own thoughts for a time."

The manner of the scout was seriously impressive, though no longer distinguished by any signs of unmanly apprehension. In such circumstances, common prudence dictated that Heyward and his companions should imitate a caution that proceeded from so intelligent a source. The young man drew a pile of the sassafras from the cave, and placing it in the chasm which separated the two caverns, it was occupied by the sisters; who were thus protected by the rocks from any missiles, while their anxiety was relieved by the assurance that no danger could approach without a warning. Heyward himself was posted at hand, so near that he might communicate with his companions without raising his voice to a dangerous elevation; while David, in imitation of the woodsmen, bestowed his person in such a manner among the fissures of the rocks that his ungainly limbs were no longer offensive to the eye.

In this manner hours passed by without further interruption. Not a sound escaped them; the most subtle examination could not have told they breathed. It was evident that this excess of caution proceeded from an experience that no subtlety on the part of their enemies could deceive. It was, however, continued without any apparent consequences until the moon had set, and a pale streak above the treetops, at the bend of the river a little below, announced the approach of day.

Then, for the first time, Hawk-eye was seen to stir. He crawled along the rock and shook Duncan from his heavy slumbers.

"Now is the time to journey," he whispered. "Awake the gentle ones, and be ready to get into the canoe when I bring it to the landing place."

"Have you had a quiet night?" said Heyward. "For myself, I believe sleep has got the better of my vigilance."

"All is yet still as midnight. Be silent, but be quick."

By this time Duncan was thoroughly awake, and he immediately lifted the shawl from the sleeping females. The motion caused Cora to raise her hand as if to repulse him, while Alice murmured, in her soft gentle voice, "No, no, dear Father, we were not deserted; Duncan was with us!"

"Yes, sweet innocence," whispered the youth. "Duncan is here, and while life continues or danger remains, he will never quit thee. Cora! Alice! awake! The hour has come to move!"

A loud shriek from the younger of the sisters, and the form of the other standing upright before him, in bewildered horror, was the unexpected answer he received. While the words were still on the lips of Heyward, there had arisen such a tumult of yells and cries as served to drive the swift currents of his own blood back from its bounding course into the fountains of his heart. It seemed, for near a minute, as if the demons of hell had possessed themselves of the air about them and were venting their savage humors in barbarous sounds. The cries came from no particular direction, though it was evident they filled the woods, and as the appalled listeners easily imagined, the caverns of the falls, the rocks, the bed of the river, and the upper air. David raised his tall person in the midst of the infernal din, with a hand on either ear, exclaiming:

"Whence comes this discord! Has hell broke loose, that man should utter sounds like these!"

The bright flashes and the quick reports of a dozen rifles, from the opposite banks of the stream followed this incautious exposure of his person, and left the unfortunate singing master senseless on that rock where he had been so long slumbering. The Mohicans boldly sent back the intimidating yell of their enemies, who raised a shout of savage triumph at the fall of Gamut. The flash of rifles was then quick and close between them, but either party was too well skilled to leave even a limb exposed to the hostile aim. Duncan listened with intense anxiety for the strokes of the paddle, believing that flight was now their only refuge. The river glanced by with its ordinary velocity, but the canoe was nowhere to be seen on its dark waters. He had just fancied they were cruelly deserted by the scout, as a stream of flame issued from the rock beneath him and a fierce yell, blended with a shriek of agony, announced that the messenger of death, sent from the fatal weapon of Hawk-eye, had found a victim. At this slight repulse the assailants instantly withdrew, and gradually the place became as still as before the sudden tumult.

Duncan seized the favorable moment to spring to the body of Gamut, which he bore within the shelter of the narrow chasm that protected the sisters. In another minute the whole party was collected in this spot of comparative safety.

"The poor fellow has saved his scalp," said Hawk-eye, coolly passing his hand over the head of David; "but he is a proof that a man may be born with too long a tongue! 'Twas downright madness to show six feet of flesh and blood, on a naked rock, to the raging savages. I only wonder he has escaped with life."

"Is he not dead!" demanded Cora, in a voice whose husky tones showed how powerfully natural horror struggled with her assumed firmness. "Can we do aught to assist the wretched man?"

"No, no! the life is in his heart yet, and after he has slept awhile he will come to himself, and be a wiser man for it, till the hour of his real time shall come," returned Hawk-eye, casting another oblique glance at the insensible body, while he filled his charger with admirable nicety. "Carry him in, Uncas, and lay him on the sassafras. The longer his nap lasts the better it will be for him, as I doubt whether he can find a proper cover for such a shape on these rocks; and singing won't do any good with the Iroquois."

"You believe, then, the attack will be renewed?" asked Heyward.

"Do I expect a hungry wolf will satisfy his craving with a mouthful! They have lost a man, and 'tis their fashion, when they meet a loss, and fail in the surprise, to fall back; but we shall have them on again, with new expedients to circumvent us, and master our scalps. Our main hope," he continued, raising his rugged countenance, across which a shade of anxiety just then passed like a darkening cloud, "will be to keep the rock until Munro can send a party to our help! God send it may be soon, and under a leader that knows the Indian customs!"

"You hear our probable fortunes, Cora," said Duncan; "and you know we have everything to hope from the anxiety and experience of your father. Come, then, with Alice, into this cavern, where you, at least, will be safe from the murderous rifles of our enemies, and where you may bestow a care suited to your gentle natures on our unfortunate comrade."

The sisters followed him into the outer cave, where David was beginning, by his sighs, to give symptoms of returning consciousness; and then commending the wounded man to their attention, he immediately prepared to leave them and join the scout and his companions, who still lay within the protection of the little chasm between the two caves.

The Indians silently repaired to their appointed stations, which were fissures in the rocks, whence they could command the approaches to the foot of the falls. In the center of the little island a few short and stunted pines had found root, forming a thicket, into which Hawk-eye darted with the swiftness of a deer, followed by the active Duncan. Here they secured themselves, as well as circumstances would permit, among the shrubs and fragments of stone that were scattered about the place. Above them was a bare, rounded rock, on each side of which the water played its gambols, and plunged into the abysses beneath, in the manner already described. As the day had now dawned, the opposite shores no longer presented a confused outline, but they were able to look into the woods and distinguish objects beneath the canopy of gloomy pines.

A long and anxious watch succeeded, but without any further evidences of a renewed attack; and Duncan began to hope that their fire had proved more fatal than was supposed, and that their enemies had been effectually repulsed. When he ventured to utter this impression to his companion, it was met by Hawk-eye with an incredulous shake of the head.

"You know not the nature of a Maqua if you think he is so easily beaten back without a scalp!" he answered. "If there was one of the imps yelling this morning, there were forty! And they know our number and quality too well to give up the chase so soon. Hist! look into the water above, just where it breaks over the rocks. I am no mortal if the risky devils haven't swam down upon the very pitch, and, as bad luck would have it, they have hit the head of the island. Hist! man, keep close or the hair will be off your crown in the turning of a knife!"

Heyward lifted his head from the cover, and beheld what he justly considered a prodigy of rashness and skill. The river had worn away the edge of the soft rock in such a manner as to render its first pitch less abrupt and perpendicular than is usual at waterfalls. With no other guide than the ripple of the stream where it met the head of the island, a party of their insatiable foes had ventured into the current, and swam down upon this point, knowing the ready access it would give, if successful, to their intended victims. As Hawk-eye ceased speaking, four human heads could be seen peering above a few logs of driftwood that had lodged on these naked rocks, and which had probably suggested the idea of the practicability of the hazardous undertaking. At the next moment, a fifth form was seen floating over the green edge of the fall, a little from the line of the island. The savage struggled powerfully to gain the point of safety, and, favored by the glancing water, he was already stretching forth an arm to meet the grasp of his companion when he shot away again with the whirling current, appeared to rise into the air, with uplifted arms and starting eyeballs, and fell, with a sullen plunge, into that deep and yawning abyss over which he hovered. A single, wild, despairing shriek rose from the cavern, and all was hushed again, as the grave.

The first generous impulse of Duncan was to rush to the rescue of the hapless wretch; but he felt himself bound to the spot by the iron grasp of the immovable scout.

"Would ye bring certain death upon us by telling the Mingoes where we lie?" demanded Hawk-eye sternly. "'Tis a charge of powder saved, and ammunition is as precious now as breath to a worried deer! Freshen the priming of your pistols – the mist of the falls is apt to dampen the brimstone – and stand firm for a close struggle, while I fire on their rush."

He placed a finger in his mouth, and drew a long, shrill whistle, which was answered from the rocks that were guarded by the Mohicans. Duncan caught glimpses of heads above the scattered driftwood, as the signal rose on the air, but they disappeared again as suddenly as they had glanced upon his sight. A low, rustling sound next drew his attention behind him, and turning his head, he beheld Uncas within a few feet, creeping to his side. Hawk-eye spoke to him in Delaware, when the young chief took his position with singular caution and undisturbed coolness. To Heyward this was a moment of feverish and impatient suspense; though the scout saw fit to select it as a fit

STAG HANDLED AMERICAN RIFLEMAN'S KNIFE

AMERICAN DAGGER · IRON QUILLONS · PEWTER BANDS ROUND WOODEN GRIP

occasion to read a lecture to his more youthful associates on the art of using firearms with discretion.

"Of all we'pons," he commenced, "the long-barreled, true-grooved, soft-metaled rifle is the most dangerous in skillful hands, though it wants a strong arm, a quick eye, and great judgment in charging, to put forth all its beauties. The gunsmiths can have but little insight into their trade when they make their fowling pieces and short horsemen's – "

He was interrupted by the low but expressive "hugh" of Uncas.

"I see them, boy, I see them!" continued Hawk-eye. "They are gathering for the rush, or they would keep their dingy backs below the logs. Well, let them," he added, examining his flint. "The leading man certainly comes on to his death, though it should be Montcalm himself!"

At that moment the woods were filled with another burst of cries, and at the signal four savages sprang from the cover of the driftwood. Heyward felt a burning desire to rush forward to meet them, so intense was the delirious anxiety of the moment; but he was restrained by the deliberate examples of the scout and Uncas. When their foes, who leaped over the black rocks that divided them with long bounds, utter-

ing the wildest yells, were within a few rods, the rifle of Hawk-eye slowly rose among the shrubs, and poured out its fatal contents. The foremost Indian bounded like a stricken deer, and fell headlong among the clefts of the island.

"Now, Uncas!" cried the scout, drawing his long knife, while his quick eyes began to flash with ardor. "Take the last of the screeching imps; of the other two we are sartain!"

He was obeyed; and but two enemies remained to be overcome. Heyward had given one of his pistols to Hawk-eye, and together they rushed down a little declivity toward their foes; they discharged their weapons at the same instant, and equally without success.

"I know'd it! And I said it!" muttered the scout, whirling the despised little implement over the falls with bitter disdain. "Come on, ye bloody-minded hellhounds! Ye meet a man without a cross!"

The words were barely uttered when he encountered a savage of gigantic stature, and of the fiercest mien. At the same moment, Duncan found himself engaged with the other, in a similar contest of hand to hand. With ready skill, Hawk-eye and his antagonist each grasped that uplifted arm of the other which held the dangerous knife. For near a minute they stood looking one another in the eye, and gradually exerting the power of their muscles for the mastery. At length, the toughened sinews of the white man prevailed over the less practised limbs of the native. The arm of the latter slowly gave way before the increasing force of the scout who, suddenly wresting his armed hand from the grasp of his foe, drove the sharp weapon through his naked bosom to the heart. In the meantime, Heyward had been pressed in a more deadly struggle. His slight sword was snapped in the first encounter. As he was destitute of any other means of defense, his safety now depended entirely on bodily strength and resolution. Though deficient in neither of these qualities, he had met an enemy every way his equal. Happily, he soon succeeded in disarming his adversary, whose knife fell on the rock at their feet; and from this moment it became a fierce struggle who should cast the other over the dizzy height into a neighboring cavern of the falls. Every successive struggle brought them nearer to the verge, where Duncan perceived the final and conquering effort must be made. Each of the combatants threw all his energies into that effort, and the result was that both tottered on the brink of the precipice. Heyward felt the grasp of the other at his throat and saw the grim smile the savage gave, under the revengeful hope that he hurried his enemy to a fate similar to his own, as he felt his body slowly yielding to a resistless power, and the young man experienced the passing agony of such a moment in all its horrors. At that instant of extreme danger, a dark hand and glancing knife appeared before him; the Indian released his hold, as the blood flowed freely from around the severed tendons of his wrist; and while Duncan was drawn backward by the saving arm of Uncas, his charmed eyes were still riveted on the fierce and disappointed countenance of his foe, who fell sullenly and disappointed down the irrecoverable precipice.

"To cover! To cover!" cried Hawkeye, who just then had dispatched his enemy. "To cover, for your lives! The work is but half ended!"

The young Mohican gave a shout of triumph, and, followed by Duncan, he glided up the acclivity they had descended to the combat, and sought the friendly shelter of the rocks and shrubs.

NO GUNPOWDER, NO CANOE

The warning call of the scout was not uttered without occasion. During the occurrence of the deadly encounter just related, the roar of the falls was unbroken by any human sound whatever. It would seem that interest in the result had kept the natives on the opposite shores in breathless suspense, while the quick evolutions and swift changes in the positions of the combatants effectually prevented a fire that might prove dangerous alike to friend and enemy. But the moment the struggle was decided, a yell arose as fierce and savage as wild and revengeful passions could throw into the air. It was followed by the swift flashes of the rifles, which sent their leaden messengers across the rock in volleys, as though the assailants would pour out their impotent fury on the insensible scene of the fatal contest.

A steady though deliberate return was made from the rifle of Chingachgook, who had maintained his post throughout the fray with unmoved resolution. When the triumphant shout of Uncas was borne to his ears, the gratified father raised his voice in a single responsive cry, after which his busy piece alone proved that he still guarded his pass with unwearied diligence. In this manner many minutes flew by with the swiftness of thought: the rifles of the assailants speaking, at times, in rattling volleys, and at others, in occasional, scattering shots. Though the rock, the trees, and the shrubs, were cut and torn in a hundred places around the besieged, their cover was so close and so rigidly maintained that, as yet, David had been the only sufferer in their little band.

"Let them burn their powder," said the deliberate scout, while bullet after bullet whizzed by the place where he securely lay. "There will be a fine gathering of lead when it is over, and I fancy the imps will tire of the sport afore these old stones cry out for mercy! Uncas, boy, you waste the kernels by overcharging: and a kicking rifle never carries a true bullet. I told you to take that loping miscreant under the line of white paint; now, if your bullet went a hairsbreadth, it went two inches above it. The life lies low in a Mingo, and humanity teaches us to make a quick end of the sarpents."

A quiet smile lighted the haughty features of the young Mohican, betraying his knowledge of the English language as well as of the other's meaning; but he suffered it to pass away without vindication or reply.

"Uncas, lad," said the scout, "go down to the canoe and bring up the big horn; it is all the powder we have left, and we shall need it to the last grain, or I am ignorant of the Mingo nature."

The young Mohican complied, leaving the scout turning over the useless contents of his pouch, and shaking the empty horn with renewed discontent. From this unsatisfactory examination, however, he was soon called by a loud and piercing exclamation from Uncas, that sounded, even to the unpracticed ears of Duncan, as the signal of some new and unexpected calamity. Every thought filled with apprehension for the precious treasure he had concealed in the cavern, the young man started to his feet, totally regardless of the hazard he incurred by such an exposure. As if actuated by a common impulse, his movement was imitated by his companions, and, together, they rushed down the pass to the friendly chasm with a rapidity that rendered the scattering fire of their enemies perfectly harmless. The unwonted cry had brought the sisters, together with the wounded David, from their place of refuge; and the whole party, at a single glance, was made acquainted with the nature of the disaster that had disturbed even the practiced stoicism of their youthful Indian protector.

At a short distance from the rock, their little bark was to be seen floating across the eddy, toward the swift current of the river, in a manner which proved that its course was directed by some hidden agent. The instant this unwelcome sight caught the eye of the scout, his rifle was leveled, as by instinct, but the barrel gave no answer to the bright sparks of the flint.

"'Tis too late, 'tis too late!" Hawk-eye exclaimed, dropping the useless piece in bitter disappointment. "The miscreant has struck the rapid; and had we powder, it could hardly send the lead swifter than he now goes!"

"What is to be done?" demanded Duncan, losing the first feeling of disappointment in a more manly desire for exertion. "What will become of us?"

Hawk-eye made no other reply than by passing his finger around the crown of his head, in a manner so significant that none who witnessed the action could mistake its meaning.

"Surely, surely, our case is not so desperate!" exclaimed the youth. "The Hurons are not here; we may make good the caverns; we may oppose their landing."

"With what?" coolly demanded the scout. "The arrows of Uncas, or such tears as women shed! No, no; you are young, and rich, and have friends, and at such an age I know it is hard to die! But," glancing his eyes at the Mohicans, "let us remember we are men without a cross, and let us teach these natives of the forest that white blood can run as freely as red, when the appointed hour is come."

"Why die at all!" said Cora, advancing from the place where natural horror had, until this moment, held her riveted to the rock. "The path is open on every side; fly, then, to the woods, and call on God for succor! Go, brave men, we owe you too much already; let us no longer involve you in our hapless fortunes!"

"You but little know the craft of the Iroquois, lady, if you judge they have left the path open to the woods!"

returned Hawk-eye, who, however, immediately added in his simplicity: "The downstream current, it is certain, might soon sweep us beyond the reach of their rifles or the sounds of their voices."

"Then try the river. Why linger, to add to the number of the victims of our merciless enemies?"

"Why," repeated the scout, looking about him proudly, "because it is better for a man to die at peace with himself than to live haunted by an evil conscience! What answer could we give Munro, when he asked us where and how we left his children?"

"Go to him, and say that you left them with a message to hasten to their aid," returned Cora, advancing nigher to the scout in her generous ardor; "that the Hurons bear them into the northern wilds, but that by vigilance and speed they may yet be rescued; and if, after

CARVED POWDER HORN

all, it should please heaven that his assistance come too late, bear to him," she continued, her voice gradually lowering, until it seemed nearly choked, "the love, the blessings, the final prayers of his daughters, and bid him not mourn their early fate, but to look forward with humble confidence to the . Christian's goal to meet his children."

The hard, weather-beaten features of the scout began to work, and when she had ended, he dropped his chin to his hand, like a man musing profoundly on the nature of the proposal.

"There is reason in her words!" at length broke from his compressed and trembling lips. "Aye, and they bear the spirit of Christianity; what might be right and proper in a red skin, may be sinful in a man who has not even a cross in blood to plead for his ignorance. Chingachgook! Uncas! hear you the talk of the dark-eyed woman!"

He now spoke in Delaware to his companions, and his address, though calm and deliberate, seemed very decided. The elder Mohican heard him with deep gravity, and appeared to ponder on his words, as though he felt the importance of their import. After a moment of hesitation, he waved his hand in assent, and uttered the English word "good" with the peculiar emphasis of his people. Then, replacing his knife and tomahawk in his girdle, the warrior moved silently to the edge of the rock which was most concealed from the banks of the river. Here he paused a moment, pointed significantly to the woods below, and saying a few words in his own language, as if indicating his intended route, he dropped into the water, and sank from before the eyes of the witnesses of his movements.

The scout delayed his departure to speak to the generous girl, whose breathing became lighter as she saw the success of her remonstrance.

"Wisdom is sometimes given to the young, as well as to the old," he said, "and what you have spoken is wise, not to call it by a better word. If you are led into the woods, that is, such of you as may be spared for a while, break the twigs on the bushes as you pass, and make the marks of your trail as broad as you can, when, if mortal eyes can see them, depend on having a friend who will follow to the ends of 'arth afore he desarts you."

He gave Cora an affectionate shake of the hand, lifted his rifle, and after regarding it a moment with melancholy solicitude, laid it carefully aside, and descended to the place where Chingachgook had just disappeared. For an instant he hung suspended by the rock; and looking about him with a countenance of peculiar care, he added bitterly, "Had the powder held out, this disgrace could never have befallen!" Then, loosening his hold, the water closed above his head, and he also became lost to view.

All eyes were now turned on Uncas, who stood leaning against the ragged rock, in immovable composure. After waiting a short time, Cora pointed down the river, and said:

"Your friends have not been seen, and are now, most probably, in safety; is it not time for you to follow?"

"Uncas will stay," the young Mohican calmly answered in English.

"To increase the horror of our capture, and to diminish the chances of our release! Go, generous young man," Cora continued, lowering her eyes under the gaze of the Mohican, and, perhaps, with an intuitive consciousness of her power; "go to my father, as I have said, and be the most confidential of my messengers. Tell him to trust you with the means to buy the freedom of his daughters. Go! 'Tis my wish, 'tis my prayer, that you will go!"

The settled, calm look of the young chief changed to an expression of gloom, but he no longer hesitated. With a noiseless step he crossed the rock and dropped into the troubled stream. Hardly a breath was drawn by those he left behind, until they caught a glimpse of his head emerging for air, far down the current, when he again sank, and was seen no more.

These sudden and apparently successful experiments had all taken place in a few minutes of that time which had now become so precious. After the last look at Uncas, Cora turned, and, with a quivering lip, addressed herself to Heyward.

"I have heard of your boasted skill in the water, too, Duncan," she said. "Follow, then, the wise example set you by these simple and faithful beings."

"Is such the faith that Cora Munro would exact from her protector?" said the young man, smiling mournfully, but with bitterness.

"This is not a time for idle subtleties and false opinions," she answered, "but a moment when every duty should be equally considered. To us you can be of no further service here, but your precious life may be saved for other and nearer friends."

He made no reply, though his eyes fell wistfully on the beautiful form of Alice, who was clinging to his arm with the dependency of an infant.

"Consider," continued Cora, after a pause during which she seemed to struggle with a pang even more acute than any that her fears had excited, "that the worst to us can be but death; a tribute that all must pay at the good time of God's appointment."

"There are evils worse than death," said Duncan, speaking hoarsely, and as if fretful at her importunity, "but which the presence of one who would die in your behalf may avert."

Cora ceased her entreaties; and, veiling her face in her shawl, drew the nearly insensible Alice after her into the deepest recess of the inner cavern.

LE RENARD SUBTIL RETURNS

The sudden and almost magical change from the stirring incidents of the combat to the stillness that now reigned around him, acted on the heated imagination of Heyward like some exciting dream. In a moment of such painful doubt, Duncan did not hesitate to look about him, without consulting that protection from the rocks which just before had been so necessary to his safety. "The Hurons are not to be seen," he said, addressing David, who had by no means recovered from the effects of the stunning blow he had received. "Let us conceal ourselves in the cavern, and trust the rest to Providence."

He seized a pile of the sassafras, which he drew before the passage, studiously concealing every appearance of an aperture. Within this fragile barrier he arranged the blankets abandoned by the foresters, darkening the inner extremity of the cavern, while its outer received a chastened light from the narrow ravine, through which one arm of the river rushed, to form the junction with its sister branch, a few rods below.

He then seated himself in the center of the cavern, grasping his remaining pistol with a hand convulsively clenched, while his contracted and frowning eye announced the sullen desperation of his purpose. "The Hurons, if they come, may not gain our position so easily as they think," he lowly muttered; and dropping his head back against the rock, he seemed to await the result in patience, though his gaze was unceasingly bent on the open avenue to their place of retreat.

The fresh air of the morning had penetrated the recess, and its influence was gradually felt on the spirits of its inmates. As minute after minute passed by, leaving them in undisturbed security, the insinuating feeling of hope was gradually gaining possession of every bosom, though each one felt reluctant to give utterance to expectations that the next moment might so fearfully destroy.

David alone formed an exception to these varying emotions. A gleam of light from the opening crossed his wan countenance and fell upon the pages of the little volume, whose leaves he was again occupied in turning, as if searching for some song more fitted to their condition than any that had yet met his eye. He was, most probably, acting all this time under a confused recollection of the promised consolation of Duncan. At length it would seem, his patient industry found its reward; for, without explanation or apology, he pronounced aloud the words "Isle of Wight," drew a long, sweet sound from his pitch pipe, and then ran through the preliminary modulations of the air, whose name he had just mentioned, with the sweeter tones of his own musical voice.

"May not this prove dangerous?" asked Cora, glancing her dark eye at Major Heyward.

"Poor fellow! His voice is too feeble to be heard amid the din of the falls," was the answer. "Besides, the cavern will prove his friend. Let him indulge his passion, since it may be done without hazard."

"Isle of Wight!" repeated David, looking about him with that dignity with which he had long been wont to silence the whispering echoes of his school. "'Tis a brave tune, and set to solemn words; let it be sung with meet respect!"

After allowing a moment of stillness to enforce his discipline, the voice of the singer was heard, in low, murmuring syllables, gradually stealing on the ear

FRONT AND BACK VIEW OF FLINTLOCK PISTOL MID C18TH

until it filled the narrow vault with sounds rendered trebly thrilling by the feeble and tremulous utterance produced by his debility. The open sympathy of the listeners stirred the spirit of the votary of music, whose voice regained its richness and volume without losing that touching softness which proved its secret charm. Exerting his renovated powers to their utmost, he was yet filling the arches of the cave with long and full tones, when a yell burst into the air without, that instantly

BACK AND FRONT OF SADDLE HOLSTER FOR FLINTLOCK PISTOL.

stilled his pious strains, choking his voice suddenly, as though his heart had literally bounded into the passage of his throat.

"We are lost!" exclaimed Alice, throwing herself into the arms of Cora.

"Not yet, not yet," returned the agitated but undaunted Heyward. "The sound came from the center of the island, and it has been produced by the sight of their dead companions. We are not yet discovered, and there is still hope."

Faint and almost despairing as was the prospect of escape, the words of Duncan were not thrown away, for they awakened the powers of the sisters in such a manner that they awaited the result in silence. A second yell soon followed the first, when a rush of voices was heard pouring down the island, from its upper to its lower extremity, until they reached the naked rock above the caverns, where, after a shout of savage triumph, the air continued full of horrible cries and screams, such as man alone can utter, and he only when in a state of the fiercest barbarity.

In the midst of this tumult, a triumphant yell was raised within a few yards of the hidden entrance to the cave. Heyward abandoned every hope, with the belief it was the signal that they were discovered. Again the impression passed away, as he heard the voices collect near the spot where the white man had so reluctantly abandoned his rifle. Amid the jargon of the Indian dialects that he now plainly heard, it was easy to distinguish not only words, but sentences, in the patois of the Canadas. A burst of voices had shouted simultaneously, "La Longue Carabine!" causing the opposite woods to reecho with a name which, Heyward well remembered, had been given by his enemies to a celebrated hunter and scout of the English camp, and who, he now learned for the first time, had been his late companion.

There were now a few minutes of fearful stillness, during which Heyward well knew that the savages conducted their search with greater vigilance and method. More than once he could distinguish their footsteps as they brushed the sassafras, causing the faded leaves to rustle, and the branches to snap. At length, the pile yielded a little, a corner of a blanket fell, and a faint ray of light gleamed into the inner part of the cave. Cora folded Alice to her bosom in agony, and Duncan sprang to his feet. A shout was at that moment heard, as if issuing from the center of the rock, announcing that the neighboring cavern had at length been entered. In a minute, the number and loudness of the voices indicated that the whole party was collected in and around that secret place.

As the inner passages to the two caves were so close to each other, Duncan, believing that escape was no longer possible, passed David and the sisters, to place himself between the latter and the first onset of the terrible meeting. Grown desperate by his situation, he drew nigh the slight barrier which separated him only by a few feet from his relentless pursuers, and placing his face to the casual opening, he even looked out, with a sort of desperate indifference, on their movements.

Within reach of his arm was the brawny shoulder of a gigantic Indian, whose deep and authoritative voice appeared to give directions to the proceedings of his fellows. Beyond him

32

again, Duncan could look into the vault opposite, which was filled with savages, upturning and rifling the humble furniture of the scout. The wound of David had dyed the leaves of sassafras with a color that the natives well knew was anticipating the season. One fierce and wild looking warrior approached the chief, bearing a load of the brush and, pointing exultingly to the deep red stains with which it was sprinkled, uttered his joy in Indian yells, whose meaning Heyward was only enabled to comprehend by the frequent repetition of the name of "La Longue Carabine!" When his triumph had ceased, he cast the brush on the slight heap that Duncan had made before the entrance of the second cavern, and closed the view. His example was followed by others, who, as they drew the branches from the cave of the scout, threw them into one pile, adding unconsciously to the security of those they sought.

As the blankets yielded before the outward pressure, and the branches settled in the fissure of the rock by their own weight, forming a compact body, Duncan once more breathed freely. With a light step and lighter heart, he returned to the center of the cave and took the place he had left, where he could command a view of the opening next the river. While he was in the act of making this movement, the Indians, as if changing their purpose by a common impulse, broke away from the chasm in a body, and were heard rushing up the island again, toward the point whence they had originally descended. Here another wailing cry betrayed that they were again collected around the bodies of their dead comrades.

Duncan now ventured to look at his companions.

"They are gone, Cora!" he whispered. "Alice, they are returned whence they came, and we are saved! To heaven, that has alone delivered us from the grasp of so merciless an enemy, be all the praise!"

"Then to heaven will I return my thanks!" exclaimed the younger sister, rising from the encircling arms of Cora, and casting herself. with enthusiastic gratitude on the naked rock; "to that heaven who has spared the tears of a gray-headed father; has saved the lives of those I so much love – "

But when her lips moved, the words they should have uttered appeared frozen by some new and sudden chill. Her bloom gave place to the paleness of death; her soft and melting eyes grew hard, and seemed contracting with horror. Heyward turned, the instant she gave a direction to his suspicions, and, peering just above the ledge which formed the threshold of the open outlet of the cavern, he beheld the malignant, fierce, and savage features of Le Renard Subtil.

In that moment of surprise, the self-possession of Heyward did not desert him. He observed by the vacant expression of the Indian's countenance that his eye, accustomed to the open air, had not yet been able to penetrate the dusky light which pervaded the depth of the cavern. He had even thought of retreating beyond a curvature in the natural wall, which might still conceal him and his companions, when, by the sudden gleam of intelligence that shot across the features of the savage, he saw it was too late, and that they were betrayed.

The look of exultation and brutal triumph which announced this terrible truth was irresistibly irritating. Forgetful of everything but the impulses of his hot blood, Duncan leveled his pistol and fired. The report of the weapon made the cavern bellow like an eruption from a volcano; and when the smoke it vomited had been driven away before the current of air which issued from the ravine, the place so lately occupied by the features of his treacherous guide was vacant. Rushing to the outlet, Heyward caught a glimpse of his dark figure, stealing around a low and narrow ledge, which soon hid him entirely from sight.

Among the savages, a frightful stillness succeeded the explosion, which had just been heard bursting from the bowels of the rock. But when Le Renard raised his voice in a long and intelligible whoop, it was answered by a spontaneous yell from the mouth of every Indian within hearing of the sound. The clamorous noises again rushed down the island; and before Duncan had time to recover from the shock, his feeble barrier of brush was scattered to the winds, the cavern was entered at both its extremities, and he and his companions were dragged from their shelter and borne into the day, where they stood surrounded by the whole band of the triumphant Hurons.

AERIAL VIEW OF PROOF MARKS ON BARREL. THEY WERE ALSO STAMPED ON THE UNDERSIDE.

BRITISH BROWN BESS MUSKET

PRISONERS

The instant the shock of this sudden misfortune had abated, Duncan began to make his observations on the appearance and proceedings of their captors.

While the others were busily occupied in seeking to gratify their childish passion for finery by plundering even the miserable effects of the scout, or had been searching, with such bloodthirsty vengeance in their looks, for their absent owner, Le Renard had stood at a little distance from the prisoners, with a demeanor so quiet and satisfied as to betray that he had already effected the grand purpose of his treachery. When the eyes of Heyward first met those of his recent guide, he turned them away in horror at the sinister though calm look he encountered. Conquering his disgust, however, he was able, with an averted face, to address his successful enemy.

"Le Renard Subtil is too much of a warrior," said the reluctant Heyward, "to refuse telling an unarmed man what his conquerors say."

"They ask for the hunter who knows the paths through the woods," returned Magua, in his broken English, laying his hand at the same time, with a ferocious smile, on the bundle of leaves with which a wound on his own shoulder was bandaged. "La Longue Carabine! His rifle is good, and his eye never shut; but, like the short gun of the white chief, it is nothing against the life of Le Subtil!"

"Le Renard is too brave to remember the hurts received in war, or the hands that gave them!"

"Was it war, when the tired Indian rested at the sugar tree to taste his corn! Who filled the bushes with creeping enemies! Who drew the knife! Whose tongue was peace, while his heart was colored with blood! Did Magua say that the hatchet was out of the ground, and that his hand had dug it up?"

As Duncan dared not retort upon his accuser by reminding him of his own premeditated treachery, and disdained to deprecate his resentment by any words of apology, he remained silent. Magua seemed also content to rest the controversy as well as all further communication there, for he resumed the leaning attitude against the rock from which, in momentary energy, he had arisen. But the cry of "La Longue Carabine" was renewed the instant the impatient savages perceived that the short dialogue was ended.

"You hear," said Magua, with stubborn indifference. "The red Hurons call for the life of 'The Long Rifle,' or they will have the blood of them that keep him hid!"

"He is gone – escaped; he is far beyond their reach."

Renard smiled with cold contempt, as he answered:

"When the white man dies, he thinks he is at peace; but the Red Men know how to torture even the ghosts of their enemies. Where is his body? Let the Hurons see his scalp!"

"He is not dead, but escaped."

Magua shook his head incredulously.

"Is he a bird, to spread his wings; or is he a fish, to swim without air! The white chief reads in his books, and he believes the Hurons are fools!"

"Though no fish, 'The Long Rifle' can swim. He floated down the stream when the powder was all burned, and when the eyes of the Hurons were behind a cloud."

Magua muttered a few words inaudibly between his teeth, before he continued, aloud:

"Can the Delawares swim, too, as well as crawl in the bushes? Where is 'Le Gros Serpent'?"

Duncan, who perceived by the use of these Canadian appellations that his late companions were much better known to his enemies than to himself, answered reluctantly, "He also is gone down with the water."

"'Le Cerf Agile' is not here?"

"I know not whom you call 'The Nimble Deer'," said Duncan, gladly profiting by any excuse to create delay.

"Uncas," returned Magua, pronouncing the Delaware name with even greater difficulty than he spoke his English words. "'Bounding Elk' is what

BROWN BESS LOCK (FLINT)

the white man says when he calls to the Young Mohican."

"If you mean the younger Delaware, he too is gone down with the water."

As there was nothing improbable to an Indian in the manner of the escape, Magua admitted the truth of what he had heard with a readiness that afforded additional evidence how little he would prize such worthless captives. With his companions, however, the feeling was manifestly different.

The Hurons had awaited the result of this short dialogue with characteristic patience, and with a silence that increased until there was a general stillness in the band. When Heyward ceased to speak, they turned their eyes, as one man, on Magua, demanding in this expressive manner an explanation of what had been said. Their interpreter pointed to the river and made them acquainted with the result, as much by the action as by the few words he uttered. When the fact was generally understood, the savages raised a frightful yell, which declared the extent of their disappointment. Some ran furiously to the water's edge, beating the air with frantic gestures, while others spat upon the element, to resent the supposed treason it had committed against their acknowledged rights as conquerors. A few, and they not the least powerful and terrific of the band, threw lowering looks in which the fiercest passion was only tempered by habitual self-command, at those captives who still remained in their power. The young soldier made a desperate but fruitless effort to spring to the side of

Alice, when he saw the dark hand of a savage twisted in the rich tresses which were flowing in volumes over her shoulders, while a knife was passed around the head from which they fell, as if to denote the horrid manner in which it was about to be robbed of its beautiful ornament. But his hands were bound; and at the first movement he made he felt the grasp of the powerful Indian who directed the band, pressing his shoulder like a vice. Immediately conscious how unavailing any struggle against such an overwhelming force must prove, he submitted to his fate, encouraging his gentle companions by a few low and tender assurances that the natives seldom failed to threaten more than they performed.

As resistance was impossible and remonstrance useless, Heyward set the example of submission by leading the way into a canoe, where he was soon seated with the sisters and the still wondering David. Notwithstanding the Hurons were necessarily ignorant of the little channels among the eddies and rapids of the stream, they knew the common signs of such a navigation too well to commit any material blunder. When the pilot chosen for the task of guiding the canoe had taken his station, the whole band plunged again into the river, the vessel glided down the current, and in a few moments the captives found themselves on the south bank of the stream, nearly opposite to the point where they had struck it the preceding evening.

Here was held another short but earnest consultation, during which the

horses, to whose panic their owners ascribed their heaviest misfortune, were led from the cover of the woods and brought to the sheltered spot. The band now divided. The great chief so often mentioned, mounting the charger of Heyward, led the way directly across the river, followed by most of his people, and disappeared in the woods, leaving the prisoners in charge of six savages, at whose head was Le Renard Subtil. Duncan witnessed all their movements with renewed uneasiness.

Anxious to know the worst, and willing, in such an emergency, to try the potency of gold, he overcame his reluctance to speak to Magua. Addressing himself to his former guide, who had now assumed the authority and manner of one who was to direct the future movements of the party, he said in tones as friendly and confiding as he could assume:

"I would speak to Magua what is fit only for so great a chief to hear."

The Indian turned his eyes on the young soldier scornfully, as he answered:

"Speak; trees have no ears!"

"Le Renard Subtil has proved himself worthy of the honorable name given to him by his Canada fathers," commenced Heyward. "I see his wisdom, and all that he has done for us, and shall remember it when the hour to reward him arrives. Yes! Renard has proved that he is not only a great chief in council, but one who knows how to deceive his enemies!"

"What has Renard done?" coldly demanded the Indian.

"What! Has he not seen that the woods were filled with outlying parties of the enemies, and that the serpent could not steal through them without being seen? Then, did he not lose his path to blind the eyes of the Hurons? Did he not pretend to go back to his tribe, who had treated him ill and driven him from their wigwams like a dog? And, when we saw what he wished to do, did we not aid him by making a false face, that the Hurons might think the white man believed that his friend was his enemy? Is not all this true? And when Le Subtil had shut the eyes and stopped the ears of his nation by his wisdom, did they not forget that they had once done him wrong, and forced him to flee to the Mohawks? And did

GUNSMITH'S PROOF-MARKS

LONDON GUNMAKERS COMPANY VIEW MARK V: VIEW

LONDON GUNMAKERS COMPANY PROOF MARK GP: GUNMAKERS PROOF

LONDON FOREIGNERS MARK

PARIS PROOF MARK

they not leave him on the south side of the river, with their prisoners, while they have gone foolishly on the north? Does not Renard mean to turn like a fox on his footsteps, and carry to the rich and gray-headed Scotchman his daughters? Yes, Magua, I see it all, and I have already been thinking how so much wisdom and honesty should be repaid. First, the chief of William Henry will give as a great chief should for such a service. The medal of Magua will no longer be of tin, but of beaten gold; his horn will run over with powder; dollars will be as plenty in his pouch as pebbles on the shore of Horican; and the deer will lick his hand, for they will know it to be vain to fly from the rifle he will carry! As for myself, I know not how to exceed the gratitude of the Scotchman, but I – yes, I will – "

"What will the young chief who comes from toward the sun, give?" demanded the Huron, observing that

Heyward hesitated in his desire to end the enumeration of benefits with that which might form the climax of an Indian's wishes.

"He will make the firewater from the Islands in the salt lake flow before the wigwam of Magua, until the heart of the Indian shall be lighter than the feathers of the hummingbird, and his breath sweeter than the wild honeysuckle."

Le Renard had listened gravely as Heyward slowly proceeded in this subtle speech. When the young man mentioned the artifice he supposed the Indian to have practised on his own nation, the countenance of the listener was veiled in an expression of cautious gravity. At the allusion to the injury which Duncan affected to believe had driven the Huron from his native tribe, a gleam of such ungovernable ferocity flashed from the other's eyes as induced the adventurous speaker to believe he had struck the proper chord. And by the time he reached the part where he so artfully blended the thirst of vengeance with the desire of gain, he had at least obtained a command of the deepest attention of the savage. The question put by Le Renard had been calm, and with all the dignity of an Indian; but it was quite apparent, by the thoughtful expression of the listener's countenance, that the answer was most cunningly devised. The Huron mused a few moments, and then laying his hand on the rude bandages of his wounded shoulder, he said with some energy:

"Do friends make such marks?"

"Would 'La Longue Carabine' cut one so light on an enemy?"

"Do the Delawares crawl upon those they love like snakes, twisting themselves to strike?"

"Would 'Le Gros Serpent' have been heard by the ears of one he wished to be deaf?"

"Does the white chief burn his powder in the faces of his brothers?"

"Does he ever miss his aim, when seriously bent to kill?" returned Duncan, smiling with well acted sincerity.

Another long and deliberate pause succeeded these sententious questions and ready replies. Duncan saw that the Indian hesitated. In order to complete his victory, he was in the act of recommencing the enumeration of the rewards when Magua made an expressive gesture, and said:

"Enough; Le Renard is a wise chief, and what he does will be seen. Go, and keep the mouth shut. When Magua speaks, it will be the time to answer."

Heyward, perceiving that the eyes of his companion were warily fastened on the rest of the band, fell back immediately, in order to avoid the appearance of any suspicious confederacy with their leader. Magua approached the horses and affected to be well pleased with the diligence and ingenuity of his comrades. He then signed to Heyward to assist the sisters into the saddles, for he seldom deigned to use the English tongue, unless urged by some motive of more than usual moment.

There was no longer any plausible pretext for delay; and Duncan was obliged, however reluctantly, to comply. As he performed this office, he whispered his reviving hopes in the ears of the trembling females who, through dread of encountering the savage countenances of their captors, seldom raised their eyes from the ground. The mare of David had been taken with the followers of the large chief; in consequence its owner, as well as Duncan, were compelled to journey on foot. The latter did not, however, so much regret this circumstance, as it might enable him to retard the speed of the party; for he still turned his longing looks in the direction of Fort Edward, in the vain expectation of catching some sound from that quarter of the forest which might denote the approach of succor.

When all were prepared, Magua made the signal to proceed, advancing in front to lead the party in person. Next followed David, who was gradually coming to a true sense of his condition, as the effects of the wound became less and less apparent. The sisters rode in his rear, with Heyward at their side, while the Indians flanked the party and brought up the close of the march, with a caution that seemed never to tire.

Cora alone remembered the parting injunctions of the scout, and whenever an opportunity offered, she stretched forth her arm to bend aside the twigs that met her hands. But the vigilance of the Indians rendered this act of precaution both difficult and dangerous. She was often defeated in her purpose by encountering their watchful eyes, when it became necessary to feign an alarm she did not feel, and occupy the limb by some gesture of feminine apprehension. Once, and once only, was she completely successful; when she broke down the bough of a large sumach, and, by a sudden thought, let her glove fall at the same instant. This sign, intended for those that might follow, was observed by one of her conductors, who restored the glove, broke the remaining branches of the bush in such a manner that it appeared to proceed from the struggling of some beast in its branches, and then laid his hand on his tomahawk, with a look so significant that it put an effectual end to these stolen memorials of their passage.

Magua during all this time, seldom turned to look at his followers, and never spoke. With the sun for his only guide, or aided by such blind marks as are only known to the sagacity of a native, he held his way along the barrens of pine, through occasional little fertile vales, across brooks and rivulets and over undulating hills, with the accuracy of instinct, and nearly with the directness of a bird. He never seemed to hesitate. Whether the path was hardly distinguishable, whether it disappeared, or whether it lay beaten and plain before him, made no sensible difference in his speed or certainty. It seemed as if fatigue could not affect him. Whenever the eyes of the wearied travelers rose from the decayed leaves over which they trod, his dark form was to be seen glancing among the stems of the trees in front, his head immovably fastened in a forward position, with the light plume on his crest fluttering in a current of air made solely by the swiftness of his own motion.

But all this diligence and speed were not without an object. After crossing a low vale, through which a gushing brook meandered, he suddenly ascended a hill so steep and difficult of ascent that the sisters were compelled to alight, in order to follow. When the summit was gained, they found themselves on a level spot, but thinly covered with trees, under one of which Magua had thrown his dark form, as if willing and ready to seek that rest which was so much needed by the whole party.

ALICE SHOWS HER COURAGE

The Indian had selected for this desirable purpose one of those steep, pyramidal hills which bear a strong resemblance to artificial mounds, and which so frequently occur in the valleys of America. The one in question was high and precipitous; its top flattened, as usual; but with one of its sides more than ordinarily irregular. It possessed no other apparent advantage for a resting place than in its elevation and form, which might render defense easy, and surprise nearly impossible. As Heyward, however, no longer expected that rescue which time and distance now rendered so improbable, he regarded these little peculiarities with an eye devoid of interest, devoting himself entirely to the comfort and condolence of his feebler companions. The Narragansets were suffered to browse on the branches of the trees and shrubs that were thinly scattered over the summit of the hill, while the remains of their provisions were spread under the shade of a beech, that stretched its horizontal limbs like a canopy above them.

Notwithstanding the swiftness of their flight, one of the Indians had found an opportunity to strike a straggling fawn with an arrow, and had borne the more preferable fragments of the victim patiently on his shoulders, to the stopping place. Without any aid from the science of cookery, he was immediately employed, in common with his fellows, in gorging himself with this digestible sustenance. Magua alone sat apart, without participating in the revolting meal, and apparently buried in the deepest thought.

This abstinence, so remarkable in an Indian, when he possessed the means of satisfying hunger, at length attracted the notice of Heyward. The young man willingly believed that the Huron deliberated on the most eligible manner of eluding the vigilance of his associates. With a view to assist his plans by any suggestion of his own, and to strengthen the temptation, he left the beech and straggled as if without an object to the spot where Le Renard was seated.

"Has not Magua kept the sun in his face long enough to escape all danger from the Canadians?" he asked, as though no longer doubtful of the good intelligence established between them; "and will not the chief of William Henry be better pleased to see his daughters before another night may have hardened his heart to their loss, to make him less liberal in his reward?"

"Do the palefaces love their children less in the morning than at night?" asked the Indian coldly.

"By no means," returned Heyward, anxious to recall his error, if he had made one. "The white man may, and does often, forget the burial place of his fathers; he sometimes ceases to remember those he should love and has promised to cherish; but the affection of a parent for his child is never permitted to die."

"Go," said the Huron, suppressing the alarming exhibition in an instant, in a deathlike calmness of countenance; "go to the dark-haired daughter, and say, Magua waits to speak. The father will remember what the child promises."

Duncan, who interpreted this speech to express a wish for some additional pledge that the promised gifts should not be withheld, slowly and reluctantly repaired to the place where the sisters were now resting from their fatigue, to communicate its purport to Cora.

"You understand the nature of an Indian's wishes," he concluded, as he led her toward the place where she was expected, "and must be prodigal of your offers of powder and blankets. Ardent spirits are, however, the most prized by such as he; nor would it be amiss to add some boon from your own hand, with that grace you so well know how to practise. Remember, Cora, that on your presence of mind and ingenuity even your life, as well as that of Alice, may in some measure depend."

She waited until he had departed, and then turning to the native, with the dignity of her sex in her voice and manner, she added, "What would Le Renard say to the daughter of Munro?"

"Listen," said the Indian, laying his hand firmly upon her arm as if willing to draw her utmost attention to his words; a movement that Cora as firmly but quietly repulsed by extricating the limb from his grasp. "When his English and French fathers dug up the hatchet, Le Renard struck the warpost of the Mohawks and went out against his own nation. The palefaces have driven the redskins from their hunting grounds, and now, when they fight, a white man leads the way. The old chief of Horican, your father, was the great captain of our war party. He said to the Mohawks do this, and do that, and he was minded. He made a law, that if an Indian swallowed the firewater and came into the cloth wigwams of his warriors, it should not be forgotten. Magua foolishly opened his mouth, and the hot liquor led him into the cabin of Munro. What did the grayhead? Let his daughter say."

"He forgot not his words, and did justice, by punishing the offender," said the undaunted daughter.

"Justice!" repeated the Indian, casting an oblique glance of the most ferocious expression at her unyielding countenance. "Is it justice to make evil, and then punish for it? Magua was not himself; it was the firewater that spoke and acted for him! But Munro did not believe it. The Huron chief was tied up before all the pale-faced warriors and whipped like a dog."

Cora remained silent, for she knew not how to palliate this imprudent severity on the part of her father, in a manner to suit the comprehension of an Indian.

"When the Chippewas tied Magua to the stake and cut this gash," said the other, laying his finger on a deep scar, "the Huron laughed in their faces and told them, women struck so light! His spirit was then in the clouds! But when he felt the blows of Munro, his spirit lay under the birch. The spirit of a Huron is never drunk; it remembers forever!"

"But it may be appeased. If my father has done you this injustice, show him how an Indian can forgive an injury, and take back his daughters. You have heard from Major Heyward – "

Magua shook his head, forbidding the repetition of offers he so much despised.

"What would you have?" continued Cora, after a most painful pause, while the conviction forced itself on her mind that the too sanguine and generous Duncan had been cruelly deceived by the cunning of the savage.

"What a Huron loves – good for good; bad for bad!"

"You would then revenge the injury inflicted by Munro on his helpless daughters. Would it not be more like a man to go before his face, and take the satisfaction of a warrior?"

"The arms of the palefaces are long, and their knives sharp!" returned the savage, with a malignant laugh. "Why should Le Renard go among the muskets of his warriors, when he holds the spirit of the grayhead in his hand?"

"Name your intention, Magua," said Cora, struggling with herself to speak with steady calmness. "Is it to lead us prisoners to the woods, or do you contemplate even some greater evil? Is there no reward, no means of palliating the injury, and of softening your heart? At least, release my gentle sister, and pour out all your malice on me. Purchase wealth by her safety and satisfy your revenge with a single victim. The loss of both his daughters might bring the aged man to his grave, and where would then be the satisfaction of Le Renard?"

"Listen," said the Indian again. "The light eyes can go back to the Horican and tell the old chief what has been done, if the dark-haired woman will swear by the Great Spirit of her fathers to tell no lie."

"What must I promise?" demanded Cora, still maintaining a secret ascendancy over the fierce native by the

SCALPING KNIFE AND SHEATH

collected and feminine dignity of her presence.

"When Magua left his people, his wife was given to another chief; he has now made friends with the Hurons, and will go back to the graves of his tribe on the shores of the great lake. Let the daughter of the English chief follow, and live in his wigwam forever."

However revolting a proposal of such a character might prove to Cora, she retained, notwithstanding her powerful disgust, sufficient self-command to reply, without betraying the weakness.

"And what pleasure would Magua find in sharing his cabin with a wife he did not love; one who would be of a nation and color different from his own? It would be better to take the gold of Munro and buy the heart of some Huron maid with his gifts."

The Indian made no reply for near a minute, but bent his fierce looks on the countenance of Cora in such wavering glances that her eyes sank with shame, under an impression that, for the first time, they had encountered an expression that no chaste female might endure. While she was shrinking within herself, in dread of having her ears wounded by some proposal still more shocking than the last, the voice of Magua answered, in its tones of deepest malignancy:

"When the blows scorched the back of the Huron, he would know where to find a woman to feel the smart. The daughter of Munro would draw his water, hoe his corn, and cook his venison. The body of the grayhead would sleep among his cannon, but his heart would lie within reach of the knife of Le Subtil."

SCALPING POLE AND STRETCHER

"Monster! Well dost thou deserve thy treacherous name!" cried Cora, in an ungovernable burst of filial indignation. "None but a fiend could meditate such a vengeance! But thou overratest thy power! You shall find it is, in truth, the heart of Munro you hold, and that it will defy your utmost malice!"

The Indian answered this bold defiance by a ghastly smile that showed an unaltered purpose, while he motioned her away, as if to close the conference forever. Cora, already regretting her precipitation, was obliged to comply; for Magua instantly left the spot and approached his gluttonous comrades.

When Magua reached the cluster of lolling savages, who, gorged with their disgusting meal, lay stretched on the earth in brutal indulgence, he commenced speaking with the dignity of an Indian chief. The first syllables he uttered had the effect to cause his listeners to raise themselves in attitudes of respectful attention. As the Huron used his native language, the prisoners, notwithstanding the caution of the natives had kept them within the swing of their tomahawks, could only conjecture the substance of his harangue from the nature of those significant gestures with which an Indian always illustrates his eloquence.

At first, the language as well as the action of Magua appeared calm and deliberative. When he had succeeded in sufficiently awakening the attention of his comrades, Heyward fancied, by his pointing so frequently toward the direction of the great lakes, that he spoke of the land of their fathers, and of their distant tribe. He enumerated the warriors of the party; their several merits; their frequent services to the nation; their wounds, and the number of the scalps they had taken. Whenever he alluded to any present (and the subtle Indian neglected none), the dark countenance of the flattered individual gleamed with exultation, nor did he even hesitate to assert the truth of the words by gestures of applause and confirmation. Then the voice of the speaker fell, and lost the loud, animated tones of triumph with which he had enumerated their deeds of success and victory. He described the cataract of Glenn's; the impregnable position of its rocky island, with its caverns and its numerous rapids and whirlpools; he named the name of

La Longue Carabine, and paused until the forest beneath them had sent up the last echo of a loud and long yell, with which the hated appellation was received. He pointed toward the youthful military captive, and described the death of a favorite warrior, who had been precipitated into the deep ravine by his hand. He not only mentioned the fate of him who, hanging between heaven and earth, had presented such a spectacle of horror to the whole band, but he acted anew the terrors of his situation, his resolution and his death, on the branches of a sapling; and, finally, he rapidly recounted the manner in which each of their friends had fallen, never failing to touch upon their courage, and their most acknowledged virtues. When this recital of events was ended, his voice once more changed, and became plaintive and even musical, in its low guttural sounds. He now spoke of the wives and children of the slain; their destitution; their misery, both physical and moral; their distance; and, at last, of their unavenged wrongs. Then suddenly lifting his voice to a pitch of terrific energy, he concluded by demanding:

"Are the Hurons dogs to bear this? Who shall say to the wife of Menowgua that the fishes have his scalp, and that his nation have not taken revenge!"

His voice was no longer audible in the burst of rage which now broke into the air, as if the wood, instead of containing so small a band, was filled with the nation. Giving utterance to their rage in the most frantic cries, they rushed upon their prisoners in a body with drawn knives and uplifted tomahawks. Heyward threw himself between the sisters and the foremost, whom he grappled with a desperate strength that for a moment checked his violence. This unexpected resistance gave Magua time to interpose, and with rapid enunciation and animated gesture, he drew the attention of the band again to himself. In that language he knew so well how to assume, he diverted his comrades from their instant purpose, and invited them to prolong the misery of their victims. His proposal was received with acclamations, and executed with the swiftness of thought.

Two powerful warriors cast themselves on Heyward, while another was occupied in securing the less active singing master. Neither of the captives, however, submitted without a desperate though fruitless struggle. Even David hurled his assailant to the earth; nor was Heyward secured until the victory over his companion enabled the Indians to direct their united force to that object. He was then bound and fastened to the body of the sapling on whose branches Magua had acted the pantomime of the falling Huron. When the young soldier regained his recollection, he had the painful certainty before his eyes that a common fate was intended for the whole party. On his right was Cora, in a durance similar to his own, pale and agitated, but with an eye whose steady look still read the proceedings of their enemies. On his left, the withes which bound her to a pine performed that office for Alice which her trembling limbs refused, and alone kept her fragile form from sinking. Her hands were clasped before her in prayer, but instead of looking upward toward that power which alone could rescue them, her unconscious looks wandered to the countenance of Duncan with infantile dependency. David had contended, and the novelty of the circumstance held him silent, in deliberation on the propriety of the unusual occurrence.

The vengeance of the Hurons had now taken a new direction, and they prepared to execute it with that barbarous ingenuity with which they were familiarized by the practice of centuries. Some sought knots, to raise the blazing pile; one was riving the splinters of pine, in order to pierce the flesh of their captives with the burning fragments; and others bent the tops of two saplings to the earth, in order to suspend Heyward by the arms between the recoiling branches. But the vengeance of Magua sought a deeper and a more malignant enjoyment.

While the less refined monsters of the band prepared, before the eyes of those who were to suffer, these well-known and vulgar means of torture, he approached Cora and pointed out, with the most malign expression of countenance, the speedy fate that awaited her.

"Ha!" he added. "What says the daughter of Munro? Her head is too good to find a pillow in the wigwam of Le Renard; will she like it better when it rolls about this hill a plaything for the wolves? Her bosom cannot nurse the children of a Huron; she will see it spit upon by Indians!"

"What means the monster!" demanded the astonished Heyward.

"Nothing!" was the firm reply. "He is a savage, a barbarous and ignorant savage, and knows not what he does. Let us find leisure, with our dying breath, to ask for him penitence and pardon."

"Pardon!" echoed the fierce Huron, mistaking, in his anger, the meaning of her words. "The memory of an Indian is longer than the arm of the palefaces; his mercy shorter than their justice! Say; shall I send the yellow hair to her father, and will you follow Magua to the great lakes, to carry his water and feed him with corn?"

"What says he, dearest Cora?" asked the trembling voice of Alice. "Did he speak of sending me to our father?"

For many moments the elder sister looked upon the younger, with a countenance that wavered with powerful and contending emotions. At length she spoke, though her tones had lost their rich and calm fullness, in an expression of tenderness that seemed maternal.

"Alice," she said, "the Huron offers us both life – nay, more than both; he offers to restore Duncan – our invaluable Duncan, as well as you, to our friends – to our father – to our heart-stricken, childless father, if I will bow down this rebellious, stubborn pride of mine, and consent – "

Her voice became choked, and clasping her hands, she looked upward as if seeking in her agony intelligence from a wisdom that was infinite. "What says my Alice? For her will I submit without another murmur."

Although both Heyward and Cora listened with painful suspense and the deepest attention, no sounds were heard in reply. It appeared as if the delicate and sensitive form of Alice would shrink into itself, as she listened to this proposal. Her arms had fallen lengthwise before her, the fingers moving in slight convulsions; her head dropped upon her bosom, and her whole person seemed suspended against the tree, looking like some beautiful emblem of the wounded delicacy of her sex, devoid of animation, and yet keenly conscious. In a few moments, however, her head began to move slowly, in a sign of deep, unconquerable disapprobation.

"No, no, no; better that we die as we have lived, together!"

"Then die!" shouted Magua, hurling his tomahawk with violence at the unresisting speaker, and gnashing his teeth with a rage that could no longer be bridled, at this sudden exhibition of firmness in the one he believed the weakest of the party. The ax cleaved the air in front of Heyward, and cutting some of the flowing ringlets of Alice, quivered in the tree above her head. The sight maddened Duncan to desperation. Collecting all his energies in one effort, he snapped the twigs which bound him, and rushed upon another savage, who was preparing, with loud yells and a more deliberate aim, to repeat the blow. They encountered, grappled, and fell to the earth together. The naked body of his antagonist afforded Heyward no means of holding his adversary, who glided from his grasp and rose again with one knee on his chest, pressing him down with the weight of a giant. Duncan already saw the knife gleaming in the air, when a whistling sound swept past him, and was rather accompanied than followed by the sharp crack of a rifle. He felt his breath relieved from the load it had endured; he saw the savage expression of his adversary's countenance change to a look of vacant wildness, when the Indian fell dead on the faded leaves by his side.

AMERICAN INDIAN CANOES

CANOE IN FIRST STAGES OF CONSTRUCTION
THIN WOODEN RIBS WERE COVERED WITH STITCHED BARK
STAKES HELD THE CANOE IN POSITION WHILST UNDER
CONSTRUCTION. THE CANOE WAS RENDERED WATER-TIGHT
WITH PINE GUM

ROLLED BIRCH OR ELM BARK

FINISHED CANOE
BIRCH BARK WAS COMMON IN NORTHERN
FORESTS. ELM THE MORE POPULAR TREE
FARTHER SOUTH

BULL BOAT AND PADDLE
A CIRCULAR BOAT MADE
BY PLAINS INDIANS FROM
BUFFALO SKINS. IT WAS
COLLAPSIBLE AND USED
FOR SHORT RIVER CROSSINGS

NORTH WEST COAST CANOE

HOLLOWED OUT OF A SINGLE CEDAR LOG THE TREE WAS ORIGINALLY FELLED BY APPLYING CLAY TO
THE BASE AND A FIRE STARTED BELOW IT. THIS WAS REPEATED UNTIL THE TREE WAS FELLED

AMERICAN KENTUCKY RIFLE

FLINTS

REAR END OF WOODEN RAMROD SHOWING CORKSCREW "WORM" FOR PULLING CLEANING CLOTH THROUGH BARREL

.50

HUNTING BAG

BUCKSKIN COAT

HUNTING KNIFE WITH MAPLE

HIDE LEGGINGS

COON SKIN CAP
THIS CAP WAS NOT AS POPULAR WITH THE WOODSMAN AS IS USUALLY BELIEVED

MOCCASINS

AMERICAN FRONTIERSMAN

THE AMERICAN FRONTIERSMAN ACTED AS GUIDE, EXPLORER AND SOLDIER IN THE EARLY DAYS OF AMERICAN DEVELOPMENT. HE USUALLY ADOPTED PART OF THE INDIAN DRESS, AND BECAME DEPENDENT UPON THE GAME AND NATURAL RESOURCES OF THE WOODS.

...ED PATCHES OF CLOTH OR BUCKSKIN
...RAPPING AROUND BALLS PRIOR TO
...NG

SMALL POWDER HORN
FOR FINE GRAIN
PRIMING POWDER

BULLET MOULD

LARGE HORN FOR
MUZZLE LOADING
POWDER

...ALLS

LOADING BLOCK USED
TO CARRY THREE
WRAPPED BALLS READY
FOR IMMEDIATE USE

STAG HORN
MEASURING
CUP

HANDLE

BUCKSKIN COAT

THE KENTUCKY RIFLE WAS MADE OF CURLY MAPLE WOOD, USUALLY
62 INCHES LONG, WEIGHING 9½ POUNDS WITH A BARREL LENGTH
OF 46 INCHES AND A FIXED REAR SIGHT. THE BUTTPLATE,
RAMROD PIPES, TRIGGER GUARD AND PATCHBOX WERE BRASS
AND ORNAMENTS ON
REVERSE SIDE SILVER.

STONE

BAIT

BOX TRAP

THE TRAP PRESSING DOWN ON
(A) KEEPS THE TRIGGER (B) IN
PLACE AND HOLDS THE CAGE UP.
MOVEMENT OF THE BAITED END DISPLACES
THIS BALANCE AND THE TRAP FALLS

RECIPES (INDIAN FOOD)

THE THREE STAPLE FOODS OF THE INDIAN DIET WERE CORN, SQUASH AND BEANS.

SUCCOTASH
BOIL BEANS WITH A LUMP OF PORK FAT FOR TWO HOURS. ADD GREEN CORN SCRAPED OFF THE COB AND BOIL FOR A FURTHER TWENTY MINUTES   ADD SALT.

IRON SKILLET

ROAST CORN HUSKS
RAKE AWAY COALS OF FIRE AND LAY GREEN CORN ON HOT GROUND. COVER WITH HOT ASHES AND REBUILD FIRE OVER THEM. ALTERNATIVELY BUILD A FIRE BETWEEN TWO LOGS AND LAY THE EARS BETWEEN THEM.

PARCHED CORN
USED BY HUNTERS AND WARRIORS AS, WHEN GROUND, THE FLOUR COULD BE MADE INTO A GRUEL WITHOUT COOKING. STRIP CORN FROM COB, STIR INTO A SKILLET FULL OF SALT AND ALLOW TO SWELL AND BROWN OVER A FIRE. POUND INTO A FINE MEAL. THE IROQUOIS ADDED DRIED CHERRIES OR MAPLE SUGAR.

ACORN MUSH
SPLIT KERNELS AND DRY IN SUN TO LEACH TANNIN FROM THEM. THEN GRIND TO A FLOUR SEASON WITH SALT AND BOIL IN A LYE OF BASSWOOD ASHES TWO QUARTS DOUGH TO THREE GALLONS OF WATER

MAPLE SUGAR
COLLECT SAP IN BARK BUCKETS IN SPRING. THEN BOIL DOWN. MAKE CANDY BY POURING IN SNOW TO COOL RAPIDLY.

BEVERAGES
BOIL SASSAFRAS ROOTS OR SWEET-BIRCH TWIGS TO MAKE A TEA.

IROQUOIS CORN MORTAR AND PESTLE

PEMMICAN
A CAKE MADE OF DRIED AND POUNDED MEAT. MIXED WITH KIDNEY FAT FROM ELK OR DEER. AND BERRIES. KEPT IN BARK CONTAINER AND USED AS IRON RATIONS ON LONG JOURNEYS.

WOODEN TANKARD

AMERICAN FOOD

WESTERN SANDWICH
INVENTED BY PIONEERS. EGGS WERE OFTEN 'HIGH' AFTER A LONG HAUL, SO TO KILL THE BAD TASTE, THEY WERE MIXED WITH ONIONS OR OTHER STRONG SEASONING COOKED AS AN OMELETTE AND EATEN BETWEEN SLICES OF BUTTERED BREAD.

JOHNNYCAKES
ADD BOILING WATER TO CORN MEAL, SALT AND SUGAR TO FORM A BATTER. FRY ON WELL-GREASED GRIDDLE. SERVE WITH BUTTER AND MAPLE SYRUP.

BATTLE

The Hurons stood aghast at this sudden visitation of death on one of their band. But, as they regarded the fatal accuracy of an aim which had dared to immolate an enemy at so much hazard to a friend, the name of La Longue Carabine burst simultaneously from every lip and was succeeded by a wild and a sort of plaintive howl. The cry was answered by a loud shout from a little thicket, where the incautious party had piled their arms; and, at the next moment, Hawk-eye, too eager to load the rifle he had regained, was seen advancing upon them, brandishing the clubbed weapon, and cutting the air with wide and powerful sweeps. Bold and rapid as was the progress of the scout, it was exceeded by that of a light and vigorous form which, bounding past him, leaped, with incredible activity and daring, into the very center of the Hurons, where it stood, whirling a tomahawk and flourishing a glittering knife, with fearful menaces, in front of Cora. Quicker than the thoughts could follow these unexpected and audacious movements, an image, armed in the emblematic panoply of death, glided before their eyes and assumed a threatening attitude at the other's side. The savage tormentors

recoiled before these warlike intruders, and uttered as they appeared in such quick succession, the often repeated and peculiar exclamation of surprise, followed by the well-known and dreaded appellations of –

"Le Cerf Agile! Le Gros Serpent!"

But the wary and vigilant leader of the Hurons was not so easily disconcerted. Casting his keen eyes around the little plain, he comprehended the nature of the assault at a glance, and encouraging his followers by his voice as well as by his example, he unsheathed his long and dangerous knife, and rushed with a loud whoop upon the expecting Chingachgook. It was the signal for a general combat. Neither party had firearms, and the contest was to be decided in the deadliest manner; hand to hand, with weapons of offense, and none of defense.

Uncas answered the whoop, and leaping on an enemy, with a single, well-directed blow of his tomahawk, cleft him to the brain. Heyward tore the weapon of Magua from the sapling, and rushed eagerly toward the fray. As the combatants were now equal in number, each singled an opponent from the adverse band. The rush and blows passed with the fury of a whirlwind and the swiftness of lightning. Hawk-eye soon got another enemy within reach of his arm, and with one sweep of his formidable weapon he beat down the slight and inartificial defenses of his antagonist, crushing him to the earth with the blow. Heyward ventured to hurl the tomahawk he had seized, too ardent to await the moment of closing. It struck the Indian he had selected on the forehead, and checked for an instant his onward rush. Encouraged by this slight advantage, the impetuous young man continued his onset, and sprang upon his enemy with naked hands. A single instant was sufficient to assure him of the rashness of the measure, for he immediately found himself fully engaged, with all his activity and courage, in endeavoring to ward the desperate thrusts made with the knife of the Huron. Unable longer to foil an enemy so alert and vigilant, he threw his arms about him, and succeeded in pinning the limbs of the other to his side with an iron grasp, but one that was far too exhausting to himself to continue long. In this extremity he heard a voice near him, shouting:

"Extarminate the varlets! No quarter to an accursed Mingo!"

At the next moment, the breech of Hawk-eye's rifle fell on the naked head of his adversary, whose muscles appeared to wither under the shock as he sank from the arms of Duncan, flexible and motionless.

When Uncas had brained his first antagonist, he turned, like a hungry lion, to seek another. The fifth and only Huron disengaged at the first onset had paused a moment, and then seeing that all around him were employed in the deadly strife, he had sought, with hellish vengeance, to complete the baffled work of revenge. Raising a shout of triumph, he sprang toward the defenseless Cora, sending his keen ax as the dreadful precursor of his approach. The tomahawk grazed her shoulder, and cutting the withes which bound her to the tree, left the maiden at liberty to fly. She eluded the grasp of the savage, and reckless of her own safety, threw herself on the bosom of Alice, striving, with convulsed and ill-directed fingers, to tear asunder the twigs which confined the person of her sister. Any other than a monster would have relented at such an act of generous devotion to the best and purest affection; but the breast of the Huron was a stranger to sympathy. Seizing Cora by the rich tresses which fell in confusion about her form, he tore her from her frantic hold and bowed her down with brutal violence to her knees. The savage drew the flowering curls through his hand, and raising them on high with an outstretched arm, he passed the knife around the exquisitely molded head of his victim, with a taunting and exulting laugh. But he purchased this moment of fierce gratification with the loss of the fatal opportunity. It was just then the sight caught the eye of Uncas. Bounding from his footsteps he appeared for an instant darting through the air, and descending in a ball he fell on the chest of his enemy, driving him many yards from the spot, headlong and prostrate. The violence of the exertion cast the young Mohican at his side. They arose together, fought, and bled, each in his turn. But the conflict was soon decided; the tomahawk of Heyward and the rifle of Hawk-eye descended on the skull of the Huron, at the same moment that the knife of Uncas reached his heart.

INDIAN BEAVER TAIL KNIFE WITH BUCKSKIN SHEATH

The battle was now entirely terminated, with the exception of the protracted struggle between Le Renard Subtil and Le Gros Serpent. Well did these barbarous warriors prove that they deserved those significant names which had been bestowed for deeds in former wars. When they engaged, some little time was lost in eluding the quick and vigorous thrusts which had been aimed at their lives. Suddenly darting on each other, they closed, and came to the earth twisted together like twining serpents, in pliant and subtle folds. At the moment when the victors found themselves unoccupied, the spot where these experienced and desperate combatants lay could only be distinguished by a cloud of dust and leaves which moved from the center of the little plain toward its boundary, as if raised by the passage of a whirlwind. Urged by the different motives of filial affection, friendship, and gratitude, Heyward and his companions rushed with one accord to the place, encircling the little canopy of dust which hung above the warriors. In vain did Uncas dart around the cloud, with a wish to strike his knife into the heart of his father's foe; the threatening rifle of Hawk-eye was raised and suspended in vain, while Duncan endeavored to seize the limbs of the Huron with hands that appeared to have lost their power. Covered, as they were, with dust and blood, the swift evolutions of the combatants seemed to incorporate their bodies into one. The deathlike looking figure of the Mohican, and the dark form of the Huron, gleamed before their eyes in such quick and confused succession that the friends of the former knew not where nor when to plant the succoring blow. It is true there were short and fleeting moments when the fiery eyes of Magua were seen glittering, like the fabled organs of the basilisk, through the dusty wrath by which he was enveloped, and he read by those short and deadly glances the fate of the combat in the presence of his enemies; ere, however, any hostile hand could descend on his devoted head, its place was filled by the scowling visage of Chingachgook. In this manner the scene of the combat was removed from the center of the little plain to its verge. The Mohican now found an opportunity to make a powerful thrust with his knife; Magua suddenly relinquished his grasp, and fell backward without motion, and seemingly without life. His adversary leaped on his feet, making the arches of the forest ring with the sounds of triumph.

"Well done for the Delawares! Victory to the Mohican!" cried Hawk-eye, once more elevating the butt of the long and fatal rifle. "A finishing blow from a man without a cross will never tell against his honor, nor rob him of his right to the scalp."

But, at the very moment when the dangerous weapon was in the act of descending, the subtle Huron rolled swiftly from beneath the danger, over the edge of the precipice, and falling on his feet, was seen leaping, with a single bound, into the center of a thicket of low bushes which clung along its sides. The Delawares, who had believed their enemy dead, uttered their exclamation of surprise, and were following with speed and clamor, like hounds in open view of the deer, when a shrill and peculiar cry from the scout instantly changed their purpose, and recalled them to the summit of the hill.

"'Twas like himself," cried the inveterate forester, whose prejudices contributed so largely to veil his natural sense of justice in all matters which concerned the Mingoes; "a lying and deceitful varlet as he is."

So saying, the honest but implacable scout made the circuit of the dead, into whose senseless bosoms he thrust his long knife with as much coolness as though they had been so many brute carcasses. He had, however, been anticipated by the elder Mohican, who had already torn the emblems of victory from the unresisting heads of the slain.

But Uncas, denying his habits, we had almost said his nature, flew with instinctive delicacy, accompanied by Heyward, to the assistance of the females, and quickly releasing Alice, placed her in the arms of Cora. We shall not attempt to describe the gratitude to the Almighty Disposer of events which glowed in the bosoms of the sisters, who were thus unexpectedly restored to life and to each other. Their thanksgivings were deep and silent; the offerings of their gentle spirits, burning brightest and purest on the secret altars of their hearts; and their renovated and more earthly feelings exhibiting themselves in long and fervent though speechless caresses.

During this display of emotions so natural in their situation, Hawk-eye, whose vigilant distrust had satisfied itself that the Hurons, who disfigured the heavenly scene, no longer possessed the power to interrupt its harmony, approached David, and liberated him from the bonds he had, until that moment, endured with the most exemplary patience.

"There," exclaimed the scout, casting the last withe behind him, "you are once more master of your own limbs, though you seem not to use them with much greater judgment than that in which they were first fashioned."

"Arms and the clarion for the battle, but the song of thanksgiving to the victory!" answered the liberated David. "Friend," he added, thrusting forth his lean, delicate hand toward Hawk-eye in kindness, while his eyes twinkled and grew moist, "I thank thee that the hairs of my head still grow where they were first rooted by Providence; for, though those of other men may be more glossy and curling, I have ever found mine own well suited to the brain they shelter. That I did not join myself to the battle was less owing to disinclination, than to the bonds of the heathen. Valiant and skillful hast thou proved thyself in the conflict, and I hereby thank thee, before proceeding to discharge other and more important duties, because thou hast proved thyself well worthy of a Christian's praise."

The scout walked away to collect and to examine into the state of the captured arsenal of the Hurons. In this office he was now joined by Chingachgook, who found his own, as well as the rifle of his son, among the arms. Even Heyward and David were furnished with weapons; nor was ammunition wanting to render them all effectual.

When the foresters had made their selection and distributed their prizes, the scout announced that the hour had arrived when it was necessary to move. The sisters, aided by Duncan and the younger Mohican, descended the precipitous sides of that hill which they had so lately ascended under so very different auspices, and whose summit had so nearly proved the scene of their massacre. At the foot, they found the Narragansets browsing the herbage of the bushes; and having mounted, they followed the movements of a guide, who, in the most deadly straits, had so often proved himself their friend. The journey was, however, short. Hawk-eye, leaving the blind path that the Hurons had followed, turned short to his right and, entering the thicket, he crossed a babbling brook and halted in a narrow dell, under the shade of a few water elms. Their distance from the base of the fatal hill was but a few rods, and the steeds had been serviceable only in crossing the shallow stream.

The scout and the Indians appeared to be familiar with the sequestered place where they now were; for, leaning their rifles against the trees, they commenced throwing aside the dried leaves and opening the blue clay, out of which a clear and sparkling spring of bright, glancing water quickly bubbled. The white man then looked about him, as though seeking for some object which was not to be found as readily as he expected.

"Them careless imps, the Mohawks, with their Tuscarora and Onondaga brethren, have been here slaking their thirst," he muttered, "and the vagabonds have thrown away the gourd!"

Uncas silently extended toward him the desired gourd, which the spleen of Hawk-eye had hitherto prevented him from observing, on a branch of an elm. Filling it with water, he retired a short distance to a place where the ground was more firm and dry; here he coolly seated himself, and after taking a long and apparently a grateful draught, he commenced a very strict examination of the fragments of food left by the Hurons, which had hung in a wallet on his arm.

Heyward, perceiving that their guides now set about their repast in sober earnest, assisted the ladies to alight and placed himself at their side, not unwilling to enjoy a few moments of grateful rest after the bloody scene he had just gone through. While the culinary process was in hand, curiosity induced him to inquire into the circumstances which had led to their timely and unexpected rescue.

"How is it that we see you so soon, my generous friend," he asked, "and without aid from the garrison of Edward?"

"Had we gone to the bend in the river, we might have been in time to rake the leaves over your bodies, but too late to have saved your scalps," coolly answered the scout. "No, no; instead of throwing away strength and opportunity by crossing to the fort, we lay by, under the bank of the Hudson, waiting to watch the movements of the Hurons."

"You were, then, witnesses of all that passed?"

"Not of all; for Indian sights is too keen to be easily cheated, and we kept close. A difficult matter it was, too, to keep this Mohican boy snug in the ambushment. Ah! Uncas, Uncas, your behavior was more like that of a curious woman than of a warrior on his scent."

Uncas permitted his eyes to turn for an instant on the sturdy countenance of the speaker, but he neither spoke nor gave any indication of repentance. On the contrary, Heyward thought the manner of the young Mohican was disdainful, if not a little fierce, and that he suppressed passions that were ready to explode, as much in compliment to the listeners, as from the deference he usually paid to his white associate.

"You saw our capture?" Heyward next demanded.

"We heard it," was the significant answer. "An Indian yell is plain language to men who have passed their days in the woods. But when you landed, we were driven to crawl, like sarpents, beneath the leaves; and then we lost sight of you entirely, until we placed eyes on you again, trussed to the trees, and ready bound for an Indian massacre."

"Our rescue was the deed of Providence. It was nearly a miracle that you did not mistake the path, for the Hurons divided, and each band had its horses."

"Aye! There we were thrown off the scent, and might, indeed, have lost the trail, had it not been for Uncas; we took the path, however, that led into the wilderness; for we judged, and judged rightly, that the savages would hold that course with their prisoners. But when we had followed it for many miles without finding a single twig broken, as I had advised, my mind misgave me; especially as all the footsteps had the prints of moccasins."

"Our captors had the precaution to see us shod like themselves," said Duncan, raising a foot, and exhibiting the buckskin he wore.

"Aye! 'twas judgmatical, and like themselves; though we were too expart to be thrown from a trail by so common an invention."

"To what, then, are we indebted for our safety?"

"To what, as a white man who has no taint of Indian blood, I should be ashamed to own; to the judgment of the young Mohican, in matters which I should know better than he, but which I can now hardly believe to be true, though my own eyes tell me it is so."

"'Tis extraordinary! Will you not name the reason?"

"Uncas was bold enough to say that

the beasts ridden by the gentle ones," continued Hawk-eye, glancing his eyes, not without curious interest, on the fillies of the ladies, "planted the legs of one side on the ground at the same time, which is contrary to the movements of all trotting four-footed animals of my knowledge, except the bear. And yet here are horses that always journey in this manner, as my own eyes have seen, and as their trail has shown for twenty long miles."

"'Tis the merit of the animal! They come from the shores of Narraganset Bay, in the small province of Providence Plantations, and are celebrated for their hardihood and the ease of this peculiar movement; though other horses are not unfrequently trained to the same."

"It may be – it may be," said Hawk-eye, who had listened with singular attention to this explanation. "Though I am a man who has the full blood of the whites, my judgment in deer and beaver is greater than in beasts of burden."

The Mohicans had suspended their operations about the glimmering fire, to listen; and when Duncan had done, they looked at each other significantly, the father uttering the never-failing exclamation of surprise. The scout ruminated, like a man digesting his newly acquired knowledge, and once more stole a curious glance at the horses.

"I dare to say there are even stranger sights to be seen in the settlements!" he said, at length. "Natur' is sadly abused by man, when he once gets the mastery. But, go sidling or go straight, Uncas had seen the movement, and their trail led us on to the broken bush. The outer branch, near the prints of one of the horses, was bent upward, as a lady breaks a flower from its stem, but all the rest were ragged and broken down, as if the strong hand of a man had been tearing them! So I concluded that the cunning varments had seen the twig bent, and had torn the rest, to make us believe a buck had been feeling the boughs with his antlers."

"I do believe your sagacity did not deceive you; for some such thing occurred!"

"That was easy to see," added the scout, in no degree conscious of having exhibited any extraordinary sagacity; "and a very different matter it was from a waddling horse! It then struck me the Mingoes would push for this spring, for the knaves well know the vartue of its waters!"

"Is it, then, so famous?" demanded Heyward, examining with a more curious eye the secluded dell, with its bubbling fountain, surrounded as it was by earth of a deep dingy brown.

"Few redskins who travel south and east of the great lakes but have heard of its qualities. Will you taste for yourself?"

Heyward took the gourd, and after swallowing a little of the water, threw it aside with grimaces of discontent. The scout laughed in his silent but heartfelt manner, and shook his head with vast satisfaction.

Then Hawk-eye announced his determination to proceed. The sisters resumed their saddles; Duncan and David grasped their rifles, and followed on their footsteps; the scout leading the advance, and the Mohicans bringing up the rear. The whole party moved swiftly through the narrow path, toward the north, leaving the healing waters to mingle unheeded with the adjacent brook, and the bodies of the dead to fester on the neighboring mount, without the rites of sepulture; a fate but too common to the warriors of the woods to excite either commiseration or comment.

INDIAN MOCCASINS

A NIGHT AMONG THE DEAD

The route taken by Hawk-eye lay across those sandy plains, relieved by occasional valleys and swells of land, which had been traversed by their party on the morning of the same day, with the baffled Magua for their guide. The sun had now fallen low toward the distant mountains; and as their journey lay through the interminable forest, the heat was no longer oppressive. Their progress, in consequence, was proportionate; and long before the twilight gathered about them, they had made good many miles on their return.

While the eyes of the sisters were endeavoring to catch glimpses through the trees of the flood of golden glory which formed a glittering halo around the sun, tingeing here and there with ruby streaks, or bordering with narrow edgings of shining yellow, a mass of clouds that lay piled at no great distance above the western hills, Hawk-eye turned suddenly, and, pointing upward toward the gorgeous heavens, he spoke.

"Yonder is the signal given to man to seek his food and natural rest," he said. "Better and wiser would it be, if he could understand the signs of nature, and take a lesson from the fowls of the air, and the beasts of the fields! Our night, however, will soon be over; for, with the moon, we must be up and moving again. I remember to have fought the Maquas, hereaways, in the first war in which I ever drew blood from man; and we threw up a work of blocks to keep the ravenous varments from handling our scalps. If my marks do not fail me, we shall find the place a few rods farther to our left."

Without waiting for an assent, or,

indeed, for any reply, the sturdy hunter moved boldly into a dense thicket of young chestnuts, shoving aside the branches of the exuberant shoots which nearly covered the ground, like a man who expected, at each step, to discover some object he had formerly known. The recollection of the scout did not deceive him. After penetrating through the brush, matted as it was with briers, for a few hundred feet, he entered an open space that surrounded a low, green hillock which was crowned by the decayed blockhouse in question. This rude and neglected building was one of those deserted works, which, having been thrown up on an emergency, had been abandoned with the disappearance of danger, and was now quietly crumbling in the solitude of the forest, neglected and nearly forgotten, like the circumstances which had caused it to be reared. The roof of bark had long since fallen, and mingled with the soil; but the huge logs of pine, which had been hastily thrown together, still preserved their relative positions, though one angle of the work had given way under the pressure, and threatened a speedy downfall to the remainder of the rustic edifice. While Heyward and his companions hesitated to approach a building so decayed, Hawk-eye and the Indians entered within the low walls, not only without fear, but with obvious interest. While the former surveyed the ruins, both internally and externally, with the curiosity of one whose recollections were reviving at each moment, Chingachgook related to his son, in the language of the Delawares and with the pride of a conqueror, the brief history of the skirmish which had been fought, in his youth, in that secluded spot. A strain of melancholy, however, blended with his triumph, rendering his voice, as usual, soft and musical.

In the meantime, the sisters gladly dismounted and prepared to enjoy their halt in the coolness of the evening, and in a security which they believed nothing but the beasts of the forest could invade.

"Would not our resting place have been more retired, my worthy friend," demanded the more vigilant Duncan, perceiving that the scout had already finished his short survey, "had we chosen a spot less known, and one more rarely visited than this?"

WHIP-POOR-WILL

"Few live who know the blockhouse was ever raised," was the slow and musing answer. "'Tis not often that books are made, and narratives written, of such a scrimmage as was here fought atween the Mohicans and the Mohawks, in a war of their own waging. I was then a younker, and went out with the Delawares, because I know'd they were a scandalized and wronged race. Forty days and forty nights did the imps crave our blood around this pile of logs, which I designed and partly reared, being, as you'll remember, no Indian myself, but a man without a cross. The Delawares lent themselves to the work, and we made it good, ten to twenty, until our numbers were nearly equal, and then we sallied out upon the hounds, and not a man of them ever got back to tell the fate of his party. Yes, yes; I was then young, and new to the sight of blood; and not relishing the thought that creatures who had spirits like myself should lay on the naked ground, to be torn asunder by beasts, or to bleach in the rains, I buried the dead with my own hands, under that very little hillock where you have placed yourselves; and no bad seat does it make neither, though it be raised by the bones of mortal men."

Heyward and the sisters arose, on the instant, from the grassy sepulcher; nor could the two latter, notwithstanding the terrific scenes they had so recently passed through, entirely suppress an emotion of natural horror when they found themselves in such familiar contact with the grave of the dead Mohawks. The gray light, the gloomy little area of dark grass, surrounded by its border of brush, beyond which the pines rose, in breathing silence, apparently into the very clouds, and the deathlike stillness of the vast forest, were all in unison to deepen such a sensation.

"They are gone, and they are harmless," continued Hawk-eye, waving his hand, with a melancholy smile, at their manifest alarm. "They'll never shout the war whoop nor strike a blow with the tomahawk again! And of all those who aided in placing them where they lie, Chingachgook and I only are living! The brothers and family of the Mohicans formed our war party; and you see before you all that are now left of his race."

The eyes of the listeners involuntarily

sought the forms of the Indians, with a compassionate interest in their desolate fortune. Their dark persons were still to be seen within the shadows of the blockhouse, the son listening to the relation of his father with that sort of intenseness which would be created by a narrative that redounded so much to the honor of those whose names he had long revered for their courage and savage virtues.

The hunter and his companions busied themselves in preparations for the comfort and protection of those they guided. A spring, which many long years before had induced the natives to select the place for their temporary fortification, was soon cleared of leaves, and a fountain of crystal gushed from the bed, diffusing its waters over the verdant hillock. A corner of the building was then roofed in such a manner as to exclude the heavy dew of the climate, and piles of sweet shrubs and dried leaves were laid beneath it for the sisters to repose on.

While the diligent woodsmen were employed in this manner, Cora and Alice partook of that refreshment which duty required much more than inclination prompted them to accept. They then retired within the walls, and first offering up their thanksgivings for past mercies, and petitioning for a continuance of the Divine favor throughout the coming night, they laid their tender forms on the fragrant couch, and in spite of recollections and forebodings, soon sank into those slumbers which nature so imperiously demanded, and which were sweetened by hopes for the morrow. Duncan had prepared himself to pass the night in watchfulness near them, just without the ruin, but the scout, perceiving his intention, pointed toward Chingachgook, as he coolly disposed his own person on the grass, and said:

"The eyes of a white man are too heavy and too blind for such a watch as this! The Mohican will be our sentinel, therefore let us sleep."

"I proved myself a sluggard on my post during the past night," said Heyward, "and have less need of repose than you, who did more credit to the character of a soldier. Let all the party seek their rest, then, while I hold the guard."

"If we lay among the white tents of the

60th, and in front of an enemy like the French, I could not ask for a better watchman," returned the scout. "But in the darkness and among the signs of the wilderness your judgment would be like the folly of a child, and your vigilance thrown away. Do then, like Uncas and myself, sleep, and sleep in safety." Hawk-eye, believing he had prevailed, soon fell asleep, and a silence as deep as the solitude in which they had found it pervaded the retired spot.

For many minutes Duncan succeeded in keeping his senses on the alert, and alive to every moaning sound that arose from the forest. His vision became more acute as the shades of evening settled on the place; and even after the stars were glimmering above his head, he was able to distinguish the recumbent forms of his companions as they lay stretched on the grass, and to note the person of Chingachgook, who sat upright and motionless as one of the trees, which formed the dark barrier on every side of them. He still heard the gentle breathings of the sisters, who lay within a few feet of him, and not a leaf was ruffled by the passing air of which his ear did not detect the whispering sound. At length, however, the mournful notes of a whippoorwill became blended with the moanings of an owl; his heavy eyes occasionally sought the bright rays of the stars, and then he fancied he saw them through the fallen lids. At instants of momentary wakefulness he mistook a bush for his associate sentinel; his head next sank upon his shoulder, which, in its turn, sought the support of the ground; and, finally, his whole person became relaxed and pliant, and the young man sank into a deep sleep, dreaming that he was a knight of ancient chivalry, holding his midnight vigils before the tent of a recaptured princess, whose favor he did not despair of gaining, by such a proof of devotion and watchfulness.

How long the tired Duncan lay in this insensible state he never knew himself, but his slumbering visions had been long lost in total forgetfulness, when he was awakened by a light tap on the shoulder. Aroused by this signal, slight as it was, he sprang upon his feet with a confused recollection of the self-imposed duty he had assumed with the commencement of the night.

"Who comes?" he demanded, feeling

SMALL SWORDS

for his sword at the place where it was usually suspended. "Speak! Friend or enemy?"

"Friend," replied the low voice of Chingachgook; who, pointing upward at the luminary which was shedding its mild light through the opening in the trees, directly on their bivouac, immediately added, in his rude English, "Moon comes, and white man's fort far – far off; time to move, when sleep shuts both eyes of the Frenchman!"

"You say true! Call up your friends, and bridle the horses, while I prepare my own companions for the march!"

"We are awake, Duncan," said the soft, silvery tones of Alice within the building, "and ready to travel very fast, after so refreshing a sleep; but you have watched through the tedious night in our behalf, after having endured so much fatigue the livelong day!"

"Say, rather, I would have watched, but my treacherous eyes betrayed me; twice have I proved myself unfit for the trust I bear."

"Nay, Duncan, deny it not," interrupted the smiling Alice, issuing from the shadows of the building into the light of the moon, in all the loveliness of her freshened beauty. "Can we not tarry here a little longer, while you find the rest you need? Cheerfully, most cheerfully, will Cora and I keep the vigils, while you, and all these brave men, endeavor to snatch a little sleep!"

The young man was relieved from the awkwardness of making any further protestations of his own demerits, by an exclamation from Chingachgook, and the attitude of riveted attention assumed by his son.

"The Mohicans hear an enemy!" whispered Hawk-eye, who by this time, in common with the whole party, was awake and stirring. "They scent danger!"

"God forbid!" exclaimed Heyward. "Surely we have had enough of bloodshed!"

While he spoke, however, the young soldier seized his rifle, and advancing toward the front, prepared to atone for his venial remissness by freely exposing his life in defense of those he attended.

"'Tis some creature of the forest prowling around us in quest of food," he said in a whisper, as soon as the low and apparently distant sounds which had startled the Mohicans, reached his own ears.

"Hist!" returned the attentive scout. "'Tis man; even I can now tell his tread, poor as my senses are when compared to an Indian's! That scampering Huron has fallen in with one of Montcalm's outlying parties, and they have struck upon our trail. I shouldn't like, myself, to spill more human blood in this spot," he added, looking around with anxiety in his features at the dim objects by which he was surrounded; "but what must be, must! Lead the horses into the blockhouse, Uncas; and, friends, do you follow to the same shelter. Poor and old as it is, it offers a cover, and has rung with the crack of a rifle afore tonight!"

He was instantly obeyed, the Mohicans leading the Narragansets within the ruin, whither the whole party repaired, with the most guarded silence.

The sounds of approaching footsteps were now too distinctly audible to leave any doubts as to the nature of the interruption. They were soon mingled with voices calling to each other in an Indian dialect, which the hunter, in a whisper, affirmed to Heyward was the language of the Hurons. When the party reached the point where the horses had entered the thicket which surrounded the blockhouse, they were evidently at fault, having lost those marks which, until that moment, had directed their pursuit.

It would seem by the voices that twenty men were soon collected at that one spot, mingling their different opinions and advice in noisy clamor. It was not long before the restless savages were heard beating the brush, and gradually approaching the inner edge of that dense border of young chestnuts which encircled the little area.

Duncan cast his eyes behind him, and saw that the trembling sisters were cowering in the far corner of the building, while the Mohicans stood in the shadow, like two upright posts, ready, and apparently willing, to strike when the blow should be needed. Curbing his impatience, he again looked out upon the area, and awaited the result in silence. At that instant the thicket opened, and a tall and armed Huron advanced a few paces into the open space. As he gazed upon the silent blockhouse, the moon fell full upon his swarthy countenance, and betrayed its surprise and curiosity. He made the exclamation which usually accompanies the former emotion in an Indian, and,

THROUGH ENEMY LINES

BLOCK HOUSE — SLITS WERE FOR FIRING THROUGH

calling in a low voice, soon drew a companion to his side.

These children of the woods stood together for several moments pointing at the crumbling edifice, and conversing in the unintelligible language of their tribe. The savages were so near that the least motion in one of the horses, or even a breath louder than common, would have betrayed the fugitives. But, in discovering the character of the mound, the attention of the Hurons appeared directed to a different object. They spoke together, and the sounds of their voices were low and solemn, as if influenced by a reverence that was deeply blended with awe. Then they drew warily back, keeping their eyes riveted on the ruin, as if they expected to see the apparitions of the dead issue from its silent walls until, having reached the boundary of the area, they moved slowly into the thicket, and disappeared.

Hawk-eye waited until a signal from the listening Chingachgook assured him that every sound from the retiring party was completely swallowed by the distance, when he motioned to Heyward to lead forth the horses, and to assist the sisters into their saddles. The instant this was done, they issued through the broken gateway, and stealing out by a direction opposite to the one by which they had entered, they quitted the spot, the sisters casting furtive glances at the silent grave and crumbling ruin, as they left the soft light of the moon, to bury themselves in the gloom of the woods.

During the rapid movement from the blockhouse, and until the party was deeply buried in the forest, each individual was too much interested in the escape to hazard a word even in whispers. At such moments, it seemed as if a vast range of country lay buried in eternal sleep; not the least sound arising from the forest, unless it was the distant and scarcely audible rippling of a watercourse. Birds, beasts, and man, appeared to slumber alike, if, indeed, any of the latter were to be found in that wide tract of wilderness. But the sounds of the rivulet, feeble and murmuring as they were, relieved the guides, and toward it they immediately held their way.

When the banks of the little stream were gained, Hawk-eye made another halt; and, taking the moccasins from his feet, he invited Heyward and Gamut to follow his example. He then entered the water, and for near an hour they traveled in the bed of the brook, leaving no trail.

"We are then at no great distance from William Henry?" said Heyward, advancing nigher to the scout.

"It is yet a long and weary path, and when and where to strike it, is now our greatest difficulty. See," he said, pointing through the trees toward a spot where a little basin of water reflected the stars from its placid bosom, "here is the

48

'bloody pond'; and I am on ground that I have not only often traveled, but over which I have fought the enemy, from the rising to the setting sun."

"It was a convenient, and, I trust, will prove a peaceful grave for a soldier. You have, then, seen much service on this frontier?"

"I!" said the scout, erecting his tall person with an air of military pride. "There are not many echoes among these hills that haven't rung with the crack of my rifle, nor is there the space of a square mile atwixt Horican and the river, that 'Kill-Deer' hasn't dropped a living body on, be it an enemy or be it a brute beast. By heaven! There is a human form, and it approaches! Stand to your arms, my friends; for we know not whom we encounter."

"Qui vive?" demanded a stern, quick voice, which sounded like a challenge from another world, issuing out of that solitary and solemn place.

"What says it?" whispered the scout. "It speaks neither Indian nor English!"

"Qui vive?" repeated the same voice, which was quickly followed by the rattling of arms, and a menacing attitude.

"France!" cried Heyward, advancing from the shadow of the trees to the shore of the pond, within a few yards of the sentinel.

"D'où venez-vous – où allez-vous, d'aussi bonne heure?" demanded the grenadier, in the language and with the accent of a man from old France.

"Je viens de la découverte, et je vais me coucher."

"Etes-vous officier du roi?"

"Sans doute, mon camarade; me prends-tu pour un provincial! Je suis capitaine de chasseurs."

The soldier made a bow; and Heyward adding a "Bonne nuit, mon camarade," they moved deliberately forward, leaving the sentinel pacing the banks of the silent pond, little suspecting an enemy of so much effrontery.

"'Tis well you understand the knave!" whispered the scout when they had gained a little distance from the place, and letting his rifle fall into the hollow of his arm again.

He was interrupted by a long and heavy groan which arose from the little basin, as though, in truth, the spirits of the departed lingered about their watery sepulcher.

"Surely it was of flesh!" continued the scout. "No spirit could handle its arms so steadily!"

"It *was* of flesh; but whether the poor fellow still belongs to this world may well be doubted," said Heyward, glancing his eyes around him, and missing Chingachgook from their little band. Another groan, more faint than the former, was succeeded by a heavy and sullen plunge into the water, and all was as still again as if the borders of the dreary pool had never been awakened from the silence of creation. While they yet hesitated in uncertainty, the form of the Indian was seen gliding out of the thicket. As the chief rejoined them, with one hand he attached the reeking scalp of the unfortunate young Frenchman to his girdle, and with the other he replaced the knife and tomahawk that had drunk his blood. He then took his wonted station, with the air of a man who believed he had done a deed of merit.

The scout dropped one end of his rifle to the earth, and leaning his hands on the other, he stood musing in profound silence. Then shaking his head in a mournful manner, he muttered:

"'Twould have been a cruel and an unhuman act for a whiteskin; but 'tis the gift and natur' of an Indian, and I suppose it should not be denied. I could wish, though, it had befallen an accursed Mingo, rather than that gay young boy from the old countries."

"Enough!" said Heyward, apprehensive the unconscious sisters might comprehend the nature of the detention, and conquering his disgust by a train of reflections very much like that of the hunter. "'Tis done; and though better it were left undone, cannot be amended. You see we are, too obviously, within the sentinels of the enemy; what course do you propose to follow?"

"We must then turn on our trail, and get without the line of their lookouts, when we will bend short to the west, and enter the mountains; where I can hide you, so that all the devil's hounds in Montcalm's pay would be thrown off the scent for months to come."

"Let it be done, and that instantly."

Further words were unnecessary; for Hawk-eye, merely uttering the mandate to "follow," moved along the route by which they had just entered their present critical and even dangerous situa-

MARQUIS OF MONTCALM

tion. Their progress, like their late dialogue, was guarded, and without noise; for none knew at what moment a passing patrol or a crouching picket of the enemy might rise upon their path.

Hawk-eye soon deviated from the line of their retreat, and striking off toward the mountains which form the western boundary of the narrow plain, he led his followers, with swift steps, deep within the shadows that were cast from their high and broken summits. At length the party began slowly to rise a steep and rugged ascent, by a path that curiously wound among rocks and trees, avoiding the one, and supported by the other, in a manner that showed it had been devised by men long practised in the arts of the wilderness. When they issued from the stunted woods which clung to the barren sides of the mountain, upon a flat and mossy rock that formed its summit, they met the morning, as it came blushing above the green pines of a hill that lay on the opposite side of the valley of the Horican.

The scout now told the sisters to dismount; and taking the bridles from the mouths, and the saddles off the backs of the jaded beasts, he turned them loose to glean a scanty subsistence among the shrubs and meager herbage of that elevated region.

"Have we no further need of them?" demanded Heyward.

"See, and judge with your own eyes," said the scout, advancing toward the eastern brow of the mountain, whither he beckoned for the whole party to follow. "If it was as easy to look into the heart of man as it is to spy out the nakedness of Montcalm's camp from this spot, hypocrites would grow scarce, and the cunning of a Mingo might prove a losing game, compared to the honesty of a Delaware."

When the travelers reached the verge of the precipice, they saw at a glance the truth of the scout's declaration, and the admirable foresight with which he had led them to their commanding station.

The mountain on which they stood, elevated perhaps a thousand feet in the air, was a high cone that rose a little in advance of that range which stretches for miles along the western shores of the lake, until meeting its sister piles, beyond the water, it ran off toward the Canadas, in confused and broken masses of rock thinly sprinkled with evergreens. Immediately at the feet of the party, the southern shore of the Horican swept in a broad semi-circle, from mountain to mountain, marking a wide strand that soon rose into an uneven and somewhat elevated plain. To the north stretched the limpid, and, as it appeared from that dizzy height, the narrow sheet of the "holy lake," indented with numberless bays, embellished by fantastic headlands, and dotted with countless islands.

Directly on the shore of the lake, and nearer to its western than to its eastern margin, lay the extensive earthen ramparts and low buildings of William Henry. Two of the sweeping bastions appeared to rest on the water which washed their bases, while a deep ditch and extensive morasses guarded its other sides and angles. The land had been cleared of wood for a reasonable distance around the work, but every other part of the scene lay in the green livery of nature, except where the limpid water mellowed the view, or the bold rocks thrust their black and naked heads above the undulating outline of the mountain ranges. In its front might be

seen the scattered sentinels, who held a weary watch against their numerous foes; and within the walls themselves, the travelers looked down upon men still drowsy with a night of vigilance. Toward the southeast, but in immediate contact with the fort, was an entrenched camp, posted on a rocky eminence, that would have been far more eligible for the work itself, in which Hawk-eye pointed out the presence of those auxiliary regiments that had so recently left the Hudson in their company. From the woods, a little farther to the south, rose numerous dark and lurid smokes that were easily to be distinguished from the purer exhalations of the springs, and which the scout also showed to Heyward, as evidences that the enemy lay in force in that direction.

But the spectacle which most concerned the young soldier was on the western bank of the lake, though quite near to its southern termination. On a stripe of land, which appeared, from his stand, too narrow to contain such an army, but which, in truth, extended many hundreds of yards from the shores of the Horican to the base of the mountain, were to be seen the white tents and military engines of an encampment of ten thousand men.

The direction taken by Hawk-eye soon brought the travelers to the level of the plain, nearly opposite to a sally port in the western curtain of the fort, which lay, itself, at the distance of about half a mile from the point where he halted to allow Duncan to come up with his charge. In their eagerness, and favored by the nature of the ground, they had anticipated the fog, which was rolling heavily down the lake, and it became necessary to pause until the mists had wrapped the camp of the enemy in their fleecy mantle. The Mohicans profited by the delay to steal out of the woods, and to make a survey of surrounding objects. They were followed at a little distance by the scout, with a view to profit early by their report, and to obtain some faint knowledge for himself of the more immediate localities.

In a very few moments he returned, his face reddened with vexation, while he muttered his disappointment in words of no very gentle import.

"Here has the cunning Frenchman been posting a picket directly in our

RED

BLUE

PRIVATE (THE ROYAL AMERICAN REGIMENT) BRITISH 60ᵗʰ FOOT

path," he said. "Redskins and whites; and we shall be as likely to fall into their midst as to pass them in the fog!"

"Cannot we make a circuit to avoid the danger," asked Heyward, "and come into our path again when it is passed?"

They had made their little circuit to the left, and were already inclining again toward the right, having, as Heyward thought, got over nearly half the distance to the friendly works, when his ears were saluted with the fierce summons, apparently within twenty feet of them, of –

"Qui va là?"

"Push on!" whispered the scout, once more bending to the left.

"Push on!" repeated Heyward; when the summons was renewed by a dozen voices, each of which seemed charged with menace.

"C'est moi," cried Duncan, dragging rather than leading those he supported swiftly onward.

"Bête! – qui? – moi!"

"They will believe it a sortie, and give way, or they will wait for reinforcements."

The scheme was well conceived, but failed in its effect. The instant the French heard the pieces, it seemed as if the plain was alive with men, muskets rattling along its whole extent, from the shores of the lake to the farthest boundary of the woods.

Cries, oaths, voices calling to each other, and the reports of muskets, were now quick and incessant, and, apparently, on every side of them. Suddenly, a strong glare of light flashed across the scene, the fog rolled upward in thick wreaths, and several cannon belched across the plain, and the roar was thrown heavily back from the bellowing echoes of the mountain.

"'Tis from the fort!" exclaimed Hawk-eye, turning short on his tracks. "And we, like stricken fools, were rushing to the woods, under the very knives of the Maquas."

in the awful tones of parental agony, the sound reaching even to the woods, and rolling back in solemn echo. "'Tis she! God has restored me my children! Throw open the sally port; to the field, 60ths, to the field; pull not a trigger, lest ye kill my lambs! Drive off these dogs of France with your steel."

Duncan heard the grating of the rusty hinges, and darting to the spot, directed by the sound, he met a long line of dark-red warriors, passing swiftly toward the glacis. He knew them for his own battalion of the royal Americans, and flying to their head, soon swept every trace of his pursuers from before the works.

For an instant, Cora and Alice had stood trembling and bewildered by this unexpected desertion; but, before either had leisure for speech, or even thought, an officer of gigantic frame, whose locks were bleached with years and service, but whose air of military grandeur had been rather softened than destroyed by time, rushed out of the body of the mist,

FRENCH MUSKET

"Ami de la France."

"Tu m'as plus l'air d'un *ennemi* de la France; arrête! Ou pardieu je te ferai ami du diable. Non! Feu; camarades; feu!"

The order was instantly obeyed, and the fog was stirred by the explosion of fifty muskets. Happily, the aim was bad, and the bullets cut the air in a direction a little different from that taken by the fugitives; though still so nigh them that to the unpracticed ears of David and the two females, it appeared as if they whistled within a few inches of the organs. The outcry was renewed, and the order, not only to fire again, but to pursue, was too plainly audible. When Heyward briefly explained the meaning of the words they heard, Hawk-eye halted, and spoke with quick decision and great firmness.

"Let us deliver our fire," he said.

The instant their mistake was rectified, the whole party retraced the error with the utmost diligence. Duncan willingly relinquished the support of Cora to the arm of Uncas, and Cora as readily accepted the welcome assistance. Men, hot and angry in pursuit, were evidently on their footsteps, and each instant threatened their capture, if not their destruction.

"Point de quartier aux coquins!" cried an eager pursuer, who seemed to direct the operations of the enemy.

"Stand firm, and be ready, my gallant 60ths!" suddenly exclaimed a voice above them. "Wait to see the enemy; fire low, and sweep the glacis."

"Father! Father!" exclaimed a piercing cry from out the mist. "It is I! Alice! Thy own Elsie! Spare, oh! save your daughters!"

"Hold!" shouted the former speaker,

and folded them to his bosom, while large scalding tears rolled down his pale and wrinkled cheeks, and he exclaimed, in the peculiar accent of Scotland:

"For this I thank thee, Lord! Let danger come as it will, thy servant is now prepared!"

HEYWARD BECOMES AN ENVOY

A few succeeding days were passed amid the privations, the uproar, and the dangers of the siege, which was vigorously pressed by a power against whose approaches Munro possessed no competent means of resistance. It appeared as if Webb, with his army, which lay slumbering on the banks of the Hudson, had utterly forgotten the strait to which his countrymen were reduced. Montcalm had filled the woods of the portage with his savages, every yell and whoop from whom rang through the British encampment, chilling the hearts of men who were already but too much disposed to magnify the danger.

The evils of this state of things pressed heavily on the fortunes of the resolute Scotsman who now defended William Henry. Though his adversary neglected the hills, he had planted his batteries with judgment on the plain, and caused them to be served with vigor and skill. Against this assault, the besieged could only oppose the imperfect and hasty preparations of a fortress in the wilderness.

It was in the afternoon of the fifth day of the siege, and the fourth of his own service in it, that Major Heyward profited by a parley that had just been beaten, by repairing to the ramparts of one of the water bastions, to breathe the cool air from the lake, and to take a survey of the progress of the siege. He was alone, if the solitary sentinel who paced the mound be excepted; for the artillerists had hastened also to profit by the temporary suspension of their arduous duties. The evening was delightfully calm, and the light air from the limpid water fresh and soothing.

Duncan had stood in a musing attitude, contemplating this scene a few minutes, when his eyes were directed to the glacis in front of the sally port already mentioned, by the sounds of approaching footsteps. He walked to an angle of the bastion, and beheld the scout advancing, under the custody of a French officer, to the body of the fort. The countenance of Hawk-eye was haggard and careworn, and his air dejected, as though he felt the deepest degradation at having fallen into the power of his enemies. He was without his favorite weapon, and his arms were even bound behind him with thongs, made of the skin of a deer. Heyward started with surprise and turned to descend from the bastion into the bosom of the work.

Moving rapidly across the parade, he was quickly in the presence of Munro, who was pacing his narrow apartment with a disturbed air and gigantic strides as Duncan entered.

"I am sorry to see, sir, that the messenger I so warmly recommended has returned in custody of the French! I hope there is no reason to distrust his fidelity?"

"The fidelity of 'The Long Rifle' is well known to me," returned Munro, "and is above suspicion; though his usual good fortune seems, at last, to have failed. Montcalm has got him, and with the accursed politeness of his nation, he has sent him in with a doleful tale of 'knowing how I valued the fellow, he could not think of retaining him.' A Jesuitical way, that, Major Duncan Heyward, of telling a man of his misfortunes!"

"But the general and his succor? – "

"Did ye look to the south as ye entered, and could ye not see them?"

said the old soldier, laughing bitterly. "Hoot! Hoot! You're an impatient boy, sir, and cannot give the gentlemen leisure for their march!"

"They are coming then? The scout has said as much?"

"When? And by what path? For the dunce has omitted to tell me this. There is a letter, it would seem, too; and that is the only agreeable part of the matter. For the customary attentions of your Marquis of Montcalm – I warrant me, Duncan, that he of Lothian would buy a dozen such marquisates – but, if the news of the letter were bad, the gentility of this French monsieur would certainly compel him to let us know it."

"He keeps the letter, then, while he releases the messenger?"

"Ay, that does he, and all for the sake of what you call your 'bonhomie.' I would venture, if the truth was known, the fellow's grandfather taught the noble science of dancing."

"But what says the scout? He has eyes and ears, and a tongue: what verbal report does he make?"

"Oh! sir, he is not wanting in natural organs, and he is free to tell all that he has seen and heard. The whole amount is this; there is a fort of his majesty's on the banks of the Hudson, called Edward, in honor of his gracious highness of York, you'll know; and it is well filled with armed men, as such a work should be."

"But was there no movement, no signs of any intention to advance to our relief?"

"There were the morning and evening parades; and when one of the provincial loons – you'll know, Duncan, you're half a Scotsman yourself – when one of them dropped his powder over his porretch, if it touched the coals, it just burnt!" Then suddenly changing his bitter, ironical manner to one more grave and thoughtful, he continued. "And yet there might, and must be, something in that letter which it would be well to know!"

"And can I be of service in the matter?"

"Sir, you can; the Marquis of Montcalm has, in addition to his other civilities, invited me to a personal interview between the works and his own camp; in order, as he says, to impart some additional information. Now, I think it would not be wise to show any undue solicitude to meet him, and I would employ you, an officer of rank, as my substitute; for it would but ill comport with the honor of Scotland to let it be said one of her gentlemen was outdone in civility by a native of any other country on earth."

Without assuming the supererogatory task of entering into a discussion of the comparative merits of national courtesy, Duncan cheerfully assented to supply the place of the veteran in the approaching interview. A long and confidential communication now succeeded, during which the young man received some additional insight into his duty, from the experience and native acuteness of his commander, and then the former took his leave.

As Duncan could only act as the representative of the commandant of the fort, the ceremonies which should have accompanied a meeting between the heads of the adverse forces were of course dispensed with. The truce still existed, and with a roll and beat of the drum, and covered by a little white flag, Duncan left the sally port within ten minutes after his instructions were ended. He was received by the French officer in advance with the usual formalities, and immediately accompanied to a distant marquee of the renowned soldier who led the forces of France.

The general of the enemy received the youthful messenger, surrounded by his principal officers, and by a swarthy band of the native chiefs, who had followed him to the field, with the warriors of their several tribes. Heyward paused short, when, in glancing his eyes rapidly over the dark group of the latter, he beheld the malignant countenance of Magua, regarding him with the calm but sullen attention which marked the expression of that subtle savage. A slight exclamation of surprise even burst from the lips of the young man; but, instantly recollecting his errand, and the presence in which he stood, he suppressed every appearance of emotion, and turned to the hostile leader, who had already advanced a step to receive him.

The Marquis of Montcalm was, at the period of which we write, in the flower of his age, and, it may be added, in the zenith of his fortunes. But, even in that enviable situation, he was affable, and distinguished as much for his attention

to the forms of courtesy as for that chivalrous courage which, only two short years afterward, induced him to throw away his life on the plains of Abraham. Duncan, in turning his eyes from the malign expression of Magua, suffered them to rest with pleasure on the smiling and polished features and the noble military air of the French general.

BRITIƧH MILITARY DRUM ƧHOWING THE ROYAL COAT OF ARMƧ

"Monsieur," said the latter, "j'ai beaucoup de plaisir à – bah! – où est cet interprète?"

"Je crois, monsieur, qu'il ne sera pas nécessaire," Heyward modestly replied. "Je parle un peu français."

Montcalm, after a pause of a moment, as if to collect his thoughts, proceeded:

"Your commandant is a brave man, and well qualified to repel my assault. Mais, monsieur, is it not time to begin to take more counsel of humanity, and

less of your courage? The one as strongly characterizes the hero as the other."

"We consider the qualities as inseparable," returned Duncan, smiling; "but while we find in the vigor of your excellency every motive to stimulate the one, we can as yet see no particular call for the exercise of the other."

Montcalm, in his turn, slightly bowed, but it was with the air of a man too practiced to remember the language of flattery. After musing a moment, he added:

"I trust, monsieur, you come authorized to treat for the surrender of the place?"

"Has your excellency found our defense so feeble as to believe the measure necessary?"

"I should be sorry to have the defense protracted in such a manner as to irritate my red friends there," continued Montcalm, glancing his eyes at the group of grave and attentive Indians, without attending to the other's question. "I find it difficult, even now, to limit them to the usages of war."

Heyward was silent; for a painful recollection of the dangers he had so recently escaped came over his mind, and recalled the images of those defenseless beings who had shared in all his sufferings.

Both mused a little while in silence, when Montcalm renewed the conversation in a way that showed he believed the visit of his guest was solely to propose terms of capitulation. On the other hand, Heyward began to throw sundry inducements in the way of the French general, to betray the discoveries he had made through the intercepted letter. The artifice of neither, however, succeeded; and after a protracted and fruitless interview, Duncan took his leave, favorably impressed with an opinion of the courtesy and talents of the enemy's captain, but as ignorant of what he came to learn as when he arrived. Montcalm followed him as far as the entrance of the marquee, renewing his invitations to the commandant of the fort to give him an immediate meeting in the open ground, between the two armies.

There they separated, and Duncan returned to the advanced post of the French, accompanied as before; whence he instantly proceeded to the fort, and to the quarters of his own commander.

COLONEL MUNRO SURRENDERS

Major Heyward found Munro attended only by his daughters. Alice sate upon his knee, parting the gray hairs on the forehead of the old man with her delicate fingers; and, whenever he affected to frown on her trifling, appeasing his assumed anger by pressing her ruby lips fondly on his wrinkled brow. Cora was seated nigh them, a calm and amused looker-on; regarding the wayward movements of her more youthful sister with that species of maternal fondness which characterized her love for Alice. Of this scene, Duncan, who in his eagerness to report his arrival had entered unannounced, stood many moments an unobserved and a delighted spectator. But the quick and dancing eyes of Alice soon caught a glimpse of his figure reflected from a glass, and she sprang blushing from her father's knee, exclaiming aloud:

"Major Heyward!"

"What of the lad?" demanded her father: "I have sent him to crack a little with the Frenchman. Ha! sir, you are young, and you're nimble! Away with you, ye baggage; as if there were not troubles enough for a soldier, without having his camp filled with such prattling hussies as yourself!"

Alice laughingly followed her sister, who instantly led the way from an apartment where she perceived their presence was no longer desirable. Munro, instead of demanding the result of the young man's mission, paced the room for a few moments, with his hands behind his back and his head inclined toward the floor, like a man lost in thought. At length he raised his eyes, glistening with a father's fondness, and exclaimed:

"They are a pair of excellent girls, Heyward, and such as anyone may boast of."

"You are not now to learn my opinion of your daughters, Colonel Munro."

"True, lad, true," interrupted the impatient old man. "You were about opening your mind more fully on that matter the day you got in; but I did not think it becoming in an old soldier to be talking of nuptial blessings and wedding jokes when the enemies of his king were likely to be unbidden guests at the feast! But I was wrong, Duncan, boy, I was wrong there; and I am now ready to hear what you have to say."

"Notwithstanding the pleasure your assurance gives me, dear sir, I have, just now, a message from Montcalm –"

"Let the Frenchman and all his host go to the devil, sir!" exclaimed the hasty veteran.

Heyward, who perceived that his superior took a malicious pleasure in exhibiting his contempt for the message of the French general, was fain to humor a spleen that he knew would be short-lived; he, therefore, replied with as much indifference as he could assume on such a subject:

"My request, as you know, sir, went so far as to presume to the honor of being your son."

"Aye, boy, you found words to make yourself very plainly comprehended. But, let me ask ye, sir, have you been as intelligible to the girl?"

"On my honor, no," exclaimed Duncan warmly. "There would have been an abuse of a confided trust, had I taken advantage of my situation for such a purpose."

"Your notions are those of a gentleman, Major Heyward, and well enough in their place. But Cora Munro is a maiden too discreet, and of a mind too elevated and improved, to need the guardianship even of a father."

"Cora!"

"Aye – Cora! We are talking of your pretensions to Miss Munro, are we not, sir?"

"I – I – I was not conscious of having mentioned her name," said Duncan, stammering.

"And to marry whom, then, did you wish my consent, Major Heyward?" demanded the old soldier, erecting himself in the dignity of offended feeling.

"You have another, and not less lovely child."

"Alice!" exclaimed the father, in an astonishment equal to that with which Duncan had just repeated the name of his sister.

"Such was the direction of my wishes, sir."

The young man awaited in silence the result of the extraordinary effect produced by a communication which, as it now appeared, was so unexpected. For several minutes Munro paced the chamber with long and rapid strides, his rigid features working convulsively and every faculty seemingly absorbed in the musings of his own mind. At length, he paused directly in front of Heyward, and riveting his eyes upon those of the other, he said, with a lip that quivered violently:

"Duncan Heyward, I have loved you for the sake of him whose blood is in your veins; I have loved you for your own good qualities; and I have loved you, because I thought you would contribute to the happiness of my child. But all this love would turn to hatred were I assured that what I so much apprehend is true."

"God forbid that any act or thought of mine should lead to such a change!" exclaimed the young man.

"You would be my son, Duncan, and you're ignorant of the history of the man you wish to call your father. Sit ye down, young man, and I will open to you the wounds of a seared heart, in as few words as may be suitable."

By this time, the message of Montcalm was as much forgotten by him who bore it as by the man for whose ears it was intended. Each drew a chair, and while the veteran communed a few moments with his own thoughts, apparently in sadness, the youth suppressed his impatience in a look and attitude of respectful attention. At length the former spoke.

"You'll know already, Major Heyward, that my family was both ancient and honorable," commenced the Scotsman; "though it might not altogether be endowed with that amount of wealth that should correspond with its degree. I was, may be, such an one as yourself when I plighted my faith to Alice Graham: the only child of a neighboring laird of some estate. But the connection was disagreeable to her father, on more accounts than my poverty. I did therefore what an honest man should – restored the maiden her troth, and departed the country in the service of my king. I had seen many regions, and had shed much blood in different lands, before duty called me to the islands of the West Indies. There it was my lot to form a connection with one who in time became my wife, and the mother of Cora. She was the daughter of a gentleman of those isles, by a lady whose misfortune it was, if you will," said the old man, proudly, "to be descended, remotely, from that unfortunate class who are so basely enslaved to administer to the wants of a luxurious people. Ha! Major Heyward, you are yourself born at the south, where these unfortunate beings are considered of a race inferior to your own."

"'Tis most unfortunately true, sir," said Duncan, unable any longer to prevent his eyes from sinking to the floor in embarrassment.

"And you cast it on my child as a reproach! You scorn to mingle the blood of the Heywards with one so degraded –

lovely and virtuous though she be?" fiercely demanded the jealous parent.

"Heaven protect me from a prejudice so unworthy of my reason!" returned Duncan. "The sweetness, the beauty, the witchery of your younger daughter, Colonel Munro, might explain my motives, without imputing to me this injustice."

"Ye are right, sir," returned the old man, again changing his tones to those of gentleness, or rather softness. "The girl is the image of what her mother was at her years, and before she had become acquainted with grief. When death deprived me of my wife I returned to Scotland, enriched by the marriage; and would you think it, Duncan! the suffering angel had remained in the heartless state of celibacy twenty long years, and that for the sake of a man who could forget her! She did more, sir; she overlooked my want of faith, and all difficulties being now removed, she took me for her husband."

"And became the mother of Alice?" exclaimed Duncan, with an eagerness that might have proved dangerous at a moment when the thoughts of Munro were less occupied than at present.

"She did, indeed," said the old man, "and dearly did she pay for the blessing she bestowed. I had her but a single year, though; a short term of happiness for one who had seen her youth fade in hopeless pining."

There was something so commanding in the distress of the old man, that Heyward did not dare to venture a syllable of consolation. Munro sat utterly unconscious of the other's presence, his features exposed and working with the anguish of his regrets, while heavy tears fell from his eyes and rolled unheeded from his cheeks to the floor. At length he moved, as if suddenly recovering his recollection; when he arose, and taking a single turn across the room, he approached his companion with an air of military grandeur, and demanded:

"Have you not, Major Heyward, some communication that I should hear from the Marquis de Montcalm?"

Duncan started, in his turn, and immediately commenced, in an embarrassed voice, the half-forgotten message. As Munro listened to the detail of Duncan, the excited feelings of the father gradually gave way before the obligations of his station, and when the other

was done, he saw before him nothing but the veteran, swelling with the wounded feelings of a soldier.

"You have said enough, Major Heyward!" exclaimed the angry old man; "enough to make a volume of commentary on French civility. Here has this gentleman invited me to a conference, and when I send him a capable substitute, for ye're all that, Duncan, though your years are but few, he answers me with a riddle."

"He may have thought less favorably of the substitute, my dear sir; and you will remember that the invitation, which he now repeats, was to the commandant of the works, and not to his second."

"I will meet the Frenchman, and that without fear or delay; promptly, sir, as becomes a servant of my royal master. Go, Major Heyward, and give them a flourish of the music; and send out a messenger to let them know who is coming. We will follow with a small guard, for such respect is due to one who holds the honor of his king in keeping; and hark'ee, Duncan," he added, in a half whisper, though they were alone, "it may be prudent to have some aid at hand, in case there should be treachery at the bottom of it all."

As soon as the usual ceremonials of a military departure were observed, the veteran and his more youthful companion left the fortress, attended by the escort.

They had proceeded only a hundred yards from the works, when the little array which attended the French general to the conference was seen issuing from the hollow way, which formed the bed of a brook that ran between the batteries of the besiegers and the fort. From the moment that Munro left his own works to appear in front of his enemies, his air had been grand, and his step and countenance highly military. The instant he caught a glimpse of the white plume that waved in the hat of Montcalm, his eye lighted, and age no longer appeared to possess any influence over his vast and still muscular person.

"Speak to the boys to be watchful, sir," he said, in an undertone, to Duncan; "and to look well to their flints and steel, for one is never safe with a servant of these Louises; at the same time, we will show them the front of men in deep security. Ye'll understand me, Major Heyward!"

He was interrupted by the clamor of a drum from the approaching Frenchmen, which was immediately answered, when each party pushed an orderly in advance, bearing a white flag, and the wary Scotsman halted, with his guard close at his back. As soon as this slight salutation had passed, Montcalm moved toward them with a quick but graceful step, baring his head to the veteran, and dropping his spotless plume nearly to the earth in courtesy. If the air of Munro was more commanding and manly, it wanted both the ease and insinuating polish of that of the Frenchman. Neither spoke for a few moments, each regarding the other with curious and interested eyes. Then, as became his superior rank and the nature of the interview, Montcalm broke the silence. After uttering the usual words of greeting, he turned to Duncan, and continued, with a smile of recognition, speaking always in French:

"I am rejoiced, monsieur, that you have given us the pleasure of your company on this occasion. There will be no necessity to employ an ordinary interpreter; for, in your hands, I feel the same security as if I spoke your language myself."

Duncan acknowledged the compliment, when Montcalm, turning to his guard, which, in imitation of that of their enemies, pressed close upon him, continued:

"En arrière, mes enfants – il fait chaud; retirez-vous un peu."

Before Major Heyward would imitate this proof of confidence, he glanced his eyes around the plain, and beheld with uneasiness the numerous dusky groups of savages who looked out from the margin of the surrounding woods, curious spectators of the interview.

"Monsieur de Montcalm will readily acknowledge the difference in our situation," he said, with some embarrassment, pointing at the same time toward those dangerous foes who were to be seen in almost every direction. "Were we to dismiss our guard, we should stand here at the mercy of our enemies."

"Monsieur, you have the plighted faith of 'un gentilhomme français' for your safety," returned Montcalm, laying his hand impressively on his heart. "It should suffice."

"It shall. Fall back," Duncan added to the officer who led the escort; "fall back, sir, beyond hearing, and wait for orders."

Montcalm drew nigher, and opened the subject of their conference.

"I have solicited this interview from your superior, monsieur," he said, "because I believe he will allow himself to be persuaded that he has already done everything which is necessary for the honor of his prince, and will now listen to the admonitions of humanity. I will forever bear testimony that his resistance has been gallant, and was continued as long as there was hope."

When this opening was translated to Munro, he answered with dignity, but with sufficient courtesy:

"However I may prize such testimony from Monsieur Montcalm, it will be more valuable when it shall be better merited."

The French general smiled, as Duncan gave him the purport of this reply, and observed:

"What is now so freely accorded to approved courage, may be refused to useless obstinacy. Monsieur would wish to see my camp, and witness for himself our numbers, and the impossibility of his resisting them, with success?"

"Ask the French general if his glasses can reach to the Hudson," said Munro, proudly; "and if he knows when and where to expect the army of Webb."

"Let General Webb be his own interpreter," returned the politic Montcalm, suddenly extending an open letter toward Munro, as he spoke. "You will there learn, monsieur, that his movements are not likely to prove embarrassing to my army."

The veteran seized the offered paper, without waiting for Duncan to translate the speech, and with an eagerness that betrayed how important he deemed its contents. As his eye passed hastily over the words, his countenance changed from its look of military pride to one of deep chagrin: his lip began to quiver; and, suffering the paper to fall from his hand, his head dropped upon his chest like that of a man whose hopes were withered at a single blow. Duncan caught the letter from the ground, and without apology for the liberty he took, he read at a glance its cruel purport. Their common superior, so far from encouraging them to resist, advised a speedy surrender, urging in the plainest language as a reason, the utter impos-

RED

BLUE

UNION JACK 1756

sibility of his sending a single man to their rescue.

"Here is no deception!" exclaimed Duncan, examining the billet both inside and out. "This is the signature of Webb, and must be the captured letter."

"The man has betrayed me!" Munro at length bitterly exclaimed. "He has brought dishonor to the door of one where disgrace was never before known to dwell, and shame has he heaped heavily on my gray hairs."

"Say not so," cried Duncan. "We are yet masters of the fort, and of our honor. Let us then sell our lives at such a rate as shall make our enemies believe the purchase too dear."

"Boy, I thank thee," exclaimed the old man, rousing himself from his stupor. "You have, for once, reminded Munro of his duty. We will go back, and dig our graves behind those ramparts."

"Messieurs," said Montcalm, advancing toward them a step, in generous interest, "you little know Louis de St. Véran, if you believe him capable of profiting by this letter to humble brave men, or to build up a dishonest reputation for himself. Listen to my terms before you leave me."

"What says the Frenchman?" demanded the veteran, sternly. "Does he make a merit of having captured a scout, with a note from headquarters? Sir, he had better raise this siege, to go and sit down before Edward if he wishes to frighten his enemy with words."

BRITISH & FRENCH UNIFORMS MID C18TH

YELLOW

MITRE CAP

WIG

OFFICER'S TRICORN HAT

WIG

BLANKET

BLUE

YELLOW

YELLOW FACINGS

SPATTERDASHES

GREY

BRITISH GRENADIER
20TH REGIMENT OF FOOT

FRENCH GRENADIER
ROYAL LORRAINE INFANTRY REGIMENT

BRITISH LIGHT INFANTRYMAN
NOTE THE AXE BENEATH THE CARTRIDGE BOX

HOW TO LOAD AND FIRE A FLINTLOCK

POUR CORRECT
MEASURE OF COARSE
GRAINED-POWDER
FROM FLASK INTO
MUZZLE OF GUN

PATCH – TO ENSURE
SNUG FIT
BETWEEN
BARREL & BALL

BALL

PATCH AND BALL

PUSH PATCHED BALL
INTO MUZZLE WITH
RAMROD

RAM BALL DOWN THE
BARREL UNTIL IT
REACHES BUT DOES NOT
CRUSH THE POWDER

CHARGE LOADED, THE RAM
HALF COCKED AND THE
THE PRINCIPLE OF THE
STRUCK METAL (FLINT IN
THE TRIGGER WAS RELEA
FRIZZEN CREATING SPA
TO SNAP BACK EXPOSIN
PRIMING POWDER WH
TOUCH HOLE) CHARGE

BUTT

LEATHER SHOT POUCH
SPOUT FILLS WHEN FLASK IS TIPPED UPSIDE DOWN
END INSERTED INTO MUZZLE AND VALVE LEVER
PRESSED, AUTOMATICALLY CLOSING FLASK AND
RELEASING MEASURE OF SHOT INTO BARREL

KNUCKLE BOW

SWORD KNOT

CHASE

REINFORCE

BREECH

BLAD

WEDGE
FOR ALTERING
ELEVATION

OFF
WIT

TRUNNION

COPPER POWDER FLASK
SPOUT CAN BE ADJUSTED FOR
DESIRED AMOUNT OF POWDER

MORTAR • A WEAPON FOR THROWING A BALL OR
GRENADE (ABOUT 12 INCHES DIAMETER) AT HIGH ANGL

...URNED, THE HAMMER
('LASH PAN) OPENED.
WAS THAT FLINT
TTING FRIZZEN) WHEN
R FELL STRIKING
SING THE FRIZZEN
HOLE AND IGNITING
N IGNITED (THROUGH
HUS PROPELLING BALL.

PRIMING WITH FINE GRAINED POWDER FROM SMALL
FLASK. THE CORRECT AMOUNT WAS IMPORTANT

FRIZZEN CLOSED, HAMMER FULLY COCKED AND GUN
TILTED TO THE LEFT TO ENSURE A FEW GRAINS OF
POWDER ENTER THE TOUCHHOLE.

WHEN THE TRIGGER WAS RELEASED. HAMMER
STRUCK FRIZZEN IGNITING POWDER AND FIRING
CHARGE IN BARREL.

POMMEL

GRIP

PAS D'ANE

QUILLON

RICASSO

WORD
RD KNOT

CAVALRY BACKSWORD
(I.E. SINGLE EDGED)

CASCABEL

BUTTON

FOR ATTACHING A
ROPE WHEN LIFTING

TRUNNION

CHASE

MUZZLE

AERIAL VIEW OF BARREL

FIELD GUN (18TH.
THE BARREL IS RAISED SLIGHTLY
TO SHOW PROFILE OF BARREL

UNIFORMS CONTINUED :-

CARTRIDGE BOX
SHOWING PAPER
CARTRIDGES

BELT FOR SWORD
AND BAYONET

SCOTS
BONN

MUSKET
BALL

PAPER CARTRIDGES

TOUCH-
HOLE
PRICKER

PRIMING
FLASK

AXE INSTEAD
OF BAYONET

POWDER
FLASK

FLAPS
COVER
TELESCOPE

BRITISH PATTERN
CARTRIDGE BOX

FRENCH INFANTRY SOLDIER'S
CARTOUCHIÈRE (CARTRIDGE POUCH)

THE GREEN TUNIC
OF THE RANGERS
WAS FIRST ISSUED
IN 1758

ROGERS RANGER
GREEN TUNIC LEATHER LEGGINGS

Duncan explained the other's meaning.

"Monsieur de Montcalm, we will hear you," the veteran added, more calmly, as Duncan ended.

"To retain the fort is now impossible," said his liberal enemy. "It is necessary to the interests of my master that it should be destroyed; but, as for yourselves, and your brave comrades, there is no privilege dear to a soldier that shall be denied."

"Our colors?" demanded Heyward.

"Carry them to England, and show them to your king."

"Our arms?"

"Keep them; none can use them better."

"Our march; the surrender of the place?"

"Shall all be done in a way most honorable to yourselves."

Duncan now turned to explain these proposals to his commander, who heard him with amazement and a sensibility that was deeply touched by so unusual and unexpected generosity.

"Go you, Duncan," he said; "go with this marquess, as indeed marquess he should be; go to his marquee, and arrange it all. I have lived to see two things in my old age, that never did I expect to behold. An Englishman afraid to support a friend, and a Frenchman too honest to profit by his advantage."

So saying, the veteran again dropped his head to his chest, and returned slowly toward the fort, exhibiting by the dejection of his air, to the anxious garrison, a harbinger of evil tidings.

From the shock of this unexpected blow the haughty feelings of Munro never recovered; but from that moment there commenced a change in his determined character, which accompanied him to a speedy grave. Duncan remained to settle the terms of the capitulation. He was seen to reenter the works during the first watches of the night, and immediately after a private conference with the commandant, to leave them again. It was then openly announced that hostilities must cease — Munro having signed a treaty, by which the place was to be yielded to the enemy, with the morning; the garrison to retain their arms, their colors, and their baggage, and consequently, according to military opinion, their honor.

MASSACRE

CROSS OF THE ORDER
ST. LOUIS

The hostile armies, which lay in the wilds of the Horican, passed the night of the ninth of August, 1757, much in the manner they would had they encountered on the fairest field of Europe. While the conquered were still, sullen, and dejected, the victors triumphed. But there are limits, alike, to grief and joy; and long before the watches of the morning came, the stillness of those boundless woods was only broken by a gay call from some exulting young Frenchman of the advanced pickets, or a menacing challenge from the fort, which sternly forbade the approach of any hostile footsteps before the stipulated moment. Even these occasional threatening sounds ceased to be heard in that dull hour which precedes the day, at which period a listener might have sought in vain any evidence of the presence of those armed powers that then slumbered on the shores of the "holy lake."

It was during these moments of deep silence that the canvas which concealed the entrance to a spacious marquee in the French encampment was shoved aside, and a man issued from beneath the drapery into the open air. He was enveloped in a cloak that might have been intended as a protection from the chilling damps of the woods, but which served equally well as a mantle, to conceal his person. He was permitted to pass the grenadier, who watched over the slumbers of the French commander, without interruption, the man making the usual salute which betokens military deference, as the other passed swiftly through the little city of tents, in the direction of William Henry. Whenever this unknown individual encountered one of the numberless sentinels who crossed his path, his answer was prompt, and as it appeared satisfactory; for he was uniformly allowed to proceed, without further interrogation.

The officer proceeded until he had reached the low strand, and in a somewhat dangerous vicinity to the western water bastion of the fort. His gaze at the ramparts was not that of a curious or idle spectator; but his looks wandered from point to point, denoting his knowledge of military usages, and betraying that his search was not unaccompanied by distrust. At length he appeared satisfied; and having cast his eyes impatiently upward toward the summit of the eastern mountain, as if anticipating the approach of the morning, he was in the act of turning on his footsteps, when a light sound on the nearest angle of the bastion caught his ear, and induced him to remain.

Just then a figure was seen to approach the edge of the rampart, where it stood, apparently contemplating in its turn the distant tents of the French encampment. The melancholy air, the hour, together with the vast frame of the man who thus leaned, in musing, against the English ramparts, left no doubt as to his person in the mind of the observant spectator. Delicacy, no less than prudence, now urged him to retire; and he had moved cautiously round the body of the tree for that purpose, when another sound drew his attention, and once more arrested his footsteps. In a moment he saw a dark form rise, as it were out of the lake, and steal without further noise to the land, within a few feet of the place where he himself stood. A rifle next slowly rose between his eyes and the watery mirror; but before it could be discharged his own hand was on the lock.

"Hugh!" exclaimed the savage, whose treacherous aim was so singularly and so unexpectedly interrupted.

Without making any reply, the French officer laid his hand on the shoulder of the Indian, and led him in profound silence to a distance from the spot, where their subsequent dialogue might have proved dangerous, and where it seemed that one of them, at least, sought a victim. Then, throwing open his cloak, so as to expose his uniform and the cross of St. Louis which was suspended at his breast, Montcalm sternly demanded:

"What means this! Does not my son know that the hatchet is buried between the English and his Canadian Father?"

"What can the Hurons do?" returned the savage, speaking also, though imperfectly, in the French language. "Not a warrior has a scalp, and the palefaces make friends!"

"But Magua is pledged not to sully the lilies of France. The enemies of the great king across the salt lake are his enemies; his friends, the friends of the Hurons."

"Friends!" repeated the Indian, in scorn. Then recollecting himself, with sudden and native dignity, he added,

THE FRENCH ROYAL FLAG

"Go; teach your young men it is peace. Le Renard Subtil knows how to speak to a Huron warrior."

Without deigning to bestow further words, or to wait for any answer, the savage cast his rifle into the hollow of his arm, and moved silently through the encampment toward the woods where his own tribe was known to lie. Every few yards as he proceeded he was challenged by the sentinels; but he stalked sullenly onward, utterly disregarding the summons of the soldiers, who only spared his life because they knew the air and tread no less than the obstinate daring of an Indian.

Montcalm lingered long and melancholy on the strand, where he had been left by his companion, brooding deeply on the temper which his ungovernable ally had just discovered. Already had his fair fame been tarnished by one horrid scene, and in circumstances fearfully resembling those under which he now found himself. In the meantime the day had dawned, and when the line of the French army was ready to receive its general the rays of a brilliant sun were glancing along the glittering array.

A very different scene presented itself within the lines of the Anglo-American army. As soon as the warning signal was given, it exhibited all the signs of a hurried and forced departure. The sullen soldiers shouldered their empty tubes and fell into their places, like men whose blood had been heated by the past contest, and who only desired the opportunity to revenge an indignity which was still wounding to their pride, concealed as it was under all the observances of military etiquette. Women and children ran from place to place, some bearing the scanty remnants of their baggage, and others searching in the ranks for those countenances they looked up to for protection.

Munro appeared among his silent troops firm but dejected. It was evident that the unexpected blow had struck deep into his heart, though he struggled to sustain his misfortune with the port of a man.

Duncan was touched at the quiet and impressive exhibition of his grief. He had discharged his own duty, and he now pressed to the side of the old man, to know in what particular he might serve him.

"My daughters," was the brief but expressive reply.

"Good heavens! Are not arrangements already made for their convenience?"

"Today I am only a soldier, Major Heyward," said the veteran. "All that you see here claim alike to be my children."

Duncan had heard enough. Without losing one of those moments which had now become so precious, he flew toward the quarters of Munro, in quest of the sisters. He found them on the threshold of the low edifice. Though the cheeks of Cora were pale, and her countenance anxious, she had lost none of her firmness; but the eyes of Alice were inflamed, and betrayed how long and bitterly she had wept. They both, however, received the young man with undisguised pleasure; the former, for a novelty, being the first to speak.

"The fort is lost," she said, with a melancholy smile; "though our good name, I trust, remains."

"Dearest Miss Munro, it is time to make some provision for yourself. Military usage – pride – that pride on which you so much value yourself, demands that your father and I should for a little while continue with the troops. Then where to seek a proper protector for you against the confusion and chances of such a scene?"

"You may be right," Cora replied, smiling again, but far more sadly than before. "Listen; chance has already sent us a friend when he is most needed."

Duncan did listen, and on the instant comprehended her meaning. The low and serious sounds of the sacred music, so well known to the eastern provinces, caught his ear, and instantly drew him to an apartment in an adjacent building, which had already been deserted by its customary tenants. There he found David, pouring out his pious feelings through the only medium in which he ever indulged. Duncan waited, until, by the cessation of the movement of the hand, he believed the strain was ended, when, by touching his shoulder, he drew the attention of the other to himself, and in a few words explained his wishes.

"It will be your duty to see that none

dare to approach the ladies with any rude intention, or to offer insult or taunt at the misfortune of their brave father. In this task you will be seconded by the domestics of their household."

"Even so."

"It is possible that the Indians and stragglers of the enemy may intrude, in which case you will remind them of the terms of the capitulation, and threaten to report their conduct to Montcalm. A word will suffice."

"If not, I have that here which shall," returned David, exhibiting his book, with an air in which meekness and confidence were singularly blended. "Here are words which, uttered, or rather thundered, with proper emphasis, and in measured time, shall quiet the most unruly temper:

AMERICAN COVERED WAGON

"Why rage the heathen furiously !"

"Enough," said Heyward, interrupting the burst of his musical invocation. "We understand each other; it is time that we should now assume our respective duties."

By this time the signal of departure had been given, and the head of the English column was in motion. The sisters started at the sound, and glancing their eyes around, they saw the white uniforms of the French grenadiers, who

had already taken possession of the gates of the fort. At that moment, an enormous cloud seemed to pass suddenly above their heads, and looking upward, they discovered that they stood beneath the wide folds of the standard of France.

"Let us go," said Cora. "This is no longer a fit place for the children of an English officer."

Alice clung to the arm of her sister, and together they left the parade, accompanied by the moving throng that surrounded them.

As they passed the gates, the French officers, who had learned their rank, bowed often and low, forbearing, however, to intrude those attentions which they saw, with peculiar tact, might not be agreeable. As every vehicle and each

beast·of burden was occupied by the sick and wounded, Cora had decided to endure the fatigues of a foot march, rather than interfere with their comforts. Indeed, many a maimed and feeble soldier was compelled to drag his exhausted limbs in the rear of the columns, for the want of the necessary means of conveyance, in that wilderness. The whole, however, was in motion; the weak and wounded, groaning, and in suffering; their comrades, silent and sullen; and the women and children in terror, they knew not of what.

Living masses of the English, to the amount in the whole of near three thousand, were moving slowly across the plain, toward the common center, and gradually approached each other, as they converged to the point of their march, a vista cut through the lofty trees, where the road to the Hudson entered the forest. Along the sweeping borders of the woods hung a dark cloud of savages, eyeing the passage of their enemies, and hovering at a distance like vultures, who were only kept from stooping on their prey by the presence and restraint of a superior army. A few had straggled among the conquered columns, where they stalked in sullen discontent; attentive, though, as yet, passive observers of the moving multitude.

The advance, with Heyward at its head, had already reached the defile and was slowly disappearing, when the attention of Cora was drawn to a collection of stragglers, by the sounds of contention. A truant provincial was paying the forfeit of his disobedience, by being plundered of those very effects which had caused him to desert his place in the ranks. The man was of powerful frame, and too avaricious to part with his goods without a struggle. Individuals from either party interfered; the one side to prevent, and the other to aid in the robbery. Voices grew loud and angry, and a hundred savages appeared, as it were by magic, where a dozen only had been seen a minute before. It was than that Cora saw the form of Magua gliding among his countrymen, and speaking with his fatal and artful eloquence. The mass of women and children stopped, and hovered together like alarmed and fluttering birds. But the cupidity of the Indian was soon gratified, and the different bodies again moved slowly onward.

The savages now fell back, and seemed content to let their enemies advance without further molestation. But as the female crowd approached them, the gaudy colors of a shawl attracted the eyes of a wild and untutored Huron. He advanced to seize it, without the least hesitation. The woman, more in terror than through love of the ornament, wrapped her child in the coveted article, and folded both more closely to her bosom. Cora was in the act of speaking, with an intent to advise the woman to abandon the trifle, when the savage

EARLY AMERICAN FEMALE DRESS MID C18TH

relinquished his hold of the shawl, and tore the screaming infant from her arms. Abandoning everything to the greedy grasp of those around her, the mother darted, with distraction in her mien, to reclaim her child. The Indian smiled grimly, and extended one hand in sign of a willingness to exchange, while, with the other, he flourished the babe over

his head, holding it by the feet as if to enhance the value of the ransom.

"Here – here – there – all – any – everything" exclaimed the breathless woman; tearing the lighter articles of dress from her person, with ill-directed and trembling fingers: "Take all, but give me my babe!"

The savage spurned the worthless rags, and perceiving that the shawl had already become a prize to another, his bantering but sullen smile changing to a gleam of ferocity, he dashed the head of the infant against a rock, and cast its quivering remains to her very feet. For an instant, the mother stood like a statue of despair, looking wildly down at the unseemly object, which had so lately nestled in her bosom and smiled in her face; and then she raised her eyes and countenance toward heaven, as if calling on God to curse the perpetrator of the foul deed. She was spared the sin of such a prayer; for, maddened at his disappointment, and excited at the sight of blood, the Huron mercifully drove his tomahawk into her own brain. The mother sank under the blow, and fell, grasping at her child, in death, with the same engrossing love that had caused her to cherish it when living.

At that dangerous moment Magua placed his hands to his mouth, and raised the fatal and appalling whoop. The scattered Indians started at the well-known cry, as coursers bound at the signal to quit the goal; and, directly, there arose such a yell along the plain, and through the arches of the wood, as seldom burst from human lips before. They who heard it listened with a curdling horror at the heart, little inferior to that dread which may be expected to attend the blasts of the final summons.

More than two thousand raving savages broke from the forest at the signal, and threw themselves across the fatal plain with instinctive alacrity. We shall not dwell on the revolting horrors that succeeded. Death was everywhere, and in his most terrific and disgusting aspects. Resistance only served to inflame the murderers, who inflicted their furious blows long after their victims were beyond the power of their resentment. The flow of blood might be likened to the outbreaking of a torrent; and as the natives became heated and maddened by the sight, many among them even kneeled to the earth, and drank freely, exultingly, hellishly, of the crimson tide.

The trained bodies of the troops threw themselves quickly into solid masses, endeavoring to awe their assailants by the imposing appearance of a military front. The experiment in some measure succeeded, though far too many suffered their unloaded muskets to be torn from their hands, in the vain hope of appeasing the savages.

In such a scene none had leisure to note the fleeting moments. It might have been ten minutes [it seemed an age], that the sisters had stood riveted to one spot, horror-stricken and nearly helpless. At this moment, Alice caught a glimpse of the vast form of her father, moving rapidly across the plain, in the direction of the French army. He was, in truth, proceeding to Montcalm, fearless of every danger, to claim the tardy escort for which he had before conditioned. Fifty glittering axes and barbed spears were offered unheeded at his life, but the savages respected his rank and calmness, even in their fury. The dangerous weapons were brushed aside by the still nervous arm of the veteran, or fell of themselves, after menacing an act that it would seem no one had courage to perform. Fortunately, the vindictive Magua was searching for his victim in the very band the veteran had just quitted.

"Father – Father – we are here!" shrieked Alice, as he passed, at no great distance, without appearing to heed them. "Come to us, Father, or we die!"

The cry was repeated, and in terms and tones that might have melted a heart of stone, but it was unanswered. Once, indeed, the old man appeared to catch the sounds, for he paused and listened; but Alice had dropped senseless on the earth, and Cora had sunk at her side, hovering in untiring tenderness over her lifeless form. Munro shook his head in disappointment, and proceeded, bent on the high duty of his station.

"Lady," said Gamut, who, helpless and useless as he was, had not yet dreamed of deserting his trust, "it is the jubilee of the devils, and this is not a meet place for Christians to tarry in. Let us up and fly."

"Go," said Cora, still gazing at her unconscious sister; "save thyself. To me thou canst not be of further use."

David comprehended the unyielding character of her resolution by the simple but expressive gesture that accompanied her words.

Then raising his voice to its highest tones, he poured out a strain so powerful as to be heard even amid the din of that bloody field. More than one savage rushed toward them, thinking to rifle the unprotected sisters of their attire, and bear away their scalps; but when they found this strange and unmoved figure riveted to his post, they paused to listen. The unwonted sounds caught the ears of a distant savage, who flew raging from group to group, like one who, scorning to touch the vulgar herd, hunted for some victim more worthy of his renown. It was Magua, who uttered a yell of pleasure when he beheld his ancient prisoners again at his mercy.

"Come," he said, laying his soiled hands on the dress of Cora, "the wigwam of the Huron is still open. Is it not better than this place?"

"Away!" cried Cora, veiling her eyes from his revolting aspect.

The Indian laughed tauntingly, as he held up his reeking hand, and answered, "It is red, but it comes from white veins!"

"Monster! There is blood, oceans of blood, upon thy soul: thy spirit has moved this scene."

"Magua is a great chief!" returned the exulting savage. "Will the dark-hair go to his tribe?"

"Never! Strike, if thou wilt, and complete thy revenge."

He hesitated a moment; and then catching the light and senseless form of Alice in his arms, the subtle Indian moved swiftly across the plain toward the woods.

"Hold!" shrieked Cora, following wildly on his footsteps. "Release the child! Wretch! What is't you do?"

But Magua was deaf to her voice; or rather he knew his power, and was determined to maintain it.

"Stay – lady – stay," called Gamut, after the unconscious Cora. "The holy charm is beginning to be felt, and soon shalt thou see this horrid tumult stilled."

Perceiving that, in his turn, he was unheeded, the faithful David followed the distracted sister, raising his voice again in sacred song, and sweeping the air to the measure with his long arm in

diligent accompaniment. In this manner they traversed the plain, through the flying, the wounded, and the dead. The fierce Huron was, at any time, sufficient for himself and the victim that he bore; though Cora would have fallen, more than once, under the blows of her savage enemies, but for the extraordinary being who stalked in her rear, and who now appeared to the astonished natives gifted with the protecting spirit of madness.

Magua, who knew how to avoid the more pressing dangers, and also to elude pursuit, entered the woods through a low ravine, where he quickly found the Narragansets, which the travelers had abandoned so shortly before, awaiting his appearance, in custody of a savage as fierce and as malign in his expression as himself. Laying Alice on one of the horses, he made a sign to Cora to mount the other.

David, perceiving that he was left alone, utterly disregarded as a subject too worthless even to destroy, threw his long limb across the saddle of the beast they had deserted, and made such progress in the pursuit as the difficulties of the path permitted.

THE PURSUIT BEGINS . . .

The third day from the capture of the fort was drawing to a close, but the business of the narrative must still detain the reader on the shores of the "holy lake." When last seen, the environs of the works were filled with violence and uproar. They were now possessed by stillness and death. The bloodstained conquerors had departed; and their camp, which had so lately run with the merry rejoicings of a victorious army, lay a silent and deserted city of huts. The fortress was a smoldering ruin; charred rafters, fragments of exploded artillery, and rent masonwork covering its earthen mounds in confused disorder.

A frightful change had also occurred in the season. The sun had hid its warmth behind an impenetrable mass of vapor, and hundreds of human forms, which had blackened beneath the fierce heats of August, were stiffening in their deformity before the blasts of a premature November. The curling and spotless mists, which had been seen sailing above the hills toward the north, were now returning in an interminable dusky sheet that was urged along by the fury of a tempest. The crowded mirror of the Horican was gone; and, in its place, the green and angry waters lashed the shores, as if indignantly casting back its impurities to the polluted strand.

The fiercer element had cropped the verdure of the plain, which looked as though it were scathed by the consuming lightning. But, here and there, a dark green tuft rose in the midst of the desolation; the earliest fruits of a soil that had been fattened with human blood.

The wind blew unequally; sometimes sweeping heavily along the ground, seeming to whisper its moanings in the cold ears of the dead, then rising in a shrill and mournful whistling, it entered the forest with a rush that filled the air with the leaves and branches it scattered in its path. Amid the unnatural shower, a few hungry ravens struggled with the gale; but no sooner was the green ocean of woods which stretched beneath them passed, than they gladly stopped, at random, to their hideous banquet.

In short, it was a scene of wildness and desolation; and it appeared as if all who had profanely entered it had been stricken, at a blow, by the relentless arm of death.

About an hour before the setting of the sun, on the day already mentioned, the forms of five men might have been seen issuing from the narrow vista of trees, where the path to the Hudson entered the forest, and advancing in the direction of the ruined works. At first their progress was slow and guarded, as though they entered with reluctance amid the horrors of the spot, or dreaded the renewal of its frightful incidents. A light figure preceded the rest of the party, with the caution and activity of a native; ascending every hillock to reconnoiter, and indicating, by gestures to his companions, the route he deemed it most prudent to pursue. Nor were those in the rear wanting in every caution and foresight known to forest warfare. One among them, he also was an Indian, moved a little on one flank, and watched the margin of the woods with eyes long accustomed to read the smallest sign of danger. The remaining three were white, though clad in vestments adapted, both in quality and color, to their present hazardous pursuit – that of hanging on the skirts of a retiring army in the wilderness.

The reader will perceive at once, in these respective characters, the Mohicans and their white friend, the scout; together with Munro and Heyward. It was, in truth, the father in quest of his children, attended by the youth who felt so deep a stake in their happiness, and those brave and trusty foresters, who had already proved their skill and fidelity through the trying scenes related.

When Uncas, who moved in front, had reached the center of the plain, he raised a cry that drew his companions in a body to the spot. The young warrior had halted over a group of females who lay in a cluster, a confused mass of dead. Notwithstanding the revolting horror of the exhibition, Munro and Heyward flew toward the festering heap, endeavoring, with a love that no unseemliness could extinguish, to discover whether any vestiges of those they sought were to be seen among the tattered and many-colored garments. The father and the lover found instant relief in the search; though each was condemned again to experience the misery of an uncertainty that was hardly less insupportable than the most revolting truth.

"Hugh!" exclaimed the young Mohican, rising on the extremities of his feet, and gazing intently in his front, frightening the raven to some other prey by the sound and the action.

"What is it, boy?" whispered the scout, lowering his tall form into a crouching attitude, like a panther about to take his leap. "God send it be a tardy Frencher, skulking for plunder. I do believe 'Kill-deer' would take an oncommon range today!"

Uncas, without making any reply, bounded away from the spot, and in the next instant he was seen tearing from a bush, and waving in triumph, a fragment of the green riding veil of Cora. The movement, the exhibition, and the cry, which again burst from the lips of the young Mohican, instantly drew the whole party about him.

"My child!" said Munro, speaking quick and wildly. "Give me my child!"

"Uncas will try," was the short and touching answer.

The simple but meaning assurance was lost on the father who seized the piece of gauze and crushed it in his hand, while his eyes roamed fearfully among the bushes, as if he equally dreaded and hoped for the secrets they might reveal.

"Here are no dead," said Heyward; "the storm seems not to have passed this way."

"That's manifest; and clearer than the heavens above our heads," returned the undisturbed scout; "but either she, or they that have robbed her, have passed the bush; for I remember the rag she wore to hide a face that all did love to look upon. Uncas, you are right; the dark-hair has been here, and she has fled, like a frightened fawn, to the wood; none who could fly would remain to be murdered. Let us search for the marks she left; for to Indian eyes, I sometimes think even a hummingbird leaves his trail in the air."

The young Mohican darted away at the suggestion, and the scout had hardly done speaking before the former raised a cry of success from the margin of the forest. On reaching the spot, the anxious party perceived another portion of the veil fluttering on the lower branch of a beech.

"Softly, softly," said the scout, extending his long rifle in front of the eager Heyward. "We now know our

CALLIOPE HUMMING-BIRD

work, but the beauty of the trail must not be deformed. A step too soon may give us hours of trouble. We have them though; that much is beyond denial."

"Bless ye, bless ye, worthy man!" exclaimed Munro. "Whither, then, have they fled, and where are my babes?"

"The path they have taken depends on many chances. If they have gone alone, they are quite as likely to move in a circle as straight, and they may be within a dozen miles of us; but if the Hurons, or any of the French Indians, have laid hands on them, 'tis probable they are now near the borders of the Canadas. But what matters that?"

"Hugh!" exclaimed Chingachgook, who had been occupied in examining an opening that had been evidently made through the low underbrush which skirted the forest; and who now stood erect as he pointed downward, in the attitude and with the air of a man who beheld a disgusting serpent.

"Here is the palpable impression of the footstep of a man," cried Heyward, bending over the indicated spot. "He has trod in the margin of this pool, and the mark cannot be mistaken. They are captives."

"Better so than left to starve in the wilderness," returned the scout; "and they will leave a wider trail. I would wager fifty beaver skins against as many flints, that the Mohicans and I enter

their wigwams within the month! Stoop to it, Uncas, and try what you can make of the moccasin; for moccasin it plainly is, and no shoe."

The young Mohican bent over the track, and removing the scattered leaves from around the place, he examined it with much of that sort of scrutiny that a money dealer, in these days of pecuniary doubts, would bestow on a suspected due bill. At length, he arose from his knees, satisfied with the result of the examination.

"Well, boy," demanded the attentive scout, "what does it say? Can you make anything of the telltale?"

"Le Renard Subtil!"

"Ha! That rampaging devil again! There never will be an end of his loping till "Kill-deer" has said a friendly word to him. Aye, 'tis a settled thing; here then have passed the dark-hair and Magua."

"And not Alice?" demanded Heyward.

"Of her we have not yet seen the signs," returned the scout, looking closely around at the trees, the bushes, and the ground. "What have we there! Uncas, bring hither the thing you see dangling from yonder thornbush."

When the Indian had complied, the scout received the prize, and holding it on high, he laughed in his silent but heartfelt manner.

"'Tis the tooting we'pon of the singer! Now we shall have a trail a priest might travel," he said. "Uncas, look for the marks of a shoe that is long enough to uphold six feet two of tottering human flesh. I begin to have some hopes of the fellow, since he has given up squalling to follow some better trade."

"At least, he has been faithful to his trust," said Heyward; "and Cora and Alice are not without a friend. As we now possess these infallible signs, let us commence our march. A moment, at such a time, will appear an age to the captives."

"It is not the swiftest leaping deer that gives the longest chase," returned Hawk-eye, without moving his eyes from the different marks that had come under his view. "We know that the rampaging Huron has passed – and the dark-hair – and the singer – but where is she of the yellow locks and blue eyes? Though little, and far from being as bold

DEER

broad St. Lawrence, or, perhaps, the Great Lakes themselves, are atwixt us."

"So much the more reason why we should not delay our march," returned Heyward. "Let us proceed."

"Young blood and hot blood, they say, are much the same thing. We are not about to start on a squirrel hunt, or to drive a deer into the Horican, but to outlie for days and nights, and to stretch across a wilderness where the feet of men seldom go, and where no bookish knowledge would carry you through harmless. An Indian never starts on such an expedition without smoking over his council fire; and though a man of white blood, I honor their customs in this particular, seeing that they are deliberate and wise. We will, therefore, go back, and light our fire tonight in the ruins of the old fort, and in the morning we shall be fresh, and ready to undertake our work like men, and not like babbling women or eager boys."

Heyward saw by the manner of the scout that altercation would be useless. Munro had again sunk into that sort of apathy which had beset him since his late overwhelming misfortunes, and from which he was apparently to be roused only by some new and powerful excitement. Making a merit of necessity, the young man took the veteran by the arm, and followed in the footsteps of the Indians and the scout, who had already begun to retrace the path which conducted them to the plain.

as her sister, she is fair to the view, and pleasant in discourse. Has she no friend, that none care for her?"

"God forbid she should ever want hundreds! Are we not now in her pursuit? For one, I will never cease the search till she be found."

"In that case we may have to journey by different paths; for here she has not passed, light and little as her footstep would be."

Heyward drew back, all his ardor to proceed seeming to vanish on the instant. Without attending to this sudden change in the other's humor, the scout, after musing a moment, continued:

"There is no woman in this wilderness could leave such a print as that, but the dark-hair or her sister. We know that the first has been here, but where are the signs of the other?"

"Unless the shining bauble Uncas has just lifted from the ground should prove one. Pass it this way, lad, that we may look at it."

Heyward instantly knew it for a trinket that Alice was fond of wearing, and which he recollected, with the tenacious memory of a lover, to have seen, on the fatal morning of the massacre, dangling from the fair neck of his mistress. He seized the highly prized jewel; and as he proclaimed the fact, it vanished from the eyes of the wondering scout, who in vain looked for it on the ground long after it was warmly pressed against the beating heart of Duncan.

"Pshaw!" said the disappointed Hawk-eye, ceasing to rake the leaves with the breech of his rifle. "'Tis a certain sign of age when the sight begins to weaken. Such a glittering gewgaw, and not to be seen! Well, well, I can squint along a clouded barrel yet, and that is enough to settle all disputes between me and the Mingoes. I should like to find the thing too, if it were only to carry it to the right owner, and that would be bringing the two ends of what I call a long trail together – for by this time the

... AND
CONTINUES

urged Munro to enter. Leaving the bereaved old man alone with his sorrows, Duncan immediately returned into the open air, too much excited himself to seek the repose he had recommended to his veteran friend.

While Hawk-eye and the Indians lighted their fire, and took their evening's repast, a frugal meal of dried bear's meat, the young man paid a visit to that curtain of the dilapidated fort which looked out on the sheet of the Horican. The wind had fallen, and the waves were already rolling on the sandy beach beneath him in a more regular and tempered succession.

Of this scene, so chillingly in accordance with the past, Duncan stood for many minutes a rapt observer. His eyes wandered from the bosom of the mound, where the foresters were seated around their glimmering fire, to the fainter light which still lingered in the skies, and then rested long and anxiously on the embodied gloom which lay like a dreary void on that side of him where the dead reposed. He soon fancied that inexplicable sounds arose from the place, though so indistinct and stolen as

to render not only their nature but even their existence uncertain. Ashamed of his apprehension the young man turned toward the water, and strove to divert his attention to the mimic stars that dimly glimmered on its moving surface. Still, his too conscious ears performed their ungrateful duty, as if to warn him of some lurking danger. At length a swift trampling seemed, quite audibly, to rush athwart the darkness. Unable any longer to quiet his uneasiness, Duncan spoke in a low voice to the scout, requesting him to ascend the mound to that place where he stood. Hawk-eye threw his rifle across an arm, and complied, but with an air so unmoved and calm as to prove how much he counted on the security of their position.

"Listen," said Duncan, when the other placed himself deliberately at his elbow. "There are suppressed noises on the plain which may show that Montcalm has not yet entirely deserted his conquest. Listen! You hear the noise I mean!"

"Aye, aye; when food is scarce, and when food is plenty, a wolf grows bold,"

The shades of evening had come to increase the dreariness of the place, when the party entered the ruins of William Henry. The scout and his companions immediately made their preparations to pass the night there; but with an earnestness and sobriety of demeanor that betrayed how much the unusual horrors they had just witnessed worked on even their practiced feelings. A few fragments of rafters were reared against a blackened wall; and when Uncas had covered them slightly with brush, the temporary accommodations were deemed sufficient. The young Indian pointed toward his rude hut, when his labor was ended; and Heyward, who understood the meaning of the silent gesture, gently

WOLF

E

said the unmoved scout. "There would be picking, too, among the skins of the devils, if there was light and time for the sport. What goes there?"

"Is it not the rushing of the wolves you have mentioned?"

Hawk-eye slowly shook his head and beckoned for Duncan to follow him to a spot to which the glare from the fire did not extend. When he had taken this precaution, the scout placed himself in an attitude of intense attention, and listened long and keenly for a repetition of the low sound that had so unexpectedly startled him. His vigilance, however, seemed exercised in vain; for, after a fruitless pause, he whispered to Duncan:

SHORT EARED OWL.

"We must give a call to Uncas. The boy has Indian senses, and may hear what is hid from us; for being a white-skin, I will not deny my nature."

The young Mohican, who was conversing in a low voice with his father, started as he heard the moaning of an owl, and springing on his feet, he looked toward the black mounds as if seeking the place whence the sounds proceeded. The scout repeated the call, and in a few

moments Duncan saw the figure of Uncas stealing cautiously along the rampart to the spot where they stood.

Hawk-eye explained his wishes in a very few words, which were spoken in the Delaware tongue. So soon as Uncas was in possession of the reason why he was summoned, he threw himself flat on the turf; where, to the eyes of Duncan, he appeared to lie quiet and motionless. Surprised at the immovable attitude of the young warrior, and curious to observe the manner in which he employed his faculties to obtain the desired information, Heyward advanced a few steps, and bent over the dark object, on which he had kept his eyes riveted. Then it was he discovered that the form of Uncas had vanished, and that he beheld only the dark outline of an inequality in the embankment.

"What has become of the Mohican?" he demanded of the scout, stepping back in amazement. "It was here that I saw him, fall, and I could have sworn that here he yet remained."

"Hist! Speak lower; for we know not what ears are open, and the Mingoes are a quick-witted breed. As for Uncas, he is out on the plain, and the Maquas, if any such are about us, will find their equal."

"You think that Montcalm has not called off all his Indians? Let us give the alarm to our companions, that we may stand to our arms. Here are five of us, who are not unused to meet an enemy."

"Not a word to either, as you value life. Look at the Sagamore, how like a grand Indian chief he sits by the fire. If there are any skulkers out in the darkness, they will never discover, by his countenance, that we suspect danger at hand."

"But they may discover him, and it will prove his death. His person can be too plainly seen by the light of that fire, and he will become the first and most certain victim."

"It is undeniable that now you speak the truth," returned the scout, betraying more anxiety than was usual. "Yet what can be done? A single suspicious look might bring on an attack before we are ready to receive it. He knows, by the call I gave to Uncas, that we have struck a scent: I will tell him that we are on the trail of the Mingoes; his Indian nature will teach him how to act."

The scout applied his fingers to his mouth, and raised a low hissing sound that caused Duncan, at first, to start aside, believing that he heard a serpent. The head of Chingachgook was resting on a hand, as he sat musing by himself; but the moment he heard the warning of the animal whose name he bore, it arose to an upright position, and his dark eyes glanced swiftly and keenly on every side of him. With his sudden and perhaps involuntary movement, every appearance of surprise or alarm ended. His rifle lay untouched, and apparently unnoticed, within reach of his hand. The tomahawk that he had loosened in his belt for the sake of ease, was even suffered to fall from its usual situation to the ground, and his form seemed to sink, like that of a man whose nerves and sinews were suffered to relax for the purpose of rest. Cunningly resuming his former position, though with a change of hands, as if the movement had been made merely to relieve the limb, the native awaited the result with a calmness and fortitude that none but an Indian warrior would have known how to exercise.

But Heyward saw that, while to a less instructed eye the Mohican chief appeared to slumber, his nostrils were expanded, his head was turned a little to one side, as if to assist the organs of hearing, and that his quick and rapid glances ran incessantly over every object within the power of his vision.

"See the noble fellow!" whispered Hawk-eye, pressing the arm of Heyward. "He knows that a look or a motion might disconsart our schemes, and put us at the mercy of them imps – "

He was interrupted by the flash and report of a rifle. The air was filled with sparks of fire, around that spot where the eyes of Heyward were still fastened, with admiration and wonder. A second look told him that Chingachgook had disappeared in the confusion. In the meantime, the scout had thrown forward his rifle, like one prepared for service, and awaited impatiently the moment when an enemy might rise to view. But with the solitary and fruitless attempt made on the life of Chingachgook, the attack appeared to have terminated. Once or twice the listeners thought they could distinguish the distant rustling of bushes, as bodies of some unknown description rushed through them; nor

INDIAN STONE AND CLAY PIPES.

was it long before Hawk-eye pointed out the "scampering of the wolves," as they fled precipitately before the passage of some intruder on their proper domains. After an impatient and breathless pause, a plunge was heard in the water, and it was immediately followed by the report of another rifle.

"There goes Uncas!" said the scout. "The boy bears a smart piece! I know its crack, as well as a father knows the language of his child, for I carried the gun myself until a better offered."

"What can this mean?" demanded Duncan. "We are watched, and, as it would seem, marked for destruction."

"Yonder scattered brand can witness that no good was intended, and this Indian will testify that no harm has been done," returned the scout, dropping his rifle across his arm again, and following Chingachgook, who just then reappeared within the circle of light, into the bosom of the works. "How is it, Sagamore? Are the Mingoes upon us in earnest, or is it only one of those reptiles who hang upon the skirts of a war party, to scalp the dead, go in, and make their boast among the squaws of the valiant deeds done on the palefaces?"

Chingachgook very quietly resumed his seat; nor did he make any reply, until after he had examined the fire-brand which had been struck by the bullet that had nearly proved fatal to himself. After which, he was content to reply, holding a single finger up to view, with the English monosyllable:

"One."

"I thought as much," returned Hawk-eye, seating himself; "and as he had got

the cover of the lake afore Uncas pulled upon him, it is more than probable the knave will sing his lies about some great ambushment, in which he was outlying on the trail of two Mohicans and a white hunter – for the officers can be considered as little better than idlers in such a scrimmage. Well, let him – let him."

Just then Uncas glided into the circle, and seated himself at the fire, with the same appearance of indifference as was maintained by his father.

"What has become of our enemy, Uncas?" demanded Duncan. "We heard your rifle, and hoped you had not fired in vain."

The young chief removed a fold of his hunting shirt and quietly exposed the fatal tuft of hair, which he bore as the symbol of victory.

Heyward withdrew to the rampart, too uneasy and too little accustomed to the warfare of the woods to remain at ease under the possibility of such insidious attacks.

The warriors, not excepting Hawk-eye, took their seats within the curl of smoke from the replenished fire with much gravity and decorum. Placing himself at an angle of the works, where he might be a spectator of the scene within, while he kept a watchful eye against any danger from without, he awaited the result with as much patience as he could summon.

After a short and impressive pause, Chingachgook lighted a pipe whose bowl was curiously carved in one of the soft stones of the country, and whose stem was a tube of wood, and commenced smoking. When he had inhaled enough

of the fragrance of the soothing weed, he passed the instrument into the hands of the scout. In this manner the pipe had made its rounds three several times, amid the most profound silence, before either of the party opened his lips. Then the Sagamore, as the oldest and highest in rank, in a few calm and dignified words, proposed the subject for deliberation. He was answered by the scout; and Chingachgook rejoined, when the other objected to his opinions. But the youthful Uncas continued a silent and respectful listener, until Hawk-eye, in complaisance, demanded his opinion. Heyward gathered from the manners of the different speakers that the father and son espoused one side of a disputed question, while the white man maintained the other. The contest gradually grew warmer until it was quite evident 'the feelings of the speakers began to be somewhat enlisted in the debate.

The language of the Mohicans was accompanied by gestures so direct and natural, that Heyward had but little difficulty in following the thread of their argument. On the other hand, the scout was obscure; because, from the lingering pride of color, he rather affected the cold and artificial manner which characterizes all classes of Anglo-Americans, when unexcited. By the frequency with which the Indians described the marks of a forest trail, it was evident they urged a pursuit by land, while the repeated sweep of Hawk-eye's arm toward the Horican denoted that he was for a passage across its waters.

The latter was, to every appearance, fast losing ground, and the point was about to be decided against him, when he arose to his feet and, shaking off his apathy, he suddenly assumed the manner of an Indian, and adopted all the arts of native eloquence. Elevating an arm, he pointed out the track of the sun, repeating the gesture for every day that was necessary to accomplish their object. Then he delineated a long and painful path, amid rocks and watercourses. The age and weakness of the slumbering and unconscious Munro were indicated by signs too palpable to be mistaken. Duncan perceived that even his own powers were spoken lightly of, as the scout extended his palm and mentioned him by the appellation of the "Open Hand" – a name his liberality had purchased of all the friendly tribes. Then came a representation of the light and graceful movements of a canoe, set in forcible contrast to the tottering steps of one enfeebled and tired. He concluded by pointing to the scalp of the Oneida, and apparently urging the necessity of their departing speedily, and in a manner that should leave no trail.

The Mohicans listened gravely, and with countenances that reflected the sentiments of the speaker. Conviction gradually wrought its influence, and toward the close of Hawk-eye's speech, his sentences were accompanied by the customary exclamation of commendation. In short, Uncas and his father became converts to his way of thinking, abandoning their own previously expressed opinions with a liberality and candor, that, had they been the representatives of some great and civilized people, would have infallibly worked their political ruin, by destroying forever their reputation for consistency.

The instant the matter in discussion was decided, the debate, and everything connected with it, except the result, appeared to be forgotten. Hawk-eye, without looking round to read his triumph in applauding eyes, very com-posedly stretched his tall frame before the dying embers, and closed his own organs in sleep.

Left now in a measure to themselves, the Mohicans, whose time had been so much devoted to the interests of others, seized the moment to devote some attention to themselves. Casting off, at once, the grave and austere demeanor of an Indian chief, Chingachgook commenced speaking to his son in the soft and playful tones of affection. Uncas gladly met the familiar air of his father; and before the hard breathing of the scout announced that he slept, a complete change was effected in the manner of his two associates.

After an hour passed in the indulgence of their better feelings, Chingachgook abruptly announced his desire to sleep, by wrapping his head in his blanket and stretching his form on the naked earth. The merriment of Uncas instantly ceased; and carefully raking the coals in such a manner that they should impart their warmth to his father's feet, the youth sought his own pillow among the ruins of the place.

Imbibing renewed confidence from the security of these experienced foresters, Heyward soon imitated their example; and long before the night had turned, they who lay in the bosom of the ruined work seemed to slumber as heavily as the unconscious multitude whose bones were already beginning to bleach on the surrounding plain.

A WATER CHASE

The heavens were still studded with stars when Hawk-eye came to arouse the sleepers. Casting aside their cloaks, Munro and Heyward were on their feet while the woodsman was still making his low calls at the entrance of the rude shelter where they had passed the night. When they issued from beneath its concealment, they found the scout awaiting their appearance nigh by.

"Come," he said, turning toward a curtain of the works; "let us get into the ditch on this side, and be regardful to step on the stones and fragments of wood as you go."

His companions complied, though to two of them the reasons of this extraordinary precaution were yet a mystery. When they were in the low cavity that surrounded the earthen fort on three of its sides, they found the passage nearly choked by the ruins. With care and patience, however, they succeeded in clambering after the scout, until they reached the sandy shore of the Horican.

"That's a trail that nothing but a nose can follow," said the satisfied scout, looking back along their difficult way. "Grass is a treacherous carpet for a flying party to tread on, but wood and stone take no print from a moccasin. Had you worn your armed boots, there might, indeed, have been something to fear; but with the deerskin suitably prepared, a man may trust himself, generally, on rocks with safety. Shove in the canoe nigher to the land, Uncas; this sand will take a stamp as easily as the butter of the Jarmans on the Mohawk. Softly, lad, softly, it must not touch the beach, or the knaves will know by what road we have left the place."

The young man observed the precaution; and the scout, laying a board from the ruins to the canoe, made a sign for the two officers to enter. When this was done, everything was studiously restored to its former disorder; and then Hawk-eye succeeded in reaching his little birchen vessel without leaving behind him any of those marks which he appeared so much to dread. Heyward was silent until the Indians had cautiously paddled the canoe some distance from the fort, and within the broad and dark shadow that fell from the eastern mountain, on the glassy surface of the lake; then he demanded:

"What need have we for this stolen and hurried departure?"

"If the blood of an Oneida could stain such a sheet of pure water as this we float on," returned the scout, "your two eyes would answer your own question. Have you forgotten the skulking reptile that Uncas slew?"

"By no means. But he was said to be alone, and dead men give no cause for fear."

"Aye, he was alone in his deviltry! But an Indian whose tribe counts so many warriors, need seldom fear his blood will run, without the death shriek coming speedily from some of his enemies."

"But our presence – the authority of Colonel Munro would prove a sufficient protection against the anger of our allies, especially in a case where the wretch so well merited his fate. I trust in Heaven you have not deviated a single foot from the direct line of our course, with so slight a reason."

"Do you think the bullet of that varlet's rifle would have turned aside, though his sacred Majesty the King had stood in its path?" returned the stubborn scout. "Why did not the grand Frencher, he who is captain-general of the Canadas, bury the tomahawks of the Hurons, if a word from a white can work so strongly on the natur' of an Indian?"

The reply of Heyward was interrupted by a groan from Munro; but after he had paused a moment, in deference to the sorrow of his aged friend, he resumed the subject.

"The Marquis of Montcalm can only settle that error with his God," said the young man solemnly.

Just as the day dawned, they entered the narrows of the lake, and stole swiftly and cautiously among their numberless little islands. It was by this road that Montcalm had retired with his army, and the adventurers knew not but he had left some of his Indians in ambush, to protect the rear of his forces, and collect the stragglers. They, therefore, approached the passage with the customary silence of their guarded habits.

Chingachgook laid aside his paddle; while Uncas and the scout urged the light vessel through crooked and intricate channels, where every foot that they advanced exposed them to the danger of some sudden rising on their progress. The eyes of the Sagamore moved warily from islet to islet, and copse to copse, as the canoe proceeded; and when a clearer sheet of water permitted, his keen vision was bent along the bald rocks and impending forests that frowned upon the narrow straight.

Heyward, who was a doubly interested spectator, as well from the beauties of the place as from the apprehension natural to his situation, was just believing that he had permitted the latter to be excited without sufficient reason, when the paddle ceased moving, in obedience to a signal from Chingachgook.

"Hugh!" exclaimed Uncas, nearly at the moment that the light tap his father

had made on the side of the canoe notified them of the vicinity of danger.

"What now?" asked the scout. "The lake is as smooth as if the winds had never blown, and I can see along its sheet for miles; there is not so much as the black head of a loon dotting the water."

The Indian gravely raised his paddle and pointed in the direction in which his own steady look was riveted. Duncan's eyes followed the motion. A few rods in their front lay another of the low wooded islets, but it appeared as calm and peaceful as if its solitude had never been disturbed by the foot of man.

"I see nothing," he said, "but land and water; and a lovely scene it is."

"Hist!" interrupted the scout. "Aye, Sagamore, there is always a reason for what you do. 'Tis but a shade, and yet it is not natural. You see the mist, Major, that is rising above the island; you can't call it a fog, for it is more like a streak of thin cloud – "

"It is vapor from the water."

"That a child could tell. But what is the edging of blacker smoke that hangs along its lower side, and which you may trace down into the thicket of hazel? 'Tis from a fire; but one that, in my judgment, has been suffered to burn low."

"Let us then push for the place, and relieve our doubts," said the impatient Duncan. "The party must be small that can lie on such a bit of land."

GREAT NORTHERN DIVER (LOON)

"There they are, by all the truth of signs," whispered the scout; "two canoes and a smoke. The knaves haven't yet got their eyes out of the mist, or we should hear the accursed whoop. Together, friends – we are leaving them, and are already nearly out of whistle of a bullet."

The well-known crack of a rifle, whose ball came skipping along the placid surface of the strait, and a shrill yell from the island, interrupted his speech and announced that their passage was discovered. In another instant several savages were seen rushing into the canoes, which were soon dancing over the water in pursuit. These fearful precursors of a coming struggle produced no change in the countenances and movements of his three guides, so far as Duncan could discover, except that the strokes of their paddles were longer and more in unison, and caused the little bark to spring forward like a creature possessing life and volition.

"Hold them there, Sagamore," said Hawk-eye, looking coolly backward over his left shoulder, while he still plied his paddle. "Keep them just there. Them Hurons have never a piece in their nation that will execute at this distance; but 'Kill-deer' has a barrel on which a man may calculate."

The scout having ascertained that the Mohicans were sufficient of themselves to maintain the requisite distance, deliberately laid aside his paddle and raised the fatal rifle. Three several times he brought the piece to his shoulder, and when his companions were expecting its report, he as often lowered it to request the Indians would permit their enemies to approach a little nigher. At length his accurate and fastidious eye seemed satisfied, and throwing out his left arm on the barrel, he was slowly elevating the muzzle, when an exclamation from Uncas, who sat in the bow, once more caused him to suspend the shot.

"What now, lad?" demanded Hawk-eye. "You saved a Huron from the death shriek by that word; have you reason for what you do?"

Uncas pointed toward the rocky shore a little in their front, whence another war canoe was darting directly across their course. It was too obvious now that their situation was imminently perilous to need the aid of language to confirm it. The scout laid aside his rifle, and resumed the paddle, while Chingachgook inclined the bows of the canoe a little toward the western shore, in order to increase the distance between them and this new enemy. In the meantime they were reminded of the presence of those who pressed upon their rear, by wild and exulting shouts. The stirring scene awakened even Munro from his apathy.

"Let us make for the rocks on the main," he said, with the mien of a tried soldier, "and give battle to the savages. God forbid that I, or those attached to me and mine, should ever trust again to the faith of any servant of the Louises!"

"He who wishes to prosper in Indian warfare," returned the scout, "must not be too proud to learn from the wit of a native. Lay her more along the land, Sagamore; we are doubling on the varlets, and perhaps they may try to strike our trail on the long calculation."

"They are preparing for a shot," said Heyward; "and as we are in a line with them, it can scarcely fail."

"Get you then into the bottom of the canoe," returned the scout; "you and the colonel; it will be so much taken from the size of the mark."

Heyward smiled, as he answered:

"It would be but an ill example for the highest in rank to dodge, while the warriors were under fire!"

"Lord! Lord! That is now a white man's courage!" exclaimed the scout; "and like too many of his notions, not to be maintained by reason. Do you think the Sagamore, or Uncas, or even I, who am a man without a cross, would deliberate about finding a cover in the scrimmage, when an open body would do no good? For what have the Frenchers reared up their Quebec, if fighting is always to be done in the clearings?"

"All that you say is very true, my friend," replied Heyward. "Still, our customs must prevent us from doing as you wish."

A volley from the Hurons interrupted the discourse, and as the bullets whistled about them, Duncan saw the head of Uncas turned, looking back at himself and Munro. Notwithstanding the nearness of the enemy, and his own great personal danger, the countenance of the young warrior expressed no other emotion, as the former was compelled to think, than amazement at finding men willing to encounter so useless an exposure. Chingachgook was probably better acquainted with the notions of white men, for he did not even cast a glance aside from the riveted look his eye maintained on the object by which he governed their course. A ball soon struck the light and polished paddle from the hands of the chief, and drove it through the air, far in the advance. A shout arose from the Hurons, who seized the opportunity to fire another volley. Uncas described an arc in the water with his own blade, and as the canoe passed swiftly on, Chingachgook recovered his paddle, and flourishing it on high, he gave the war whoop of the Mohicans, and then lent his strength and skill again to the important task.

The clamorous sounds of "Le Gros Serpent!" "La Longue Carabine!" "Le Cerf Agile!" burst at once from the canoes behind, and seemed to give new zeal to the pursuers. The scout seized "Kill-deer" in his left hand, and elevating it above his head, he shook it in triumph at his enemies.

Duncan was glad to find that owing to their superior dexterity they were very sensibly obtaining the advantage. The Hurons soon fired again, and a bullet struck the blade of Hawk-eye's paddle without injury.

"That will do," said the scout, examining the slight indentation with a curious eye. "It would not have cut the skin of an infant, much less of men who, like us, have been blown upon by the Heavens in their anger. Now, Major, if you will try to use this piece of flattened wood, I'll let 'Kill-deer' take a part in the conversation."

Heyward seized the paddle, and applied himself to the work with an eagerness that supplied the place of skill, while Hawk-eye was engaged in inspecting the priming of his rifle. The latter then took a swift aim, and fired. The Huron in the bows of the leading canoe had risen with a similar object, and he now fell backward, suffering his gun to escape from his hands into the water. In an instant, however, he recovered his feet, though his gestures were wild and bewildered. At the same moment his companions suspended their efforts, and the chasing canoes clustered together and became stationary.

"We forget our errand," said the diligent Duncan. "For God's sake let us profit by this advantage, and increase our distance from the enemy."

"Give me my children," said Munro hoarsely. "Trifle no longer with a father's agony, but restore me my babes."

Long and habitual deference to the mandates of his superiors had taught the scout the virtue of obedience. Throwing a last and lingering glance at the distant canoes, he laid aside his rifle, and relieving the wearied Duncan, resumed the paddle, which he wielded with sinews that never tired. His efforts were seconded by those of the Mohicans, and a very few minutes served to place such a sheet of water between them and their enemies that Heyward once more breathed freely.

Instead of following the western shore, whither their errand led them, the wary Mohican inclined his course more toward those hills behind which Montclam was known to have led his army into the formidable fortress of Ticonderoga. As the Hurons, to every appearance, had abandoned the pursuit, there was no apparent reason for this excess of caution. It was, however, maintained for hours, until they had reached a bay, nigh the northern termination of the lake. Here the canoe was driven upon the beach, and the whole party landed. Hawk-eye and Heyward ascended an adjacent bluff, where the former, after considering the expanse of water beneath him, pointed out to the latter a small black object, hovering under a headland, at the distance of several miles.

"Do you see it?" demanded the scout. "Now, what would you account that spot, were you left alone to white experience to find your way through this wilderness?"

"But for its distance and its magnitude, I should suppose it a bird. Can it be a living object?"

"'Tis a canoe of good birchen bark, and paddled by fierce and crafty Mingoes. Though Providence has lent to those who inhabit the woods eyes that would be needless to men in the settlements, where there are inventions to assist the sight, yet no human organs can see all the dangers which at this moment circumvent us.

"Let us not delay a moment, without some good and obvious cause."

"I little like that smoke, which you may see worming up along the rock above the canoe," interrupted the abstracted scout. "My life on it, other eyes than ours see it, and know its meaning. Well, words will not mend the matter, and it is time that we were doing."

Hawk-eye moved away from the lookout, and descended, musing profoundly, to the shore. He communicated the result of his observations to his companions, in Delaware, and a short and earnest consultation succeeded. When it terminated, the three instantly set about executing their new resolutions.

The canoe was lifted from the water and borne on the shoulders of the party. They proceeded into the wood, making as broad and obvious a trail as possible. They soon reached a watercourse which they crossed, and continued onward until they came to an extensive and naked rock. At this point, where their footsteps might be expected to be no longer visible, they retraced their route to the brook, walking backwards, with the utmost care. They now followed the bed of the little stream to the lake, into which they immediately launched their canoe again. A low point concealed them from the headland, and the margin of the lake was fringed for some distance with dense and overhanging bushes. Under the cover of these natural advantages, they toiled their way with patient industry, until the scout pronounced that he believed it would be safe once more to land.

The halt continued until evening rendered objects indistinct and uncertain to the eye. Then they resumed their route, and, favored by the darkness, pushed silently and vigorously toward the western shore. Although the rugged outline of mountain to which they were steering presented no distinctive marks to the eyes of Duncan, the Mohican entered the little haven he had selected with the confidence and accuracy of an experienced pilot.

The boat was again lifted and borne into the woods, where it was carefully concealed under a pile of brush. The adventurers assumed their arms and packs, and the scout announced to Munro and Heyward that he and the Indians were at last in readiness to proceed.

DUNCAN IS DECEIVED

The party had landed on the border of a region that is, even to this day, less known to the inhabitants of the states than the deserts of Arabia, or the steppes of Tartary. It was the sterile and rugged district which separates the tributaries of Champlain from those of the Hudson, the Mohawk, and the St. Lawrence. Since the period of our tale, the active spirit of the country has surrounded it with a belt of rich and thriving settlements, though none but the hunter or the savage is ever known, even now, to penetrate its wild recesses.

As Hawk-eye and the Mohicans had, however, often traversed the mountains and valleys of this vast wilderness, they did not hesitate to plunge into its depths, with the freedom of men accustomed to its privations and difficulties.

After proceeding a few miles, the progress of Hawk-eye, who led the advance, became more deliberate and watchful. He often stopped to examine the trees; nor did he cross a rivulet without attentively considering the quantity, the velocity, and the color of its waters. Distrusting his own judgment, his appeals to the opinion of Chingachgook were frequent and earnest. During one of these conferences, Heyward observed that Uncas stood a patient and silent, though, as he imagined, an interested listener. At last, the scout spoke in English, and at once explained the embarrassment of their situation.

"When I found that the home path of the Hurons runs north," he said, "it did not need the judgment of many long years to tell that they would follow the valleys, and keep atween the waters of the Hudson and the Horican, until they might strike the springs of the Canada streams, which would lead them into the heart of the country of the Frenchers. Yet here are we, within a short range of the Scaroon, and not a sign of a trail have we crossed! Human natur' is weak, and it is possible we may not have taken the proper scent."

"Heaven protect us from such an error!" exclaimed Duncan. "Let us retrace our steps, and examine as we go, with keener eyes. Has Uncas no counsel to offer in such a strait?"

The young Mohican cast a glance at his father, but maintaining his quiet and reserved mien, he continued silent. Chingachgook had caught the look, and motioning with his hand, he bade him speak. The moment this permission was accorded, the countenance of Uncas changed from its grave composure to a gleam of intelligence and joy. Bounding forward like a deer, he sprang up the side of a little acclivity, a few rods in advance, and stood, exultingly, over a spot of fresh earth that looked as though it had been recently upturned by the passage of some heavy animal. The eyes of the whole party followed the unexpected movement, and read their success in the air of triumph that the youth assumed.

"'Tis the trail!" exclaimed the scout, advancing to the spot. "The lad is quick of sight and keen of wit for his years."

"'Tis extraordinary that he should have withheld his knowledge so long," muttered Duncan, at his elbow.

"It would have been more wonderful had he spoken without a bidding. No, no; your young white, who gathers his learning from books and can measure what he knows by the page, may conceit that his knowledge, like his legs, outruns that of his father; but where experience is the master, the scholar is made to know the value of years, and respects them accordingly."

"See!" said Uncas, pointing north and south, at the evident marks of the broad trail on either side of him. "The dark-hair has gone toward the frost."

The spirits of the scout, and the astonishing success of the chase, in which a circuitous distance of more than forty miles had been passed, did not fail to impart a portion of hope to the whole party. Their advance was rapid; and made with as much confidence as a traveler would proceed along a wide highway.

By the middle of the afternoon they had passed the Scaroon, and were following the route of the declining sun. After descending an eminence to a low bottom, through which a swift stream glided, they suddenly came to a place where the party of Le Renard had made a halt. Extinguished brands were lying around a spring, the offals of a deer were scattered about the place, and the trees bore evident marks of having been

BEAVER

THE BEAVER BED IN THE CUT-AWAY DRAWING OF THE LODGE IS RAISED ABOVE THE AREA IN WHICH THE BEAVER EATS. THE DAM IS FACED WITH MUD AND SMALL STONES. THEN STICKS ARE LAID WITH THE GNAWED-AWAY ENDS FACING UPSTREAM.

browsed by the horses. At a little distance, Heyward discovered, and contemplated with tender emotion, the small bower under which he was fain to believe that Cora and Alice had reposed. But while the earth was trodden, and the footsteps of both men and beasts were so plainly visible around the place, the trail appeared to have suddenly ended.

It was easy to follow the tracks of the Narragansets, but they seemed only to have wandered without guides or any other object than the pursuit of food. At length Uncas, who, with his father, had endeavored to trace the route of the horses, came upon a sign of their presence that was quite recent. Before following the clue, he communicated his success to his companions; and while the latter were consulting on the circumstance, the youth reappeared, leading the two fillies, with their saddles broken and the housings soiled, as though they had been permitted to run at will for several days.

"What should this prove?" said Duncan, turning pale, and glancing his eyes around him, as if he feared the brush and leaves were about to give up some horrid secret.

"That our march is come to a quick end, and that we are in an enemy's country," returned the scout. "Had the

knave been pressed, and the gentle ones wanted horses to keep up with the party, he might have taken their scalps; but without an enemy at his heels, and with such rugged beasts as these he would not hurt a hair of their heads. It is true that the horses are here, but the Hurons are gone; let us then hunt for the path by which they departed."

Hawk-eye and the Mohicans now applied themselves to their task in good earnest. A circle of a few hundred feet in circumference was drawn, and each of the party took a segment for his portion. The examination, however, resulted in no discovery.

"We must get down to it, Sagamore, beginning at the spring, and going over the ground by inches. The Huron shall never brag in his tribe that he has a foot which leaves no print."

Setting the example himself, the scout engaged in the scrutiny with renewed zeal. Not a leaf was left unturned. At length Uncas, whose activity had enabled him to achieve his portion of the task the soonest, raked the earth across the turbid little rill which ran from the spring, and diverted its course into another channel. So soon as its narrow bed below the dam was dry, he stooped over it with keen and curious eyes. A cry of exultation immediately announced the success of the young warrior. The

ISLAND LODGE IN POND MADE BY BEAVER. .

whole party crowded to the spot, where Uncas pointed out the impression of a moccasin in the moist alluvion.

"The lad will be an honor to his people," said Hawk-eye, regarding the trail with as much admiration as a naturalist would expend on the tusk of a

BEAVER LODGE

BEAVER DAM

73

mammoth or the rib of a mastodon. "Aye, and a thorn in the sides of the Hurons. Yet that is not the footstep of an Indian! Run back, Uncas, and bring me the size of the singer's foot. You will find a beautiful print of it just opposite yon rock, ag'in the hillside."

While the youth was engaged in this commission, the scout and Chingachgook were attentively considering the impressions. The measurements agreed, and the former unhesitatingly pronounced that the footstep was that of David, who had, once more, been made to exchange his shoes for moccasins.

"I can now read the whole of it, as plainly as if I had seen the arts of Le Subtil," he added. "The singer being a man whose gifts lay chiefly in his throat and feet, was made to go first, and the others have trod in his steps, imitating their formation."

"But," cried Duncan, "I see no signs of – "

"The gentle ones," interrupted the scout. "The varlet has found a way to carry them, until he supposed he had thrown any followers off his scent. My life on it, we see their pretty little feet again before many rods go by."

The whole party now proceeded, following the course of the rill, keeping anxious eyes on the regular impressions. The water soon flowed into its bed again, but watching the ground on either side, the foresters pursued their way, content with knowing that the trail lay beneath.

As the Hurons had made no further efforts to conceal their footsteps, the progress of the pursuers was no longer delayed by uncertainty. Before an hour had elapsed, however, the speed of Hawk-eye sensibly abated, and his head, instead of maintaining its former direct and forward look, began to turn suspiciously from side to side, as if he were conscious of approaching danger. He soon stopped again and waited for the whole party to come up.

"I scent the Hurons," he said, speaking to the Mohicans. "Yonder is open sky, through the treetops, and we are getting too nigh their encampment. Sagamore, you will take the hillside, to the right; Uncas will bend along the brook to the left, while I will try the trail. If anything should happen, the call will be three croaks of a crow. I saw one of the birds fanning himself in the air, just beyond the dead oak – another sign that we are touching an encampment."

The Indians departed their several ways without reply, while Hawk-eye cautiously proceeded with the two gentlemen.

The trees of many acres had been felled, and the glow of a mild summer's evening had fallen on the clearing, in beautiful contrast to the gray light of the forest. A short distance from the place where Duncan stood, the stream had seemingly expanded into a little lake, covering most of the low land from mountain to mountain. The water fell out of this wide basin in a cataract so regular and gentle that it appeared rather to be the work of human hands than fashioned by nature. A hundred earthen dwellings stood on the margin of the lake, and even in its water, as though the latter had overflowed its usual banks. Their rounded roofs, admirably molded for defense against the weather, denoted more of industry and foresight than the natives were wont to bestow on their regular habitations, much less on those they occupied for the temporary purposes of hunting and war. In short, the whole village or town, whichever it might be termed, possessed more of method and neatness of execution than the white men had been accustomed to believe belonged, ordinarily, to the Indian habits. It appeared, however, to be deserted. At least, so thought Duncan for many minutes; but, at length, he fancied he discovered several human forms advancing toward him on all fours, and apparently dragging in their train some heavy, and as he was quick to apprehend, some formidable engine. Just then a few dark-looking heads gleamed out of the dwellings, and the place seemed suddenly alive with beings, which, however, glided from cover to cover so swiftly as to allow no opportunity of examining their humors or pursuits. Alarmed at these suspicious and inexplicable movements, he was about to attempt the signal of the crows, when the rustling of leaves at hand drew his eyes in another direction.

The young man started, and recoiled a few paces instinctively, when he found himself within a hundred yards of a stranger Indian. Recovering his recollection on the instant, instead of sounding an alarm, which might prove fatal to himself, he remained stationary, an attentive observer of the other's motions.

Duncan was still curiously observing the person of his neighbor, when the scout stole silently and cautiously to his side.

"You see we have reached their settlement or encampment," whispered the young man; "and here is one of the savages himself, in a very embarrassing position for our further movements."

Hawk-eye started, and dropped his rifle, when, directed by the finger of his companion, the stranger came under his view. Then lowering the dangerous muzzle, he stretched forward his long neck, as if to assist a scrutiny that was already intensely keen.

"The imp is not a Huron," he said, "nor of any of the Canada tribes; and yet you see, by his clothes, the knave has been plundering a white. Aye, Montcalm has raked the woods for his inroad, and a whooping, murdering set of varlets has he gathered together. Can you see where he has put his rifle or his bow?"

"He appears to have no arms; nor does he seem to be viciously inclined. Unless he communicate the alarm to his fellows, who, as you see, are dodging about the water, we have but little to fear from him."

The scout turned to Heyward, and regarded him a moment with unconcealed amazement. Then opening wide his mouth, he indulged in unrestrained and heartfelt laughter, though in that silent and peculiar manner which danger had so long taught him to practice.

Repeating the words, "Fellows who are dodging about the water!" he added, "So much for schooling and passing a boyhood in the settlements! The knave has long legs, though, and shall not be trusted. Do you keep him under your rifle while I creep in behind, through the bush, and take him alive. Fire on no account."

In the next moment he was concealed by the leaves. Duncan waited several minutes in feverish impatience, before he caught another glimpse of the scout. Then he reappeared, creeping along the earth, from which his dress was hardly distinguishable, directly in the rear of his intended captive. Having reached within a few yards of the latter, he arose to his feet, silently and slowly. At that instant, several loud blows were struck on the water, and Duncan turned his eyes just in time to perceive that a hundred dark forms were plunging, in a body, into the troubled little sheet. Grasping his rifle, his looks were again bent on the Indian near him. Instead of taking the alarm, the unconscious savage stretched forward his neck, as if he also watched the movements about the gloomy lake, with a sort of silly curiosity. In the meantime, the uplifted hand of Hawk-eye was above him. But, without any apparent reason, it was withdrawn, and its owner indulged in a long, though silent, fit of merriment. When the peculiar and hearty laughter of Hawk-eye was ended, instead of grasping his victim by the throat, he tapped him lightly on the shoulder, and exclaimed aloud:

"How now, friend! Have you a mind to teach the beavers to sing?"

"Even so," was the ready answer. "It would seem that the Being that gave them power to improve his gifts so well, would not deny them voices to proclaim his praise."

DAVID REGAINS HIS PITCH PIPE

The reader may better imagine than we describe, the surprise of Heyward. His lurking Indians were suddenly converted into four-footed beasts; his lake into a beaver pond; his cataract into a dam, constructed by those industrious and ingenious quadrupeds; and a suspected enemy into his tried friend, David Gamut, the master of psalmody. The presence of the latter created so many unexpected hopes relative to the sisters that, without a moment's hesitation, the young man broke out of his ambush, and sprang forward to join the two principal actors in the scene.

The merriment of Hawk-eye was not easily appeased. Without ceremony, and with a rough hand, he twirled the supple Gamut around on his heel, and more than once affirmed that the Hurons had done themselves great credit in the fashion of his costume. Then seizing the hand of the other, he squeezed it with a grip that brought the tears into the eyes

MOOSE

of the placid David, and wished him joy of his new condition.

"We see that you are safe; now tell us what has become of the maidens."

"They are captives to the heathen," said David; "and though greatly troubled in spirit, enjoying comfort and safety in the body."

"Both?" demanded the breathless Heyward.

"Even so. Though our wayfaring has been sore and our sustenance scanty, we have had little other cause for complaint, except the violence done our feelings, by being thus led in captivity into a far land."

"Bless ye for these very words!" exclaimed the trembling Munro. "I shall then receive my babes, spotless and angel-like, as I lost them!"

"I know not that their delivery is at hand," returned the doubting David. "The leader of these savages is possessed of an evil spirit that no power short of Omnipotence can tame. I have tried him sleeping and waking, but neither sounds nor language seem to touch his soul."

"Where is the knave?" bluntly interrupted the scout.

"He hunts the moose today, with his young men; and tomorrow, as I hear, they pass further into these forests, and nigher to the borders of Canada. The elder maiden is conveyed to a neighboring people, whose lodges are situate beyond yonder black pinnacle of rock; while the younger is detained among the women of the Hurons, whose dwellings are but two short miles hence, on a tableland, where the fire has done the office of the ax and prepared the place for their reception."

"Alice, my gentle Alice!" murmured Heyward. "She has lost the consolation of her sister's presence!"

"Even so. But so far as praise and thanksgiving in psalmody can temper the spirit in affliction, she has not suffered."

"And why are you permitted to go at large, unwatched?"

David composed his features into what he intended should express an air of modest humility, before he meekly replied:

"Little be the praise to such a worm as I. But, though the power of psalmody was suspended in the terrible business of that field of blood through which we passed, it has recovered its influence even over the souls of the heathen, and I am suffered to go and come at will."

The scout laughed, and tapping his own forehead significantly, he perhaps explained the singular indulgence more satisfactorily when he said:

"The Indians never harm a noncomposser. Here, friend; I did intend to kindle a fire with this tooting whistle of thine; but as you value the thing, take it, and blow your best on it!"

Gamut received his pitch pipe with as strong an expression of pleasure as he believed compatible with the grave functions he exercised. After essaying its virtues repeatedly, in contrast with his own voice, and satisfying himself that none of its melody was lost, he made a very serious demonstration toward achieving a few stanzas of one of the longest effusions in the little volume so often mentioned.

Heyward, however, hastily interrupted his pious purpose by continuing questions concerning the past and present condition of his fellow captives, and in a manner more methodical than had been permitted by his feelings in the opening of their interview. The narrative of David was simple, and the facts but few.

Magua had waited on the mountain until a safe moment to retire presented itself, when he had descended, and taken the route along the western side of the Horican, in the direction of the Canadas. As the subtle Huron was familiar with the paths, and well knew there was no immediate danger of pursuit, their progress had been moderate, and far from fatiguing. It appeared, from the unembellished statement of David, that his own presence had been rather endured than desired; though even Magua had not been entirely exempt from that veneration with which the Indians regard those whom the Great Spirit has visited in their intellects. At night, the utmost care had been taken of the captives, both to prevent injury from the damps of the woods and to guard against an escape. At the spring, the horses were turned loose, as has been seen; and notwithstanding the remoteness and length of their trail, the artifices already named were resorted to, in order to cut off every clue to their place of retreat. On their arrival at the encampment of his people, Magua, in obedience to a policy seldom departed from, separated his prisoners. Cora had been sent to a tribe that temporarily occupied an adjacent valley, though David was far too ignorant of the customs and history of the natives to be able to declare anything satisfactory concerning their name or character. He only knew that they had not engaged in the late expedition against William Henry; that, like the Hurons themselves, they were allies of Montcalm; and that they maintained an amicable though a watchful intercourse with the warlike and savage people, whom chance had, for a time, brought in such close and disagreeable contact with themselves.

The Mohicans and the scout listened to his interrupted and imperfect narrative, with an interest that obviously increased as he proceeded; and it was while attempting to explain the pursuits of the community in which Cora was detained, that the latter abruptly demanded:

"Did you see the fashion of their knives? Were they of English or French formation?"

"My thoughts were bent on no such vanities, but rather mingled on consolation with those of the maidens."

"The time may come when you will not consider the knife of a savage such a despisable vanity," returned the scout, with a strong expression of contempt for the other's dullness. "Had they held their corn-feast – or can you say anything of the totems of their tribe?"

"Of corn, we had many and plentiful feasts; for the grain, being in the milk, is both sweet to the mouth and comfortable to the stomach. Of totem, I know not the meaning; but I have seen strange and fantastic images drawn in their paint, of which their admiration and care savored of spiritual pride; especially one, and that, too, a foul and loathsome object."

"Was it a sarpent?" quickly demanded the scout.

"Much the same. It was in the likeness of an abject and creeping tortoise."

"Hugh!" exclaimed both the attentive Mohicans in a breath; while the scout shook his head with the air of one who had made an important but by no means a pleasing discovery. Then the father spoke, in the language of the Delawares, and with a calmness and dignity that

INDIAN TOTEMS   USED TO DENOTE CLANS WITHIN A TRIBE

instantly arrested the attention even of those to whom his words were unintelligible. His gestures were impressive, and at times energetic. Once he lifted his arm on high; and as it descended, the action threw aside the folds of his light mantle, a finger resting on his breast, as if he would enforce his meaning by the attitude. Duncan's eyes followed the movement, and he perceived that the animal just mentioned was beautifully, though faintly, worked in a blue tint, on the swarthy breast of the chief. All that he had ever heard of the violent separation of the vast tribes of the Delawares rushed across his mind, and he awaited the proper moment to speak, with a suspense that was rendered nearly intolerable by his interest in the stake. His wish, however, was anticipated by the scout, who turned from his red friend, saying:

"We have found that which may be good or evil to us, as Heaven disposes. The Sagamore is of the high blood of the Delawares, and is the great chief of their Tortoises! That some of this stock are among the people of whom the singer tells us, is plain by his words."

"You then suspect it is a portion of that people among whom Cora resides?"

The scout nodded his head in assent, though he seemed anxious to waive the further discussion of a subject that appeared painful. The impatient Duncan now made several hasty and desperate propositions to attempt the release of the sisters. But the scout, after suffering the ardor of the lover to expend itself a little, found means to convince him of the folly of precipitation, in a matter that would require their coolest judgment and utmost fortitude.

"It would be well," he added, "to let this man go in again, as usual, and for him to tarry in the lodges, giving notice to the gentle ones of our approach, until we call him out, by signal, to consult."

"Stop," interrupted Heyward. "I will accompany him."

"You!" exclaimed the astonished Hawk-eye. "Are you tired of seeing the sun rise and set?"

"David is a living proof that the Hurons can be merciful."

"Aye, but David can use his throat, as no man in his senses would pervart the gift."

"I too can play the madman, the fool, the hero; in short, any or everything to rescue her I love. Name your objections no longer: I am resolved."

Hawk-eye regarded the young man a moment in speechless amazement.

"Come," he said, with a good-humored smile; "the buck that will take to the water must be headed, and not followed. Chingachgook has as many different paints as the engineer officer's wife, who takes down natur' on scraps of paper, making the mountains look like cocks of rusty hay, and placing the blue sky in reach of your hand. The Sagamore can use them too. Seat yourself on the log; and my life on it, he can soon make a natural fool of you, and that well to your liking."

Duncan complied; and the Mohican, who had been an attentive listener to the discourse, readily undertook the office.

In short, he entirely sacrificed every appearance of the warrior to the masquerade of a buffoon. Such exhibitions were not uncommon among the Indians; and as Duncan was already sufficiently disguised in his dress, there certainly did exist some reason for believing that, with his knowledge of French, he might pass for a juggler from Ticonderoga, straggling among the allied and friendly tribes.

When he was thought to be sufficiently painted, the scout led Heyward aside, and acquainted him with his intention to leave the veteran in some safe encampment, in charge of Chingachgook, while he and Uncas pursued their inquiries among the people they had reason to believe were Delawares. Then renewing his cautions and advice, he concluded by saying, with a solemnity and warmth of feeling with which Duncan was deeply touched:

"And now God bless you! You have shown a spirit that I like; for it is the gift of youth, more especially one of warm blood and a stout heart. But believe the warning of a man who has reason to know all he says to be true. You will have occasion for your best manhood, and for a sharper wit than what is to be gathered in books, afore you outdo the cunning, or get the better of the courage of a Mingo."

Duncan shook his worthy and reluctant associate warmly by the hand, once more recommended his aged friend to his care, and returning his good wishes, he motioned to David to proceed.

The route taken by Duncan and David lay directly across the clearing of the beavers, and along the margin of their pond.

When the former found himself alone with one so simple, and so little qualified to render any assistance in desperate emergencies, he first began to be sensible of the difficulties of the task he had undertaken. Then came the glowing image of Alice; her distress; her actual danger; and all the peril of his situation was forgotten. Cheering David, he moved on with the light and vigorous step of youth and enterprise.

Within half an hour they gained the margin of another opening that bore all the signs of having been also made by the beavers, and which those sagacious animals had probably been induced, by some accident, to abandon for the more eligible position they now occupied. A very natural sensation caused Duncan to hesitate a moment, unwilling to leave the cover of their bushy path, as a man pauses to collect his energies before he essays any hazardous experiment in which he is secretly conscious they will all be needed. He profited by the halt to gather such information as might be obtained from his hasty glances.

On the opposite side of the clearing, and near the point where the brook tumbled over some rocks, from a still higher level, some fifty or sixty lodges, rudely fabricated of logs, brush, and earth intermingled, were to be discovered. They were arranged without any order, and seemed to be constructed with very little attention to neatness or beauty. Indeed, so very inferior were they in the two latter particulars to the village Duncan had just seen, that he began to expect a second surprise, no less astonishing than the former. This expectation was in no degree diminished, when, by the doubtful twilight, he beheld twenty or thirty forms rising alternately from the cover of the tall, coarse grass in front of the lodges, and then sinking again from the sight, as it were to burrow in the earth. By the sudden and hasty glimpses that he caught of these figures, they seemed more like dark glancing specters, or some other unearthly beings, than creatures fashioned with the ordinary and vulgar materials of flesh and blood. A gaunt, naked form was seen, for a single instant, tossing its arms wildly in the air, and then the spot it had filled was vacant; the figure appearing suddenly in some other and distant place, or being succeeded by another, possessing the same mysterious character. David, observing that his companion lingered, pursued the direction of his gaze, and in some measure recalled the recollection of Heyward, by speaking.

"There is much fruitful soil uncultivated here," he said; "and I may add, without the sinful leaven of self-commendation, that since my short sojourn in these heathenish abodes, much good seed has been scattered by the wayside."

"The tribes are fonder of the chase than of the arts of men of labor," returned the unconscious Duncan, still gazing at the objects of his wonder.

"It is rather joy than labor to the spirit, to lift up the voice in praise; but sadly do these boys abuse their gifts. Rarely have I found any of their age, on whom nature has so freely bestowed the elements of psalmody; and surely, surely, there are none who neglect them more. Three nights have I now tarried here, and three several times have I assembled the urchins to join in sacred song; and as often have they responded to my efforts with whoopings and howlings that have chilled my soul!"

"Of whom speak you?"

"Of those children of the devil who waste the precious moments in yonder idle antics. Ah! The wholesome restraint of discipline is but little known among this self-abandoned people. In a country of birches, a rod is never seen; and it ought not to appear a marvel in my eyes, that the choicest blessings of Providence are wasted in such cries as these."

David closed his ears against the juvenile pack, whose yell just then rang shrilly through the forest; and Duncan, suffering his lip to curl, as in mockery of his own superstition, said firmly:

"We will proceed."

Without removing the safeguards from his ears, the master of song complied, and together they pursued their way toward what David was sometimes wont to call "the tents of the Philistines."

INTO THE
ENEMY CAMP

It is unusual to find an encampment of the natives, like those of the more instructed whites, guarded by the presence of armed men. Well informed of the approach of every danger while it is yet at a distance, the Indian generally rests secure under his knowledge of the signs of the forest, and the long and difficult paths that separate him from those he has most reason to dread. But the enemy who, by any lucky concurrence of accidents, has found means to elude the vigilance of the scouts, will seldom meet with sentinels nearer home to sound the alarm.

When Duncan and David, therefore, found themselves in the center of the children, who played the antics already mentioned, it was without the least previous intimation of their approach. But so soon as they were observed, the whole of the juvenile pack raised, by common consent, a shrill and warning whoop; and then sank, as it were, by magic, from before the sight of their visitors. The cry of the children had

drawn a dozen warriors to the door of the nearest lodge, where they stood clustered in a dark and savage group, gravely awaiting the nearer approach of those who had unexpectedly come among them.

David, in some measure familiarized to the scene, led the way with a steadiness that no slight obstacle was likely to disconcert, into this very building. Duncan found it difficult to assume the necessary appearance of unconcern, as he brushed the dark and powerful frames of the savages who thronged its threshold; but, conscious that his existence depended on his presence of mind, he trusted to the discretion of his companion, whose footsteps he closely followed, endeavoring, as he proceeded, to rally his thoughts for the occasion.

So soon as their visitor had passed, the observant warriors fell back from the entrance, and arranging themselves about him, they seemed patiently to await the moment when it might comport with the dignity of the stranger to speak. By far the greater number stood leaning, in lazy, lounging attitudes, against the upright posts that supported the crazy building, while three or four of the oldest and most distinguished of the chiefs placed themselves on the earth a little more in advance.

At length one whose hair was beginning to be sprinkled with gray, but whose sinewy limbs and firm tread announced that he was still equal to the duties of manhood, advanced out of the gloom of a corner, whither he had probably posted himself to make his observations unseen, and spoke. He used the language of the Wyandots, or Hurons; his words were, consequently, unintelligible to Heyward, though they seemed, by the gestures that accompanied them, to be uttered more in courtesy than anger. The latter shook his head, and made a gesture indicative of his inability to reply.

"Do none of my brothers speak the French or the English?" he said, in the former language, looking about him from countenance to countenance, in hopes of finding a nod of assent.

Though more than one had turned, as if to catch the meaning of his words, they remained unanswered.

"I should be grieved to think," continued Duncan, speaking slowly, and using the simplest French of which he

was the master, "to believe that none of this wise and brave nation understand the language that the 'Grand Monarque' uses when he talks to his children."

At length, the same warrior who had before addressed him, replied, by drily demanding, in the language of the Canadas:

"When our Great Father speaks to his people, is it with the tongue of a Huron?"

"He knows no difference in his children, whether the color of the skin be red, or black, or white," returned Duncan, evasively; "though chiefly is he satisfied with the brave Hurons. See; he has bid me, who am a man that knows the art of healing, to go to his children, the red Hurons of the great lakes, and ask if any are sick!"

After a silence of a few moments, as if adjusting his thoughts, in order to make a suitable answer to the declaration their guest had just given, another warrior arose, and placed himself in an attitude to speak. While his lips were yet in the act of parting, a low but fearful sound arose from the forest, and was immediately succeeded by a high, shrill yell, that was drawn out until it equaled the longest and most plaintive howl of the wolf. The sudden and terrible interruption caused Duncan to start from his seat, unconscious of everything but the effect produced by so frightful a cry. At the same moment, the warriors glided in a body from the lodge, and the outer air was filled with loud shouts that nearly drowned those awful sounds, which were still ringing beneath the arches of the woods. Unable to command himself any longer, the youth broke from the place, and presently stood in the center of a disorderly throng that included nearly everything having life, within the limits of the encampment. Men, women, and children; the aged, the infirm, the active, and the strong, were alike abroad; some exclaiming aloud, others clapping their hands with a joy that seemed frantic, and all expressing their savage pleasure in some unexpected event. Though astounded, at first, by the uproar, Heyward was soon enabled to find its solution by the scene that followed.

There yet lingered sufficient light in the heavens to exhibit those bright openings among the treetops where different paths left the clearing to enter the depths of the wilderness. Beneath one of them, a line of warriors issued from the woods, and advanced slowly toward the dwellings. One in front bore a short pole, on which, as it afterward appeared, were suspended several human scalps. The startling sounds that Duncan had heard were what the whites have, not inappropriately, called the "death-hallo"; and each repetition of the cry was intended to announce to the tribe the fate of an enemy. Thus far the knowledge of Heyward assisted him in the explanation; and as he now knew that the interruption was caused by the unlooked-for return of a successful war party, every disagreeable sensation was quieted in inward congratulations for the opportune relief and insignificance it conferred on himself.

part in the cruel game that was at hand. Even the children would not be excluded; but boys, little able to wield the instruments, tore the tomahawks from the belts of their fathers and stole into the ranks, apt imitators of the savage traits exhibited by their parents.

Large piles of brush lay scattered about the clearing, and a wary and aged squaw was occupied in firing as many as might serve to light the coming exhibition. As the flame arose, its power exceeded that of the parting day, and assisted to render objects at the same time more distinct and more hideous. The whole scene formed a striking picture, whose frame was composed of the dark and tall border of pines. The warriors just arrived were the most distant figures. A little in advance stood

safer side of the formidable array. The artifice was answered by a hundred voices raised in imprecations; and the whole of the excited multitude broke from their order, and spread themselves about the place in wild confusion.

Nothing could be distinguished but a dark mass of human forms tossed and involved in inexplicable confusion. Arms, gleaming knives, and formidable clubs, appeared above them, but the blows were evidently given at random. The awful effect was heightened by the piercing shrieks of the women and the fierce yells of the warriors. Now and then Duncan caught a glimpse of a light form cleaving the air in some desperate bound, and he rather hoped than believed that the captive yet retained the command of his astonishing powers

IROQUOIS WAR CLUB

When at the distance of a few hundred feet from the lodges, the newly arrived warriors halted. Their plaintive and terrific cry, which was intended to represent equally the wailings of the dead and the triumph of the victors, had entirely ceased. One of their number now called aloud, in words that were far from appalling, though not more intelligible to those for whose ears they were intended, than their expressive yells. It would be difficult to convey a suitable idea of the savage ecstasy with which the news, thus imparted, was received. The whole encampment, in a moment, became a scene of the most violent bustle and commotion. The warriors drew their knives, and flourishing them, they arranged themselves in two lines, forming a lane that extended from the war party to the lodges. The squaws seized clubs, axes, or whatever weapon of offense first offered itself to their hands, and rushed eagerly to act their

two men, who were apparently selected from the rest, as the principal actors in what was to follow. The light was not strong enough to render their features distinct, though it was quite evident that they were governed by very different emotions. While one stood erect and firm, prepared to meet his fate like a hero, the other bowed his head, as if palsied by terror or stricken with shame. Just then the signal yell was given, and the momentary quiet which had preceded it was broken by a burst of cries that far exceeded any before heard. The most abject of the two victims continued motionless; but the other bounded from the place at the cry, with the activity and swiftness of a deer. Instead of rushing through the hostile lines, as had been expected, he just entered the dangerous defile, and before time was given for a single blow, turned short, and leaping the heads of a row of children, he gained at once the exterior and

of activity. Suddenly the multitude rolled backward, and approached the spot where he himself stood. The heavy body in the rear pressed upon the women and children in front, and bore them to the earth. The stranger reappeared in the confusion. Human power could not, however, much longer endure so severe a trial. Of this the captive seemed conscious. Profiting by the momentary opening, he darted from among the warriors, and made a desperate, and, what seemed to Duncan, a final effort to gain the wood. As if aware that no danger was to be apprehended from the young soldier, the fugitive nearly brushed his person in his flight. A tall and powerful Huron, who had husbanded his forces, pressed close upon his heels, and with an uplifted arm menaced a fatal blow. Duncan thrust forth a foot, and the shock precipitated the eager savage headlong, many feet in advance of his intended victim. Thought itself is not quicker than was the motion with which the latter profited by the advantage; he turned, gleamed like a meteor again before the eyes of Duncan, and at the next moment, when the latter recovered his recollection and gazed around in quest of the captive, he saw him quietly leaning against a small painted post, which stood before the door of the principal lodge.

Apprehensive that the part he had taken in the escape might prove fatal to himself, Duncan left the place without delay. He followed the crowd, which drew nigh the lodges, gloomy and sullen, like any other multitude that had been disappointed in an execution. Curiosity, or perhaps a better feeling, induced him to approach the stranger. He found him standing with one arm cast about the protecting post, and breathing thick and hard after his exertions, but disdaining to permit a single sign of suffering to escape. His person was now protected by immemorial and sacred usage, until the tribe in council had deliberated and determined on his fate. It was not difficult, however, to foretell the result, if any presage could be drawn from the feelings of those who crowded the place.

There was no term of abuse known to the Huron vocabulary that the disappointed women did not lavishly expend on the successful stranger. They flouted at his efforts, and told him, with bitter scoffs, that his feet were better than his hands; and that he merited wings, while he knew not the use of an arrow or a knife. To all this the captive made no reply; but was content to preserve an attitude in which dignity was singularly blended with disdain. Exasperated as much by his composure as by his good fortune, their words became unintelligible, and were succeeded by shrill piercing yells. His head was immovable; nor did he betray the slightest consciousness that any were present, except when his haughty eye rolled toward the dusky forms of the warriors, who stalked in the background, silent and sullen observers of the scene.

The effect of his indifference began to extend itself to the other spectators; and a youngster, who was just quitting the condition of a boy to enter the state of manhood, attempted to assist, by flourishing his tomahawk before their

victim and adding his empty boasts to the taunts of the woman. Then, indeed, the captive turned his face toward the light, and looked down on the stripling with an expression that was superior to contempt. At the next moment he resumed his quiet and reclining attitude against the post. But the change of posture had permitted Duncan to exchange glances with the firm and piercing eyes of Uncas.

Breathless with amazement, and heavily oppressed with the critical situation of his friend, Heyward recoiled before the look, trembling lest its meaning might, in some unknown manner, hasten the prisoner's fate. There was not, however, any instant cause for such an apprehension. Just then a warrior forced his way into the exasperated crowd. Motioning the women and children aside with a stern gesture, he took Uncas by the arm and led him toward the door of the council lodge. Thither all the chiefs, and most of the distinguished warriors, followed; among whom the anxious Heyward found means to enter without attracting any dangerous attention to himself.

A few minutes were consumed in disposing of those present in a manner suitable to their rank and influence in the tribe. An order very similar to that adopted in the preceding interview was observed; the aged and superior chiefs occupying the area of the spacious apartment, within the powerful light of a glaring torch, while their juniors and inferiors were arranged in the background, presenting a dark outline of swarthy and marked visages. In the very center of the lodge, immediately under an opening that admitted the twinkling light of one or two stars, stood Uncas – calm, elevated, and collected.

The case was different with the individual whom Duncan had observed to stand forth with his friend, previously to the desperate trial of speed; and who, instead of joining in the chase, had remained, throughout its turbulent uproar, like a cringing statue, expressive of shame and disgrace. Instead of mingling with his tribe, he sat apart, a solitary being in a multitude, his form shrinking into a crouching and abject attitude, as if anxious to fill as little space as possible. When each individual had taken his proper station, and silence reigned in the place, the gray-haired chief already

introduced to the reader spoke aloud, in the language of the Lenni Lenape.

"Delaware," he said, "though one of a nation of women, you have proved yourself a man. I would give you food; but he who eats with a Huron should become his friend. Rest in peace till the morning sun, when our last words shall be spoken."

"Seven nights, and as many summer days, have I fasted on the trail of the Hurons," Uncas coldly replied. "The children of the Lenape know how to travel the path of the just without lingering to eat."

"Two of my young men are in pursuit of your companion," resumed the other, without appearing to regard the boast of his captive. "When they get back, then will our wise men say to you, live or die."

"Has a Huron no ears?" scornfully exclaimed Uncas. "Twice, since he has been your prisoner, has the Delaware heard a gun that he knows. Your young men will never come back."

A short and sullen pause succeeded this bold assertion. Duncan, who understood the Mohican to allude to the fatal rifle of the scout, bent forward in earnest observation of the effect it might produce on the conquerors; but the chief was content with simply retorting:

"If the Lenape are so skillful, why is one of their bravest warriors here?"

"He followed in the steps of a flying coward, and fell into a snare. The cunning beaver may be caught."

As Uncas thus replied, he pointed with his finger toward the solitary Huron, but without deigning to bestow any other notice on so unworthy an object.

The young Huron was in his war paint, and very little of a finely molded form was concealed by his attire. The light rendered every limb and joint discernible, and Duncan turned away in horror when he saw they were writhing in irrepressible agony.

"Reed-that-bends," said the chief, addressing the young culprit by name, and in his proper language, "though the Great Spirit has made you pleasant to the eyes, it would have been better that you had not been born. Your tongue is loud in the village, but in battle it is still. None of my young men strike the tomahawk deeper into the war post – none of them so lightly on the Yengeese.

The enemy know the shape of your back, but they have never seen the color of your eyes. Three times have they called on you to come, and as often did you forget to answer. Your name will never be mentioned again in your tribe – it is already forgotten."

As the chief slowly uttered these words, pausing impressively between each sentence, the culprit raised his face, in deference to the other's rank and years. Shame, horror, and pride struggled in its lineaments. His eye, which was contracted with inward anguish, gleamed on the persons of those whose breath was his fame; and the latter emotion for an instant predominated. He arose to his feet, and baring his bosom, looked steadily on the keen, glittering knife that was already upheld by his inexorable judge. As the weapon passed slowly into his heart he even smiled, as if in joy at having found death less dreadful than he had anticipated, and fell heavily on his face, at the feet of the rigid and unyielding form of Uncas.

The whole shuddering group of spectators glided from the lodge, like troubled sprites; and Duncan thought that he and the yet throbbing body of the victim of an Indian judgment had now become its only tenants.

UNCAS
IN DANGER

A single moment served to convince the youth that he was mistaken. A hand was laid, with a powerful pressure, on his arm, and the low voice of Uncas muttered in his ears:

"The Hurons are dogs. The sight of a coward's blood can never make a warrior tremble. The Gray Head and the Sagamore are safe, and the rifle of Hawk-eye is not asleep. Go – Uncas and the Open Hand are now strangers. It is enough."

Heyward would gladly have heard more, but a gentle push from his friend urged him toward the door and admonished him of the danger that might attend the discovery of their intercourse. Slowly and reluctantly yielding to the necessity, he quitted the place and mingled with the throng that hovered nigh. The dying fires in the clearing cast a dim and uncertain light on the dusky figures that were silently stalking to and fro; and occasionally a brighter gleam than common glanced into the lodge, and exhibited the figure of Uncas still maintaining its upright attitude near the dead body of the Huron.

A knot of warriors soon entered the

place again, and reissuing, they bore the senseless remains into the adjacent woods. After this termination of the scene, Duncan wandered among the lodges, unquestioned and unnoticed, endeavoring to find some trace of her in whose behalf he incurred the risk he ran. In the present temper of the tribe, it would have been easy to have fled and rejoined his companions, had such a wish crossed his mind. But, in addition to the never-ceasing anxiety on account of Alice, a fresher though feebler interest in the fate of Uncas assisted to chain him to the spot. He continued, therefore, to stray from hut to hut, looking into each only to encounter additional disappointment, until he had made the entire circuit of the village. Abandoning a species of inquiry that proved so fruitless, he retraced his steps to the council lodge, resolved to seek and question David, in order to put an end to his doubts.

Without seeming to hesitate, he walked into the lodge, and took his seat with a gravity that accorded admirably with the deportment of his hosts. He had not long occupied the seat wisely taken a little in the shade, when another of the elder warriors, who spoke the French language, addressed him.

"My Canada father does not forget his children," said the chief. "I thank him. An evil spirit lives in the wife of one of my young men. Can the cunning stranger frighten him away?"

Heyward possessed some knowledge of the mummery practised among the Indians in the cases of such supposed visitations. He saw at a glance that the circumstance might possibly be improved to further his own ends. Aware of the necessity of preserving the dignity of his imaginary character, however, he repressed his feelings, and answered with suitable mystery:

"Spirits differ; some yield to the power of wisdom, while others are too strong."

"My brother is a great medicine," said the cunning savage. "He will try?"

A gesture of assent was the answer. The Huron was content with the assurance, and resuming his pipe, he awaited the proper moment to move. Just then, a warrior of powerful frame darkened the door, and stalking silently among the attentive group, he seated himself on one end of the low pile of

TRADE TOMAHAWK PIPES
1. ENGLISH
2. FRENCH

1.

2.

suffered their wild and glaring eyeballs to roll in the direction of a white-headed savage who sat between two of the most venerated chiefs of the tribe. There was nothing in the air or attire of this Indian that would seem to entitle him to such a distinction. The former was rather depressed, than remarkable for the bearing of the natives; and the latter was such as was commonly worn by the ordinary men of the nation. Like most around him, for more than a minute his look too was on the ground; but, trusting his eyes at length to steal a glance aside, he perceived that he was becoming an object of general attention. Then he arose and lifted his voice in the general silence.

"It was a lie," he said. "I had no son. He who was called by that name is forgotten; his blood was pale, and it came not from the veins of a Huron; the wicked Chippewas cheated my squaw. The Great Spirit has said that the family of Wiss-en-tush should end – he is happy who knows that the evil of his race dies with himself. I have done."

The speaker, who was the father of the recreant young Indian, looked round and about him, as if seeking commendation of his stoicism in the eyes of his auditors. But the stern customs of his people had made too severe an exaction of the feeble old man.

The Indians, who believe in the hereditary transmission of virtues and defects in character, suffered him to depart in silence. Then, with an elevation of breeding that many in a more cultivated state of society might profitably emulate, one of the chiefs drew the attention of the young men from the weakness they had just witnessed, by saying in a cheerful voice, addressing himself in courtesy to Magua, as the newest comer:

"The Delawares have been like bears after the honey-pots, prowling around my village. But who has ever found a Huron asleep?"

The darkness of the impending cloud which precedes a burst of thunder was not blacker than the brow of Magua as he exclaimed:

"The Delawares of the Lakes!"

"Not so. They who wear the petticoats of squaws, on their own river. One of them has been passing the tribe."

"Did my young men take his scalp?"

"His legs were good, though his arm

brush which sustained Duncan. The latter cast an impatient look at his neighbor, and felt his flesh creep with uncontrollable horror when he found himself in actual contact with Magua.

The sudden return of this artful and dreaded chief caused a delay in the departure of the Huron. Several pipes that had been extinguished, were lighted again; while the newcomer, without speaking a word, drew his tomahawk from his girdle, and filling the bowl on its head, began to inhale the vapors of the weed through the hollow handle with as much indifference as if he had not been absent two weary days on a

long and toilsome hunt. Ten minutes, which appeared so many ages to Duncan, might have passed in this manner; and the warriors were fairly enveloped in a cloud of white smoke before any of them spoke.

"Welcome!" one at length uttered. "Has my friend found the moose?"

"The young men stagger under their burdens," returned Magua. "Let Reed-that-bends go on the hunting path; he will meet them."

A deep and awful silence succeeded the utterance of the forbidden name. Each pipe dropped from the lips of its owner as though all had inhaled an impurity at the same instant. The smoke wreathed above their heads in little eddies, and curling in a spiral form, it ascended swiftly through the opening in the roof of the lodge, leaving the place beneath clear of its fumes, and each dark visage distinctly visible. The looks of most of the warriors were riveted on the earth; though a few of the younger and less gifted of the party is better for the hoe than the toma-hawk," returned the other, pointing to the immovable form of Uncas.

Instead of manifesting any womanish curiosity to feast his eyes with the sight of a captive from a people he was known to have so much reason to hate, Magua continued to smoke, with the meditative air that he usually maintained when there was no immediate call on his cunning or his eloquence. Although secretly amazed at the facts communicated by the speech of the aged father, he permitted himself to ask no questions, reserving his inquiries for a more suitable moment. It was only after a sufficient interval that he shook the ashes from his pipe, replaced the toma-hawk, tightened his girdle, and arose, casting for the first time a glance in the direction of the prisoner, who stood a little behind him. The wary though seemingly abstracted Uncas caught a glimpse of the movement, and turning suddenly to the light, their looks met. Near a minute these two bold and un-tamed spirits stood regarding one another steadily in the eye, neither quailing in the least before the fierce gaze he encountered. The form of Uncas dilated, and his nostrils opened like those of a tiger at bay; but so rigid and unyielding was his posture, that he might easily have been converted by the imagination into an exquisite and faultless representation of the warlike deity of his tribe. The lineaments of the quivering features of Magua proved more ductile; his countenance gradually lost its character of defiance in an expression of ferocious joy, and heaving a breath from the very bottom of his chest, he pronounced aloud the formid-able name of –

"Le Cerf Agile!"

Each warrior sprang upon his feet at the utterance of the well-known appella-tion, and there was a short period during which the stoical constancy of the natives was completely conquered by surprise. Uncas enjoyed his victory, but was content with merely exhibiting his triumph by a quiet smile – an emblem of scorn which belongs to all time and every nation.

Magua caught the expression, and raising his arm, he shook it at the cap-tive – the light silver ornaments attached to his bracelet rattling with the trem-bling agitation of the limb, as, in a tone of vengeance, he exclaimed, in English:
"Mohican, you die!"

"The healing waters will never bring the dead Hurons to life," returned Uncas, in the music of the Delawares. "The tumbling river washes their bones; their men are squaws; their women owls. Go – call together the Huron dogs, that they may look upon a warrior. My nostrils are offended; they scent the blood of a coward."

"A stain on the name of a Huron can only be hid by blood that comes from the veins of an Indian. Let this Dela-ware die."

The effect could scarcely be mistaken. Magua had so artfully blended the natural sympathies with the religious superstition of his auditors, that their minds, already prepared by custom to sacrifice a victim to the manes of their countrymen, lost every vestige of humanity in a wish for revenge. One warrior in particular, a man of wild and ferocious mien, had been conspicuous for the attention he had given to the words of the speaker. His countenance had changed with each passing emotion, until it settled into a look of deadly malice. As Magua ended he arose, and uttering the yell of a demon, his polished little ax was seen glancing in the torch-light as he whirled it above his head. The motion and the cry were too sudden for words to interrupt his bloody inten-tion. It appeared as if a bright gleam shot from his hand, which was crossed at the same moment by a dark and powerful line. The former was the tomahawk in its passage; the latter the arm that Magua darted forward to divert its aim. The quick and ready motion of the chief was not entirely too late. The keen weapon cut the war plume from the scalping tuft of Uncas, and passed through the frail wall of the lodge as though it were hurled from some formidable engine.

Duncan had seen the threatening action, and sprang upon his feet with a heart which, while it leaped into his throat, swelled with the most generous resolution in behalf of his friend. A glance told him that the blow had failed, and terror changed to admiration. Uncas stood still, looking his enemy in the eye with features that seemed superior to emotion. Marble could not be colder, calmer, or steadier than the countenance he put upon this sudden and vindictive attack. Then, as if pitying a want of skill which had proved so fortunate to himself, he smiled, and muttered a few words of contempt in his own tongue.

"No!" said Magua, after satisfying himself of the safety of the captive. "The sun must shine on his shame; the squaws must see his flesh tremble, or our revenge will be like the play of boys. Go – take him where there is silence; let us see if a Delaware can sleep at night, and in the morning die."

The young men whose duty it was to guard the prisoner instantly passed their ligaments of bark across his arms, and led him from the lodge, amid a profound and ominous silence. It was only as the figure of Uncas stood in the opening of the door that his firm step hesitated. There he turned, and, in the sweeping and haughty glance that he threw around the circle of his enemies, Duncan caught a look which he was glad to construe into an expression that he was not entirely deserted by hope.

When the chief who had solicited the aid of Duncan finished his pipe, he made a final and successful movement toward departing. A motion of a finger was the intimation he gave the supposed physician to follow; and passing through the clouds of smoke, Duncan was glad, on more accounts than one, to be able, at last, to breathe the pure air of a cool and refreshing summer evening.

Instead of pursuing his way among those lodges where Heyward had already made his unsuccessful search, his com-panion turned aside and proceeded directly toward the base of an adjacent mountain, which overhung the tem-porary village. At a little distance from a bald rock, and directly in its front, they entered a grassy opening which they prepared to cross. Just then fresh fuel was added to the fire, and a powerful light penetrated even to that distant spot. It fell upon the white surface of the mountain, and was reflected down-ward upon a dark and mysterious look-ing being that arose, unexpectedly, in their path.

The Indian paused, as if doubtful whether to proceed, and permitted his companion to approach his side. A large black ball, which at first seemed station-ary, now began to move in a manner that to the latter was inexplicable. Again the fire brightened, and its glare fell more distinctly on the object. Then even Duncan knew it, by its restless and sidling attitudes, which kept the upper part of its form in constant motion, while the animal itself appeared seated, to be a bear.

Duncan, who knew that the animal was often domesticated among the Indians, followed the example of his companion, believing that some favorite of the tribe had found its way into the thicket, in search of food. They passed it unmolested. Though obliged to come nearly in contact with the monster, the Huron, who had at first so warily determined the character of his strange visitor, was now content with proceeding without wasting a moment in further examination; but Heyward was unable to prevent his eyes from looking backward, in salutary watchfulness against attacks in the rear. His uneasiness was in no degree diminished when he perceived the beast rolling along their path, and following their footsteps. He

would have spoken, but the Indian at that moment shoved aside a door of bark, and entered a cavern in the bosom of the mountain.

Profiting by so easy a method of retreat, Duncan stepped after him, and was gladly closing the slight cover to the opening, when he felt it drawn from his hand by the beast, whose shaggy form immediately darkened the passage. They were now in a straight and long gallery, in a chasm of the rocks, where retreat without encountering the animal was impossible. Making the best of the circumstances, the young man pressed forward, keeping as close as possible to his conductor. The bear growled frequently at his heels, and once or twice its enormous paws were laid on his person, as if disposed to prevent his further passage into the den.

A large cavity in the rock had been rudely fitted to answer the purposes of many apartments. The apartment into which Duncan and his guide first

entered, had been exclusively devoted to the sick woman. The latter approached her bedside, which was surrounded by females, in the center of whom Heyward was surprised to find his missing friend David.

A single look was sufficient to apprise the pretended leech that the invalid was far beyond his powers of healing. She lay in a sort of paralysis, indifferent to the objects which crowded before her sight, and happily unconscious of suffering.

Gamut, who had stood prepared to pour forth his spirit in song when the visitors entered, after delaying a moment, drew a strain from his pipe, and commenced a hymn that might have worked a miracle, had faith in its efficacy been of much avail. He was allowed to proceed to the close, the Indians respecting his imaginary infirmity, and Duncan too glad of the delay to hazard the slightest interruption. As the dying cadence of his strains was falling on the ears of the latter, he started aside at hearing them repeated behind him, in a voice half human and half sepulchral. Looking around, he beheld the shaggy monster seated on end in a shadow of the cavern, where, while his restless body swung in the uneasy manner of the animal, it repeated, in a sort of low growl, sounds, if not words, which bore some slight resemblance to the melody of the singer.

The effect of so strange an echo on David may better be imagined than described. His eyes opened as if he doubted their truth; and his voice became instantly mute in excess of wonder. A deep-laid scheme of communicating some important intelligence to Heyward was driven from his recollection by an emotion which very nearly resembled fear, but which he was fain to believe was admiration. Under its influence, he exclaimed aloud – "She expects you, and is at hand"; and precipitately left the cavern.

AMERICAN BLACK BEAR

A BEAR
TRIUMPHS

There was a strange blending of the ridiculous with that which was solemn in this scene. The beast still continued its rolling and apparently untiring movements, though its ludicrous attempt to imitate the melody of David ceased the instant the latter abandoned the field. The words of Gamut were, as has been seen, in his native tongue; and to Duncan they seemed pregnant with some hidden meaning, though nothing present assisted him in discovering the object of their allusion. A speedy end was, however, put to every conjecture

on the subject by the manner of the chief, who advanced to the bedside of the invalid and beckoned away the whole group of female attendants that had clustered there to witness the skill of the stranger.

"Now let my brother show his power."

Thus unequivocally called on to exercise the functions of his assumed character, Heyward was apprehensive that the smallest delay might prove dangerous. It is more than probable that, in the disordered state of his thoughts, he would soon have fallen into some suspicious, if not fatal error, had not his incipient attempts been interrupted by a fierce growl from the quadruped. Three several times did he renew his efforts to proceed, and as often as he met by the same unaccountable opposition, each interruption seeming more savage and threatening than the preceding.

"The cunning ones are jealous," said the Huron. "I go. Brother, the woman is the wife of one of my bravest young men; deal justly by her. Peace," he added, beckoning to the discontented beast to be quiet. "I go."

The chief was as good as his word, and Duncan now found himself alone in that wild and desolate abode, with the helpless invalid and the fierce and dangerous brute. The latter listened to the movements of the Indian with that air of sagacity that a bear is known to possess, until another echo announced that he had also left the cavern, when it turned and came waddling up to Duncan, before whom it seated itself, in its natural attitude, erect like a man. The youth looked anxiously about him for some weapon with which he might make a resistance against the attack he now seriously expected.

It seemed, however, as if the humor of the animal had suddenly changed. Instead of continuing its discontented growls, or manifesting any further signs of anger, the whole of its shaggy body shook violently, as if agitated by some strange internal convulsion. The huge and unwieldy talons pawed stupidly about the grinning muzzle, and while Heyward kept his eyes riveted on its movements with jealous watchfulness, the grim head fell on one side, and in its place appeared the honest, sturdy countenance of the scout, who was

indulging, from the bottom of his soul, in his own peculiar expression of merriment.

"Hist!" said the wary woodsman, interrupting Heyward's exclamation of surprise. "The varlets are about the place, and any sounds that are not natural to witchcraft would bring them back upon us in a body."

"Tell me the meaning of this masquerade; and why you have attempted so desperate an adventure?"

"Ah! reason and calculation are often outdone by accident," returned the scout. "But as a story should always commence at the beginning, I will tell you the whole in order. After we parted I placed the commandant and the Sagamore in an old beaver lodge, where they are safer from the Hurons than they would be in the garrison of Edward; for your high northwest Indians, not having as yet got the traders among them, continue to venerate the beaver. After which Uncas and I pushed for the other encampment, as was agreed; have you seen the lad?"

"To my great grief! – He is captive, and condemned to die at the rising of the sun."

"I had misgivings that such would be his fate," resumed the scout, in a less confident and joyous tone. But soon regaining his naturally firm voice, he continued: "His bad fortune is the true reason of my being here, for it would never do to abandon such a boy to the Hurons. But all our work is yet before us: where is the gentle one?"

"Heaven knows; I have examined every lodge in the village, without discovering the slightest trace of her presence in the tribe."

"You heard what the singer said, as he left us – 'She is at hand, and expects you.'"

"I have been compelled to believe he alluded to this unhappy woman."

"The simpleton was frightened, and blundered through his message; but he had a deeper meaning. Here are walls enough to separate the whole settlement. A bear ought to climb; therefore will I take a look above them. There may be honeypots hid in these rocks, and I am a beast, you know, that has a hankering for the sweets."

The scout looked behind him, laughing at his own conceit, while he clambered up the partition, imitating, as he went, the clumsy motions of the beast he represented; but the instant the summit was gained he made a gesture for silence, and slid down with the utmost precipitation.

"She is here," he whispered, "and by that door you will find her. I would have spoken a word of comfort to the afflicted soul; but the sight of such a monster might upset her reason. Though for that matter, Major, you are none of the most inviting yourself in your paint."

Duncan, who had already sprung eagerly forward, drew instantly back on hearing these discouraging words.

"Am I, then, so very revolting?" he demanded with an air of chagrin.

"You might not startle a wolf, or turn the Royal Americans from a charge; but I have seen the time when you had a better-favored look; your streaked countenances are not ill-judged of by the squaws, but young women of white blood give the preference to their own color. See," he added, pointing to a place where the water trickled from a rock, forming a little crystal spring before it found an issue through the

COMB BACK WINDSOR CHAIR

adjacent crevices. "You may easily get rid of the Sagamore's daub, and when you come back I will try my hand at a new embellishment. It's as common for a conjurer to alter his paint as for a buck in the settlements to change his finery."

The deliberate woodsman had little occasion to hunt for arguments to enforce his advice. He was yet speaking when Duncan availed himself of the water. In a moment every frightful or offensive mark was obliterated, and the youth appeared again in the lineaments with which he had been gifted by nature. Thus prepared for an interview with his mistress, he took a hasty leave of his companion, and disappeared through the indicated passage which led to a further apartment of the cavern. It was profusely strewed with the plunder of William Henry fortress. In the midst of this confusion he found her he sought, pale, anxious, and terrified, but lovely. David had prepared her for such a visit.

"Duncan!" she exclaimed, in a voice that seemed to tremble at the sounds created by itself.

"Alice!" he answered, leaping carelessly among trunks, boxes, arms, and furniture, until he stood at her side.

"I knew that you would never desert me," she said, looking up with a momentary glow on her otherwise dejected countenance. "But you are alone! Grateful as it is to be thus remembered, I could wish to think you are not entirely alone."

Duncan observing that she trembled in a manner which betrayed her inability to stand, gently induced her to be seated while he recounted those leading incidents which it has been our task to record. Alice listened with breathless interest; and though the young man touched lightly on the sorrows of the stricken father, taking care, however, not to wound the self-love of his auditor, the tears ran as freely down the cheeks of the daughter as though she had never wept before. The soothing tenderness of Duncan, however, soon quieted the first burst of her emotions, and she then heard him to the close with undivided attention, if not with composure.

"And now, Alice," he added, "you will see how much is still expected of you. By the assistance of our experienced and invaluable friend, the

scout, we may find our way from this savage people, but you will have to exert your utmost fortitude. Remember that you fly to the arms of your venerable parent, and how much his happiness, as well as your own, depends on those exertions."

"Can I do otherwise for a father who has done so much for me?"

The youth was about to answer, when he was interrupted by a light tap on his shoulder. Starting to his feet, he turned, and, confronting the intruder, his looks fell on the dark form and malignant visage of Magua. The deep guttural laugh of the savage sounded at such a moment to Duncan like the hellish taunt of a demon. Had he pursued the sudden and fierce impulse of the instant, he would have cast himself on the Huron, and committed their fortunes to the issue of a deadly struggle. But, without arms of any description, ignorant of what succor his subtle enemy could command, and charged with the safety of one who was just then dearer than ever to his heart, he no sooner entertained than he abandoned the desperate intention.

"What is your purpose?" said Alice, meekly folding her arms on her bosom, and struggling to conceal an agony of apprehension in behalf of Heyward, in the usual cold and distant manner with which she received the visits of her captor.

The exulting Indian had resumed his austere countenance, though he drew warily back before the menacing glance of the young man's fiery eye. He regarded both his captives for a moment with a steady look, and then stepping aside, he dropped a log of wood across a door different from that by which Duncan had entered. The latter now comprehended the manner of his surprise, and believing himself irretrievably lost, he drew Alice to his bosom, and stood prepared to meet a fate which he hardly regretted, since it was to be suffered in such company. But Magua meditated no immediate violence.

"The palefaces trap the cunning beavers; but the redskins know how to take the Yengeese."

"Huron, do your worst!" exclaimed the excited Heyward, forgetful that a double stake was involved in his life. "You and your vengeance are alike despised."

"Will the white man speak these words at the stake?" asked Magua; manifesting, at the same time, how little faith he had in the other's resolution by the sneer that accompanied his words.

"Here; singly to your face, or in the presence of your nation."

"Le Renard Subtil is a great chief!" returned the Indian. "He will go and bring his young men, to see how bravely a paleface can laugh at the tortures."

He turned away while speaking, and was about to leave the place through the avenue by which Duncan had approached, when a growl caught his ear and caused him to hesitate. The figure of the bear appeared in the door, where it sat, rolling from side to side in its customary restlessness. Magua, like the father of the sick woman, eyed it keenly for a moment, as if to ascertain its character.

"Fool!" exclaimed the chief, in Huron. "Go play with the children and squaws; leave men to their wisdom."

He once more endeavored to pass the supposed empiric, scorning even the parade of threatening to use the knife, or tomahawk, that was pendent from his belt. Suddenly the beast extended its arms, or rather legs, and inclosed him in a grasp that might have vied with the far-famed power of the "bear's hug" itself. Heyward had watched the whole procedure, on the part of Hawk-eye, with breathless interest. At first he relinquished his hold of Alice; then he caught up a thong of buckskin which had been used around some bundle, and when he beheld his enemy with his two arms pinned to his side by the iron muscles of the scout, he rushed upon him, and effectually secured them there. Arms, legs, and feet were encircled in twenty folds of the thong, in less time than we have taken to record the circumstance. When the formidable Huron was completely pinioned, the scout released his hold, and Duncan laid his enemy on his back, utterly helpless.

Throughout the whole of this sudden and extraordinary operation, Magua, though he had struggled violently, until assured he was in the hands of one whose nerves were far better strung than his own, had not uttered the slightest exclamation. But when Hawk-eye, by way of making a summary explanation of his conduct, removed the shaggy jaws of the beast and exposed his own

rugged and earnest countenance to the gaze of the Huron, the philosophy of the latter was so far mastered as to permit him to utter the never-failing:

"Hugh!"

"Aye! You've found your tongue," said his undisturbed conqueror. "Now, in order that you shall not use it to our ruin, I must make free to stop your mouth."

As there was no time to be lost, the scout immediately set about effecting so necessary a precaution; and when he had gagged the Indian, his enemy might safely have been considered as *hors de combat*.

"By what place did the imp enter?" asked the industrious scout, when his work was ended. "Not a soul has passed my way since you left me."

Duncan pointed out the door by which Magua had come, and which now presented too many obstacles to a quick retreat.

"Bring on the gentle one then," continued his friend. "We must make a push for the woods by the other outlet."

Duncan took the light person of Alice in his arms, and followed on the footsteps of the scout. They found the sick woman as they had left her, still alone, and passed swiftly on, by the natural gallery, to the place of entrance. As they approached the little door of bark, a murmur of voices without announced that the friends and relatives of the invalid were gathered about the place, patiently awaiting a summons to reenter.

The door opened a little, as if one without was listening to the proceedings within. A fierce growl repelled the eavesdropper, and then the scout boldly threw open the covering of bark, and left the place, enacting the character of the bear as he proceeded. Duncan kept close at his heels, and soon found himself in the center of a cluster of twenty anxious relatives and friends.

The crowd fell back a little, and permitted the father, and one who appeared to be the husband of the woman, to approach.

"Has my brother driven away the evil spirit?" demanded the former. "What has he in his arms?"

"Thy child," returned Duncan gravely. "The disease has gone out of her; it is shut up in the rocks. I take the woman to a distance, where I will

strengthen her against any further attacks. She shall be in the wigwam of the young man when the sun comes again."

When the father had translated the meaning of the stranger's words into the Huron language, a suppressed murmur announced the satisfaction with which this intelligence was received. The chief himself waved his hand for Duncan to proceed.

Hawk-eye was not ignorant that they were rather tolerated than relied on by the wisest of the chiefs. Taking the path, therefore, that was most likely to avoid observation, he rather skirted than entered the village. The warriors were still to be seen in the distance, by the fading light of the fires, stalking from lodge to lodge. But the children had abandoned their sports for their beds of skins, and the quiet of night was already beginning to prevail over the turbulence and excitement of so busy and important an evening.

Alice revived under the renovating influence of the open air, and as her physical rather than her mental powers had been the subject of weakness, she stood in no need of any explanation of that which had occurred.

"Now let me make an effort to walk," she said, when they had entered the forest, blushing, though unseen, that she had not been sooner able to quit the arms of Duncan. "I am indeed restored."

"Nay, Alice, you are yet too weak."

The maiden struggled gently to release herself, and Heyward was compelled to part with his precious burden. The representative of the bear had certainly been an entire stranger to the delicious emotions of the lover while his arms encircled his mistress; and he was, perhaps, a stranger also to the nature of that feeling of ingenuous shame that oppressed the trembling Alice. But when he found himself at a suitable distance from the lodges he made a halt, and spoke on a subject of which he was thoroughly the master.

"This path will lead you to the brook," he said. "Follow its northern bank until you come to a fall; mount the hill on your right, and you will see the fires of the other people. There you must go, and demand protection; if they are true Delawares, you will be safe. A distant flight with that gentle one, just now, is

AMERICAN INDIAN TIPI

TIPI COVER
SHOWING
HUNTING SCENE

CONSTRUCTION OF TIPI
SHOWING POSITION
OF LINING

LINING

TIPI LINING PREVENTED DRAFTS, DAMPNESS AND GAVE INCREASED VENTILATION. PERSONAL STORIES AND WAR RECORDS WERE ALSO PAINTED ON THESE LININGS

LINING DESIGN

SMOKE FLAPS

SIDE VIEW OF TIPI

COMPLETED TIPI

FOX CHIEF

ROACH

CORNPLANTER A SENECA CHIEF
SENECAS WERE A WOODLAND TRIBE OF THE IROQUOIS OR FIVE NATIONS

THE FALSE FACE CEREMONY OF THE IROQUOIS WAS HELD TO DRIVE AWAY DISEASES AND BANISH EVIL SPIRITS. THE MASK WAS CARVED FROM THE LIVING TREE, THE TREE THEN BEING CUT DOWN

CLAY POT

IROQUOIS BIRCH BARK VESSEL

FALSE FACE

IROQUOIS WOODEN SPOON

SENECA WOODEN SPOON

WOODLAND AND PLAINS INDIANS

PLAINS INDIANS HEADDRESS

PLAINS SHIELD

PLAINS INDIAN ABOUT 1840

FOLD

STITCH

MAKING A WOODLAND MOCCASIN FROM ONE PIECE OF HIDE

NORTHERN CLAM (QUAHOG)

WAMPUM WAS MADE BY BREAKING OFF THE OUTER SHELL LEAVING THE CORE WHICH WAS THEN DRILLED THROUGH ITS CENTRE. WHITE WAMPUM WAS MORE PLENTIFUL BEING MADE FROM THE PERIWINKLE. PURPLE BEADS WERE MADE FROM CLAMS (QUAHOG) AND HIGHLY PRIZED BY THE INDIANS.

WOODLAND INDIANS BEADED DESIGNS

IROQUOIS LONGHOUSE

THE IROQUOIS LONGHOUSE WAS BUILT OF EL[M] BARK LAID ON A WOODEN FRAME. ABOUT TWENTY FEET WIDE, PRACTICALLY AS HIG[H] AND SOMETIMES WAS BETWEEN EIGHTY AND ONE HUNDRED & FIFTY FEET LONG. IT SHELTERED MANY FAMILIES OF THE S[A] CLAN. EACH FAMILY HAD ITS OWN ROO[M] WITH A COOKING FIRE IN THE MIDDLE OF THE HOUSE AND A SMOKE HOLE ABOV[E]

INTERIOR OF LONGHOUSE SHOWING ROOMS OFF THE CENTRE AISLE, COOKING FIRES AND SMOKE HOLES.

AN IROQUOIS VILLAGE SURROUNDED BY A WOODEN PALISADE. THE TREE STUMPS WERE CLEARED TO ALLOW THE LAND TO BE CULTIVATED.

impossible. The Hurons would follow up our trail and master our scalps before we had got a dozen miles. Go, and Providence be with you."

"And you!" demanded Heyward, in surprise. "Surely we part not here?"

"The Hurons hold the pride of the Delawares; the last of the high blood of the Mohicans is in their power," returned the scout. "I go to see what can be done in his favor. Had they mastered your scalp, Major, a knave should have fallen for every hair it held; but if the young Sagamore is to be led to the stake, the Indians shall see also how a man without a cross can die."

Duncan released his hold on the arm of the scout, who turned, and steadily retraced his steps toward the lodges. After pausing a moment to gaze at his retiring form, the successful and yet sorrowful Heyward, and Alice, took their way together toward the distant village of the Delawares.

UNCAS IN DISGUISE

Notwithstanding the high resolution of Hawk-eye, he fully comprehended all the difficulties and dangers he was about to incur. In his return to the camp, his acute and practiced intellects were intently engaged in devising means to counteract a watchfulness and suspicion on the part of his enemies, that he knew were in no degree inferior to his own.

Throwing himself into a suitable posture for the beast he represented, Hawk-eye crawled to a neglected hut. First making the circuit of the hut, and ascertaining that it stood quite alone, and that the character of its inmate was likely to protect it from visitors, he ventured through its low door into the very presence of Gamut. The position of the latter brought the fire between them; and when Hawk-eye had seated himself on end, near a minute elapsed during which the two remained regarding each other without speaking. The suddenness and the nature of the surprise had nearly proved too much for – we will not say the philosophy – but for the faith and resolution of David. He fumbled for his pitch pipe, and arose with a confused intention of attempting a musical exorcism.

"Dark and mysterious monster!" he exclaimed, while with trembling hands he disposed of his auxiliary eyes, and sought his never-failing resource in trouble, the gifted version of the Psalms. "I know not your nature nor intents; but if aught you meditate against the person and rights of one of the humblest servants of the temple, listen to the inspired language of the youth of Israel, and repent."

The bear shook his shaggy sides, and then a well-known voice replied:

"Put up the tooting we'pon, and teach your throat modesty. Five words of plain and comprehendible English are worth, just now, an hour of squalling."

"What art thou?" demanded David, utterly disqualified to pursue his original intention, and nearly gasping for breath.

"A man like yourself; and one whose blood is as little tainted by the cross of a bear, or an Indian, as your own. Have you so soon forgotten from whom you received the foolish instrument you hold in your hand?"

"Can these things be?" returned David, breathing more freely as the truth began to dawn upon him. "I have

HEAD OF BLACK BEAR.

found many marvels during my sojourn with the heathen, but surely nothing to excel this!"

"Come, come," returned Hawk-eye, uncasing his honest countenance, the better to assure the wavering confidence of his companion. "You may see a skin, which, if it be not as white as one of the gentle ones, has no tinge of red to it that the winds of the heaven and the sun have not bestowed. Now let us to business."

"First tell me of the maiden, and of the youth who so bravely sought her," interrupted David.

"Aye, they are happily freed from the tomahawks of these varlets. But can you put me on the scent of Uncas?"

"The young man is in bondage, and much I fear his death is decreed. I greatly mourn that one so well disposed should die in his ignorance, and I have sought a goodly hymn – "

"Can you lead me to him?"

"The task will not be difficult," returned David, hesitating; "though I greatly fear your presence would rather increase than mitigate his unhappy fortunes."

"No more words, but lead on," returned Hawk-eye, concealing his face again, and setting the example in his own person, by instantly quitting the lodge.

The lodge in which Uncas was confined was in the very center of the village, and in a situation, perhaps, more difficult than any other to approach, or leave, without observation. Most of the warriors had retired to their lodges for the night. Four or five of the latter only lingered about the door of the prison of Uncas, wary but close observers of the manner of their captive.

At the sight of Gamut, accompanied by one in the well-known masquerade of their most distinguished conjurer, they readily made way for them both. Still they betrayed no intention to depart. On the other hand, they were evidently disposed to remain bound to the place by an additional interest in the mysterious mummeries that they of course expected from such a visit.

Uncas occupied a distant corner, in a reclining attitude, being rigidly bound, both hands and feet, by strong and painful withes. When the frightful object first presented itself to the young Mohican, he did not deign to bestow a

single glance on the animal. The scout, who had left David at the door to ascertain they were not observed, thought it prudent to preserve his disguise until assured of their privacy. As soon, therefore, as David gave the preconcerted signal, a low hissing sound was heard in the lodge, in place of the fierce growlings of the bear.

Uncas had cast his body back against the wall of the hut and closed his eyes, as if willing to exclude so contemptible and disagreeable an object from his sight. But the moment the noise of the serpent was heard, he arose and cast his looks on each side of him, bending his head low, and turning it inquiringly in every direction, until his keen eye rested on the shaggy monster, where it remained riveted, as though fixed by the power of a charm. Again the same sounds were repeated, evidently proceeding from the mouth of the beast. Once more the eyes of the youth roamed over the interior of the lodge, and returning to their former resting place, he uttered, in a deep, suppressed voice:

"Hawk-eye!"

"Cut his bands," said Hawk-eye to David, who just then approached them.

The singer did as he was ordered, and Uncas found his limbs released. At the same moment the dried skin of the animal rattled, and presently the scout arose to his feet, in proper person. The Mohican appeared to comprehend the nature of the attempt his friend had made, intuitively; neither tongue nor feature betraying another symptom of surprise. When Hawk-eye had cast his shaggy vestment, which was done by simply loosing certain thongs of skin, he drew a long glittering knife, and put it in the hands of Uncas.

"The red Hurons are without," he said. "Let us be ready."

At the same time he laid his finger significantly on another similar weapon, both being the fruits of his prowess among their enemies during the evening.

"We will go," said Uncas.

"Whither?"

"To the Tortoises; they are the children of my grandfathers."

Uncas, who had already approached the door in readiness to lead the way, now recoiled; and placed himself once more in the bottom of the lodge.

"Uncas will stay," he said.

"For what?"

"To fight with his father's brother, and die with the friend of the Delawares."

"Aye, lad," returned Hawk-eye, squeezing the hand of Uncas between his own iron fingers. "'Twould have been more like a Mingo than a Mohican had you left me. But I thought I would make the offer, seeing that youth commonly loves life. Well, what can't be done by main courage, in war, must be done by circumvention. Put on the skin; I doubt not you can play the bear nearly as well as myself."

Whatever might have been the private opinion of Uncas of their respective abilities in this particular, his grave countenance manifested no opinion of his own superiority. He silently and expeditiously encased himself in the covering of the beast, and then awaited such other movements as his more aged companion saw fit to dictate.

"Now, friend," said Hawk-eye, addressing David, "an exchange of garments will be a great convenience to you, inasmuch as you are but little acustomed to the makeshifts of the wilderness. Here, take my hunting shirt and cap, and give me your blanket and hat. You must trust me with the book and spectacles, as well as the tooter, too; if we ever meet again, in better times, you shall have all back again, with many thanks into the bargain."

David parted with the several articles named with a readiness that would have done great credit to his liberality, had he not certainly profited, in many particulars, by the exchange. Hawk-eye was not long in assuming his borrowed garments; and when his restless eyes were hid behind the glasses, and his head was surmounted by the triangular beaver, as their statures were not dissimilar, he might readily have passed for the singer by starlight. As soon as these dispositions were made, the scout turned to David, and gave him his parting instructions.

"Are you much given to cowardice?" he bluntly asked, by way of obtaining a suitable understanding of the whole case before he ventured a prescription.

"My pursuits are peaceful, and my temper, I humbly trust, is greatly given to mercy and love," returned David, a little nettled at so direct an attack on his manhood. "But there are none who can say that I have ever forgotten my faith

BEAVER TRICORN HAT

in the Lord, even in the greatest straits."

"God bless you, friend; I do believe your scent is not greatly wrong, when the matter is duly considered, and keeping eternity before the eyes, though much depends on the natural gifts, and the force of temptation."

So saying, the scout returned and shook David cordially by the hand; after which act of friendship he immediately left the lodge, attended by the new representative of the beast.

The instant Hawk-eye found himself under the observation of the Hurons, he drew up his tall form in the rigid manner of David, threw out his arm in the act of keeping time, and commenced what he intended for an imitation of his psalmody. Happily for the success of this delicate adventure, he had to deal with ears but little practiced in the concord of sweet sounds, or the miserable effort would infallibly have been detected. It was necessary to pass within a dangerous proximity of the dark group of the savages, and the voice of the scout grew louder as they drew nigher. When at the nearest point, the Huron who spoke the English thrust out an arm and stopped the supposed singing master.

"The Delaware dog!" he said, leaning forward, and peering through the dim light to catch the expression of the other's features. "Is he afraid? Will the Hurons hear his groans?"

A growl so exceedingly fierce and natural proceeded from the beast that the young Indian released his hold and started aside, as if to assure himself that it was not a veritable bear, and no counterfeit, that was rolling before him. The little knot of Indians drew back in a body, and suffered, as they thought, the conjurer and his inspired assistant to proceed.

The adventurers had got clear of the village, and were now swiftly approaching the shelter of the woods, when a loud and long cry arose from the lodge where Uncas had been confined. The Mohican started on his feet, and shook his shaggy covering, as though the animal he counterfeited was about to make some desperate effort.

"Hold!" said the scout, grasping his friend by the shoulder. "Let them yell again! 'Twas nothing but wonderment."

He had no occasion to delay, for at the next instant a burst of cries filled the outer air and ran along the whole extent of the village. Uncas cast his skin, and stepped forth in his own beautiful proportions. Hawk-eye tapped him lightly on the shoulder, and glided ahead.

"Now let the devils strike our scent!" said the scout, tearing two rifles, with all their attendant accouterments, from beneath a bush, and flourishing "Killdeer" as he handed Uncas his weapon. "Two, at least, will find it to their deaths."

Then throwing their pieces to a low trail, like sportsmen in readiness for their game, they dashed forward, and were soon buried in the somber darkness of the forest.

MAGUA MAKES A SPEECH

The impatience of the savages who lingered about the prison of Uncas, as has been seen, had overcome their dread of the conjurer's breath. They stole cautiously, and with beating hearts, to a crevice, through which the faint light of the fire was glimmering. For several minutes they mistook the form of David for that of their prisoner; but the very accident which Hawk-eye had foreseen occurred. Tired of keeping the extremities of his long person so near together, the singer gradually suffered the lower limbs to extend themselves, until one of his misshapen feet actually came in contact with and shoved aside the embers of the fire. At first the Hurons believed the Delaware had been thus deformed by witchcraft. But when David, unconscious of being observed, turned his head and exposed his simple, mild countenance, in place of the haughty lineaments of their prisoner, it would have exceeded the credulity of even a native to have doubted any longer. They rushed together into the lodge, and laying their hands with but little ceremony on their captive, immediately detected the imposition. Then arose the cry first heard by the fugitives. It was succeeded by the most frantic and angry demonstrations of vengeance. David, however firm in his determination to cover the retreat of his friends, was compelled to believe that his own final hour had come. Deprived of his book and his pipe, he was fain to trust to a memory that rarely failed him on such subjects; and breaking forth in a loud and impassioned strain, he endeavored to smooth his passage into the other world by singing the opening verse of a funeral anthem. The Indians were seasonably reminded of his infirmity, and rushing into the open air, they aroused the village in the manner described.

A native warrior fights as he sleeps, without the protection of anything defensive. The sounds of the alarm were, therefore, hardly uttered, before two hundred men were afoot and ready for the battle or the chase, as either might be required. The escape was soon known; and the whole tribe crowded in a body around the council lodge, impatiently awaiting the instruction of their chiefs. In such a sudden demand on their wisdom, the presence of the cunning Magua could scarcely fail of being needed. His name was mentioned, and all looked round in wonder that he did not appear. Messengers were then dispatched to his lodge, requiring his presence.

ready to devote themselves to the public good, though, at the same time, secretly doubting the nature of the power with which they were about to contend.

The outer apartment of the cavern was silent and gloomy. The woman lay in her usual place and posture, though there were those present who affirmed they had seen her borne to the woods by the supposed "medicine of the white men." Such a direct and palpable contradiction of the tale related by the father, caused all eyes to be turned on him. Chafed by the silent imputation, and inwardly troubled by so unaccountable a circumstance, the chief advanced to the side of the bed, and stooping, cast an incredulous look at the

Huron arose, and shook himself like a lion quitting his lair. Not a word escaped him, though his hand played convulsively with the handle of his knife, while his lowering eye scanned the whole party, as if they sought an object suited to the first burst of his vengeance.

It was happy for Uncas and the scout, and even David, that they were all beyond the reach of his arm at such a moment; for, assuredly, no refinement in cruelty would then have deferred their deaths, in opposition to the promptings of the fierce temper that nearly choked him. Meeting everywhere faces that he knew as friends, the savage grated his teeth together like rasps of iron, and swallowed his pas-

CLAY PIPE

In the meantime, some of the swiftest and most discreet of the young men were ordered to make the circuit of the clearing, under cover of the woods, in order to ascertain that their suspected neighbors, the Delawares, designed no mischief. Women and children ran to and fro; and, in short, the whole encampment exhibited another scene of wild and savage confusion. Gradually, however, these symptoms of disorder diminished; and in a few minutes the oldest and most distinguished chiefs were assembled in the lodge, in grave consultation.

The father of the sick woman stepped forth, and, in a few pithy expressions, related what he knew.

Instead of rushing in a confused and disorderly throng to the cavern, ten of the wisest and firmest among the chiefs were selected to prosecute the investigation. As no time was to be lost, the instant the choice was made the individuals appointed rose in a body and left the place without speaking. On reaching the entrance, the younger men in advance made way for their seniors; and the whole proceeded along the low, dark gallery with the firmness of warriors

features, as if distrusting their reality. His daughter was dead.

The unerring feeling of nature for a moment prevailed, and the old warrior hid his eyes in sorrow. Then recovering his self-possession, he faced his companions, and pointing toward the corpse, he said in the language of his people:

"The wife of my young man has left us! The Great Spirit is angry with his children."

The mournful intelligence was received in solemn silence. After a short pause, one of the elder Indians was about to speak, when a dark-looking object was seen rolling out of an adjoining apartment, into the very center of the room where they stood. Ignorant of the nature of the beings they had to deal with, the whole party drew back a little, and gazed in admiration, until the object fronted the light, and rising on end, exhibited the distorted but still fierce and sullen features of Magua. The discovery was succeeded by a general exclamation of amazement.

As soon, however, as the true situation of the chief was understood, several ready knives appeared, and his limbs and tongue were quickly released. The

sion for want of a victim on whom to vent it. This exhibition of anger was noted by all present; and, from an apprehension of exasperating a temper that was already chafed nearly to madness, several minutes were suffered to pass before another word was uttered. When, however, suitable time had elapsed, the oldest of the party spoke.

"My friend has found an enemy," he said. "Is he nigh, that the Hurons may take revenge?"

"Let the Delaware die!" exclaimed Magua, in a voice of thunder.

Another long and expressive silence was observed, and was broken, as before, with due precaution, by the same individual.

"The Mohican is swift of foot, and leaps far," he said. "But my young men are on his trail."

"Is he gone?" demanded Magua in tones so deep and guttural that they seemed to proceed from his inmost chest.

"An evil spirit has been among us, and the Delaware has blinded our eyes."

"An evil spirit!" repeated the other mockingly. "'Tis the spirit that has taken the lives of so many Hurons. The spirit that slew my young men at the tumbling river; that took their scalps at the healing spring; and who has, now, bound the arms of Le Renard Subtil!"

"Of whom does my friend speak?"

"Of the dog who carries the heart and cunning of a Huron under a pale skin – La Longue Carabine."

The pronunciation of so terrible a name produced the usual effect among his auditors. But when time was given for reflection, and the warriors remembered that their formidable and daring enemy had even been in the bosom of their encampment, working injury, fearful rage took the place of wonder.

Magua, who had, in his turn, found leisure for reflection, now changed his manner and assumed the air of one who knew how to think and act with a dignity worthy of so grave a subject.

"Let us go to my people," he said. "They wait for us."

His companions consented in silence, and the whole of the savage party left the cavern and returned to the council lodge. When they were seated, all eyes turned on Magua, who understood from such an indication that, by common consent, they had devolved the duty of relating what had passed on him. He arose and told his tale, without duplicity or reservation. The whole deception practised by both Duncan and Hawk-eye was, of course, laid naked; and no room was found, even for the most superstitious of the tribe, any longer to affix a doubt on the character of the occurrences. It was but too apparent that they had been insultingly, shamefully, disgracefully, deceived. When he had ended, and resumed his seat, the collected tribe – for his auditors, in substance, included all the fighting men of the party – sat regarding each other like men astonished equally at the audacity and the success of their enemies. The next consideration, however, was the means and opportunities for revenge.

It has been already stated that, in obedience to a policy rarely departed from, the sisters were separated so soon as they reached the Huron village. Magua had early discovered that in retaining the person of Alice, he possessed the most effectual check on Cora. When they parted, therefore, he kept the former within reach of his hand, con-

signing the one he most valued to the keeping of their allies. The arrangement was understood to be merely temporary, and was made as much with a view to flatter his neighbors as in obedience to the invariable rule of Indian policy.

While goaded incessantly by those revengeful impulses that in a savage seldom slumber, the chief was still attentive to his more permanent personal interests. The follies and disloyalty committed in his youth were to be expiated by a long and painful penance ere he could be restored to the full enjoyment of the confidence of his ancient people; and without confidence there could be no authority in an Indian tribe. In this delicate and arduous situation, the crafty native had neglected no means of increasing his influence; and one of the happiest of his expedients had been the success with which he had cultivated the favor of their powerful and dangerous neighbors. The result of his experiment had answered all the expectations of his policy; for the Hurons were in no degree exempt from that governing principle of nature, which induces man to value his gifts precisely in the degree that they are appreciated by others.

But, while he was making this ostensible sacrifice to general considerations, Magua never lost sight of his individual motives. The latter had been frustrated by the unlooked-for events which had placed all his prisoners beyond his control; and he now found himself reduced to the necessity of suing for favors to those whom it had so lately been his policy to oblige.

Magua had now attained one great object of all his cunning and enterprise. The ground he had lost in the favor of his people was completely regained, and he found himself even placed at the head of affairs. He was, in truth, their ruler; and, so long as he could maintain his popularity, no monarch could be more despotic, especially while the tribe continued in a hostile country. Throwing off, therefore, the appearance of consultation, he assumed the grave air of authority necessary to support the dignity of his office.

Runners were dispatched for intelligence in different directions; spies were ordered to approach and feel the encampment of the Delawares; the warriors were dismissed to their lodges,

with an intimation that their services would soon be needed; and the women and children were ordered to retire, with a warning that it was their province to be silent. When these several arrangements were made, Magua passed through the village, stopping here and there to pay a visit where he thought his presence might be flattering to the individual. He confirmed his friends in their confidence, fixed the wavering, and gratified all. Then he sought his own lodge. While others slept, however, he neither knew nor sought repose.

Long before the day dawned, however, warrior after warrior entered the solitary hut of Magua, until they had collected to the number of twenty. Each bore his rifle, and all the other accouterments of war, though the paint was uniformly peaceful. The entrance of these fierce-looking beings was unnoticed; some seating themselves in the shadows of the place, and others standing like motionless statues, until the whole of the designated band was collected.

Then Magua arose and gave the signal to proceed, marching himself in advance. They followed their leader singly, and in that well-known order which has obtained the distinguishing appellation of "Indian file." Unlike other men engaged in the spirit-stirring business of war, they stole from their camp unostentatiously and unobserved, resembling a band of gliding specters more than warriors seeking the bubble reputation by deeds of desperate daring.

Instead of taking the path which led directly toward the camp of the Delawares, Magua led his party for some distance down the windings of the stream, and along the little artificial lake of the beavers. The day began to dawn as they entered the clearing which had been formed by those sagacious and industrious animals. Though Magua, who had resumed his ancient garb, bore the outline of a fox on the dressed skin which formed his robe, there was one chief of his party who carried the beaver as his peculiar symbol, or "totem." There would have been a species of profanity in the omission, had this man passed so powerful a community of his fancied kindred without bestowing some evidence of his regard. Accordingly, he paused, and spoke in words as kind and friendly as if he were addressing more intelligent beings. He called the animals his cousins, and reminded them that his protecting influence was the reason they remained unharmed, while so many avaricious traders were prompting the Indians to take their lives. He promised a continuance of his favors, and admonished them to be grateful. After which, he spoke of the expedition in which he was himself engaged, and intimated, though with sufficient delicacy and circumlocution, the expediency of bestowing on their relative a portion of that wisdom for which they were so renowned.

During the utterance of this extraordinary address, the companions of the speaker were as grave and as attentive to his language as though they were all equally impressed with its propriety. Once or twice black objects were seen rising to the surface of the water, and the Huron expressed pleasure, conceiving that his words were not bestowed in vain. Just as he had ended his address, the head of a large beaver was thrust from the door of a lodge, whose earthen walls had been much injured, and which the party had believed, from its situation, to be uninhabited. Such an extraordinary sign of confidence was received by the orator as a highly favorable omen; and though the animal retreated a little precipitately, he was lavish of his thanks and commendations.

When Magua thought sufficient time had been lost in gratifying the family affection of the warrior, he again made the signal to proceed. As the Indians moved away in a body, and with a step that would have been inaudible to the ears of any common man, the same venerable looking beaver once more ventured his head from its cover. Had any of the Hurons turned to look behind them, they would have seen the animal watching their movements with an interest and sagacity that might easily have been mistaken for reason. Indeed, so very distinct and intelligible were the devices of the quadruped, that even the most experienced observer would have been at a loss to account for its actions, until the moment when the party entered the forest, when the whole would have been explained by seeing the entire animal issue from the lodge, uncasing, by the act, the grave features of Chingachgook from his mask of fur.

THE CUNNING
OF THE HURON

The tribe, or rather half tribe, of Delawares, which has been so often mentioned, and whose present place of encampment was so nigh the temporary village of the Hurons, could assemble about an equal number of warriors with the latter people. Like their neighbors, they had followed Montcalm into the territories of the English crown, and were making heavy and serious inroads on the hunting grounds of the Mohawks; though they had seen fit, with the mysterious reserve so common

among the natives, to withhold their assistance at the moment when it was most required.

On that morning when Magua led his silent party from the settlement of the beavers into the forest, in the manner described, the sun rose upon the Delaware encampment as if it had suddenly burst upon a busy people, actively employed in all the customary avocations of high noon. The women ran from lodge to lodge, some engaged in preparing their morning's meal, a few earnestly bent on seeking the comforts necessary to their habits, but more pausing to exchange hasty and whispered sentences with their friends. The warriors were lounging in groups, musing more than they conversed; and when a few words were uttered, speaking like men who deeply weighed their opinions. And, occasionally, the eyes of a whole group were turned simultaneously toward a large and silent lodge in the center of the village, as if it contained the subject of their common thoughts.

During the existence of this scene, a man suddenly appeared at the furthest extremity of a platform of rock which formed the level of the village. He was without arms, and his paint tended rather to soften than increase the natural sternness of his austere countenance. When in full view of the Delawares he stopped, and made a gesture of amity by throwing his arm upward toward heaven, and then letting it fall impressively on his breast. The inhabitants of the village answered his salute by a low murmur of welcome, and encouraged him to advance by similar indications of friendship. Fortified by these assurances, the dark figure left the brow of the natural rocky terrace, where it had stood a moment, drawn in a strong outline against the blushing morning sky, and moved with dignity into the very center of the huts. As he approached, nothing was audible but the rattling of the light silver ornaments that loaded his arms and neck, and the tinkling of the little bells that fringed his deerskin moccasins. He made, as he advanced, many courteous signs of greeting to the men he passed, neglecting to notice the women, however, like one who deemed their favor, in the present enterprise, of no importance. When he had reached the group in which it was evident, by the haughtiness of their common mien,

1. IROQUOIS EARRING
2. NATIONAL BADGE OF IROQUOIS
3. DESIGN ON SILVER BADGE
4. HEART MOTIF (THE OWL)
5. BROOCH DESIGN

INDIANS SCRATCHED DESIGNS ON SILVER ORNAMENTS GIVEN TO THEM BY EUROPEANS.

INDIAN DESIGNS ON TRADE SILVER

thing of course, than did his hosts, notwithstanding every individual present was perfectly aware that it must be connected with some secret object, and that probably of importance to themselves. When the appetites of the whole were appeased, the squaws removed the trenchers and gourds, and the two parties began to prepare themselves for a subtle trial of their wits.

"Does my prisoner give trouble to my brothers?"

"She is welcome."

"The path between the Hurons and the Delawares is short, and it is open; let her be sent to my squaws, if she gives trouble to my brother."

"She is welcome," returned the chief of the latter nation, still more emphatically.

The baffled Magua continued silent several minutes, apparently indifferent, however, to the repulse he had received in this his opening effort to regain possession of Cora.

"Do my young men leave the Delawares room on the mountains for their hunts?" he at length continued.

"The Lenape are rulers of their own hills," returned the other, a little haughtily.

"It is well. Justice is the master of a redskin! Why should they brighten their tomahawks, and sharpen their knives against each other? Are not the palefaces thicker than the swallows in the season of flowers?"

"Good!" exclaimed two or three of his auditors at the same time.

Magua waited a little, to permit his words to soften the feelings of the Delawares, before he added:

"Have there not been strange moccasins in the woods? Have not my brothers scented the feet of white men?"

"Let my Canada father come," returned the other evasively. "His children are ready to see him."

"When the great chief comes, it is to smoke with the Indians in their wigwams. The Hurons say, too, he is welcome. But the Yengeese have long arms, and legs that never tire! My young men dreamed they had seen the trail of the Yengeese nigh the village of the Delawares!"

"They will not find the Lenape asleep."

"It is well. The warrior whose eye is open can see his enemy," said Magua,

that the principal chiefs were collected, the stranger paused, and then the Delawares saw that the active and erect form that stood before them was that of the well-known Huron chief, Le Renard Subtil.

His reception was grave, silent, and wary. The warriors in front stepped aside, opening the way to their most approved orator by the action; one who spoke all those languages that were cultivated among the northern aborigines.

"The wise Huron is welcome," said the Delaware, in the language of the Maquas. "He is come to eat his succatash, with his brothers of the lakes."

"He is come," repeated Magua, bending his head with the dignity of an eastern prince.

The chief extended his arm, and taking the other by the wrist, they once more exchanged friendly salutations. Then the Delaware invited his guest to enter his own lodge, and share his morning meal. The invitation was accepted; and the two warriors, attended by three or four of the old men, walked calmly away, leaving the rest of the tribe devoured by a desire to understand the reasons of so unusual a visit, and yet not betraying the least impatience by sign or word.

During the short and frugal repast that followed, the conversation was extremely circumspect, and related entirely to the events of the hunt, in which Magua had so lately been engaged. It would have been impossible for the most finished breeding to wear more of the appearance of considering the visit as a once more shifting his ground, when he found himself unable to penetrate the caution of his companion. "I have brought gifts to my brother. His nation would not go on the warpath, because they did not think it well; but their friends have remembered where they lived."

When he had thus announced his liberal intention, the crafty chief arose, and gravely spread his presents before the dazzled eyes of his hosts. They consisted principally of trinkets of little value, plundered from the slaughtered females of William Henry.

This well-judged and politic stroke on the part of Magua was not without instantaneous results. The Delawares lost their gravity in a much more cordial expression; and the host, in particular, after contemplating his own liberal share of the spoil for some moments with peculiar gratification, repeated with strong emphasis the words:

"My brother is a wise chief. He is welcome."

"The Hurons love their friends the Delawares," returned Magua. "Why should they not? They are colored by the same sun, and their just men will hunt in the same grounds after death. The redskins should be friends, and look with open eyes on the white men. Has not my brother scented spies in the woods?"

The Delaware whose name in English signified "Hard Heart," an appellation that the French had translated into "Le Coeur-Dur," forgot that obduracy of purpose which had probably obtained him so significant a title. His countenance grew very sensibly less stern, and he now deigned to answer more directly.

"There have been strange moccasions about my camp. They have been tracked into my lodges."

"Did my brother beat out the dogs?" asked Magua, without advertising in any manner to the former equivocation of the chief.

"It would not do. The stranger is always welcome to the children of the Lenape."

"The stranger, but not the spy."

"Would the Yengeese send their women as spies? Did not the Huron chief say he took women in the battle?"

"He told no lie. The Yengeese have sent out their scouts. They have been in my wigwams, but they found there

no one to say welcome. Then they fled to the Delawares – for, say they, the Delawares are our friends; their minds are turned from their Canada father!"

This insinuation was a home thrust, and one that in a more advanced state of society would have entitled Magua to the reputation of a skillful diplomatist. Accordingly, this alarming annunciation was received, as Magua intended, with manifest disapprobation, if not with alarm.

"Let my father look in my face," said Le Coeur-Dur. "He will see no change. It is true, my young men did not go out on the warpath; they had dreams for not doing so. But they love and venerate the great white chief."

"Will he think so when he hears that his greatest enemy is fed in the camp of his children? When he is told a bloody Yengee smokes at your fire? That the paleface who has slain so many of his friends goes in and out among the Delawares? Go – my great Canada father is not a fool!"

"Where is the Yengee that the Delawares fear?" returned the other. "Who has slain my young men? Who is the mortal enemy of my Great Father!"

"La Longue Carabine."

The Delaware warriors started at the well-known name, betraying by their amazement that they now learned, for the first time, one so famous among the Indian allies of France was within their power.

"What does my brother mean?" demanded Le Coeur-Dur, in a tone that, by its wonder, far exceeded the usual apathy of his race.

"A Huron never lies!" returned Magua coldly, leaning his head against the side of the lodge, and drawing his slight robe across his tawny breast. "Let the Delawares count their prisoners; they will find one whose skin is neither red nor pale."

A long and musing pause succeeded. The chief consulted apart with his companions, and messengers were despatched to collect certain others of the most distinguished men of the tribe.

As warrior after warrior dropped in, they were each made acquainted, in turn, with the important intelligence that Magua had just communicated. The air of surprise, and the usual low, deep, guttural exclamation, were common to them all.

The council of the Delawares was short. When it was ended, a general bustle announced that it was to be immediately succeeded by a solemn and formal assemblage of the nation. As such meetings were rare, and only called on occasions of the last importance, the subtle Huron, who still sat apart, a wily and dark observer of the proceedings, now knew that all his projects must be brought to their final issue. He, therefore, left the lodge, and walked silently forth to the place in front of the encampment whither the warriors were already beginning to collect.

It might have been half an hour before each individual, including even the women and children, was in his place. The delay had been created by the grave preparations that were deemed necessary to so solemn and unusual a conference. But when the sun was seen climbing above the tops of that mountain against whose bosom the Delawares had constructed their encampment, most were seated; and as his bright rays darted from behind the outline of trees that fringed the eminence, they fell upon as grave, as attentive, and as deeply interested a multitude as was probably ever before lighted by his morning beams. Its number somewhat exceeded a thousand souls.

At length, one of those low murmurs that are so apt to disturb a multitude was heard, and the whole nation arose to their feet by a common impulse. At that instant the door of the lodge in question opened, and three men issuing from it, slowly approached the place of consultation. They were all aged, even beyond that period to which the oldest present had reached; but one in the center, who leaned on his companions for support, had numbered an amount of years to which the human race is seldom permitted to attain. His frame, which had once been tall and erect, like the cedar, was now bending under the pressure of more than a century. The elastic, light step of an Indian was gone, and in its place he was compelled to toil his tardy way over the ground, inch by inch. His dark, wrinkled countenance was in singular and wild contrast with the long white locks which floated on his shoulders in such thickness as to announce that generations had probably passed away since they had last been shorn.

The dress of this patriarch – for such, considering his vast age, in conjunction with his affinity and influence with his people, he might very properly be termed – was rich and imposing, though strictly after the simple fashions of the tribe. His robe was of the finest skins, which had been deprived of their fur in order to admit of a hieroglyphical representation of various deeds in arms, done in former ages. His bosom was loaded with medals, some in massive silver, and one or two even in gold, the gifts of various Christian potentates during the long period of his life. He also wore armlets, and cinctures above the ankles, of the latter precious metal. His head, on the whole of which the hair had been permitted to grow, the pursuits of war having so long been abandoned, was encircled by a sort of plated diadem, which, in its turn, bore lesser and more glittering ornaments that sparkled amid the glossy hues of three drooping ostrich feathers, dyed a deep black, in touching contrast to the color of his snow-white locks. His tomahawk was nearly hid in silver, and the handle of his knife shone like a horn of solid gold.

So soon as the first hum of emotion and pleasure which the sudden appearance of this venerated individual created, had a little subsided, the name of "Tamenund" was whispered from mouth to mouth. Magua had often heard the fame of this wise and just Delaware; a reputation that even proceeded so far as to bestow on him the rare gift of holding secret communion with the Great Spirit, and

which has since transmitted his name, with some slight alteration, to the white usurpers of his ancient territory, as the imaginary tutelar saint of a vast empire. The Huron chief, therefore, stepped eagerly out a little from the throng, to a spot whence he might catch a nearer glimpse of the features of the man whose decision was likely to produce so deep an influence on his own fortunes.

The eyes of the old man were closed, as though the organs were wearied with having so long witnessed the selfish workings of the human passions. The color of his skin differed from that of most around him, being richer and darker, the latter hue having been produced by certain delicate and mazy lines of complicated and yet beautiful figures, which had been traced over most of his person by the operation of tattooing.

Nothing could surpass the reverence and affection with which this unexpected visit from one who belonged rather to another world than to this, was received by his people. After a suitable and decent pause, the principal chiefs arose; and approaching the patriarch, they placed his hands reverently on their heads, seeming to entreat a blessing.

After a short delay, a few of the young men, to whom instructions had been whispered by one of the aged attendants of Tamenund, arose, left the crowd, and entered the lodge which has already been noted as the object of so much attention throughout that morning. In a few minutes they reappeared, escorting the individuals who had caused all these solemn preparations toward the seat of judgment. The crowd opened in a lane; and when the party had reentered, it closed in again, forming a large and dense belt of human bodies, arranged in an open circle.

INDIAN BEADED HAT

Cora stood foremost among the prisoners, entwining her arms in those of Alice, in the tenderness of sisterly love. Close at their side stood Heyward, with an interest in both, that, at such a moment of intense uncertainty, scarcely knew a preponderance in favor of her whom he most loved. Hawk-eye had placed himself a little in the rear, with a deference to the superior rank of his companions, that no similarity in the state of their present fortunes could induce him to forget. Uncas was not there.

When perfect silence was again restored, and after the usual long, impressive pause, one of the two aged chiefs who sat at the side of the patriarch arose, and demanded aloud, in very intelligible English:

"Which of my prisoners is La Longue Carabine?"

Neither Duncan nor the scout answered. The former, however, glanced his eyes around the dark and silent assembly, and recoiled a pace, when they fell on the malignant visage of Magua.

"My brother has said that a snake crept into my camp," said the chief to Magua. "Which is he?"

The Huron pointed to the scout.

"Will a wise Delaware believe the barking of a wolf?" exclaimed Duncan, confirmed in the evil intentions of his ancient enemy and wishing to protect his friend. "A dog never lies, but when was a wolf known to speak the truth?"

The eyes of Magua flashed fire; but, suddenly recollecting the necessity of maintaining his presence of mind, he turned away in silent disdain, well assured that the sagacity of the Indians would not fail to extract the real merits of the point in controversy. He was not deceived; for after another short consultation, the wary Delaware turned to him again, and expressed the determination of the chiefs, though in the most considerate language.

"My brother has been called a liar," he said, "and his friends are angry. They will show that he has spoken the truth. Give my prisoners guns, and let them prove which is the man."

Magua affected to consider the expedient, which he well knew proceeded from distrust of himself, as a compliment, and made a gesture of acquiescence, well content that his veracity should be supported by so skillful a marksman as the scout. The weapons were instantly placed in the hands of the friendly opponents, and they were bid to fire, over the heads of the seated multitude, at an earthen vessel, which lay, by accident, on a stump some fifty yards from the place where they stood.

Heyward smiled to himself at the idea of a competition with the scout, though he determined to persevere in the deception until apprised of the real designs of Magua. Raising his rifle with the utmost care, and renewing his aim three several times, he fired. The bullet cut the wood within a few inches of the vessel; and a general exclamation of satisfaction announced that the shot was considered a proof of great skill in the use of the weapon. Even Hawk-eye nodded his head, as if he would say it was better than he had expected. But, instead of manifesting an intention to contend with the successful marksman, he stood leaning on his rifle for more than a minute, like a man who was completely buried in thought. From this reverie he was, however, awakened by one of the young Indians who had furnished the arms, and who now touched his shoulder, saying, in exceedingly broken English:

"Can the paleface beat it?"

"Yes, Huron!" exclaimed the scout, raising the short rifle in his right hand, and shaking it at Magua, with as much apparent ease as if it were a reed. "Yes, Huron, I could strike you now, and no power of earth 'ould prevent the deed!"

The flushed countenance, angry eye, and swelling figure of the scout produced a sensation of secret awe in all that heard him.

"Beat it," repeated the young Delaware at the elbow of the scout.

"Beat what; fool! – what!" – exclaimed Hawk-eye, still flourishing the weapon angrily above his head, though his eye no longer sought the person of Magua.

"If the white man is the warrior he pretends," said the aged chief, "let him strike nigher to the mark."

The scout laughed aloud – a noise that produced the startling effect of an unnatural sound on Heyward – then dropping the piece, heavily, into his extended left hand, it was discharged, apparently by the shock, driving the fragments of the vessel into the air, and scattering them on every side. Almost at

PANTHER
NTAIN LION – (COUGAR)
UMA – (CATAMOUNT.)

It were impossible to say what violent assertion the stubborn Hawk-eye would have next made, in his headlong wish to vindicate his identity, had not the aged Delaware once more interposed.

"The hawk which comes from the clouds can return when he will," he said. "Give them the guns."

This time the scout seized the rifle with avidity; nor had Magua, though he watched the movement of the marksman with jealous eyes, any further cause for apprehension.

"Now let it be proved, in the face of this tribe of Delawares, which is the better man," cried the scout, tapping the butt of his piece with that finger which had pulled so many fatal triggers. "You see the gourd hanging against yonder tree, Major; if you are a marksman fit for the borders, let me see you break its shell!"

Duncan noted the object, and prepared himself to renew the trial. The gourd was one of the usual little vessels used by the Indians, and it was suspended from a dead branch of a small pine by a throng of deerskin, at the full

ERMINE

distance of a hundred yards. Had his life depended on the issue, the aim of Duncan could not have been more deliberate or guarded. He fired; and three or four young Indians, who sprang forward at the report, announced with a shout that the ball was in the tree, a very little on one side of the proper object. The warriors uttered a common ejaculation of pleasure, and then turned their eyes, inquiringly, on the movements of his rival.

"It may do for the Royal Americans!" said Hawk-eye, laughing once more in his own silent, heartfelt manner. "But had my gun often turned so much from the true line, many a marten whose skin is now in a lady's muff would still be in the woods; aye, and many a bloody Mingo, who has departed to his final account, would be acting his deviltries at this very day, atween the provinces. I hope the squaw who owns the gourd has more of them in her wigwam, for this will never hold water again!"

The scout had shook his priming and cocked his piece while speaking; and, as he ended, he threw back a foot, and slowly raised the muzzle from the earth: the motion was steady, uniform, and in one direction. When on a perfect level, it remained for a single moment, without tremor or variation, as though both man and rifle were carved in stone. During

the same instant, the rattling sound of the rifle was heard, as he suffered it to fall, contemptuously, to the earth.

The first impression of so strange a scene was engrossing admiration. Then a low but increasing murmur ran through the multitude and finally swelled into sounds that denoted a lively opposition in the sentiments of the spectators. While some openly testified their satisfaction at so unexampled dexterity, by far the larger portion of the tribe were inclined to believe the success of the shot was the result of accident. Heyward was not slow to confirm an opinion that was so favorable to his own pretensions.

"It was chance!" he exclaimed. "None can shoot without an aim!"

"Chance!" echoed the excited woodsman, who was now stubbornly bent on maintaining his identity at every hazard. "Does yonder lying Huron, too, think it chance? Give him another gun, and place us face to face, without cover or dodge, and let Providence, and our own eyes, decide the matter atween us! I do not make the offer to you, Major; for our blood is of a color, and we serve the same master."

"That the Huron is a liar, is very evident," returned Heyward, coolly. "You have yourself heard him assert you to be La Longue Carabine."

BUFFALO

that stationary instant, it poured forth its contents in a bright, glancing sheet of flame. Again the young Indians bounded forward; but their hurried search and disappointed looks announced that no traces of the bullet were to be seen.

"Go," said the old chief to the scout, in a tone of strong disgust. "Thou art a wolf in the skin of a dog. I will talk to the 'Long Rifle' of the Yengeese."

"Ah! Had I that piece which furnished the name you use, I would obligate myself to cut the thong, and drop the gourd without breaking it!" returned Hawk-eye, perfectly undisturbed by the other's manner. "Fools, if you would find the bullet of a sharpshooter of these woods, you must look *in* the object and not around it!"

The Indian youths instantly compre-

PIGEON

hended his meaning – for this time he spoke in the Delaware tongue – and tearing the gourd from the tree, they held it on high with an exulting shout, displaying a hole in its bottom which had been cut by the bullet, after passing through the usual orifice in the center of its upper side. At this unexpected exhibition, a loud and vehement expression of pleasure burst from the mouth of every warrior present. It decided the question, and effectually established Hawk-eye in the possession of his dangerous reputation. Those curious and admiring eyes which had been turned again on Heyward, were finally directed to the weather-beaten form of the scout, who immediately became the principal object of attention to the simple and unsophisticated beings by

WILD CAT (BOBCAT)

whom he was surrounded. When the sudden and noisy commotion had a little subsided, the aged chief resumed his examination.

"Why did you wish to stop my ears?" he said, addressing Duncan. "Are the Delawares fools, that they could not know the young panther from the cat?"

"They will yet find the Huron a singing bird," said Duncan, endeavoring to adopt the figurative language of the natives.

"It is good. We will know who can shut the ears of men. Brother," added the chief, turning his eyes on Magua, "the Delawares listen."

Thus singled, and directly called on to declare his object, the Huron arose; and advancing with great deliberation and dignity into the very center of the circle, where he stood confronted to the prisoners, he placed himself in an attitude to speak. Before opening his mouth, however, he bent his eyes slowly along the whole living boundary of earnest faces, as if to temper his expressions to the capacities of his audience. On Hawk-eye he cast a glance of respectful enmity; on Duncan, a look of inextinguishable hatred; the shrinking figure of Alice he scarcely deigned to notice; but when his glance met the firm, commanding, and yet lovely form of Cora, his eye lingered a moment, with an expression that it might have been difficult to define. Then, filled with his own dark intentions, he spoke in the language of the Canadas, a tongue that he well knew was comprehended by most of his auditors.

"The Spirit that made men colored them differently," commenced the subtle Huron. "Some are blacker than the sluggish bear. These he said should be slaves; and he ordered them to work forever, like the beaver. You may hear them groan, when the south wind blows, louder than the lowing buffaloes, along the shores of the great salt lake, where the big canoes come and go with them in droves. Some he made with faces paler than the ermine of the forests: and these he ordered to be traders; dogs to their women, and wolves to their slaves. He gave this people the nature of the pigeon; wings that never tire: young, more plentiful than the leaves on the trees, and appetites to devour the earth. He gave them tongues like the false call of the wildcat; hearts like rabbits; the cunning of the hog [but none of the fox], and arms longer than the legs of the moose. With his tongue, he stops the ears of the Indians; his heart teaches him to pay warriors to fight his battles; his cunning tells him how to get together the goods of the earth; and his arms inclose the land from the shores of the salt water to the islands of the great lake. His gluttony makes him sick. God gave him enough, and yet he wants all. Such are the palefaces.

"Some the Great Spirit made with skins brighter and redder than yonder sun," continued Magua, pointing impressively upward to the lurid luminary, which was struggling through the misty atmosphere of the horizon, "and these did he fashion to his own mind. He gave them this island as he had made it, covered with trees, and filled with game. The wind made their clearings; the sun and rains ripened their fruits; and the snows came to tell them to be thankful. What need had they of roads to journey by! They saw through the hills! When the beavers worked, they lay in the shade and looked on. The winds cooled them in summer; in winter, skins kept them warm. If they fought among themselves, it was to prove that they were men. They were brave; they were just; they were happy."

Here the speaker paused, and again looked around him, to discover if his legend had touched the sympathies of his listeners. He met everywhere with eyes riveted on his own, heads erect, and nostrils expanded, as if each individual present felt himself able and willing, singly, to redress the wrongs of his race.

"If the Great Spirit gave different tongues to his red children," he continued, in a low, still melancholy voice, "it was that all animals might understand them. Some he placed among the snows, with their cousin the bear. Some he placed near the setting sun, on the road to the happy hunting grounds. Some on the lands around the great fresh waters; but to his greatest, and most beloved, he gave the sands of the salt lake. Do my brothers know the name of this favored people?"

"It was the Lenape!" exclaimed twenty eager voices, in a breath.

"It was the Lenni Lenape," returned Magua, affecting to bend his head in reverence to their former greatness. "It was the tribes of the Lenape! The sun rose from water that was salt, and set in water that was sweet, and never hid himself from their eyes. But why should I, a Huron of the woods, tell a wise people their own traditions? Why remind them of their injuries; their ancient greatness; their deeds; their glory; their happiness – their losses; their defeats; their misery? Is there not one among them who has seen it all, and who knows it to be true? I have done. My tongue is still, for my heart is of lead. I listen."

As the voice of the speaker suddenly ceased, every face and all eyes turned, by a common movement, toward the venerable Tamenund. He made an effort to rise, and being upheld by his supporters, he gained his feet, in a posture commanding by its dignity, while he tottered with weakness.

"Who calls upon the children of the Lenape!" he said, in a deep, guttural voice, that was rendered awfully audible by the breathless silence of the multitude. "Who speaks of things gone! Does not the egg become a worm – the worm a fly, and perish! Why tell the Delawares of good that is past? Better thank the Manitto for that which remains."

"It is a Wyandot," said Magua, stepping nigher to the rude platform on which the other stood; "a friend of Tamenund."

"A friend!" repeated the sage, on whose brow a dark frown settled, imparting a portion of that severity which had rendered his eye so terrible in middle age. "Are the Mingoes rulers of the earth? What brings a Huron here?"

"Justice. His prisoners are with his brothers, and he comes for his own."

Tamenund turned his head toward one of his supporters, and listened to the short explanation the man gave. Then facing the applicant, he regarded him a moment with deep attention; after

HARE

which he said, in a low and reluctant voice:

"Justice is the law of the great Manitto. My children, give the stranger food. Then, Huron, take thine own and depart."

Magua cast a look of triumph around the whole assembly before he proceeded to the execution of his purpose. Perceiving that the men were unable to offer any resistance, he turned his looks on her he valued most. Cora met his gaze with an eye so calm and firm that his resolution wavered. Then recollecting his former artifice, he raised Alice from the arms of the warrior against whom she leaned, and beckoning Heyward to follow, he motioned for the encircling crowd to open. But Cora, instead of obeying the impulse he had expected, rushed to the feet of the patriarch, and raising her voice, exclaimed aloud:

"Just and venerable Delaware, on thy wisdom and power we lean for mercy! Be deaf to yonder artful and remorseless monster, who poisons thy ears with

FOX

RED HEADED WOODPPECKER

THE VERDICT OF THE DELAWARES

The old man looked down upon her from his elevated stand with a benignant smile on his wasted countenance, and then casting his eyes slowly over the whole assemblage, he answered:

"Of a nation."

"For myself I ask nothing. Like thee and thine, venerable chief," she continued, pressing her hands convulsively on her heart, and suffering her head to droop until her burning cheeks were nearly concealed in the maze of dark glossy tresses that fell in disorder upon her shoulders, "the curse of my ancestors has fallen heavily on their child. But yonder is one who has never known the weight of Heaven's displeasure until now. She is the daughter of an old and failing man, whose days are near their close. She has many, very many, to love her and delight in her; and she is too good, much too precious, to become the victim of that villain. There is yet one of thine own people who has not been brought before thee; before thou lettest the Huron depart in triumph, hear him speak."

Observing Tamenund to look about him doubtingly, one of his companions said:

"It is a snake – a redskin in the pay of the Yengeese. We keep him for the torture."

"Let him come," returned the sage.

Then Tamenund once more sank into his seat, and a silence so deep prevailed while the young men prepared to obey his simple mandate, that the leaves which fluttered in the draught of the light morning air were distinctly heard rustling in the surrounding forest.

falsehoods to feed his thirst for blood. Thou that hast lived long, and that hast seen the evil of the world, should know how to temper its calamities to the miserable."

The eyes of the old man opened heavily, and he once more looked upward at the multitude.

"What art thou?"

"A woman. One of a hated race, if thou wilt – a Yengee. But one who has never harmed thee, and who cannot harm thy people, if she would; who asks for succor."

"Tell me, my children," continued the patriarch, hoarsely, motioning to those around him, though his eyes still dwelt upon the kneeling form of Cora, "where have the Delawares 'camped?"

"In the mountains of the Iroquois, beyond the clear springs of the Horican."

"Many parching summers are come and gone," continued the sage, "since I drank of the waters of my own river. The children of Minquon are the justest white men; but they were thirsty, and they took it to themselves. Do they follow us so far?"

"We follow none; we covet nothing," answered Cora. "Captives against our wills, have we been brought amongst you; and we ask but permission to depart to our own in peace. Art thou not Tamenund – the father – the judge – I had almost said, the prophet – of this people?"

"I am Tamenund of many days."

"Tell me, is Tamenund a father?"

BLUE JAY

The silence continued unbroken by human sounds for many anxious minutes. Then the waving multitude opened and shut again, and Uncas stood in the living circle. All those eyes which had been curiously studying the lineaments of the sage, as the source of their own intelligence, turned on the instant, and were now bent in secret admiration on the erect, agile, and faultless person of the captive. But neither the presence in which he found himself, nor the exclusive attention that he attracted, in any manner disturbed the self-possession of the young Mohican. He cast a deliberate and observing look on every side of him, meeting the settled expression of hostility that lowered in the visages of the chiefs with the same calmness as the curious gaze of the attentive children. But when, last in his haughty scrutiny, the person of Tamenund came under his glance, his eye became fixed, as though all other objects were already forgotten. Then advancing with a slow and noiseless step up the area, he placed himself immediately before the footstool of the sage. Here he stood unnoted, though keenly observant himself, until one of the chiefs apprised the latter of his presence.

"With what tongue does the prisoner speak to the Manitto?" demanded the patriarch, without unclosing his eyes.

"Like his fathers," Uncas replied; "with the tongue of a Delaware."

At this sudden and unexpected annunciation, a low, fierce yell ran through the multitude that might not inaptly be compared to the growl of the lion as his choler is first awakened – a fearful omen of the weight of his future anger. The effect was equally strong on the sage, though differently exhibited. He passed a hand before his eyes, as if to exclude the least evidence of so shameful a spectacle, while he repeated, in his low, guttural tones, the words he had just heard.

"A Delaware! I have lived to see the tribes of the Lenape driven from their council fires, and scattered, like broken herds of deer, among the hills of the Iroquois! I have seen the hatchets of a strange people sweep woods from the valleys that the winds of Heaven had spared! The beasts that run on the mountains and the birds that fly above the trees have I seen living in the wigwams of men; but never before have I found a Delaware so base as to creep, like a poisonous serpent, into the camps of his nation."

"Delaware!" resumed the sage, "little art thou worthy of thy name. My people have not seen a bright sun in many winters; and the warrior who deserts his tribe when hid in clouds is doubly a traitor. The law of the Manitto is just. It is so; while the rivers run and the mountains stand, while the blossoms come and go on the trees, it must be so. He is thine, my children; deal justly by him."

Throughout these trying moments, Uncas had alone preserved his serenity. He looked on the preparations with a steady eye, and when the tormenters came to seize him, he met them with a firm and upright attitude. One among them, if possible, more fierce and savage than his fellows, seized the hunting shirt of the young warrior, and at a single effort tore it from his body. Then, with a yell of frantic pleasure, he leaped toward his unresisting victim, and prepared to lead him to the stake. But at

that moment, when he appeared most a stranger to the feelings of humanity, the purpose of the savage was arrested as suddenly as if a super-natural agency had interposed in the behalf of Uncas. The eyeballs of the Delaware seemed to start from their sockets; his mouth opened, and his whole form became frozen in an attitude of amazement. Raising his hand with a slow and regulated motion, he pointed with a finger to the bosom of the captive. His companions crowded about him in wonder, and every eye was, like his own, fastened intently on the figure of a small tortoise, beautifully tattooed on the breast of the prisoner, in a bright blue tint.

For a single instant Uncas enjoyed his triumph, smiling calmly on the scene. Then motioning the crowd away with a high and haughty sweep of his arm, he advanced in front of the nation with the air of a king, and spoke in a voice louder than the murmur of admiration that ran through the multitude.

"Men of the Lenni Lenape!" he said, "my race upholds the earth! Your feeble tribe stands on my shell! What fire that a Delaware can light would burn the child of my fathers," he added, pointing proudly to the simple blazonry on his skin; "the blood that came from such a stock would smother your flames! My race is the grandfather of nations!"

"Who art thou?" demanded Tamenund, rising at the startling tones he heard more than at any meaning conveyed by the language of the prisoner.

"Uncas, the son of Chingachgook," answered the captive modestly, turning from the nation, and bending his head in reverence to the other's character and years; "a son of the great Unamis."

"The hour of Tamenund is nigh!" exclaimed the sage. "The day is come, at last, to the night! I thank the Manitto, that one is here to fill my place at the council fire. Uncas, the child of Uncas, is found! Let the eyes of a dying eagle gaze on the rising sun."

The calm and deep silence which succeeded these words sufficiently announced the awful reverence with which his people received the communication of the patriarch. None dared to answer, though all listened in breathless expectation of what might follow. Uncas, however, looking in his face with the fondness and veneration of a favored

child, presumed on his own high and acknowledged rank, to reply.

"Four warriors of his race have lived, and died," he said, "since the friend of Tamenund led his people in battle. The blood of the turtle has been in many chiefs, but all have gone back into the earth from whence they came except Chingachgook and his son."

The men of the Lenape listened to his words with all the respect that superstition could lend, finding a secret charm even in the figurative language with which the young Sagamore imparted his ideas. Uncas himself watched the effect of his brief explanation with intelligent eyes, and gradually dropped the air of authority he had assumed as he perceived that his auditors were content. Then permitting his looks to wander over the silent throng that crowded around the elevated seat of Tamenund, he first perceived Hawk-eye in his bonds. Stepping eagerly from his stand, he made way for himself to the side of his friend; and cutting his thongs with a quick and angry stroke of his own knife, he motioned to the crowd to divide. The Indians silently obeyed, and once more they stood ranged in their circle, as before his appearance among them. Uncas took the scout by the hand, and led him to the feet of the patriarch.

"Father," he said, "look at this paleface; a just man, and the friend of the Delawares."

"Is he a son of Miquon?"

"Not so; a warrior known to the Yengeese, and feared by the Maquas."

"What name has he gained by his deeds?"

"We call him Hawk-eye," Uncas replied, using the Delaware phrase, "for his sight never fails. The Mingoes know him better by the death he gives their warriors: with them he is The Long Rifle."

"La Longue Carabine!" exclaimed Tamenund, opening his eyes, and regarding the scout sternly. "My son has not done well to call him friend."

"I call him so who proves himself such," returned the young chief, with great calmness, but with a steady mien. "If Uncas is welcome among the Delawares, then is Hawk-eye with his friends."

"The paleface has slain my young men; his name is great for the blows he has struck the Lenape."

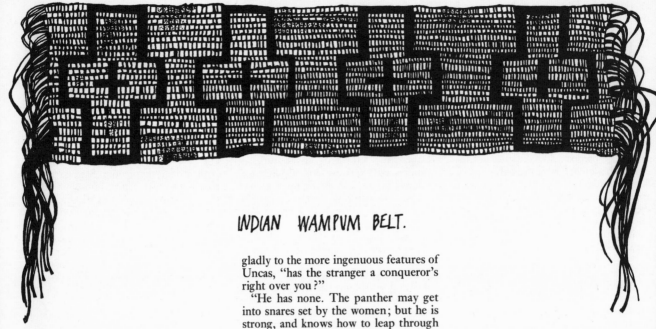

INDIAN WAMPUM BELT.

"If a Mingo has whispered that much in the ear of the Delaware, he has only shown that he is a singing bird," said the scout, who now believed that it was time to vindicate himself from such offensive charges, and who spoke in the tongue of the man he addressed, modifying his Indian figures, however, with his own peculiar notions. "That I have slain the Maquas I am not the man to deny, even at their own council fires; but that, knowingly, my hand has ever harmed a Delaware, is opposed to the reason of my gifts, which is friendly to them, and all that belongs to their nation."

A low exclamation of applause passed among the warriors, who exchanged looks with each other like men that first began to perceive their error.

"Where is the Huron?" demanded Tamenund. "Has he stopped my ears?"

Magua, whose feelings during that scene in which Uncas had triumphed may be much better imagined than described, answered to the call by stepping boldly in front of the patriarch.

"The just Tamenund," he said, "will not keep what a Huron has lent."

"Tell me, son of my brother," returned the sage, avoiding the dark countenance of Le Subtil, and turning gladly to the more ingenuous features of Uncas, "has the stranger a conqueror's right over you?"

"He has none. The panther may get into snares set by the women; but he is strong, and knows how to leap through them."

"La Longue Carabine?"

"Laughs at the Mingoes. Go, Huron, ask your squaws the color of a bear."

"The stranger and the white maiden that came into my camp together?"

"Should journey on an open path."

"And the woman that Huron left with my warriors?"

Uncas made no reply.

"And the woman that the Mingo has brought into my camp," repeated Tamenund, gravely.

"She is mine," cried Magua, shaking his hand in triumph at Uncas. "Mohican, you know that she is mine."

"My son is silent," said Tamenund, endeavoring to read the expression of the face that the youth turned from him in sorrow.

"It is so," was the low answer.

A short and impressive pause succeeded, during which it was very apparent with what reluctance the multitude admitted the justice of the Mingo's claim. At length the sage, on whom alone the decision depended, said, in a firm voice:

"Girl, what wouldst thou? A great warrior takes thee to wife. Go; thy race will not end."

"Better a thousand times it should," exclaimed the horror-struck Cora, "than meet with such a degradation!"

"Huron, her mind is in the tents of her fathers. An unwilling maiden makes an unhappy wigwam."

"She speaks with the tongue of her people," returned Magua, regarding his victim with a look of bitter irony. "She is of a race of traders, and will bargain for a bright look. Let Tamenund speak the words."

"Take you the wampum, and our love."

"Nothing hence but what Magua brought hither."

"Then depart with thine own. The Great Manitto forbids that a Delaware should be unjust."

Magua advanced, and seized his captive strongly by the arm; the Delawares fell back, in silence; and Cora, as if conscious that remonstrance would be useless, prepared to submit to her fate without resistance.

"Aye, go," cried Duncan, placing Alice in the arms of an Indian girl. "Go, Magua, go. These Delawares have their laws, which forbid them to detain you; but I – I have no such obligation. Go, malignant monster – why do you delay?"

It would be difficult to describe the expression with which Magua listened to this threat to follow. There was at first a fierce and manifest display of joy, and then it was instantly subdued in a look of cunning coldness.

"The woods are open," he was content with answering. "The Open Hand can come."

"Hold," cried Hawk-eye, seizing Duncan by the arm and detaining him by violence. "You know not the craft of the imp. He would lead you to an ambushment, and your death – "

"Huron," interrupted Uncas, who, submissive to the stern customs of his people, had been an attentive and grave listener to all that passed. "Huron, the justice of the Delawares comes from the Manitto. Look at the sun. He is now in the upper branches of the hemlock. Your path is short and open. When he is seen above the trees, there will be men on your trail."

"I hear a crow!" exclaimed Magua, with a taunting laugh. "Go," he added, shaking his hand at the crowd, which had slowly opened to admit his passage. "Where are the petticoats of the Delawares! Let them send their arrows and their guns to the Wyandots; they shall have venison to eat, and corn to hoe. Dogs, rabbits, thieves – I spit on you."

His parting gibes were listened to in a dead, boding silence, and, with these biting words in his mouth, the triumphant Magua passed unmolested into the forest, followed by his passive captive and protected by the inviolable laws of Indian hospitality.

UNCAS IN CHARGE

RED PINE (PINUS RESINOSA)

So long as their enemy and his victim continued in sight, the multitude remained motionless as beings charmed to the place by some power that was friendly to the Huron; but the instant he disappeared, it became tossed and agitated by fierce and powerful passion. Uncas maintained his elevated stand, keeping his eyes on the form of Cora until the colors of her dress were blended with the foliage of the forest; when he descended, and moving silently through the throng, he disappeared in that lodge from which he had so recently issued. A few of the graver and more attentive warriors, who caught the gleams of anger that shot from the eyes of the young chief in passing, followed him to the place he had selected for his meditations. After which, Tamenund and Alice were removed, and the women and children were ordered to disperse. During the momentous hour that succeeded, the encampment resembled a hive of troubled bees, who only awaited the appearance and example of their leader to take some distant and momentous flight.

A young warrior at length issued from the lodge of Uncas; and moving deliberately, with a sort of grave march, toward a dwarf pine that grew in the crevices of the rocky terrace, he tore the bark from its body and then returned whence he came without speaking. He was soon followed by another, who stripped the sapling of its branches, leaving it a naked and blazed trunk. A third colored the post with stripes of a dark red paint; all which indications of a hostile design in the leaders of the nation were received by the men without in a gloomy and ominous silence. Finally, the Mohican himself reappeared, divested of all his attire except his girdle and leggings, and with one half of his fine features hid under a cloud of threatening black.

Just then Uncas struck his tomahawk deep into the post, and raised his voice in a shout, which might be termed his own battle cry. The act announced that he had assumed the chief authority in the intended expedition.

The instant Uncas had struck the blow, he moved out of the circle and cast his eyes up to the sun, which was just gaining the point when the truce with Magua was to end. The fact was soon announced by a significant gesture, accompanied by a corresponding cry; and the whole of the excited multitude abandoned their mimic warfare, with shrill yells of pleasure, to prepare for the more hazardous experiment of the reality.

The whole face of the encampment was instantly changed. The warriors, who were already armed and painted, became as still as if they were incapable of any uncommon burst of emotion. On the other hand, the women broke out of the lodges, with the songs of joy and those of lamentation so strangely mingled that it might have been difficult to have said which passion preponderated. None, however, were idle. Some bore their choicest articles, others their young, and some their aged and infirm, into the forest, which spread itself like a verdant carpet of bright green against the side of the mountain. Thither Tamenund also retired, with calm composure, after a short and touching interview with Uncas; from whom the sage separated with the reluctance that a parent would quit a long lost and just recovered child. In the meantime, Duncan saw Alice to a place of safety, and then sought the scout, with a countenance that denoted how eagerly he also panted for the approaching contest.

But Hawk-eye was too much accustomed to the war song and the enlistments of the natives to betray any interest in the passing scene. He merely cast an occasional look at the number and quality of the warriors, who, from time to time, signified their readiness to accompany Uncas to the field. In this particular he was soon satisfied; for, as has been already seen, the power of the young chief quickly embraced every fighting man in the nation. After this material point was so satisfactorily decided, he dispatched an Indian boy in quest of "Kill-deer" and the rifle of Uncas, to the place where they had deposited the weapons on approaching the camp of the Delawares; a measure of double policy, inasmuch as it protected the arms from their own fate, if detained as prisoners, and gave them the advantage of appearing among the strangers rather as sufferers than as men provided with the means of defense.

The calm but still impatient Uncas now collected his chiefs, and divided his power. He presented Hawk-eye as a warrior, often tried, and always found deserving of confidence. When he found his friend met with a favorable reception, he bestowed on him the command of twenty men, like himself, active, skillful, and resolute. He gave the Delawares to understand the rank of Heyward among the troops of the Yengeese, and then tendered to him a trust of equal authority. But Duncan declined the charge, professing his readiness to serve as a volunteer by the side of the scout. After this disposition, the young Mohican appointed various native chiefs to fill the different situations of responsibility, and the time pressing, he gave forth the word to march. He was cheerfully but silently obeyed by more than two hundred men.

Their entrance into the forest was perfectly unmolested; nor did they encounter any living objects that could either give the alarm or furnish the intelligence they needed, until they came upon the lairs of their own scouts. Here a halt was ordered, and the chiefs were assembled to hold a "whispering council." At this meeting divers plans of operation were suggested, though none of a character to meet the wishes of their ardent leader. Had Uncas followed the promptings of his own inclinations, he would have led his followers to the charge without a moment's delay, and put the conflict to the hazard of an instant issue; but such a course would have been in opposition to all the received practices and opinions of his countrymen. He was, therefore, fain to adopt a caution that in the present temper of his mind he execrated, and to listen to advice at which his fiery spirit chafed, under the vivid recollection of Cora's danger and Magua's insolence.

After an unsatisfactory conference of many minutes, a solitary individual was seen advancing from the side of the enemy, with such apparent haste as to induce the belief he might be a messenger charged with pacific overtures. When within a hundred yards, however, of the cover behind which the Delaware council had assembled, the stranger hesitated, appeared uncertain what course to take, and finally halted. All eyes were now turned on Uncas, as if seeking directions how to proceed.

"Hawk-eye," said the young chief, in a low voice, "he must never speak to the Hurons again."

"His time has come," said the laconic scout, thrusting the long barrel of his rifle through the leaves, and taking his deliberate and fatal aim. But, instead of pulling the trigger, he lowered the muzzle again, and indulged himself in a fit of his peculiar mirth. "I took the imp for a Mingo, as I'm a miserable sinner!" he said. "But when my eye ranged along his ribs for a place to get the bullet in – would you think it, Uncas – I saw the musicianer's blower! And so, after all, it is the man they call Gamut, whose death can profit no one, and whose life, if his tongue can do anything but sing, may be made serviceable to our own ends. If sounds have not lost their virtue, I'll soon have a discourse with the honest fellow, and that in a voice he'll find more agreeable than the speech of 'Kill-deer'."

So saying, Hawk-eye laid aside his rifle; and crawling through the bushes until within hearing of David, he attempted to repeat the musical effort which had conducted himself, with so much safety and éclat, through the Huron encampment.

"I wonder what the Hurons will think of that!" said the scout, laughing, as he took his companion by the arm and urged him toward the rear.

David gazed about him at the fierce and wild-looking chiefs, in mute wonder; but assured by the presence of faces that he knew, he soon rallied his faculties so far as to make an intelligent reply.

"The heathen are abroad in goodly numbers," said David; "and, I fear, with evil intent. There has been much howling and ungodly revelry, together with such sounds as it is profanity to utter, in their habitations within the past hour; so much so, in truth, that I have fled to the Delawares in search of peace."

"Your ears might not have profited much by the exchange, had you been quicker of foot," returned the scout a little drily. "But let that be as it may; where are the Hurons?"

"They lie hid in the forest, between this spot and their village, in such force that prudence would teach you instantly to return."

Uncas cast a glance along the range of trees which concealed his own band and mentioned the name of –

"Magua?"

"Is among them. He brought in the maiden that had sojourned with the Delawares, and leaving her in the cave, has put himself, like a raging wolf, at the head of his savages. I know not what has troubled his spirit so greatly!"

"He has left her, you say, in the cave!" interrupted Heyward. "'Tis well that we know its situation! May not something be done for her instant relief?"

Uncas looked earnestly at the scout before he asked:

"What says Hawk-eye?"

"Give me my twenty rifles, and I will turn to the right, along the stream; and passing by the huts of the beaver, will join the Sagamore and the colonel. You shall then hear the whoop from that quarter; with this wind one may easily send it a mile. Then, Uncas, do you drive in their front; when they come within range of our pieces, we will give them a blow that, I pledge the good name of an old frontiersman, shall make their line bend like an ashen bow. After which, we will carry their village and take the woman from the cave; when the affair may be finished with the tribe, according to a white man's battle, by a blow and a victory; or, in the Indian fashion, with dodge and cover. There may be no great learning, Major, in this plan, but with courage and patience it can all be done."

"I like it much," cried Duncan, who saw that the release of Cora was the primary object in the mind of the scout. "I like it much. Let it be instantly attempted."

After a short conference, the plan was matured and rendered more intelligible to the several parties; the different signals were appointed, and the chiefs separated, each to his allotted station.

THE FINAL BATTLE

During the time Uncas was making this disposition of his forces, the woods were as still, and, with the exception of those who had met in council, apparently as much untenanted as when they came fresh from the hands of their Almighty Creator. The eye could range in every direction through the long and shadowed vistas of the trees; but nowhere was any object to be seen that did not properly belong to the peaceful and slumbering scenery. Here and there a bird was heard fluttering among the branches of the beeches, and occasionally a squirrel dropped a nut, drawing the startled looks of the party, for a moment, to the place; but the instant the casual interruption ceased, the passing air was heard murmuring above their heads, along that verdant and undulating surface of forest which spread itself unbroken, unless by stream or lake, over such a vast region of country. Across the tract of wilderness which lay between the Delawares and the village of their enemies, it seemed as if the foot of man had never trodden, so breathing and deep was the silence in which it lay. But Hawk-eye, whose duty led him foremost in the adventure, knew the character of those with whom he was about to contend too well to trust the treacherous quiet.

When he saw his little band collected, the scout threw "Kill-deer" into the hollow of his arm, and making a silent signal that he would be followed, he led them many rods toward the rear, into the bed of a little brook which they had crossed in advancing. Here he halted, and after waiting for the whole of his grave and attentive warriors to close about him, he spoke in Delaware, demanding:

"Do any of my young men know whither this run will lead us?"

A Delaware stretched forth a hand, with the two fingers separated, and indicating the manner in which they were joined at the root, he answered:

"Before the sun could go his own length, the little water will be in the big." Then he added, pointing in the direction of the place he mentioned, "The two make enough for the beavers."

"I thought as much," returned the scout, glancing his eye upward at the opening in the treetops, "from the course it takes, and the bearings of the mountains. Men, we will keep within the cover of its banks till we scent the Hurons."

The scout had stood, while making his observations, sheltered by a brake, and his companions still lay in the bed of the ravine through which the smaller stream debouched; but on hearing his low though intelligible signal, the whole party stole up the bank, like so many dark specters, and silently arranged themselves around him. Pointing in the direction he wished to proceed, Hawk-eye advanced, the band breaking off in single files, and following so accurately in his footsteps as to leave it, if we except Heyward and David, the trail of but a single man.

The party was, however, scarcely uncovered before a volley from a dozen rifles was heard in their rear; and a Delaware leaping high into the air, like a wounded deer, fell at his whole length, perfectly dead.

"Ah! I feared some devilry like this!" exclaimed the scout, in English; adding, with the quickness of thought, in his adopted tongue, "to cover, men, and charge!"

The band dispersed at the word, and before Heyward had well recovered from his surprise, he found himself standing alone with David. Luckily, the Hurons had already fallen back, and he was safe from their fire. But this state of things was evidently to be of short continuance; for the scout set the example of pressing on their retreat, by discharging his rifle and darting from tree to tree, as his enemy slowly yielded ground.

It would seem that the assault had been made by a very small party of the Hurons, which, however, continued to increase in numbers as it retired on its friends, until the return fire was very nearly, if not quite, equal to that maintained by the advancing Delawares. Heyward threw himself among the combatants, and imitating the necessary caution of his companions, he made quick discharges with his own rifle. The contest now grew warm and stationary. Few were injured, as both parties kept their bodies as much protected as possible by the trees; never, indeed, exposing any part of their persons except in the act of taking aim. But the chances were gradually growing unfavorable to Hawk-eye and his band. The quick-

sighted scout perceived his danger, without knowing how to remedy it. He saw it was more dangerous to retreat than to maintain his ground; while he found his enemy throwing out men on his flank, which rendered the task of keeping themselves covered so very difficult to the Delawares as nearly to silence their fire. At this embarrassing moment, when they began to think the whole of the hostile tribe was gradually encircling them, they heard the yell of combatants and the rattling of arms echoing under the arches of the wood, at the place where Uncas was posted; a bottom which, in a manner, lay beneath the ground on which Hawk-eye and his party were contending.

The effects of this attack were instantaneous, and to the scout and his friends greatly relieving. It would seem that, while his own surprise had been anticipated and had consequently failed, the enemy, in their turn, having been deceived in its object and in his numbers, had left too small a force to resist the impetuous onset of the young Mohican. This fact was doubly apparent by the rapid manner in which the battle in the forest rolled upward toward the village, and by an instant falling off in the number of their assailants, who rushed to assist in maintaining the front, and, as it now proved to be, the principal point of defense.

In this crisis, Hawk-eye found means to get behind the same tree as that which served for a cover to Heyward; most of his own combatants being within call, a little on his right, where they main-

tained rapid though fruitless discharges on their sheltered enemies.

"You are a young man, Major," said the scout, dropping the butt of "Kill-deer" to the earth and leaning on the barrel, a little fatigued with his previous industry; "and it may be your gift to lead armies, at some future day, ag'in these imps, the Mingoes. You may here see the philosophy of an Indian fight. It consists, mainly, in a ready hand, a quick eye, and a good cover. Now, if you had a company of the Royal Americans here, in what manner would you set them to work in this business?"

"The bayonet would make a road."

"Aye, there is white reason in what you say; but a man must ask himself, in this wilderness, how many lives he can spare. No – horse," continued the scout, shaking his head, like one who mused, "horse, I am ashamed to say, must sooner or later, decide these scrimmages. The brutes are better than men, and to horse must we come at last. Put a shodden hoof on the moccasin of a redskin; and if his rifle be once emptied he will never stop to load it again."

"This is a subject that might better be discussed another time," returned Heyward. "Shall we charge?"

"I see no contradiction to the gifts of any man in passing his breathing spells in useful reflections," the scout replied. "As to a rush I little relish such a measure; for a scalp or two must be thrown away in the attempt. And yet," he added, bending his head aside to catch the sounds of the distant combat, "if we are to be of use to Uncas, these knaves in our front must be got rid of!"

SIDE AND TOP VIEW OF A BROWN BESS BAYONET

Then turning, with a prompt and decided air, he called aloud to his Indians in their own language. Without stopping to breathe, the Delawares leaped in long bounds toward the wood, like so many panthers springing upon their prey. Hawk-eye was in front, brandishing his terrible rifle and animating his followers by his example. The Delawares broke into the cover with the ferocity of their natures, and swept away every trace of resistance by the fury of the onset.

The combat endured only for an instant, hand to hand, and then the assailed yielded ground rapidly, until they reached the opposite margin of the thicket where they clung to the cover with the sort of obstinacy that is so often witnessed in hunted brutes. At this critical moment, when the success of the struggle was again becoming doubtful, the crack of a rifle was heard behind the Hurons, and a bullet came whizzing from among some beaver lodges which were situated in the clearing, in their rear, and was followed by the fierce and appalling yell of the war whoop.

"There speaks the Sagamore!" shouted Hawk-eye, answering the cry with his own stentorian voice. "We have them now in face and back!"

The effect on the Hurons was instantaneous. Discouraged by an assault from a quarter that left them no opportunity for cover, their warriors uttered a common yell of disappointment and, breaking off in a body, they spread themselves across the opening, heedless of every consideration but flight. Many fell, in making the experiment, under the bullets and the blows of the pursuing Delawares.

The warriors, who had breathed themselves freely in the preceding struggle, were now posted on a bit of level ground, sprinkled with trees in sufficient numbers to conceal them. The land fell away rather precipitately in front, and beneath their eyes stretched for several miles a narrow, dark, and wooded vale. It was through this dense and dark forest that Uncas was still contending with the main body of the Hurons.

The Mohican and his friends advanced to the brow of the hill, and listened with practiced ears to the sounds of the combat. A few birds hovered over the leafy bosom of the valley, frightened from their secluded nests; and here and there a light vapory cloud, which seemed already blending with the atmosphere, arose above the trees and indicated some spot where the struggle had been fierce and stationary.

"The fight is coming up the ascent," said Duncan, pointing in the direction of a new explosion of firearms. "We are too much in the center of their line to be effective."

"They will incline into the hollow, where the cover is thicker," said the scout, "and that will leave us well on their flank. Go, Sagamore; you will hardly be in time to give the whoop, and lead on the young men. I will fight this scrimmage with warriors of my own color. You know me, Mohican; not a Huron of them all shall cross the swell, into your rear, without the notice of 'Kill-deer'."

It was not long before the reports of the rifles began to lose the echoes of the woods, and to sound like weapons discharged in the open air. Then a warrior appeared, here and there, driven to the skirts of the forest, and rallying as he entered the clearing, as at the place where the final stand was to be made. These were soon joined by others, until a long line of swarthy figures was to be seen clinging to the cover with the obstinacy of desperation. Heyward began to grow impatient, and turned his eyes anxiously in the direction of Chingachgook. The chief was seated on a rock, with nothing visible but his calm visage, considering the spectacle with an eye as deliberate as if he were posted there merely to view the struggle.

"The time is come for the Delaware to strike!" said Duncan.

"Not so, not so," returned the scout. "When he scents his friends, he will let them know that he is here. See, see; the knaves are getting in that clump of pines, like bees settling after their flight. By the Lord, a squaw might put a bullet into the center of such a knot of dark skins!"

At that instant the whoop was given, and a dozen Hurons fell by a discharge from Chingachgook and his band. The shout that followed was answered by a single war cry from the forest, and a yell passed through the air that sounded as if a thousand throats were united in a common effort. The Hurons staggered, deserting the center of their line, and Uncas issued from the forest through the opening they left, at the head of a hundred warriors.

Waving his hands right and left, the young chief pointed out the enemy to his followers, who separated in pursuit. The war now divided, both wings of the broken Hurons seeking protection in the woods again, hotly pressed by the victorious warriors of the Lenape. A minute might have passed, but the sounds were already receding in different directions, and gradually losing their distinctness beneath the echoing arches of the woods. One little knot of Hurons, however, had disdained to seek a cover, and were retiring, like lions at bay, slowly and sullenly up the acclivity which Chingachgook and his band had just deserted, to mingle more closely in the fray. Magua was conspicuous in this party, both by his fierce and savage mien, and by the air of haughty authority he yet maintained.

In his eagerness to expedite the pursuit, Uncas had left himself nearly alone; but the moment his eye caught the figure of Le Subtil, every other consideration was forgotten. Raising his cry of battle, which recalled some six or seven warriors, and reckless of the disparity of their numbers, he rushed upon his enemy. Le Renard, who watched the movement, paused to receive him with secret joy. But at the moment when he thought the rashness of his impetuous young assailant had left him at his mercy, another shout was given, and La Longue Carabine was seen rushing to the rescue, attended by all his white associates. The Huron instantly turned, and commenced a rapid retreat up the ascent.

But Uncas, who had vainly sought him in the mêlée, bounded forward in pursuit; Hawk-eye, Heyward, and David still pressing on his footsteps. The utmost that the scout could effect was to keep the muzzle of his rifle a little in advance of his friend, to whom, however, it answered every purpose of a charmed shield. Once Magua appeared disposed to make another and a final effort to revenge his losses; but, abandoning his intention as soon as demonstrated, he leaped into a thicket of bushes, through which he was followed by his enemies, and suddenly entered the mouth of the cave already known to the reader. Hawk-eye, who had only forborne to fire in tenderness to Uncas, raised a shout of success, and proclaimed aloud that now they were certain of their game. The pursuers dashed into the long and narrow entrance in time to catch a glimpse of the retreating forms of the Hurons. Their passage through the natural galleries and subterraneous apartments of the cavern was preceded by the shrieks and cries of hundreds of women and children. The place, seen by its dim and uncertain light, appeared like the shades of the infernal regions, across which unhappy ghosts and savage demons were flitting in multitudes.

Still Uncas kept his eye on Magua, as if life to him possessed but a single object. Heyward and the scout still pressed on his rear, actuated, though possibly in a less degree, by a common feeling. But their way was becoming intricate, in those dark and gloomy passages, and the glimpses of the retiring warriors less distinct and frequent; and for a moment the trace was believed to be lost, when a white robe was seen fluttering in the extremity of a passage that seemed to lead up the mountain.

"'Tis Cora!" exclaimed Heyward, in a voice in which horror and delight were wildly mingled.

"Cora! Cora!" echoed Uncas, bending forward like a deer.

"'Tis the maiden!" shouted the scout. "Courage, lady; we come! We come!"

The chase was renewed with a diligence rendered tenfold encouraging by this glimpse of the captive. But the way was rugged, broken, and in spots nearly impassable. Uncas abandoned his rifle, and leaped forward with headlong precipitation. Heyward rashly imitated his example, though both were, a moment afterward, admonished of its madness by hearing the bellowing of a piece that the Hurons found time to discharge down the passage in the rocks, the bullet from which even gave the young Mohican a slight wound.

"We must close!" said the scout, passing his friends by a desperate leap. "The knaves will pick us all off at this distance; and see, they hold the maiden so as to shield themselves!"

Though his words were unheeded, or rather unheard, his example was followed by his companions, who, by incredible exertions, got near enough to

the fugitives to perceive that Cora was borne along between the two warriors, while Magua prescribed the direction and manner of their flight. At this moment the forms of all four were strongly drawn against an opening in the sky, and they disappeared. Nearly frantic with disappointment, Uncas and Heyward increased efforts that already seemed superhuman, and they issued from the cavern on the side of the mountain in time to note the route of the pursued. The course lay up the ascent, and still continued hazardous.

Encumbered by his rifle, and, perhaps, not sustained by so deep an interest in the captive as his companions, the scout suffered the latter to precede him a little, Uncas, in his turn, taking the lead of Heyward. In this manner, rocks, precipices, and difficulties were surmounted in an incredibly short space that at another time, and under other circumstances, would have been deemed almost insuperable. But the impetuous young men were rewarded by finding that, encumbered with Cora, the Hurons were losing ground in the race.

"Stay, dog of the Wyandots!" exclaimed Uncas, shaking his bright tomahawk at Magua. "A Delaware girl calls stay!"

"I will go no further," cried Cora, stopping unexpectedly on a ledge of rocks that overhung a deep precipice, at no great distance from the summit of the mountain. "Kill me if thou wilt, detestable Huron; I will go no further."

The supporters of the maiden raised their ready tomahawks with the impious joy that fiends are thought to take in mischief, but Magua stayed the uplifted arms. The Huron chief, after casting the weapons he had wrested from his companions over the rock, drew his knife and turned to his captive with a look in which conflicting passions fiercely contended.

"Woman," he said, "choose; the wigwam or the knife of Le Subtil!"

Cora regarded him not, but dropping on her knees, she raised her eyes and stretched her arms toward heaven, saying in a meek and yet confiding voice:

"I am thine! Do with me as thou seest best!"

"Woman," repeated Magua hoarsely, and endeavoring in vain to catch a glance from her serene and beaming eye, "choose!"

But Cora neither heard nor heeded his demand. The form of the Huron trembled in every fiber, and he raised his arm on high, but dropped it again with a bewildered air, like one who doubted. Once more he struggled with himself and lifted the keen weapon again – but just then a piercing cry was heard above them, and Uncas appeared, leaping frantically from a fearful height, upon the ledge. Magua recoiled a step; and one of his assistants, profiting by the chance, sheathed his own knife in the bosom of Cora.

The Huron sprang like a tiger on his offending and already retreating countryman, but the falling form of Uncas separated the unnatural combatants. Diverted from his object by this interruption, and maddened by the murder he had just witnessed, Magua buried his weapon in the back of the prostrate Delaware, uttering an unearthly shout as he committed the dastardly deed. But Uncas arose from the blow, as the wounded panther turns upon his foe, and struck the murderer of Cora to his feet, by an effort in which the last of his failing strength was expended. Then, with a stern and steady look, he turned to Le Subtil and indicated, by the expression of his eye, all that he would do, had not the power deserted him. The latter seized the nerveless arm of the unresisting Delaware, and passed his knife into his bosom three several times, before his victim, still keeping his gaze riveted on his enemy with a look of inextinguishable scorn, fell dead at his feet.

"Mercy! Mercy! Huron," cried Heyward, from above, in tones nearly choked by horror. "Give mercy, and thou shalt receive it!"

Whirling the bloody knife up at the imploring youth, the victorious Magua uttered a cry so fierce, so wild, and yet so joyous, that it conveyed the sounds of savage triumph to the ears of those who fought in the valley, a thousand feet below.

He was answered by a burst from the lips of the scout, whose tall person was just then seen moving swiftly toward him, along those dangerous crags, with steps as bold and reckless as if he possessed the power to move in air. But when the hunter reached the scene of the ruthless massacre, the ledge was tenanted only by the dead.

His keen eye took a single look at the victims, and then shot its glances over the difficulties of the ascent in his front. A form stood at the brow of the mountain, on the very edge of the giddy height, with uplifted arms, in an awful attitude of menace. Without stopping to consider his person, the rifle of Hawkeye was raised; but a rock, which fell on the head of one of the fugitives below, exposed the indignant and glowing countenance of the honest Gamut. Then Magua issued from a crevice, and stepping with calm indifference over the body of the last of his associates, he leaped a wide fissure, and ascended the rocks at a point where the arm of David could not reach him. A single bound would carry him to the brow of the precipice, and assure his safety. Before taking the leap, however, the Huron paused and, shaking his hand at the scout, he shouted:

"The palefaces are dogs! The Delawares women! Magua leaves them on the rocks, for the crows!"

Laughing hoarsely, he made a desperate leap, and fell short of his mark; though his hands grasped a shrub on the verge of the height. The form of Hawkeye had crouched like a beast about to take its spring, and his frame trembled so violently with eagerness that the muzzle of the half-raised rifle played like a leaf fluttering in the wind. Without exhausting himself with fruitless efforts, the cunning Magua suffered his body to drop to the length of his arms, and found a fragment for his feet to rest on. Then summoning all his powers, he renewed the attempt, and so far succeeded as to draw his knees on the edge of the mountain. It was now, when the body of his enemy was most collected together, that the agitated weapon of the scout was drawn to his shoulder. The surrounding rocks, themselves, were not steadier than the piece became, for the single instant that it poured out its contents. The arms of the Huron relaxed, and his body fell back a little, while his knees still kept their position. Turning a relentless look on his enemy, he shook a hand in grim defiance. But his hold loosened, and his dark person was seen cutting the air with its head downward, for a fleeting instant, until it glided past the fringe of shrubbery which clung to the mountain, in its rapid flight to destruction.

THE LAST WARRIOR

RAVEN

The sun found the Lenape, on the succeeding day, a nation of mourners. The sounds of the battle were over, and they had fed fat their ancient grudge and had avenged their recent quarrel with the Mengwe, by the destruction of a whole community. The black and murky atmosphere that floated around the spot where the Hurons had encamped, sufficiently announced, of itself, the fate of that wandering tribe; while hundreds of ravens, that struggled above the bleak summits of the mountains, or swept in noisy flocks across the wide ranges of the woods, furnished a frightful direction to the scene of the combat. In short, any eye at all practiced in the signs of a frontier warfare might easily have traced all those unerring evidences of the ruthless results which attended an Indian vengeance.

Still, the sun rose on the Lenape a nation of mourners. No shouts of success, no songs of triumph, were heard, in rejoicings for their victory. The latest straggler had returned from his fell employment, only to strip himself of the terrific emblems of his bloody calling, and to join in the lamentations of his countrymen, as a stricken people. Pride and exultation were supplanted by humility, and the fiercest of human passions was already succeeded by the most profound and unequivocal demonstrations of grief.

The lodges were deserted; but a broad belt of earnest faces encircled a spot in their vicinity whither everything possessing life had repaired, and where all were now collected, in deep and awful silence. Though beings of every rank and age, of both sexes, and of all pursuits, had united to form this breathing wall of bodies, they were influenced by a single emotion. Each eye was riveted on the center of that ring, which contained the objects of so much, and of so common, an interest.

Six Delaware girls, with their long, dark, flowing tresses falling loosely across their bosoms, stood apart, and only gave proofs of their existence as they occasionally strewed sweet-scented herbs and forest flowers on a litter of fragrant plants that, under a pall of Indian robes, supported all that now remained of the ardent, high-souled, and generous Cora. Her form was concealed in many wrappers of the same simple manufacture, and her face was shut forever from the gaze of men. At her feet was seated the desolate Munro. His aged head was bowed nearly to the earth, in compelled submission to the stroke of Providence; but a hidden anguish struggled about his furrowed brow, that was only partially concealed by the careless locks of gray that had fallen, neglected, on his temples. Gamut stood at his side, his meek head bared to the rays of the sun, while his eyes, wandering and concerned, seemed to be equally divided between that little volume, which contained so many quaint but holy maxims, and the being in whose behalf his soul yearned to administer consolation. Heyward was also nigh, supporting himself against a tree, and endeavoring to keep down those sudden risings of sorrow that it required his utmost manhood to subdue.

But sad and melancholy as this group may easily be imagined, it was far less touching than another, that occupied the opposite space of the same area. Seated, as in life, with his form and limbs arranged in grave and decent composure, Uncas appeared, arrayed in the most gorgeous ornaments that the wealth of the tribe could furnish. Rich plumes nodded above his head; wampum, gorgets, bracelets, and medals adorned his person in profusion; though his dull eye and vacant lineaments too strongly contradicted the idle tale of pride they would convey.

Directly in front of the corpse Chingachgook was placed, without arms, paint, or adornment of any sort, except the bright blue blazonry of his race, that was indelibly impressed on his naked bosom. During the long period that the tribe had been thus collected, the Mohican warrior had kept a steady, anxious look on the cold and senseless countenance of his son. So riveted and intense had been that gaze, and so changeless his attitude, that a stranger might not have told the living from the dead, but for the occasional gleamings of a troubled spirit that shot athwart the dark visage of one, and the death-like calm that had forever settled on the lineaments of the other.

The scout was hard by, leaning in a pensive posture on his own fatal and avenging weapon; while Tamenund, supported by the elders of his nation, occupied a high place at hand, whence he might look down on the mute and sorrowful assemblage of his people.

Just within the inner edge of the circle stood a soldier, in the military attire of a strange nation; and without it was his war-horse, in the center of a collection of mounted domestics, seemingly in readiness to undertake some distant journey. The vestments of the stranger announced him to be one who held a responsible situation near the person of the Captain of the Canadas; and who, as it would now seem, finding his errand of peace frustrated by the fierce impetuosity of his allies, was content to become a silent and sad spectator of the fruits of a contest that he had arrived too late to anticipate.

The day was drawing to the close of its first quarter, and yet had the multitude maintained its breathing stillness since its dawn. No sound louder than a stifled sob had been heard among them, nor had even a limb been moved throughout that long and painful period, except to perform the simple and touching offerings that were made, from time to time, in commemoration of the dead. The patience and forbearance of Indian fortitude could alone support such an appearance of abstraction as seemed now to have turned each dark and motionless figure into stone.

At length, the sage of the Delawares stretched forth an arm, and leaning on the shoulders of his attendants, he arose with an air as feeble as if another age had already intervened between the man who had met his nation the preceding day, and him who now tottered on his elevated stand.

"Men of the Lenape!" he said, in hollow tones, that sounded like a voice charged with some prophetic mission. "The face of the Manitto is behind a cloud! His eye is turned from you; his ears are shut; his tongue gives no answer. You see him not; yet his judgments are before you. Let your hearts be open and your spirits tell no lie. Men of the Lenape! The face of the Manitto is behind a cloud."

As this simple and yet terrible annunciation stole on the ears of the multitude, a stillness as deep and awful succeeded, as if the venerated spirit they worshiped had uttered the words without the aid of human organs; and even the inanimate Uncas appeared a being of life, compared with the humbled and submissive throng by whom he was surrounded. As the immediate effect, however, gradually passed away, a low murmur of voices commenced a sort of chant in honor of the dead. The sounds were those of females, and were thrillingly soft and wailing. The words were connected by no regular continuation, but as one ceased another took up the eulogy, or lamentation, whichever it might be called, and gave vent to her emotions in such language as was suggested by her feelings and the occasion. At intervals the speaker was interrupted by general and loud bursts of sorrow, during which the girls around the bier of Cora plucked the plants and flowers blindly from her body, as if bewildered with grief. But, in the milder moments of their plaint, these emblems of purity and sweetness were cast back to their places, with every sign of tenderness and regret. Though rendered less connected by many and general interruptions and outbreakings, a translation of their language would have contained a regular descant, which, in substance, might have proved to possess a train of consecutive ideas.

A girl, selected for the task by her rank and qualifications, commenced by modest allusions to the qualities of the deceased warrior, embellishing her expressions with those oriental images that the Indians have probably brought with them from the extremes of the other continent, and which form of themselves a link to connect the ancient histories of the two worlds.

Then they who succeeded, changing their tones to a milder and still more tender strain, alluded, with the delicacy and sensitiveness of women, to the stranger maiden, who had left the upper earth at a time so near his own departure as to render the will of the Great Spirit too manifest to be disregarded. They admonished him to be kind to her, and to have consideration for her ignorance of those arts which were so necessary to the comfort of a warrior like himself. They dwelt upon her matchless beauty, and on her noble resolution, without the taint of envy, and as angels may be thought to delight in a superior excellence; adding, that these endowments should prove more than equivalent for any little imperfections in her education.

Then, with another transition in voice and subject, allusions were made to the virgin who wept in the adjacent lodge. They compared her to flakes of snow; as pure, as white, as brilliant, and as liable to melt in the fierce heats of summer, or congeal in the frosts of winter. They doubted not that she was lovely in the eyes of the young chief, whose skin and whose sorrow seemed so like her own; but, though far from expressing such a preference, it was evident they deemed her less excellent than the maid they mourned. Still they denied her no meed her rare charms might properly claim. Her ringlets were compared to the exuberant tendrils of the vine, her eye to the blue vault of the heavens, and the most spotless cloud, with its glowing flush of the sun, was admitted to be less attractive than her bloom.

The scout, to whom alone of all the white men the words were intelligible, suffered himself to be a little aroused from his meditative posture, and bent his face aside to catch their meaning, as the girls proceeded. But when they spoke of the future prospects of Cora and Uncas, he shook his head, like one who knew the error of their simple creed, and resuming his reclining attitude, he maintained it until the ceremony – if that might be called a ceremony in which feeling was so deeply imbued – was finished. Happily for the self-command of both Heyward and Munro, they knew not the meaning of the wild sounds they heard.

Chingachgook was a solitary exception to the interest manifested by the native part of the audience. His look never changed throughout the whole of the scene, nor did a muscle move in his rigid countenance, even at the wildest or the most pathetic parts of the lamentation. The cold and senseless remains of his son was all to him, and every other sense but that of sight seemed frozen, in order that his eyes might take their final gaze at those lineaments he had so long loved, and which were now about to be closed forever from his view.

In this stage of the funeral obsequies, a warrior much renowned for deeds in arms, and more especially for services in the recent combat, a man of stern and grave demeanor, advanced slowly from the crowd, and placed himself nigh the person of the dead.

"Why hast thou left us, pride of the Wapanachki?" he said, addressing himself to the dull ears of Uncas, as if the empty clay retained the faculties of the animated man. "Thy time has been like that of the sun when in the trees; thy glory brighter than his light at noonday. Thou art gone, youthful warrior, but a hundred Wyandots are clearing the briers from thy path to the world of spirits. Who that saw thee in battle would believe that thou couldst die? Who before thee has ever shown Uttawa the way into the fight? Thy feet were like the wings of eagles; thine arm heavier than falling branches from the pine; and thy voice like the Manitto when he speaks in the clouds. The tongue of Uttawa is weak," he added, looking about him with a melancholy gaze, "and his heart exceeding heavy. Pride of the Wapanachki, why hast thou left us?"

He was succeeded by others, in due order, until most of the high and gifted men of the nation had sung or spoken their tribute of praise over the manes of the deceased chief. When each had ended, another deep and breathing silence reigned in all the place.

A signal was given by one of the elder chiefs to the women, who crowded that part of the circle near which the body of Cora lay. Obedient to the sign, the girls raised the bier to the elevation of their heads, and advanced with slow and regulated steps, chanting, as they proceeded, another wailing song in praise of the deceased. Gamut, who had been a close observer of rites he deemed so heathenish, now bent his head over the shoulder of the unconscious father, whispering:

"They move with the remains of thy child; shall we not follow, and see them interred with Christian burial?"

Munro started, as if the last trumpet had sounded in his ear, and bestowing one anxious and hurried glance around him, he arose and followed in the simple train, with the mien of a soldier, but bearing the full burden of a parent's suffering. His friends pressed around him with a sorrow that was too strong to be termed sympathy – even the young Frenchman joining in the procession, with the air of a man who was sensibly touched at the early and melancholy fate of one so lovely. But when the last and humblest female of the tribe had joined in the wild and yet ordered array, the men of the Lenape contracted their circle, and formed again around the person of Uncas, as silent, as grave, and as motionless as before.

The place which had been chosen for the grave of Cora was a little knoll, where a cluster of young and healthful pines had taken root, forming of themselves a melancholy and appropriate shade over the spot. On reaching it the girls deposited their burden, and continued for many minutes waiting, with characteristic patience and native timidity, for some evidence that they whose feelings were most concerned were content with the arrangement. At length the scout, who alone understood their habits, said, in their own language:

"My daughters have done well; the white men thank them."

Satisfied with this testimony in their favor, the girls proceeded to deposit the body in a shell ingeniously and not inelegantly fabricated of the bark of the birch; after which they lowered it into its dark and final abode. The ceremony of covering the remains, and concealing the marks of the fresh earth, by leaves and other natural and customary objects, was conducted with the same simple and silent forms.

The females stood modestly aside, and, from having been the principal actors in the scene, they now became the meek and attentive observers of that which followed. During the time David was occupied in pouring out the pious feelings of his spirit in this manner, not a sign of surprise nor a look of impatience escaped them. They listened like those who knew the meaning of the strange words, and appeared as if they felt the mingled emotions of sorrow, hope, and resignation they were intended to convey.

Excited by the scene he had just witnessed, and perhaps influenced by his own secret emotions, the master of song exceeded his usual efforts. His full, rich voice was not found to suffer by a comparison with the soft tones of the girls; and his more modulated strains possessed, at least for the ears of those to whom they were peculiarly addressed, the additional power of intelligence. He ended the anthem, as he had commenced it, in the midst of a grave and solemn stillness.

When, however, the closing cadence had fallen on the ears of his auditors, the secret, timorous glances of the eyes, and the general and yet subdued movement of the assemblage, betrayed that something was expected from the father of the deceased. Munro seemed sensible that the time was come for him to exert what is, perhaps, the greatest effort of which human nature is capable. He bared his gray locks and looked around the timid and quiet throng by which he was encircled with a firm and collected countenance.

Then motioning with his hand for the scout to listen, he said:

"Say to these kind and gentle females, that a heartbroken and failing man returns them his thanks. Tell them, that the Being we all worship, under different names, will be mindful of their charity; and that the time shall not be distant when we may assemble around his throne without distinction of sex, or rank, or color."

The scout listened to the tremulous voice in which the veteran delivered these words, and shook his head slowly when they were ended, as one who doubted their efficacy.

"To tell them this," he said, "would be to tell them that the snows come not in the winter, or that the sun shines fiercest when the trees are stripped of their leaves."

Then turning to the women, he made such a communication of the other's gratitude as he deemed most suited to the capacities of his listeners. The head of Munro had already sunk upon his chest, and he was again fast relapsing into melancholy, when the young Frenchman before named ventured to touch him lightly on the elbow. As soon as he had gained the attention of the mourning old man, he pointed toward a group of young Indians, who approached with a light but closely covered litter, and then pointed upward toward the sun.

"I understand you, sir," returned Munro, with a voice of forced firmness. "I understand you. It is the will of Heaven, and I submit. Cora, my child! If the prayers of a heartbroken father could avail thee now, how blessed shouldst thou be! Come, gentlemen," he added, looking about him with an air of lofty composure, though the anguish that quivered in his faded countenance was far too powerful to be concealed, "our duty here is ended; let us depart."

Heyward gladly obeyed a summons that took them from a spot where, each instant, he felt his self-control was about to desert him. While his companions were mounting, however, he found time to press the hand of the scout, and to repeat the terms of an engagement they had made, to meet again within the posts of the British army. Then gladly throwing himself into the saddle, he spurred his charger to the side of the litter, whence low and stifled sobs alone announced the presence of Alice. In this manner, the head of Munro again dropping on his bosom, with Heyward and David following in sorrowing silence, and attended by the aide of Montcalm with his guard, all the white men, with the exception of Hawk-eye, passed from before the eyes of the Delawares, and were soon buried in the vast forests of that region.

But the tie which, through their common calamity, had united the feelings of these simple dwellers in the woods with the strangers who had thus transiently visited them, was not so easily broken. Years passed away before the traditionary tale of the white maiden, and of the young warrior of the Mohicans, ceased to beguile the long nights and tedious marches, or to animate their youthful and brave with a desire for vengeance. Neither were the secondary actors in these momentous incidents forgotten. Through the medium of the scout, who served for years afterward as a link between them and civilized life, they learned, in answer to their inquiries, that the "Gray Head" was speedily gathered to his fathers – borne down, as was erroneously believed, by his military misfortunes; and that the Open Hand had conveyed his surviving daughter far into the settlements of the palefaces, where her tears had at last ceased to flow, and had been succeeded by the bright smiles which were better suited to her joyous nature.

But these were events of a time later than that which concerns our tale. Deserted by all of his color, Hawk-eye returned to the spot where his own sympathies led him, with a force that no ideal bond of union could bestow. He was just in time to catch a parting look of the features of Uncas, whom the Delawares were already inclosing in his last vestments of skins. They paused to permit the longing and lingering gaze of the sturdy woodsman, and when it was ended, the body was enveloped, never to be unclosed again. Then came a procession like the other, and the whole nation was collected about the temporary grave of the chief – temporary, because it was proper that, at some future day, his bones should rest among those of his own people.

The movement, like the feeling, had been simultaneous and general. The same grave expression of grief, the same rigid silence, and the same deference to the principal mourner, were observed around the place of interment as have been already described. The body was deposited in an attitude of repose, facing the rising sun, with the implements of war and of the chase at hand, in readiness for the final journey. An opening was left in the shell, by which it was protected from the soil, for the spirit to communicate with its earthly tenement, when necessary; and the whole was concealed from the instinct, and protected from the ravages of the beasts of prey, with an ingenuity peculiar to the natives. The manual rites then ceased, and all present reverted to the more spiritual part of the ceremonies.

Chingachgook became once more the object of the common attention. He had not yet spoken and something consolatory and instructive was expected from so renowned a chief on an occasion of such interest. Conscious of the wishes of the people, the stern and self-restrained warrior raised his face, which had latterly been buried in his robe, and looked about him with a steady eye. His firmly compressed and expressive lips then severed, and for the first time during the long ceremonies his voice was distinctly audible.

"Why do my brothers mourn!" he said, regarding the dark race of dejected warriors by whom he was environed. "Why do my daughters weep! That a young man has gone to the happy hunting grounds; that a chief has filled his time with honor? He was good: he was dutiful; he was brave. Who can deny it? The Manitto had need of such a warrior, and he has called him away.

As for me, the son and the father of Uncas, I am a blazed pine, in a clearing of the palefaces. My race has gone from the shores of the salt lake, and the hills of the Delawares. But who can say that the serpent of his tribe has forgotten his wisdom? I am alone – "

"No, no," cried Hawk-eye, who had been gazing with a yearning look at the rigid features of his friend, with something like his own self-command, but whose philosophy could endure no longer. "No, Sagamore, not alone. The gifts of our colors may be different, but God has so placed us as to journey in the same path. I have no kin, and I may also say, like you, no people. He was your son, and a redskin by nature; and it may be that your blood was nearer – but if ever I forget the lad who has so often fought at my side in war, and slept at my side in peace, may He who made us all, whatever may be our color or our gifts, forget me! The boy has left us for a time; but, Sagamore, you are not alone."

Chingachgook grasped the hand that, in the warmth of feeling, the scout had stretched across the fresh earth, and in that attitude of friendship these two sturdy and intrepid woodsmen bowed their heads together, while scalding tears fell to their feet, watering the grave of Uncas like drops of falling rain.

In the midst of the awful stillness with which such a burst of feeling, coming, as it did, from the two most renowned warriors of that region, was received, Tamenund lifted his voice to disperse the multitude.

"It is enough," he said. "Go, children of the Lenape, the anger of the Manitto is not done. Why should Tamenund stay? The palefaces are masters of the earth, and the time of the Red Men has not yet come again. My day has been too long. In the morning I saw the sons of Unamis happy and strong; and yet, before the night has come, have I lived to see the last warrior of the wise race of the Mohicans."

CHARACTERS IN THIS BOOK

Bounding Elk	*see* Uncas
Bumppo, Natty (Nathaniel)	*see* Hawk-eye
Cerf Agile, Le	*see* Uncas
Chingachgook	Mohican chief, also called the Sagamore, and Le Gros Serpent. Father of Uncas, descendant of Unamis, loyal to the British
Coeur Dur, Le	Delaware chief, also called Hard Heart. Conversant with many Indian languages. Formerly allied to the French
Effingham, Major	Officer in the 60th Regiment of the Royal Americans, colleague of Major Duncan Heyward
Gamut, David	Instructor in the art of Psalmody and faithful companion to Heyward's group
Gray Head	*see* Colonel Munro
Gros Serpent, Le	*see* Chingachgook
Hard Heart	*see* Le Coeur Dur
Hawk-eye	American frontier scout and woodsman, also called La Longue Carabine or Long Rifle. Intensely loyal friend of the British and of Chingachgook and Uncas, brilliant shot, hated and feared by the Hurons and their allies. His proper name is Natty (Nathaniel) Bumppo, and he features in five novels by James Fenimore Cooper, *Leather-Stocking Tales*, of which *The Last of the Mohicans* (1826) is the second
Heyward, Major Duncan	Officer in the 60th Regiment of the Royal Americans, also called Open Hand. In love with Alice Munro, young, rich, a loyal friend and a gallant gentleman.
Long Rifle	*see* Hawk-eye
Longue Carabine, La	*see* Hawk-eye
Magua	Huron chief, also called Le Renard Subtil. Intensely evil, consumed by hatred for the British, especially Colonel Munro, untrustworthy formerly drunken.
Menowgua	Huron warrior, killed at Glenn's Falls.
Munro, Alice	Younger daughter of Colonel Munro. Also called Elsie. In love with Major Duncan Heyward, more frail and timid than her elder sister Cora
Munro, Colonel	Commander of the besieged Fort William Henry on Lake George ("Horican"). Also called Gray Head. Father of Cora and Alice, the latter by his second wife and first love, Alice Graham. An imperious Scot and fine soldier.
Munro, Cora	Elder daughter of Colonel Munro. Admired by all, especially Uncas. A dark beauty of great strength of will and courage. An object of Magua's lust and cunning
Montcalm, Major-General	Fully, Louis-Joseph de Montcalm-Gozon, Marquis de Saint-Véran (1712–59). Commander of French forces in Canada from 1756. Highly successful and honorable soldier. Regained control of Lake Ontario by the capture of Oswego (1756). Took Fort William Henry (1757), resisted Abercromby at Ticonderoga (1758). Defended Quebec against Wolfe, but the English climbed the Heights of Abraham and entered the city. Both he and Wolfe were killed in the Plains of Abraham in the ensuing battle. Cooper remarks that an otherwise honorable record was scarred by two lapses, one the Massacre of Fort William Henry described in the book.
Nimble Deer	*see* Uncas
Open Hand	*see* Major Duncan Heyward
Reed-that-bends	Cowardly Huron warrior
Renard Subtil, Le	*see* Magua
St Véran, Louis de	*see* Montcalm
Tamenund	Delaware chief. A half-legendary figure, said to have greeted William Penn and the white settlers (end of 17th century). A man of great character and power. The Americans considered him their patron saint in the 1770s. Also spelt Tamenay and Tammany.
Unamis	Mohican chief, ancestor of Chingachgook and Uncas. The name means 'Turtle', hence the tattoo on Uncas' chest. The turtle signified membership of the senior clan of the tribe.
Uncas	Mohican chief, also called Bounding Elk, Le Cerf Agile, Nimble Deer. Son of Chingachgook and protégé of Hawk-eye. The successor as supreme chieftain of all the tribes of the Delaware confederacy. Young, daring, and loyal; admirer of Cora.
Wassawattimie	Huron warrior, killed at Glenn's Falls

GLOSSARY

Abraham, Heights of – Natural fortifications of Quebec, scaled by British troops under Wolfe in 1759.

Abraham, Plains of – Site of battle between Wolfe and Montcalm, 1759.

big river – The Mississippi – Hawk-eye, in conversation with Chingachgook, alludes to a tradition that the Atlantic states Indian tribes came from the west.

Burgoyne, John – English general (1722–92), made commander-in-chief of the northern army during the revolution. Captured Fort Ticonderoga, 1777. '

castle – Used to describe a principal Indian village, even though it may be no more than a scatter of huts. They were usually protected by a strong wooden stockade.

catbird – The American thrush. The true American mockingbird is not found so far north as the state of New York, where this story is set. The catbird and the ground-thresher are its two, inferior substitutes, though both are said to be superior to the European nightingale.

Champlain, Lake – Lake due south of Quebec, extending for about 110 miles, on whose south-westerly shore is Fort Ticonderoga.

Chippewas – A hunting Indian tribe of the Great Lakes region, also called Ojibway. They sided with the French. In the seventeenth century they had become the first tribe in the region to receive firearms from white people, the Dutch.

Delawares – The Delaware Indians were a large grouping together (or confederacy) of Algonquian tribes. (Algonquin was originally the name given to the wandering tribes of Quebec and Ontario, but was later used to include all tribes of a certain linguistic group, including the Chippewas, Delawares, Mohegans and Narragansetts.) In 1682 they made a treaty with William Penn (which lasted for 50 years). The Iroquois defeated them in 1720, and they later sided with the French against the British. They were related to the members of the Mahican (Mohican) Confederacy, which occupied the higher reaches of the Hudson river. Other people who can be considered in *The Last of the Mohicans* to be tribes of the same stock are the Lenni-Lenape, the Lenope, and the Wapanachki (members of the Wappinger Confederacy).

Dieskau, Baron – A German in the service of France. A few years before this tale he had been defeated by Sir William Johnson on the shores of Lake George.

empiric – conjurer.

Five Nations – See Iroquois.

Fort du Quesne – Founded 1754 and renamed Pittsburgh in 1758, after the British Prime Minister. Twice (in 1754 and 1755) the British were cut to pieces there by the French and their allies, the most important of whom were the Delawares.

Fort Edward – British fort, to the south-east of Lake George, commanded by General Webb.

Fort Ticonderoga – On a main route to Canada, this strategic fort was built at the foot of Lake Champlain by the French (who called it Fort Carillon) in 1755. See also *Champlain, Lake* and *Burgoyne, John*.

Glenn's Falls – On the Hudson River, some 40–50 miles above the head of tide, where the river becomes navigable for large sailing ships. The description given by Hawk-eye is more or less accurate.

Great Lakes – The string of vast lakes (Superior, Michigan, Huron, Erie and Ontario) which span the border between Canada and the United States of America.

Hollanders – New York state was originally a Dutch colony. Together with New Jersey, it was claimed for the Dutch in 1609 by Hudson, and New Amsterdam (now New York City) was settled by the New Netherland Company.

Horican – The name used by Hawk-eye for Lake George (also called Le Lac du Saint Sacrement and Holy Lake), a beautiful lake which forms a sort of tail to the south of Lake Champlain. Cooper, disliking the name Lake George, found that a tribe, whom the French called Les Horicans, formerly dwelt on its shores, and so coined the new name.

Hudson – The Hudson river flows due south from Lake Champlain to flow out at New York City.

hunting shirt – Hawk-eye's hunting shirt was a picturesque deerskin smock frock, rather short, and decorated with fringes and tassels. Its green and yellow coloration blended with the forest. American rifle corps members used frequently to wear this type of garment, though it was often white.

Huron – A confederacy of nomadic Iroquoian Indians. Among the first fur-trading partners of the French, they were bitter enemies of the true Iroquois. Under Samuel de Champlain, together with an Algonquin war party, they defeated the Mohawks on Lake Champlain. They are properly called Wyandots.

Iroquois – This confederacy of Five Nations had existed since about 1570 in northwestern New York State. The original tribes were the Mohawks, the Oneidas, the Senecas, the Cayugas and the Onondagaes. They were joined in 1715 by the Tuscarora Indians to form the Six Nations. After defeats in the 17th century (see *Huron*) they came back as an extremely powerful and warlike nation. They skilfully played off the French against the British in the late 1600s and later, but generally gave their support to the British cause.

Johnson, Sir William (1715–74) – Colonial superintendent of Indian affairs north of the Ohio. He owned enormous tracts of land and his second and third marriages were to Mohawk girls. The British defeat at Fort du Quesne (q.v.) persuaded most Indians to support the French, but Johnson persuaded the Iroquois to lend some 200 or 300 brave warriors, and in the battle of Lake George their presence had great propaganda value. It was after this battle that Johnson received a baronetcy.

Kill-deer – Hawk-eye's rifle (La Longue Carabine). It was of great length, as is

usual with hunting rather than military firearms.

Lac du Saint Sacrement – See Horican.

Lake George – See Horican.

league – A unit of measurement which may differ. Usually about three miles.

Lenni-Lenape-Lenope – See Delawares.

licks – Spots where salt springs are found. Many animals resort to these places for their necessary salt intake. They are favourite places for hunters, because of the number of animals which gather at them.

Loudo(u)n, Earl of – John Campbell (1705–82). British soldier, commander-in-chief of British forces in North America (1756), failed to defeat Montcalm, and, highly unpopular with his subordinates, was recalled at the end of 1757.

Mahicans – An Algonquian confederacy (see *Delawares*), closely affiliated with the Mohegans (q.v.) and the Delawares. They originally occupied both banks of the upper Hudson River. Cooper, in his Mohicans, seems to have confused the Mahicans with the Mohegans.

Manitto – Also Manitou. Algonquin word for a good or evil spirit. Cooper here uses it as an alternative for Great Spirit.

Maqua – Maqua, Mengwe and Mingo were names given to certain tribes of the Iroquoian confederacy. Mingo, and to a lesser extent Maqua, are used as terms of abuse in the book.

Massacre of Fort William Henry – Vividly described in all its ghastly detail in *The Last of the Mohicans*, this rout of the British by the Indians took place on 9 August 1757. Montcalm's Indian allies are said to have killed or made prisoner 1500 people. Cooper saw this massacre as a blot on Montcalm's reputation, but it may be that Montcalm was simply unable to control his unpredictable allies.

medal – When Heyward tempts Magua with a medal, he is following a custom whereby the whites would try to con-

ciliate a chief by presenting him with a medal with the reigning monarch's head embossed on it.

Mengwe – See Maqua.

Mingo – See Maqua.

Minquon – Name used by the Delawares for William Penn. As he was always strictly just in his dealings with the Indians, and never used violence, his reputation for honesty became proverbial.

moccasin – Animal skin (usually deerskin) covering for the feet.

Mohawks – The easternmost tribe of the Iroquois Confederacy (q.v.). Ferocious fighters, their name (corrupted to Mohock), like that of the Apaches, has passed into the language.

Mohegans – An Algonquian Indian tribe (see *Delawares*), allied with the English. After 1676 they became the only important tribe south of Maine. One of their chiefs in the first half of the 17th century was indeed called Uncas, and it is with this tribe and the Mahicans that Cooper appears to have become confused.

Mohicans – See *Mahicans* and *Mohegans*. Cooper himself appears to have realized his own muddle, without quite admitting it, for in the "Author's Introduction", written 24 years after the book was published he says: "The whites have assisted greatly in rendering the traditions of the aborigines more obscure by their own manner of corrupting names. Thus, the term used in the title of this book has undergone the changes of Mahicanni, Mohicans, and Mohegans; the latter being the word commonly used by the whites."

moose – Huge, antlered North American animal, very closely related to the European Elk.

Narraganset – A bay in Rhode Island, named after a powerful tribe of Algonquian Indians (see *Delawares*), all but wiped out in 1675. From the region came a breed of reddish-brown (sorrel) horses, small, hardy and sure-footed. Their chief peculiarity was their habit of "pacing" or "ambling", that is lifting both the feet on one side at the same time.

nemo me impune laccessit – "No-one attacks me with impunity".

non-composser – Hawk-eye's description of David Gamut, meaning he was mad or a lunatic. The Indians, like many other peoples, held lunatics in great awe, believing them to be specially gifted by the Great Spirit.

Oneida – One of the tribes of the Five Nations (see *Iroquois*).

Onondaga – A tribe from New York State, belonging to the Five Nations (see *Iroquois*).

Oswego – The scene of Montcalm's victory over the British in 1756, when he regained control of Lake Ontario.

panther – Cougar (puma), North American big cat.

Potomac(k) – River forming part of the border between Maryland and Virginia, flowing out into Chesapeake Bay.

Quebec – The scene of the battle of the Plains of Abraham (q.v.) in which the French under Montcalm were defeated by the British under Wolfe, both commanders being killed (1759). After the British took Quebec, the French and Indian Wars, which had been fought for nearly 100 years over territorial rights in Canada and the West, were at an end. In the Treaty of Paris (1763) the St Lawrence Valley and land west of the Mississippi was relinquished by the French to the British.

relish – The condiments accompanying a meal. Hawk-eye would here be referring to salt.

Sachem – Supreme chief of Indian tribe (same as Sagamore).

Sagamore – As Sachem (see above), but in the book almost exclusively used of Chingachgook.

St Lawrence – Great river flowing through Montreal and Quebec, fed by the Great Lakes and the Ottawa River and flowing out into the Gulf of St Lawrence. A vitally important waterway strategically.

Salique (Salic) laws – An ancient law-book, from which the French drew a fundamental rule of monarchy, that no female could succeed to the throne. This rule was drawn from a misinterpretation of the passage "The crown of France shall never degrade the lance to the distaff".

scalping tuft – The practice of scalping their enemies was not uncommon among several tribes, but it became far more common after the colonizing Europeans introduced 'scalp bounties'. Scalps became big business – in Massachusetts, £12 per scalp in 1703, and £100 in 1722. According to Cooper, the North American warrior plucked hair from his body except for a small tuft on the crown of the head. This was left as a courtesy to a victorious enemy, who was thus provided with something to grip while executing his horrid task.

Six Nations – See Iroquois.

succatash or succotash – A dish of green maize and beans.

Ticonderoga – See Fort Ticonderoga.

tomahawk – Indian war-axe, often with a hollow shaft and a pipe bowl inserted opposite the axe head, so that it could be smoked.

torture – Captured victims were often slowly and horribly tortured by the Indians, the purpose being to prolong the death sometimes for days. The manner in which the victim withstood these cruelties reflected greatly on his honour and therefore the honour of his tribe.

Tuscarora – The Sixth Nation (see *Iroquois*).

wampum – Beads strung together and used for decoration or money.

Wapanachki – See Delawares.

Webb, General – Commander of Fort Edward, whose failure to relieve Colonel Munro provides one of the tragic elements in the book.

wigwam – Indians' hut or tent, usually made of skins, bark or matting.

Yengeese – Indian pronunciation of English. This word is possibly the origin of Yankees, the white inhabitants of New England, and the Federal soldiers in the American civil war.